EQUINOX
THE GODDESS RISES

BY

J.S. COMISKEY

Other books by J.S. Comiskey:
The Goddess Trilogy

Book I - Solstice – The Goddess Awakens

With all that is in me, I dedicate this book

to the two men who have transformed my life.

To my husband Neil and to our beloved baby son

Theo, who could only stay for a short while.

"It's I who know that well: when it was dark, you always carried the sun in your hand for me."

    - Seán O'Casey, Red Roses for Me

"All the variety, all the charm, all the beauty of life is made up of light and shadow."

    - Leo Tolstoy, Anna Karenin

~ 1 ~

anus Moriarty's soft rubber soles kissed the worn floor of the Long Library. A calming silence had descended on the room as the last trickle of summer visitors to the university's historic book collection finally subsided. The professor inhaled the comforting fusion of sunlight and polish. Like a sedative, it soothed his increasing agitation.

The library and all its literary treasures at Trinity College Dublin had been his home for thirty years. Normally, he'd linger amongst the dust and rosewood stacks with their aged books and sun-bleached spines – here he never felt alone. When he found himself harboured in the confines of the library he was always in the company of greatness. Busts of Newton, Socrates and Shakespeare stared from iron eyes, oblivious to his anguish as he strode past them. His temper still smouldered and his empty stomach felt as though it had been wrapped in tight binding.

The rare manuscripts professor was a touch out of breath by the time he reached his office, which lay embedded deep in the womb of the building. His hands were limp and clumsy as they tried to fish the keys from his trouser pocket but finally they allowed him to unlock the door.

The meeting had unsettled him and while he was getting what he wanted, he hadn't once imagined that it would come at such a cost. His mind toiled as if trying to decipher some ancient codex. It searched for the merits in the offer he'd received, but came up short.

Offer, he thought, was perhaps a touch misleading, it didn't feel much like an offer. It didn't feel as though he had a choice at all.

The professor's face burned beneath its heavy auburn stubble and light pearls of sweat settled on his forehead. He needed something to calm his nerves.

Following the trajectory of the evening sun as it floated through the port window high up on the office wall, he made straight for the drinks cabinet that lay beside his desk. He rubbed the film of dust off a small cut-class whiskey tumbler with the sleeve of his blazer and reached for the vintage bottle of Bushmills, a delicacy that was normally reserved for special occasions. Today certainly marked such an occasion, he thought, as he poured the ten-year single malt.

Exhausted and unsure if his legs would hold him any longer, he slumped into his cracked green Chesterfield and knocked back the contents, quickly pouring himself a second as the warm amber liquid slid down his throat, subduing his churning gut and agitated mind.

Bloody Americans. Think they know everything. All money and not an ounce of class. What do they know about culture? Bastardised brutes that they are. To think that I can just take something so old and valuable on a plane, like I was carrying a bloody newspaper. I won't do it. No. I won't risk destroying it!

As if challenging this internal monologue, the phone on his desk gave out a loud shrill, slapping him from his debate. With a quick flick of his head, he downed the rest of the whiskey before lifting the receiver.

'Hello,' he said dryly. He knew who it would be. He had walked out on his boss and now he would be chided like an errant schoolboy.

'I trust you've calmed down, Professor Moriarty?' said the cool voice at the other end of the line. Manus could tell that the provost was still furious with him but the whiskey had silenced his reserve – he didn't care. Besides, some things were more important than donations to the university from wealthy Americans.

Manus slid further into the chair as the absurdity of his own words assaulted him. How naïve and petulant his argument sounded. The truth, however unpalatable, was that he could not continue his research without these 'patrons'. Tourism brought the university and his work revenue. Over half a million people came to see the renowned artefact each year, but his boss was right, it was nowhere near enough to continue his research. He was so close to a major discovery and he couldn't do it alone, he needed the new technology and he needed these Yanks to supply it. The thought made his stomach lurch again. What had he done?

'I trust you've had a little time to, let's say, reflect on your current stance?'

'Yes, John,' said the professor. As quickly as it had erupted, all gusto seemed to abandon him. He knew that he must be pragmatic. 'But,' he offered meekly, 'I still think it's a huge risk to transport such an old document to America. Why can't we travel to Oxford? They have the same multi-spectrometer, tried and tested on the Codex, no less. It has yielded fantastic results.'

He could tell the provost was growing impatient again.

'Jeesus, Manus, we've been through all of this,' he hissed down the phone. 'If the bloody thing survived the bloody Vikings and every other pillaging invader this country has endured, it'll survive a first class flight across the Atlantic.'

Manus almost smiled. He was right, it had survived many conquests and tribulations; indeed it was a miracle that it was still in such pristine condition.

'The Butler Library at Columbia is one of the most remarkable in its field. You of all people don't need me to remind you of its importance. Their new purpose built preservation and conservation facility has the most up to date equipment and expertise. There is no better place on this earth for you to conduct the last of your research.'

He was right. Manus knew he couldn't argue. The Butler Library housed over four million cuneiform tablets, cylinder seals, Coptic ostraca and medieval and renaissance manuscripts. It was a treasure trove of antiquity and he had been promised access to it all.

'Our patrons have also guaranteed us that the book will be transported in a state of the art container and ensured that no damage or harm will come to it. More to the point, they are sending you out with it and paying you a handsome fee as well as donating a substantial sum to the university. I just don't understand what the problem is, Manus, I really don't. You said it yourself, you are so close to a major discovery and now that you have the chance of a lifetime you're balking at it all because of something as futile as logistics.' In his mind's eye Manus could see the provost's jowls shake and colour as he spat his rage down the line.

'Dammit man, wake-up! You are a research director, not to mention keeper of manuscripts, and you had better dam well start acting like it. It's not as though people are knocking the door down to give you money. Your plane leaves for New York in two days and you and that book of yours had better bloody well be on it.'

The line went dead. The professor's head felt light again. He was forty-eight but tonight he felt like a child again. John was right. This was a great opportunity. Funding of this kind was something researchers dreamed of, something he had pursued relentlessly for years. So why did success feel so hollow? Why did it make him feel so uneasy? If his theory was correct, he might just have to give up the book for good. Manus wasn't sure he was ready to do that just yet.

Sweeping the thick fall of hair back off his clammy forehead he made his way to the set of double doors on the back wall of the homely office, the effect on his mood was immediate.

His earlier anxiety was repelled by simultaneous streams of excitement and serenity, which seemed to flow through him each time he approached the oaken doors. This was the professor's private office and only he knew what lay behind them. During the semester, when he wasn't lecturing, he could be found in his room at the School of Antiquities. It was a hive of activity throughout the academic year as students and lecturers came and went. But down here in the womb of the library, this was his sanctuary, his harbour, and it proved to be the perfect place to secure the ancient folio.

A wave of satisfaction rippled through his body when he unlocked the doors. It moved him to know that Ireland's most valuable treasure lay behind two humble pieces of wood and that he was its sole guardian.

Spinning the combination wheel, he listened as the key code secured the cogs into place. In all the years he had been doing this, Manus Moriarty never tired of that sound.

The book lay in effigy in a darkened container. For almost thirty years he had laboured over and devoured each of the one hundred and eighty-five pages of elaborate ornamentation and writing and yet it remained an enigma to him.

Of course he knew, like every tourist that came to Trinity, that it was penned on the finest calf vellum and written in iron gall ink. He knew every theory there was about its origins, from Saint Columba as its scribe to those who believed it was written in honour of the humble Irish saint from Donegal.

However, his theory was much more controversial and if he was correct, Ireland's most valuable piece of antiquity would find its rightful place amongst the other celebrated antiquarian documents like the Paris and Dresden Codices and the Herculaneum Scrolls.

After he slipped on a pair of worn cotton gloves, the professor gently lifted the large folio from its cradle and carried it like a new born to his desk. Lifting the bleached page turner, he allowed his thumb to trace over the triple spiral that had been engraved at the bottom of the piece of alder.

The wooden page turner had been a gift from a visiting professor many years ago. Manus couldn't recall his name now but he did remember the vast knowledge the man had about the manuscripts in the university's archives. It had made quite an impression on him as a young student. He had come to love the page turner as much as he loved the Leabhar Cheanannais. Even after one thousand two hundred and forty years, the Book of Kells was still immaculate.

The professor's eyes absorbed the gold and silver leaf, the rich Mediterranean pigments of yellow and red ochre, of lapis lazuli. All this made it, in his opinion, stand out as the finest example of medieval writing and art. But the book, as he hoped to prove, was older still.

He remembered when as a young boy his father had brought him to the Long Room at Trinity to see the Book of Kells. It was love at first sight. It was as though he'd not been whole until that very moment when he stood at the display case with his hands spread out on the glass, his nose pressed down tight, his eyes wide as a fawn's, absorbing everything the book had to offer. He didn't know what the term was back then, but that very day over forty years ago he knew he would become a palaeographer.

He was hooked instantly, as if under a spell. It felt as though the book spoke to a part of him that he couldn't feel or see or touch until that very moment. He felt like he'd always known it as its colourful pages gazed back at him. Every day of his life after that chance encounter had been dedicated to getting him one step closer to unravelling its mysteries.

The professor turned the pages gently. It wasn't until he was studying for his doctorate that he became privy to the truth, that the book in the library on display to the unassuming public, was not the real Book of Kells but a replica. After months of postgraduate research, he was finally allowed to look at the real manuscript.

Like a tentative lover he lavished all his time and energy on the text. He spent every working hour trying to unlock her beauty and unravel her mystique. All these years of effort had stemmed from a singular, in-explicable vision decades before, but the professor himself struggled to understand what he had seen. Even now as he tried to wade through the fog of his memory, he still wondered if it had been real.

That late night in his youth, hunched over the book, somewhere between the veil of sleep and lucidness, the book had opened itself up to him like a lotus flower, revealing her golden forms and symbols etched underneath the Latin script. The single word 'equinox' had permeated off the page like mist before his reluctant and sceptical eyes.

Initially, he suspected that the dim light and sheer exhaustion had conspired against him, but cold reason, although he wished to embrace it, was banished by something much stronger burrowed deep inside his very being.

He knew he could never speak of the events of that night; he valued his career too much. Manus Moriarty knew what his work had cost him, a chance at marriage, children, a family. But now he was almost there, after years of research and work, and he couldn't allow these fears, whether real or imagined, to jeopardise that. All he had to do was get on that plane to America.

The thought made his stomach lurch again. Perhaps it was his lack of control, his fear of failure, his fear of success. Or, perhaps the motives and interests of his old mentor and these anonymous patrons were what concerned him. As he closed the book and lay it softly back in the safe, he understood that his entire career rested on this trip across the tempestuous Atlantic.

The rainfall on the tunnel to the plane beat a steady tattoo to Lola's thoughts as the snaking line, filled with holidaymakers, students and business travellers, came to a halt.

She'd been watching the man in front of her for quite some time as he fidgeted and fussed with his hand luggage. She could see he was on edge.

The line crawled forward again as the flight attendant checked their cards permitting some to board the plane.

It was his aura that had initially lured her eye with its fusion of royal blue, indigo and grey. Lola had become so efficient at reading auras now that it was effortless. She could turn it on and off like the flick of a switch. It was a game she played sometimes when she was waiting for a bus, or sitting in the doctor's or even at lectures. When she trusted the clarity of her eyes, allowing them to guide her, she was able to unveil people, little facets of their personality, their current mood, their concerns, and their emotions.

In this sense, she thought, what lay within always reflected without, if you knew how to see it. This new gift and the knowledge that came with it fascinated her. Any one person could have so many silhouettes but she could see the truth. So what could her talent reveal about this man who seemed so distant and preoccupied?

His colours, thought Lola as she scrutinised him further, suggested a conservative disposition, but she could have told that from his clothes – a Harris Tweed jacket, crisp white shirt and a mint green tie with matching chinos.

No, there were other traits that the royal blue exposed, like loyalty and integrity, yet the hues of indigo around the edges seemed to contradict this theory. They said that this man had a deeper connection with himself than the rigidness of academia would allow – that was Lola's guess, he was a lecturer of some sort, humanities, not science.

She wondered if that was what now occupied his mind.

Then there were the grey speckles. They flashed intermittently like a blinking bulb. It was as if they sparked in rhythm with the neurons that were exploding in his head, declaring the birth of some new thought or concern.

Lola knew the grey was what troubled him, the grey of compromise, the grey of indecision, the grey of trepidation, the grey of uncertainty. That's what troubled most people. Where there was grey, there was doubt.

Lola quickened her step as the line lurched forward again breaking her hold on her subject. As she walked her path was blocked by a thick stack of papers that had slipped from under

the arm of her study. Stooping to pick them up, she felt an immediate sense of triumph and pleasure when she saw the title page.

The Equinox Theory declared the rigid bold type on the white page; she'd been right, he was an academic. Lola ahem-ed and excused herself several times before putting her hand on the man's shoulder to get his attention.

The very instant her hand touched his body, the tunnel, the rain, the passengers, the stranger, and Lola herself, seemed to dematerialise in a blast of light and sound, only to re-emerge somewhere else, a place that was now as familiar to her as her home at Brook Mill Manor.

Shadows danced off the granite walls of the Brú na Bóinne in front of Lola, or was it Brigid, she couldn't be sure because the image before her was so fragmented and clouded that her mind couldn't quite grasp hold of it. She was presenting something to a young man, whose face remained elusive but she could see the dark wings of fear and that panic flew into his eyes. Then as quickly as the image had come it was gone.

The tunnel, the sound of the rain tapping on its roof, the passengers, the stranger, they were all back where they had been just seconds before.

'Thanks. I must have dropped that,' said the owner of the bundle.

'Yes,' said Lola smiling before handing him the pages back carefully, terrified she might make physical contact with the man again.

Everyone around her continued to move on towards the craft, including the stranger, each of them oblivious to her momentary excursion. He thanked her again before disappearing into first class.

Disorientated, Lola blindly settled into her seat. Her head throbbed as her jumbled thoughts washed from side to side; she felt all at sea. Pressing her head against the coolness of the rounded window, she concentrated on nothing but the rain as it fell in sweeping slants across the airfield.

The plane's engines roared to life and the Boeing 757 taxied out towards the slick runway. Lola tried to make the effort to watch the hostess as she delivered the usual safety advice, noting the exits as asked and praying that she would never need them.

As the plane left the busy terminal behind, she thought for the first time about the entourage that she'd abandoned in the Dublin departure lounge. It had felt so final when she hugged and waved her parents and the girls a hasty goodbye. Thinking about them made her morose.

She'd hoped to see Aíbgréne there, but her friend hadn't shown. Friendships, thought Lola, were frail things. No matter how old or how strong, sometimes the only glue that held them together were memories of the way things had once been, interests once shared, lives once intricately interwoven, but things changed, people changed, life was always evolving.

Perhaps Celeste hadn't been fit for the journey and that was why Aíbgréne hadn't come. She didn't like to leave her mum on her own for too long now.

In fact Aíbgréne hadn't left her mum's side since the two women had been reunited on that Samhain night, when she and Lola had rescued her from certain death. Celeste hadn't been the same since. A shiver crawled over Lola's skin thinking about how close they had come to losing her.

After everything that had happened, she could understand why her parents had pleaded with her not to go, but she couldn't get her head around Aíbgréne's resistance to the idea. More than anyone, she should have known why she had to seize this opportunity.

It all felt like ancient history.

Ancient history. The notion made Lola laugh. She had so much of that. To think that in the space of a year, just twelve short months, her life had changed so completely and so had she. Lola Paige. Who is Lola Paige? She repeated the name to herself hoping that she would receive an answer. Lola Paige. The truth was that even she didn't know anymore.

She now felt like two women inside one person. One steeped in ancient wisdom and knowledge and the other trying desperately to recall it, all the while navigating a world where light and shadow were so chequered that the right choices, the right paths, were often blurred and distorted.

Her ma and da understood that she was not the same young woman anymore, as did the girls, but they all played the game, pretending that her life and theirs had gone unaltered.

Lola was grateful for the reprieve from the burdens that her own past and Arthur's murder had placed on her shoulders.

She was grateful because she could pretend too – even if only for a while. She could pretend that she had never learned the truth about who and what she really was.

She could pretend that she was just a normal nineteen year old. She could pretend that she had never heard of Carl Stein, or that she hadn't loved Alex Stein. If she pushed herself, she could even pretend that Arthur wasn't gone.

But pretence was fleeting. She'd been through too much and seen too much of the world to remain the same, and yet despite this Aíbgréne continued to underestimate her.

Aíbgréne's resistance to her idea had hurt her more than she cared to admit. She was eager to prove to her friend that she was a worthy custodian and conduit of the Order's secrets.

Perhaps Aíbgréne resented this? After all she had been born into the culture and magick of the Ancient Order of Golden Dawn. She had said it herself on the night that they first met; she couldn't believe how Arthur had entrusted everything to someone that knew little or nothing of the Order.

She had been right back then, but that was then and this is now. After everything that they had been through together Aíbgréne should have known better. She should have trusted her more.

But Lola knew she was selling her friend short, distorting her character to ease her own guilt. Aíbgréne wasn't petty or jealous. She cared about Lola and had only ever tried to protect her.

When approached by her lecturer at university about applying for the prestigious internship at the New York Torch Lola wasn't really interested; she thought she wouldn't stand a chance and she told him as much.

Yet that night when she tossed and turned in her bed, the idea grew in her mind from the seed which had been planted. Something beckoned her and by the time she'd woken the next morning she was resolute. She would at least apply.

When Lola got the letter a month later to say that she had been accepted and that she would be spending three months in New York, she was elated.

She would be working at the very same paper as her favourite journalist, Isaac Kane. Lola could hardly contain her excitement; Aíbgréne was the first person she had called to share her good news but their exchange hadn't gone to plan.

'I don't really think that would be a good idea, Lola,' she'd said. Lola had tried to convince her what a great opportunity this was for her as a journalist and that she felt she needed to be in New York. For what, Lola herself wasn't sure at that point, but her friend wasn't prepared to listen.

'You've no idea what you would be walking into, Lo.' By then she'd had enough of Aíbgréne's lecture and hung up the phone.

Things had been awkward between them at Arthur's anniversary commemoration. Lola had organised for all his friends to come to Brook Mill Manor on the evening of the summer solstice to pay their respects to their old friend.

Celeste hadn't tried to dissuade her from going and nor had Markus, in fact he'd thought it a great idea. That didn't go down well with Aíbgréne and she had called her the night before she was due to leave, begging her to reconsider.

'Lo, please think about what you are about to do. You're walking into Hell Fire Club HQ, ground zero. You'll be like a lamb to the slaughter. You have no idea what these people are capable of.'

Her condescension made Lola's temper flare again. She, more than anyone, knew what they were capable of.

The Hell Fire Club had murdered Arthur and had enough power to try and conceal it. They murdered Victoria Jones and they kidnaped and tortured Celeste and attempted to kill Lola herself. Yes, Lola knew exactly what they were capable of.

But this wasn't about Lola's vulnerability to the Hell Fire Club or to Carl Stein; this was about her vulnerability to one of its members.

Aíbgréne suspected Lola was still in love with Alex Stein and she outright refused to believe that he could be different from his father, even if he did take a knife to the chest to prove that he was.

Lola wasn't so sure that her friend was wrong. There had been no contact from Alex Stein or the Hell Fire Club since they had drugged her and brought her to Tara and the Brú na Bóinne on the eve of the winter solstice. They had both disappeared without a trace and the Cosmic Cube with them.

Lola looked down through the grey rain as the green fields below stitched together like one glorious patchwork quilt before finally disappearing from view and with them the little island that she called home.

In a few hours she would be in New York and hopefully ready for what lay ahead. Her intuition had brought her there and that, along with the small ring that hung on a chain around her neck, would have to be enough to keep her safe. Exhausted, her eyelids sore and tired, she finally permitted them to close.

~3~

Aíbgréne Moone pretended she was oblivious to her mother's tentative gaze as she continued to dust the same Tibetan singing bowl for the umpteenth time. Mystic Moone was slow today. This was nothing out of the ordinary for this time of year; it was always slow after the summer solstice celebrations.

Compared to the events of the previous year, Aíbgréne was content to have her mother with her, even if she did feel like she was under the microscope of her shrewd eyes.

The driving rain washed against the shop's large front window – typical summer weather in Belfast. Outside on the street, the few pedestrians who braved the elements scuttled like insects from one shop to another in search of shelter.

Aíbgréne couldn't settle, she kept on checking her watch. It was almost three o'clock. Lola would have left by now. The thought of her friend boarding the plane depressed her and added to her unrest.

Why hadn't Lola listened to her? She was so headstrong and sometimes it frustrated Aíbgréne. But Aíbgréne understood enough to know that it wasn't Lola's pig-headed determination that was the root of her frustration. She knew perfectly well the cause of that was her own guilt. Why had she not gone to the airport and made things right? Who was the pig-headed one now?

'Aíbgréne pet, why don't you take the rest of the day off?' said her mum as she shuffled some paper work around on the shop counter.

Aíbgréne leaned awkwardly from one foot to another. 'I'm fine, Celeste,' her rebuff sounded more petulant than she'd intended.

Her mother took off her glasses and looked at her daughter. Celeste Moone was barley a shell of her former self. Her once gleaming nut-brown hair was diluted by thick bands of ash-grey and her pallor never reached its former iridescent heights. Carl Stein's shadowy mark still lingered in and around her and she never felt truly free from its grip. Despite all they had done to help her heal, she felt ravaged and spent. An agitation constantly smouldered in her, so she had to carefully handpick her words before she spoke them.

'It was Lola's decision to go to New York, Aíbgréne,' said Celeste. 'She felt compelled to go. Why? Well that will only be revealed in time.'

This wasn't the first occasion that she'd had this debate with her daughter and it was growing old. Only Celeste knew the full story and because of that only she could see the whole of the moon while the others could only see the crescent.

But this understanding was as much a burden as it was a blessing to her especially when she had to lie to her own flesh and blood.

At times Celeste marvelled at how intuitive her daughter was, she'd been that way ever since she was a child. Aíbgréne could always see the subtext. But for all its beauty, her daughter's intuition was fast becoming a source of great trepidation for Celeste.

'Mum, don't,' said Aíbgréne still in pursuit. 'Do you not understand what she is walking into? She'll be like a lamb to the slaughter and yet you and Markus practically sent her off with a smile on your faces, as if it's nothing. After all she has done for you. For us.'

Aíbgréne paused, before moving to the incense stand to continue. 'More to the point, why was Markus so eager to get her onto that plane? We haven't seen him in almost a year and suddenly he's a bloody expert on what's best for Lola Paige. I know crap when I smell it.'

'Aíbgréne!' admonished Celeste bringing her hand down with force on to the wooden counter causing the wind chimes to play their music. 'I don't like you talking like that. You're not too old to get cuff around the ear, you know. Markus didn't just disappear, he was out in the field working, trying to gather information on what Carl Stein has been up to.'

Aíbgréne's eyes lit up at this revelation. Her mother's tongue had loosened and she knew she'd caught her off guard but for now she let the question sit on a to-do shelf at the back of her mind, she didn't want to push her mother.

'Besides,' said Celeste, her neck flushing crimson, 'Lola won't be alone if she's staying with your great-aunt Rocha. She couldn't be in better hands.

Auntie Rocha has been in the Order since she was just nine, such was her talent for healing. Where do you think you get it from?'

'And,' said Celeste, her tone softening. 'Don't presume to lecture me on what I owe Lola Paige. I don't need reminding. What you need to accept, pet, is that the Lola Paige you met twelve months ago, is no longer. That scared, naive girl has now become a young woman. Her awareness has grown, her powers have grown and her understanding of what she faces has grown.'

'And so have the stakes, Mum,' countered Aíbgréne, still unconvinced.

'You ought to have a little more faith in our friend and stop treating her with kid gloves, Aíbgréne.'

Tears began to leak from Aíbgréne's eyes, acknowledgment of the truth that her mother had just imparted.

'I know, Mum. I do believe in her. I do have faith,' said Aíbgréne reduced to a child again by her mother's scolding. 'But it's him, Mum, she can't see past him. He'll be the death of her, I know he will.'

Celeste slid out from behind the counter to wipe her daughter's tears away with the soft sleeve of her velvet dress. Aíbgréne saw the milky white scars on her mother's thin arms and she felt bad for pushing her when she'd been through so much already.

'I think you underestimate my nephew and your cousin,' said Celeste, holding her daughter's face in her hands.

'He is nothing to me. That man is nothing to me,' said Aíbgréne recoiling as though she had been struck across the face by the words.

'You cannot blame Alex Stein for what he is, Aíbgréne. The child has seen nothing but darkness and fear. He has been taught to dominate and to use. You might not ever admit it, but you must see that Lola is his only salvation. Whether they know it or not, their story is as old as time itself.'

Shaking off the assertion that the souls of Lola and Alex where in some way bonded, Aíbgréne pulled her mum into a tight hug.

'I don't want to fight with you, Mum,' said Aíbgréne, sniffing back the urge to cry again. 'I love you and I'm going home,' she smiled.

Aíbgréne fetched her raincoat from the back store and pulling it on stepped out into the rain.

The doorbell tinkled behind her as she took her phone and dialled her best friend's number. She felt a bit cowardly leaving a voice mail but she needed to clear the air.

As the door chimed closed Celeste retrieved the letter, which she'd buried surreptitiously underneath the stack of invoices, concealing it from her daughter. The postmark said it was from New York City.

Celeste read it over, carefully this time. Lola was on her way to New York and everything was falling into place.

~4~

wry smile spread across Markus Holmes's face as he lay dying on the floor of his drawing room.

'Chess 101, Markus my old friend, any or all sacrifice,' said Carl Stein looking down on him with a bemused expression on his face.

'I hope you understand that it's nothing personal just the tying up of some loose ends. You've been a good servant to our family and that is why, despite your personal conflict, I wanted to come and see to this myself.'

Carl stepped over the frail body and walked towards a walnut bureau where he lifted a framed photo.

'Unfortunately for you, you forgot whose side you were on. You grew weak for the old man and his ways,' said Carl throwing the picture with a crack onto the floor where Markus lay rigid with pain.

'Not to worry, you'll be meeting him soon. Tell him I said hello and that I miss him. He was the only one worth a damn.' Carl walked out of the room, leaving Markus alone and dying.

It was amazing how different the room looked from a worm's eye view. For Markus Holmes, life was all about perspective. He wasn't afraid, he wasn't panicked, he wasn't even bitter. That was the chance he'd taken. Life was always the bargaining chip and now he had cashed out.

He'd simply been outfoxed, and karma had a wonderful way of evening out the chips. Besides he'd felt drained by the many masks he wore; each one wrenched something from his soul, which now lay, like him, dried and wizened.

The hand he had dealt his best friend – his only true friend – was now being dealt to him. Poetic justice, grimaced Markus as a shrill pain shot up his legs. He was dying but his body and senses had never felt so alive.

The ghost of Arthur Delphian rose before him again and he wondered if his old friend had known he'd slipped the hemlock into his brandy that summer night over a year ago. When he recalled the look in Arthur's eyes that last evening, he believed he did know, which only served to compound his guilt and his sorrow in the days and months after Arthur's murder. What Markus saw in those eyes wasn't fear or anger or hurt but forgiveness, and that small observation had haunted and unsettled Markus every day of his life since. Arthur Delphian had forgiven his betrayal, or so he suspected.

Markus had danced between the light and shadow so much he didn't even know himself why he had done what he did.

Markus had met Carl Stein – betrothed at that time to Aurora Moone – for the first time in the same drawing room in Brook Mill Manor that he ended his best friend's life. Arthur had high hopes for the young associate and such was the level of Carl Stein's duplicity and treachery that Arthur never once suspected that he was the heir apparent of the Hell Fire Club.

Markus had been quite surprised that Carl had come in person to do the job, in a convoluted way he felt privileged. It was dignified and clean, he thought, but if Carl had known the truth, if he'd known the extent of his betrayal, it would have certainly been a more painful departure. That could only mean that Carl wasn't in possession of all the facts – at least that was a comfort.

Markus didn't put up a fight because he believed he deserved to die; he had helped to destroy the Order and the little that he had done in the past year to aid it would never atone for the sins he had committed.

The Ancient Order of the Golden Dawn was in tatters and its future was hanging by a ragged thread; a fragile silver string of light in the form of a nineteen-year-old girl.

From the instant he'd met her, Arthur Delphian was convinced that she was his old charge. The one who had been promised. Lola Paige was to be the Order's – and the world's – last hope and who'd have thought she would have been found in a council estate in Ballyvalley. The image brought a smile to Markus's hollow face.

Markus had not been convinced at all and was even less convinced when he met the girl at Arthur's funeral. If he'd had his way she wouldn't have been at the Fort at all, but then unlike Celeste, Markus wasn't executor to Arthur's will, she was and that is what Arthur had wanted.

Celeste Moone was nothing like her sister Aurora and what she lacked in talent, she made up for in savvy. She was a shrewd and beautiful woman and Markus came to realise that she had suspected him all along. That was why she had insisted on dealing with Arthur's remains herself.

But even Celeste, the most faithful of Arthur's disciples, came to understand than in order to get a job done you sometimes had to get your hands dirty.

Celeste's pragmatism ensured that she never questioned how Markus came by the inside information he fed her; she took what he served her and left him to his games.

By then everything that he had been telling her was the truth. His trips to Iraq had proven to be fruitful but his curiosity didn't go unnoticed and that was what had ultimately led him to his current predicament – lying in a semi-paralysed state as an ancient poison slowly crawled through his body.

Markus couldn't feel his legs or torso now but using what little strength he had left in his sinewy arms, he pulled himself, like a snake across the carpet. With a veined and wrinkled out-stretched hand he grasped the walnut picture frame that lay face down on the plush but worn rug.

It was funny the things you observed when you were dying. A stray tear slid from his eyes as he looked down at the photo of the two young men staring back at him.

The picture had been taken in the forties. He and Arthur had just moved to the university's observatory in Oxford Parks when the picture had been taken. They had been involved in the construction of the new solar telescope and spectroscope in 1953 and 1954 before Arthur returned to Ireland. They were much simpler times, he lamented.

Markus gazed at the two strangers as they stood squinting in the sun with their arms around each other. Comrade. Friend. Where did it all go wrong?

He had been so taken by Arthur when they first met at university all those years ago. He was so gentle, so knowledgeable. Markus remembered how loyal he had been to Arthur back then, nothing could have shattered their bond.

Another blast of pain made his body convulse and twist and he knew it wouldn't be long until the hemlock reached his heart.

But over time, Markus had grown to resent always being in the shadow, always the follower and never the leader. His mind was as great as Arthur Delphian's after all, so by the time he met Carl Stein on that fateful December night Markus never stood a chance.

Stein could sense the dark tumour of treachery that Markus harboured in his heart and he exploited it with clinical precision. That was Carl Stein's particular talent, he could mould and manipulate, foster and corrupt even the most righteous of souls, not that Markus could ever have claimed to be righteous.

However, Lola Paige could not be won over so easily and it unsettled Carl Stein. Markus had seen something unfamiliar in his eyes. The fear that resided there was alien to its host, and she would have to pay the price for it.

Letting his head rest on the floor, Markus Holmes could smell the dust and sense the years of footsteps that had worn down the fabric beneath him. The poison was moving quickly as the chill now spread beyond his torso to his chest. His time was almost up.

He couldn't put things right, not now. By this time Lola would be well on her way. She should have listened to Aíbgréne; the young healer was right, she was walking into the lion's den.

Carl Stein needed to level the playing field; he needed Lola Paige out in the open, away from the Moones, away from the Manor and away from Ireland, whose rich magick coursed through her very veins.

Bit by bit Markus's body died. It was quite a peaceful way to go, he mused. The numbness was strange and cold as though his body was being frozen solid one cell at a time.

He clasped the picture to his flailing chest. 'Sorry, Arthur,' he declared to the empty room. 'You were my best friend and I betrayed you, please forgive me, old chap.'

Markus Holmes looked down on his dead body, an empty vessel now. His time in this life had come to an end and now he would have to account for it.

~5~

'Alright, Mr Kane, just sit back and enjoy the ride. We should land in the United States of America at exactly oh-four-hundred hours.' Isaac Kane nodded and smiled politely at the US Marine that had just buckled him into his seat. He couldn't have been more than twenty- three, like the rows and rows of young Americans who were sandwiched into the large carrier.

At twenty-three Isaac had been studying for his Masters at Columbia, not fighting in a foreign country. The thought depressed him; he let his head fall back and closed his stinging eyes. Months of dry desert sun and dust clung to them and to him and he couldn't wait to step into a shower or have a proper bath. If only the water could wash away more than the dust and the dirt, he thought.

The silence hit him like a wall. It hadn't surprised him on the outward journey to Iraq – none of them knew if they would be returning after all. However, he had expected some sort of excitement from the troops on the return home. But then he didn't feel that way either. Each of the battle-weary soldiers wore the same look of relief on their sombre faces – relief that they were alive and going home.

Isaac, like them, was grateful to be returning home but what they had seen and done, what they had lost, made it impossible to be anything as normal as excited.

Yet, they were the lucky ones and it showed in every single worn and exhausted face. Isaac Kane would never be back in Iraq, he was sure of that. The whole thing made him sick to the pit of his empty stomach.

The war, the plane, the dust, the heat, the constant smell of death, the corpses of innocent women and children cut down like animals in the street, the flashbacks of young soldiers crying for their mothers, their bodies ripped asunder at the side of some desert road, their lives extinguished by a faceless and invisible enemy.

He would never forget it, indeed he would never allow himself the luxury of forgetting. What right had he? How privileged he was that he could make the decision never to return. Those around him were not that fortunate. They belonged to the state and they could be put in harm's way again should their masters wish it.

There was movement beside him as a body filled the empty seat but still he kept his eyes closed. Isaac heard the click of the seatbelt.

'Well if it isn't Mr Isaac Kane.' The weary journalist opened his eyes. It was a young soldier he'd met the first time he'd gone out to Iraq. He hadn't seen him since. 'I must say you look like shit, brother!'

'There's no doubt about that,' said Isaac breaking into a wide grin and shaking the young corporal's outstretched hand. 'This place seems to have that effect on everyone.' Isaac looked around the silent carrier.

'For sure,' acknowledged Lemar Jenkins nodding his head. 'They tell us that we've done our bit, that we won't have to come back to this godforsaken place again but I don't know about that, Mr Kane. I say if it's not Al Qaeda it'll be some other faceless enemy. Thank God, unlike some of these good men and women here, I'm out. Uncle Sam can kiss my black ass.' The young man laughed and shook his head again. 'I can't wait to hit 125th Street, back to Sylvia's. You know her pie is the only thing that kept me going, that, and my moms. I've paid my dues, Mr Kane, and now it's time for me to have a life. I start college in the fall and I'm damn sure no child of mine will ever have to see what I've seen just to get to college.'

'I hear you, son,' agreed Isaac. The young soldier's wisdom was beyond his years. 'So 125th Street? You're a Harlem boy then?'

The young Marine smiled a proud grin. 'Yes indeed, sir. I grew up in the Grant Housing projects. It's rough, but it's home. I can tell you, brothers on the block thought I'd gone crazy when I told them that I was joining the army. "Army ain't no place for the Blackman" they told me. Hell, they might've been right – some parts of Harlem make Iraq look like the Hamptons. You know what I'm sayin?'

They both laughed. Isaac was grateful for the boy's light spirit. Four years had passed since he had met Lemar Jenkins on the plane over to Iraq. Back then, the young soldier had just graduated from high school top of his class but couldn't afford to go to college. The Marines visited his school one day and told him that if signed up there and then that the Corp would pay for college. Here he was, still alive, and now they would have to keep that promise to the kid. No child should have to go to war to get an education, thought Isaac with disgust.

Isaac had made the trip to Iraq four times since he'd last met Lemar. Each time he left with a new unit but he never returned home with them. He never learned their fate and for him it was easier that way.

'So where you from, man?'

Isaac laughed again. 'I'm from Harlem too would you believe? Washington Heights, Sugar Hill.'

'Oh, you a rich boy then? That's how you could afford to go to that Ivy League University. I didn't know the New York Torch employed Harlemites. But then that rule doesn't really apply when you from Sugar Hill.' Despite his curtness there was no animosity in the young Marine's tone.

'It's a good area alright,' said Isaac, talking it all in good humour. 'I still live there.'

'My moms says Harlem has changed a lot since I've been gone,' said Lemar, his eyebrows drawing together in deep furrows. 'She said that this so-called "gentrification",' Lemar held up both hands and made quotation marks with his fingers indicating his distaste for the word, 'is driving the local folks out. Driving up prices, causing tension. My moms said that she was at the market the other day, you know on 125th and Lexington and old Cecil, you know the crab vender? You know him?'

Isaac nodded, 'Yeah I know old Cecil. I used to run errands for him when I was kid, to earn a few extra dollars. He taught me all I know about Jazz. Used to let me borrow his Dizzy and Miles records. I haven't seen him in a while though.'

'Well then you know he has been at that same spot for over forty years. Mamma says he moved on up to 135th Street, he said he didn't know any of his customers no more, said he used to know them all. Their names, their families, their problems.'

'It has changed even from when I was a boy,' agreed Isaac. 'The heart and soul of Harlem, the very essence of its culture, its music, its creed is being opened up to other people, which can be a good thing, but that will always come at a price. Stein Corp has been buying up old buildings and land for the last decade. So many churches have closed, shops, stalls, and homes and now the local folks can't afford to live there anymore. But it's not just happening in Harlem, it's happening all over the city.'

'Well I doubt Mr Stein will be buying over Grant House anytime soon,' said Lemar laughing. 'So, Mr Kane, where were you stationed?'

'I was embedded with a unit just north of Fallujah,' said Isaac feeling a little awkward, they were all forbidden from discussing locations or missions for security reasons. 'I've been with them a few times,' continued Isaac, 'it's tough.' Isaac's words seemed hollow when he heard them back.

Tough didn't cover it. There were so many other adjectives that he could have used like dehumanising, barbaric, vile, pointless. He knew he couldn't say too much about their location, OPSEC forbid it and he did understand that hundreds of lives were at stake. Still as he sat in the airfield in Kuwait, waiting to return home, he understood that most Americans didn't really want to know the truth. It was easier to cling to the fallacy that what their government was doing in Iraq was righteous, justified and for the greater good.

'Yeah, it was tough alright,' said Lemar, 'especially in the early days. I came over with a few guys from the Bronx. I heard this one guy, Tre, got killed first patrol. He was blown to bits by the side of the road. Now ain't that some shit?'

For Isaac, there were too many Tres. Too many stories just the same, all retelling the same story of the senseless and gratuitous loss of life.

'We were based in Kandahar, to start with,' continued Lemar. Then myself and about four others were moved to another unit about eighty kilometres south in al-Basrah.'

Lemar leant in closer to Isaac, lowering his voice, not that anyone could have heard him over the roar of the C-17 as its four large engines ignited.

'Mr Kane,' he hushed, 'it was strange. They had us escorting archaeologists and scientists. I mean it was strictly top secret. We didn't get to hear too much but you know you heard a bit and they were looking for something.'

'WMDs?' asked Isaac, intrigued.

'No, sir. That's what was weird about it all. It was a document or a book of some kind. They had aerial pictures of the area, called it Babylon.'

'What, the operation?'

'Yes. They called the Op Babylon. The project was called Inanna, named after some Sumerian Goddess, or something.'

Isaac Kane showed no inclination that he had any intelligence on the subject. He could tell the young Marine was nervous, scared, so he didn't want to spook him.

'That's why I'm glad to get home, Mr Kane. Those four guys that went on that op with me, they are all dead and to be honest I was afraid that I would end up the same way.'

'They died on the mission?'

Lemar began to laugh. 'Come on, brother, that would make it too obvious. We both know how cunning the Man can be. It was different missions, after we were called back to our original divisions. I just found out by chance.'

Lemar let the words settle between them as he closed his eyes and rested his head on the back of the seat.

The Globmaster III taxied the runway readying itself for take-off. The next stop was Ireland, to refuel and then Lejeune Marine Corps Base Camp, USA.

As the light dimmed in the carrier, Isaac reached in to the inside pocket of his New York Torch windbreaker and pulled out a small black notebook. He flipped the leather-bound cover over, exposing the two solitary words that sat glaring up at him from the dusty white page. Operation Babylon. They weren't written in his own hand but that of a logistics manager that had come looking for him the night before he was due to leave Iraq.

'You can call me Brad,' he'd told Isaac as he closed the door of the small sleeping cell. Isaac assumed that Brad wasn't his real name. The man, who was in his late thirties and about 5 foot 7, had a pleasant face and a short military buzz cut. He didn't strike Isaac as the typical jarhead, he was softly spoken and measured, almost gentle, all the things that could get you killed in the field, which was why he sat behind a computer all day.

Brad wasn't exactly jittery but his eyes travelled around the tiny room slowly and enquiringly as if scanning for some hidden object.

'Mr Kane, I'm afraid I can't say a lot, not here, not now but I'm very conscious that you will be leaving this god-awful place in a few hours and as a result time is not on our side. The walls have eyes,' said Brad. That's when he lifted Isaac's notebook from the night stand and scrawled the words Operation Babylon with his left hand, smudging the ink as his hand moved awkwardly across the thin page.

'I happen to believe that you are one of the last pillars of the fourth estate, Mr Kane. I also just happen to know that you have been tracking Stein Corp for some time. Have you managed to dig up anything yet?' he asked.

Isaac could only shake his head blankly because his mind was reeling trying to figure out who this young man was and how he knew so much about him. It was unnerving.

'Well your birthday and Christmas has come all at once, Mr Kane,' smiled Brad.

'If it were to get out that I've been in contact with you, I could spend the rest of my life in a prison cell, that's if I'm lucky. What I've seen, Mr Kane, the horrors that have been perpetrated in our great country's name is a lie and you are going to expose it and the vile men that have sold it to the American people.'

Isaac had explained that none of this made sense to him as he read out the note on the page. 'And what is Operation Babylon?' he'd quizzed him.

Brad took a step closer to him. 'Careful, Mr Kane,' he said looking around him cautiously. 'You'll need to find that out yourself. Follow the money and good luck.' Then as quick as Brad had materialised he was gone.

The plane was airborne and the conversation between both men had fallen dormant. Isaac Kane suspected that the logistics manager had seen to it that he had found himself sat beside Lemar Jenkins on the flight home so being the investigative journalist he was, Isaac resolved to catch up with the young Marine when they both got back to New York.

Fishing a pencil from his backpack he added the words Project Inanna to his ink-smudged page.

~6~

lex Stein inhaled deeply the fresh morning air as the streets of Manhattan hummed to life. It was just before dawn, his favourite time of day. Downtown lay in a semi-slumber and this was the only stage of the day that he could remain anonymous. Among the legions of yellow taxis, the homeless and the street cleaners who occupied the avenues in these early hours, he was just another faceless New Yorker, not Alex Stein, socialite and heir to the Stein Empire.

Adjusting the volume on his phone, Alex selected the appropriate playlist and began his ritual morning run from the Pierre Hotel.

Fifth Avenue was born anew, shimmering as the heat rose from the damp sidewalks that had just been hosed. Every morning each street was allowed to cast off the previous day's grime and dirt. Alex wondered what it would be like if he was afforded the same luxury. To cleanse himself each morning of the decisions and faces that haunted him by night. It was never that easy for him so instead he had learned how to hide it under an immaculate mantle of charm and designer suits, making it almost impossible for anyone to see what lay below his marble façade.

Almost everyone. Not his father. His father could read his face and every part of him. His father could sniff out any hint of weakness no matter how faint a trace, like a shark could smell a tiny speck of blood in an ocean of water.

Then there was her. From their very first encounter those eyes of emerald cut through his fallacy like a laser. Alex's stomach lurched at the mere thought of her name. His hand involuntarily reached for his chest where a small scar from an old puncture wound lay hidden under his damp t-shirt. He had taken that wound for the owner of those green eyes, but had it been worth it?

He didn't think so. His actions had merely prolonged the inevitable and complicated his own life beyond measure. That single act of love, of compassion, of madness or weakness, whatever it was, could have cost him everything, including his own life.

The thought angered him. He resented Lola Paige for what she had done to him, for how she had diluted him. If only he had allowed his father to end her life that night, the embarrassment, the shame, the desperate feeling of impotence could have been avoided.

Yet, although he resented her, no matter how he tried he could never bring himself to truly hate her. He could never hate something so beautiful, so pure.

Fuelled by his own self-flagellation – something that had never existed until he met Lola Paige – Alex picked up the pace, pushing his athletic frame harder as he passed the darkened windows of Tiffany's and turned off Fifth Avenue on to East 66th Street.

His heart rate intensified and like a radio he tuned into its beat and the rhythm of his stride, the control of his breath, it helped him to focus on only that. This half-hour run each morning silenced his demons, expunged Lola Paige from his mind, even if only for a short while.

Alex blazed past Trump Towers now, another building owned by his father's company, not that anyone knew that. Hammering on to FDR Drive he was momentarily blinded by the sudden burst of sunlight that ran in a thin line across the mist-shrouded horizon of the East River. It was truly majestic.

As dawn broke silently over the water, he no longer had the city to himself. A group of female joggers smiled and called out to him as he passed by. Alex tipped his cap with a reciprocal smile.

He was in the zone now as he pushed his body further. His head was clear, nothing existed beyond his breath, his legs, his sweat and finally his mind was given a reprieve from his thoughts, his duties, his job and from her.

Alex left the river turning onto East 51st Street and back towards Fifth Avenue again. This was the same route each morning.

Recently though he had been taking a short detour at the top of East 51st. Slowing to a light jog Alex crossed the road and slipped discreetly into Saint Patrick's Cathedral.

His own company, Vesta Designs, had been given the 175 million dollar contract to restore the 135-year-old church. Since he could remember, Alex had always loved the architecture of the building. He had spent his summers sketching its intricate double belfry, marble arches and stained glass window all from his father's office across the road in the Rockefeller Center and when Stein Corp moved he kept Vesta's offices there. He could see all the comings and goings of the busy church from his plush corner suite.

But back when he was young, when the church rose out of the concrete like some exotic vision, Alex couldn't understand why his father forbid him to cross the road into the church.

Then one day, not long after his ninth birthday, he decided to go without permission. Alex couldn't describe the feeling he had when he first walked through those enormous double doors into the central aisle of the church with its polished marble floor and overbearing and comforting smell of incense and beeswax. He sat for four hours drawing and examining the vaulted ceilings and Romanesque colonnades, the grand central arcade and every detail of its beautiful ornamentation.

His father was furious with him when they finally located him, hours later, as he emerged into the light of the mid-town sun.

The building, irrespective of what it was used for, was a work of art to him. That's why when it required some much-needed renovation he had tendered for the contract. He even invested some of his own money into the project, but his father would never know that.

They had done a fantastic job. The crumpling bricks had been refaced and repaired so too was the archaic heating system. The damage caused by acid rain and pollution had been eradicated, restoring the beautiful Tuckahoe marble façade. Now the Neo-Gothic masterpiece was once again the jewel in the Fifth Avenue crown thanks to him.

Alex understood what brought him to Saint Patrick's this morning was nothing to do with its fine architecture. He let the doors close behind him with a dull thud that reverberated around the empty cathedral.

Anonymously, he slid into a wooden pew that was shrouded in shadow at the back of the church and was immediately transfixed by the blue and red votive candles as their flaming heads wavered in the draught of the cavernous building.

Alex's eyes bent on the golden spears of flame as they fought against the dying of their light. But he knew that, although burning brightly, they too would join the legions that had died, sitting now darkened and in uniform rows, each one a hope, a prayer, a request snuffed out.

The building was peaceful as none of the noise and drama of the great and ferocious city beyond its thick walls was permitted to enter. Lifting the bible from its resting place in the back of the row in front, he nimbly slipped in a note and closing it again, softly placed it back in its resting place.

The tinkling of bells sounded from the altar as someone busied about making it ready for the morning service and the multitude of tourists that poured in through the Cathedral doors each day. He could see them from his top floor office.

Soft footsteps padded towards him but it was difficult for him to ascertain in which direction they proceeded.

It wasn't until the owner of the footstep spoke that Alex realised. His bare legs squeaked on the polished seat as he turned toward the cathedral rector.

'Monsignor Monaghan,' smiled Alex in his usual charming manner. 'Good Morning.'

'A good morning it is indeed, Mr Stein. Are you in to have a look at your handy work? I must say Vesta Designs did a wonderful job of the restoration and, well, your very generous donations made it all possible. God bless you, young man.'

Alex laughed. If this old man's god existed, he definitely wouldn't be bestowing his blessings on him.

'I think I'm a lost cause, Monsignor,' said Alex. The tone of his words sounded wrong, they sounded pitiful and much to his discomfort they gave rise to something paternal in the old priest as he took a seat beside Alex in the pew.

Cornered, Alex just wanted to leave now.

'Well I may get going,' said Alex, gesturing to move, 'I'll be seizing up.' But the priest continued undeterred.

'I know you're not a catholic, Alex, and I know,' laughed the Monsignor, 'that you're not the most religious person. It's fair to say, Mr Stein, you do lead a very, let's say, colourful life. But I've noticed you in and out of our church a lot lately. Is something troubling you, son?'

Alex laughed, rebuffing the sentiments. 'Are you trying to save my soul, Monsignor?'

'No, Alex, I'm just saying if you need to talk, I'm always here, that's all,' smiled the priest.

Alex rose from the seat, he was rigid. He felt angry now. His eyes fell on the bible again.

'Thanks for the offer,' said Alex, 'but my soul is beyond saving, by your god or mine.' With that he stalked out of the darkened church.

Manhattan was in full flow. The serenity that he had retreated from just thirty minutes ago had all but disappeared. The sidewalks were cluttered with workers, shoppers and tourists. He stretched and began to jog again. Picking up his pace he made it to the top of Fifth Avenue in just under sixty seconds to the Pierre Hotel where the doorman greeted him by name.

'Good run, Mr Stein?'

'Yes, thanks, John,' said Alex, lifting the morning papers at reception before riding the private lift to the penthouse that occupied the 41st, 42nd and 43rd floors of the 1930's hotel. His father called it the 'Chateau dans le Ciel' – the Chateau in the Sky. It was most certainly that.

The triplex was something of an Elysium for him, rising 525 feet like a limestone beacon above East 61st and Fifth Avenue it offered unrivalled views of Central Park, and the city. As a purveyor of fine architecture Alex often admired the resemblance to Mansard's Royal Chapel at Versailles; his father was obsessed with Versailles and every property he owned was a nod to its wonderful design.

Alex shared that love. He marvelled at the penthouse's exquisite and intricate system of Corinthian pilasters and its arch-headed windows, all this set under a copper roof punctuated with bronze dormers.

They didn't make buildings like this anymore. Beyond the soaring French doors and windows of the penthouse, New York sprawled into the urban distance, lying at his feet as if it all belonged to Alex. It was his kingdom or at least it would be.

The Pierre Hotel was an iconic building even before it became Carl Stein's, and in celebration of its legendary top-floor parties and fine design, Chateau dans le Ciel opened its doors to the public every Fourth of July.

Equipped with a large ballroom that occupied most of the 42nd floor, the room with its elegant Palladian windows offered guests three hundred and sixty degree panoramas of the city and access to two west facing terraces that were said to offer the best views in all of Manhattan and the Upper East Side. This was too much splendour not to share.

So each year they drafted up a lottery of New York's finest and sent out the much coveted golden tickets to the annual Fourth of July masquerade ball when the penthouse stepped back in time to the hedonistic 1930s when the last three floors of the Pierre Hotel's exclusive 'Super Club' were infamous for its orchestra events and society galas.

Alex's grandfather used to frequent the club and he brought his father to some of their meetings. Carl Stein had fallen in love with the old building and when it came on the market in the 1990s he snapped it up in flash.

When the lift doors slid open, Alex stepped out onto the chequered tiles that Maria, the housekeeper, had just mopped. He looked at her gingerly as he tiptoed over the wet surface.

'Master Alex, my tiles,' she protested as he passed her making for the sweeping staircase that led to the second floor. So vast was the space, with its sixteen bedrooms, six bathrooms and four kitchens that he and his father were almost able to live independently of each other, both occupying separate wings of the house.

Lately this space was much appreciated. Alex didn't like being in his company too often. He felt as though he had betrayed him, let him down.

'Mr Stein, you're back?'

'Yes,' said Alex to the old man.

'Your father left a message for you to call him. Will you have your breakfast after your shower, sir?'

'Yes, Henry, I'll take it in the service kitchen if that's okay.' 'As you like, sir.'

Alex had been dreading the phone call but he didn't want to put it off any longer so he lifted his mobile and dialled the international code along with his father's cell number.

'Alex,' answered Carl Stein. His voice was light and convivial so Alex knew that things had gone to plan. His body exhaled a touch.

'You're back from your morning run, Son?'

'Yes, sorry I missed you, Father, it took a little longer than normal this morning.'

'That's your little diversions into Saint Patrick's. You always did love that old building.'

Alex continued seamlessly as if he hadn't been taken aback by his father's knowledge of his morning trips to the church.

'I'm not sure what you're looking for in there, my boy.' Despite his revelation, Carl Stein's voice still carried an airy texture.

'Good architecture, the same thing that I have always looked for,' replied Alex impassively.

'Indeed boy, indeed. Well, I'm calling to say that I have tied up the loose ends here in England and I will back stateside by tomorrow night. There is another thing, which would explain my buoyant mood tonight,' said Carl Stein. Alex sensed the subtle sharpening of his tone and he waited for his father's words to hit their mark, like darts.

'It looks as though our mutual friend will be visiting the city this summer, now ain't that quite a pleasant surprise? Markus was not entirely useless after all.' Alex didn't believe it was a surprise to his father at all and he knew his little revelation was a test.

'What fun we will have, Father,' said Alex.

'That's my boy. The playing field is stacked in our favour and we must take full advantage. We can't have any mishaps this time.'

Alex didn't get time to respond, his father hung up the phone indicating his statement required no reply. Besides, Alex didn't have one.

All the pieces where now in place and the moment Lola Paige set foot in New York the great game would be in session.

~7~

'Y ou okay, Ms Paige? You look kinda pale. Is it the heat?' Lola's driver turned up the air con, which helped. The heat and sheer exhaustion bore down on Lola and she couldn't quite shake off the oppressive feeling that had assaulted her since she'd left the terminal at JFK airport.

She hadn't been prepared for the humidity as it coiled itself around her body, restricting her movement and breathing and while the air-conditioned car was a welcome reprieve Lola couldn't concentrate on what her driver was saying.

Dressed in a black suit with a clean crisp white shirt and black cap, Tommy Maloney was a man with a stocky build in his early forties. His face was clean shaven and soft around the edges giving him a warm disposition.

He was deceptively agile and seemed to have steel in his arms Lola noticed when he took her bags, lifting them with ease into the boot of the car.

His aura bounced between the colours of dandelions and buttercups with a splash of aqua green. Lola had never seen that combination before and it endeared the stranger to her. Tommy was jovial and polite but Lola's foggy mind was only capable of picking up fragments of his conversation.

'My people came from Ireland, my grandfather was from a town called Dune Eagle.' Lola's mind fought the fog. 'Dune Eagle?'

He said it again as if that would make it any difference. 'Dune Eagle. It's on the west coast of Ireland, up north.'

'Oh! Donegal.' Lola tried not to laugh at his pronunciation.

'Yeah, that's what I said. Dune Eagle.' Lola nodded politely. 'I guess you're not used to this weather, hey?'

'I'm Irish,' said Lola breaking into a pleasant laugh. 'We don't tend to get summers this hot.' She lifted her white arms to prove the point.

Lola tried to shake off the heaviness and when the vast phallic frame of the New York City skyline came into view she almost forgot about the suffocating presence. Nothing prepared her for the sheer scale of the buildings and the skyline that had been made so familiar to her and her brothers through childhood films and television.

Lola was tempted to take some pictures with her phone but that required too much energy so she sat and glared out the tinted windows of the car.

Even from this distance, before they crossed over the East River into Manhattan, she could feel the enmity radiating from each of the skyscrapers as they sat like steel totems housing and protecting something malignant.

Lola could feel Tommy Maloney's eyes watching her reaction through the rear-view mirror.

'You're not in Kansas anymore, Dorothy,' he said, his round face breaking into a warm grin. His accent was thick New York, just like the movies. It sounded harsher than intended, as though every word had its own exclamation mark.

'I am not indeed,' laughed Lola beginning to feel more like herself.

She thought of Aíbgréne's warnings as her wide eyes traced over every building with a childish expression of fear and curiosity. The cityscape magnified and expanded the closer the car got until Lola could no longer see the tips of the high rises.

An unconquerable sultriness assaulted her again but Lola knew that it wasn't the effects of the seven-hour flight or the punishing humidity. It was something more imposing, more sinister and while she couldn't pinpoint it Lola knew it was there and so too did her ring.

Dutifully, its indigo light expanded and stretched protecting her from the harsh energies of the sprawling metropolis. Lola slid back sinking deep in to the cool leather seat and closed her eyes. She concentrated on the movement behind her heavy lids as the light and darkness flickered on and off as they passed between each mammoth building.

'We're passing through Wall Street now, Ms Paige,' said Tommy Maloney over his shoulder. 'You might wanna see this, kid.'

So Lola forced her eyes open because she didn't want to offend Tommy. He had been very courteous.

Wall Street wasn't what Lola had expected at all. It was much smaller actually. She watched as mostly men in suits and ties came and went laughing and discussing the day's business. As the car passed by the famous Wall Street bull, which stood snarling, crouched and ready to attack, a bang of grief settled in Lola. Stirred by a shadowy remembrance of a time long forgotten.

The bull, she remembered, was once an ancient goddess symbol and now here it was used to symbolise greed and uninhibited power. She wasn't even sure where that piece of knowledge came from but she assumed that it was Brigid's not hers.

'Banksters,' said Tommy in an acrid tone. 'Getting millions of dollars in bonuses while the blue collar people fight for their jobs and their homes.' Tommy shook his head. 'What has happened to this country?' Lola felt it was a rhetorical question so she offered no reply. Besides what could she say?

'We're not too far away now, Ms Paige.' The car continued towards the Hudson River and through 12th Avenue before finally coming to a stop on 8th outside Lola's final destination.

Lola's stomach leapt as she gazed up at the glass-fronted building and the colossal sign that proudly proclaimed that this was the world-renowned New York Torch.

In there was Isaac Kane, his actual seat and his actual desk. The last she read he had been in Iraq and there was very little chance that he would be mingling with interns but still being in the same building would be enough for her.

Tommy Maloney had Lola's luggage stacked neatly on the kerb as he opened the door of the car for her.

'Good luck, kid,' he said as she thanked him and handed him a twenty-dollar tip. 'You must have some smarts to be going in there.'

Tommy reached into the inside pocket of his jacket and handed Lola his card. 'You need anything, and I mean anything, you get in touch with me. We Irish gotta stick together.'

Without knowing why, Lola reached out and hugged him. 'Thanks, Tommy. I really appreciate that,' said Lola leaving the driver blushing and awkward on the pavement.

Lola struggled clumsily with her two suitcases and bag through the grand lobby doors of the New York Torch.

This was quite an upgrade from the Ballyvalley News. The lobby was a vast space, almost like an art gallery, where well-dressed people gathered around plush chairs and talked in hushed tones to one another.

Heads lifted towards Lola and her squeaking suitcase wheels as she passed through an open corridor where hundreds of mobile phones hung along the walls on display. The grating symphony of her luggage was momentarily halted when she stopped to look more closely at the little tiny square screens that each declared a different message. 'Everything has its beauty, but not everyone sees it. Confucious', read one. Lola looked down at her jeans and the sweaty t-shirt that clung to her. She ran her hands over her fringe and the top of her hair to smooth it out.

Turning to the left she found the reception. The white cylinder desk looked out onto the busy street. The sun streamed in from the high panes and landed on Lola's neck making it sticky and uncomfortable again.

'Hi my name is Lola Paige. I'm looking for the New York Torch.'

'Come this way, Ms Paige.' The young man came out from behind his desk and, walking with more swagger than a runway model, led her to a small storeroom. 'You can leave your cases in here if you wish.'

Lola gladly deposited the luggage in the darkened store keeping her handbag.

'The elevator is just over here, Miss Paige.' Lola followed and thanked him as he scanned his pass card against the long black panel to open the lift.

'This will take you to the third floor, you're a bit late, the rest of the interns have already arrived,' he laughed. 'Nothing like making a good impression on your first day, Miss Paige.'

'Oh leave her alone, Greg,' laughed a voice behind them. 'He's only messing with you,' the woman smiled as she stepped into the lift beside Lola.

'Lookin' good, Ms Jodi,' said Greg raising his eyebrow and pursing his lip in appreciation of the vision.

The young woman was dressed in a pink pinafore dress with grey heels and her ebony skin was smooth and clear, Lola gazed at the perfect symmetry of her face, which was angular yet full. Her hair flowed to just below her ears in a mass of tiny but perfect corkscrews and Lola Paige was sure that she had never seen a more perfect woman in her life.

The contrast between them both made Lola take a subtle step away as if to distinguish her shoddy and dishevelled state from this vision that stood towering over her holding a coffee and what looked like a very expensive bag on her arm.

The woman's perfume filled the small space between them with hints of mandarin, bergamot and musk, Lola knew the smell but she couldn't place its name.

'Hi,' said the woman, her white smile in uniform with the rest of her perfections, extending her slender hand out. 'I'm Jodi. I work up in lifestyle.'

Lola rubbed the sweat from her hands onto the side of her jeans before shaking Jodi's hand. 'Nice to meet you,' smiled Lola apologetically, 'I'm Lola.'

'You're Irish!' declared Jodi, her face lighting up as if Lola was the most exciting and exotic thing that she'd ever seen.

'Yes,' nodded Lola suddenly filled with pride that being Irish could excite such enthusiasm in a woman like Jodi.

'So where are you interning, Lola?'

'News, I think, but I'll find out this morning where exactly.'

'Good,' said Jodi, her expression darkening slightly. 'I started out in news myself. It's okay but look out for Eugene, he can be a total pain in the ass for interns,' an airy laugh issued from her full lips.

The lift stopped and the doors swung open. 'Good luck, Lola. Maybe see you around.'

'Thank you,' said Lola self-consciously stepping out into another vast corporate space where the sound of computer keyboards clacked and hummed as the thrum of the printers and the general mechanics of the busy newsroom filtered up from the floor below.

'Miss Paige?' a young woman with long sleek dark hair approached Lola with a manufactured smile. Her brown eyes and arched eyebrows regarded Lola with indolence as though unsure if she'd gotten the right person. But Lola wasn't offended in the slightest she knew that she looked like a bag lady and there was a good chance she even smelled like one.

Lola nodded mumbling an apology for her unkempt appearance and followed the gentle tapping of the lady's Louboutins to a set of walnut double-doors.

'They're waiting for you in the boardroom,' she smiled, considering Lola again with a bemused look before leaving.

The boardroom doors lay open and the soft murmur of quiet conversation around the oval mahogany table halted when Lola walked in excusing her tardiness.

Her fellow interns – three men and one woman – sat poised and dressed immaculately looking professional all having arrived prepared with notepaper and pens, well ahead of time.

The man standing at the top of the room who was conducting proceedings looked up from his notes to greet her.

'Ms Paige, finally you've managed to join us.' Lola could tell that his smile was insincere not just because his eyes narrowed in a withering way when they looked at her but because his colours were muddy.

Lots of people had the same colours but instinct told Lola that not all people were the same. When the red in this man's aura pulsed and flexed she could see that it wasn't vibrant and clear red, which would have told her that this man was passionate with a healthy ego. His red was dull and murky revealing that he harboured deep resentments and anger. That he would be willing to place his own needs first even if it meant betrayal.

All this detail was formulated in seconds. Without her talent it would have been impossible to know such things after a few moments of observation, but Lola trusted her inner sight with total conviction.

'I'm very sorry, sir,' said Lola shyly. 'My flight only got in about thirty minutes ago.'

Lola's senses were on fire as her eyes flicked around the three young men and the young woman conducting a lightening quick survey of them. She took a seat beside the young girl with amiable chromes and ambers.

'Now that you've finally decided upon your seat, Miss Paige,' smiled the man, his expression withering again, 'we've a lot to get through.' He slid a welcome pack across the table to her as she perched uncomfortably on the edge of the stiff chair, trying to ignore the inquisitive stares from her fellow interns.

The young woman beside her smiled warmly and Lola reciprocated before turning her attention to the man at the head of the table.

'Right we can finally get started,' he said rolling his eyes in Lola's direction.

His balding head bent over to consult his notes again head. Lola could see his chest hair through his white shirt, either that or he had a black t-shirt on. She was too exhausted to give him a closer examination, but she didn't need to. His tone and lack of manners told her everything she needed to know.

'My name is Gene Rush.' Lola couldn't believe her rotten luck, the one man Jodi had warned her about was in charge of her every move. She would have laughed, but the fear of attracting any more unnecessary attention kept her silent.

'I am your lifeline, your supervisor and your saviour,' declared Gene Rush with all the pomp and ceremony of a preacher. 'I will oversee every aspect of your time here at the Torch. I will examine every inch of column you write, every interview you conduct and if I don't like what I see, we will be having a very serious conversation.' Perhaps she was just being paranoid but Lola thought his flinty eyes had settled a fraction longer on her with this warning.

'Each of you have been chosen because you are the best young talent that America has to offer. That's with the exception of Ms Paige here – where is it you're from? Dublin?'

Lola knew that he wasn't really expecting an answer but she politely gave him one. 'No, sir, I'm from the north of the island, Dublin is in the south.'

'It's all Ireland, isn't it,' he said dismissing her with a flick of his wrist. 'This is the first year that we've given a space to an international,' he smiled at her again so that his words sounded more like a threat than a declaration of fact. Two of the young men at the other side of the table sniggered, earning them an approving nod from their host.

Lola shot them an incendiary look.

'Now, you've all managed to secure accommodation in the city. If you look at your schedules, you can see that over the next few days we will be helping you to settle in to life in the Big Apple. After that you're on your own.'

Rush continued. 'You are at one of the greatest newspapers in the world and you will act and behave in a manner befitting the New York Torch. When you go out on a story you will act accordingly. If you bring the paper into disrepute in any way, you will be sent home on the next train. Or plane.' He looked at Lola again.

'A bank account has been set up for each of you. Your wage will be one thousand dollars per week. You will also be given a laptop and a phone, which can be used only for work purposes. I can and will monitor your emails and your browsing history.' He paused to let the full drama of the threat sink in.

'Each of you has been allocated a section of the newsroom to work in.' Rush turned to the woman seated beside Lola. 'Erin O'Connell, you will be working on the picture desk. This will include everything from news stories to fashion. I've had a look at some of your studies with the Boston Sentinel and I was very impressed.' The young woman beside Lola blushed and nodded her thanks.

'Jayden Watts, you'll be working on the metro's digital sports section, Eric Bebencowsky, you'll work up in the digital news desk and you will be joined up there by John Green. John, as you know you will be working as part of our technical team, designing and programming all our online content. Digital is where it is at, guys, print is dead. They just don't know it yet.'

Rush turned to Lola with the shadow of a smirk. 'Finally, Ms Paige, you'll be working down in print, on the metro news desk. Like your Bostonian comrade here, you'll find yourself working across all areas of news.'

Gene Rush closed over his notebook, slipping the golden pen into the inside of his jacket. He checked his phone before placing it back into his pocket.

'Guys, this is not the university newspaper or the local rag. This is a global daily. When you're in the bullpen you either sink or you swim. It is hard and it is cutthroat. Each of you will be assigned a mentor, who you will meet tomorrow. Their role is to guide you through the job, but if you want to survive in this game you must be able to work independently. Each mentor will report to me and each week we will review your progress.'

Again his gaze landed on Lola who stared at the tiny scuff marks on the table trying her best to ignore him.

'That's all for today, unfortunately something has come up that I need to deal with urgently. You are free to go home. You'll each report to your mentor in your relevant departments no later than 8.30 am tomorrow morning. I'll sent each of you an email letting you know who and where to find your designated person.'

As the interns began to pack their things away, the boardroom door opened. 'Isaac Kane.' Rush's tone was airy but there was a coldness in it.

The name made Lola start, causing her to bang her head off the underside of the table where she had been cramming her welcome pack into her bursting handbag.

'The mentors' meeting isn't until later,' Rush said, giving the impression that all mentors, like the interns around the table, should answer to him. 'To what do we owe this pleasure?'

Lola sat awestruck. Just inches in front of her, there in magnificent flesh and bone, suit and tie, was the sole reason she had wanted to become a journalist. Four-time Pulitzer Prize winning Isaac Kane.

Lola sat alert and upright her bright smile brimming from ear lobe to ear lobe staring with such reverence that everyone in the room was left in no doubt that Lola Paige's favourite journalist had just walked into the room.

Gene Rush looked from Lola to Isaac and back again and this fixed his hostility toward her from unsure to certain.

'Interns, I'm sure you don't need me to tell you who this man is,' said Rush, stepping aside to give Isaac the centre spot at the head of the table.

'Sorry, Eugene,' said Isaac smiling. 'Chris told me our meeting was later but I wanted to get an exclusive look at our crop of interns this summer.' He turned now to speak to them. 'This is the first year I've actually been at my desk and able to volunteer to be a mentor.' Isaac Kane's dark face broadened into a wide grin. 'So who have we got here?'

Immediately Gene Rush pointed to Eric Bebencowsky, one of the interns that had ingratiated themselves with the man by laughing at his jokes and insults.

Eric, a tall thin character with slicked hair, had an air of superiority and privilege. He condescended to inform Isaac what a great asset he was to the Torch and what an honour it would be to work with such an esteemed journalist. Lola watched as his colours flushed from deep reds to cloudy browns.

Isaac Kane smiled. 'Thank you, Eric, for your very kind words. What is it in particular that you like about my work?' The question threw Eric, and by now Lola was quite enjoying his discomfort. It was petty, she knew, but Eric could do with a bit of humility.

He was mumbling now about the Pulitzer Prizes before seizing up altogether and falling silent.

'You're on the print news desk, Eric?' asked Isaac sounding quite disappointed. 'No, Mr Kane, sir. No, I'm on the digital desk, sir.'

'Oh,' he smiled again, 'I only work in print, I've no real love for this whole online phenomenon, I'm a traditional man if anything.'

He turned to Gene Rush again whose face had turned puce. 'Is that it? I know the powers that be are determined to destroy us print journalists, Eugene, but I can't believe that they haven't sent us an intern. That's certainly a first,' chuckled Isaac.

'Lola, Mistah Kane, she's the intern fawr the print section.' Lola was taken aback by the interjection of the young woman beside her with a strong Bostonian accent. Lola liked the sound of how she rolled her consonants.

'You're, Lola, I take it?' Isaac Kane was actually speaking to her. Lola nodded, she couldn't seem to articulate anything.

'Right, Lola, it looks like you're with me,' he smiled.

Lola nodded her head in shock. She couldn't believe what had actually just happened.

'I'll see you at the bullpen desk at 9am sharp tomorrow.'

'Actually as the Intern Manager,' Rush interrupted, 'I've already informed Ms Paige here that she is answerable to me and that she must be in each morning by 8.30.'

'Okay, Eugene, you're the boss,' said Isaac, holding his hands up in mock surrender. '8.30 it is.' With that he walked back out of the room with Gene Rush stalking out behind him.

Lola finally managed to force the pack into her bag and pushed the chair in to the desk. The others had left the room, but Erin had stayed behind to wait on her.

'Hey, I'm Erin, it's good to meet you!'

Lola offered her hand in exchange. 'I'm Lola.'

'I've got to say I just love you're accent. So you're from Northern Ireland?'

'Yeah, I just got off the plane a while ago and I didn't have time to get changed. That would explain the absolute state of me!'

'You're fine,' said Erin, waving the comment off with her hand. 'Never listen to Eugene.' Both of them laughed. 'Is he an ass or what?'

'Yeah, he's a wee bit intense alright. I don't think I've gotten off to a very good start with him.'

'Never mind Eugene. You've only gone and landed Isaac freaking Kane as your mentor! How gorgeous is that man? I saw the way you looked at him, Lola, all wide eyed.'

Lola tried to explain that he was the reason that she wanted to be a journalist but Erin wasn't listening.

'Now don't you dare tell me it's all about the journalism,' she pointed at Lola laughing.

Erin's colours soared and melted into one another the more enthused she became. She flicked back her long honey-coloured hair away from her face. It looked so fresh and clean, while Lola's stuck to her head like glue. What with the rain at home and the heat in New York she looked a watery mess.

'Well, I'm not blind,' smiled Lola, 'but he's a bit old for us is he not?'

'Speak for yourself, Lola.' The girls laughed and made their way out into the assaulting heat.

'You want to share a cab?' Lola was about to jump into the taxi with Erin when she remembered her luggage.

'Shit,' she said stopping at the open cab door. 'I've forgotten my bags. You go on Erin and I'll see you tomorrow.'

'I'll see you in the morning,' waved Erin as she closed the door.

'See you tomorrow.' Lola waved her off before heading back inside to get the luggage from the store.

Five minutes later, Lola slid into the seat of her taxi; she was glad the ordeal was over. She was totally exhausted. Now there was only one more introduction to be made. Celeste had arranged for her to stay with her aunt. Rocha Moone had been a life-long member of the Order and had headed the American Chapter ever since her departure from Ireland as a young student in the 1960s. Now Rocha was professor of gender studies at Columbia University and Lola's host for the next three months.

'Where we goin', darling?' asked the cabbie through the screen between them.

'Sorry,' said Lola shaking the fog from her head again. '21 Princes Street, Manhattan. Please.'

The taxi driver hit the meter and they were off again, fading in to the bright yellow procession of cars.

~8~

The taxi pulled up outside a large industrial building, which had iron grids and ladders attached to the grey stone façade. The street, although off a central artery, was a hive of activity as crowds filled the terraces of cafés and bars enjoying the sunshine.

At first Lola thought that she might have come to the wrong address, but then she realised that the building had been sectioned off into apartments, each with their own bell and post box.

The taxi driver kindly lifted her luggage from the car and sat it on the pavement. She thanked him and paid the fare. Turning her attention to the door again, Lola ran her finger down the copper plate of listings. It was the last one. Pressing the corresponding bell she looked about the busy street trying to make some sense of the grid system she had just navigated. Lola had no idea what direction she'd come from or how far it was to the Torch offices.

She was wondering if she could walk to work from there when she absently hit the buzzer again, but this time the door swung open revealing a fresh-faced woman with silver hair styled into a bob. Her face was open and warm and her eyes were like Celeste's – a soft luminous brown which reminded Lola of the colour of autumn.

Rocha Moone was in her mid-sixties but there was a joie de vivre about her that meant she could easily have passed for a decade younger. The afternoon sunlight that bleached the pavements and buildings defused and radiated off her aura which matched her clothes and her spirit. Rocha wore a flowing silken dress with splashes of lilac, fuchsia and grey spilling into each other. Her nails were painted a deep purple and she smelled like violets. Her dress straps slipped off her shoulder giving her an air of carelessness and a vivaciousness that only women of her vintage could carry. Her feet were bare and the toenails were painted purple to match her fingernails. Around her neck hung a thick Celtic collaret with a triple spiral attached to the end of it. Lola thought it looked antique.

In Ireland, Rocha Moone would have been called a hippy but she exuded such a rich sensuality and satisfaction with herself that Lola found the woman completely captivating.

'Lola Paige,' she declared, pulling her into a tight embrace as if they'd know each other all their lives. 'What an honour it is to finally meet you,' said Rocha holding Lola at arm's length to examine her.

'We have so much to talk about. But come in off the street, darling,' she smiled lifting one of Lola's cases. 'You look like you could be doing with a shower and a bite to eat.'

Although she had a largely American accent now there still remained a trace of old country in Rocha's speech.

Lola followed Rocha into the lift. After pulling the steel cage shut behind them, they ascended to the fifth and top floor of the building where her loft apartment sat open and glorious.

Lola's jaw dropped at the sheer scale of the apartment and the surprising contemporary feel to it. Rocha had married the new with the antique beautifully. The entire bottom floor – comprised of a great living room and kitchen – was opened planned. The space was outlined by walls of naked, rust-coloured brick and three towering brick columns held up the roof of the apartment. But the one feature that Lola could not drag her eyes from was the vast windows that punctuated the stone, making it almost feel like the entire building was open to the world. Three thirteen feet high by twenty feet wide arched windows stretched from the floor right up to the ceiling, inviting the light of the sun to warm the room and the Swedish beech wood floors.

Two large grey sofas sat opposite each other on an enormous Persian rug. To the left stood a large wood burner that extended straight up into the high ceiling, disappearing out of the roof.

At the back of the apartment, a set of floating stairs lead to a mezzanine level which was closed off with a wall of glass cubes. All available wall space was either occupied by shelves of books or paintings, most of which depicted the Goddess in her many guises. Despite the volume of personal items, the apartment didn't feel cluttered such was the vastness of the room.

Lola couldn't believe that this was going to be her home for the next three months. She'd never want to leave here. It had everything: books, art and light. Lola thought this could even rival Arthur's book room back home in Brook Mill Manor.

'What an amazing home you have, Rocha,' said Lola in rapture as her eyes latched on to another piece of antiquity.

'I'm glad you like it, Lola,' said Rocha. 'I bought this place back in the seventies when no- one wanted to live around here and my colleagues at the university thought I'd gone crazy.' She smiled broadly.

'Your bedroom is up the stairs,' she said, pointing up to the left of the stairs. 'You'll have your own bathroom and all you need. This is your home for the next three months so please treat it as such. I've got you a set of your own keys so you can come and go as you please.'

Lola flopped down on the sofa; she had never been more grateful for a seat. Every part of her body ached and her head was still throbbing. Rocha sat down beside her giving her a once over. Her aura changed from violets and purples to apple and mossy greens with accents of daffodil yellow. The greens reminded Lola of Aíbgréne and she wondered if Rocha was a healer too.

'Is everything okay with you, Lola?' Rocha asked, her eyes alert and penetrating. Normally Lola would have been inclined to parry the question but she couldn't quite muster the energy required to put on a show.

'To be honest, Rocha,' said Lola, feeling comfortable enough already to call her by her first name, 'I've had a very strange day.'

'Okay. So how strange is strange?' said Rocha smiling and settling back in to her chair.

'Something happened to me today that has never happened before. I mean...' corrected Lola, 'I've had flashbacks before but not by actually touching someone.'

'Interesting,' said Rocha. She sat with her index finger and thumb around her chin, nodding thoughtfully for Lola to continue.

'Back home, when I was boarding the plane, there was this man in front of me. I had been looking at his aura, trying to figure him out,' said Lola smiling awkwardly, 'I like to do that sometimes when I'm bored,' she added, almost apologising.

'That's a very clever way to hone your skills, Lola. Practice makes perfect after all.'

'Well I was watching him and as we were walking on to the plane he dropped some papers so I picked them up for him.' Lola's mind drifted back to the airplane and while it was only hours ago it felt like years. 'I called out to him but when he didn't hear me I tapped him on the shoulder to hand them back.' The memory of the peculiar encounter flashed back to Lola as though it was happening all over again.

'There was a flash and then I was transported somewhere else. I mean, I know I didn't physically go somewhere else because just seconds later I was back standing in the same place.'

'Did you recognise the place you went to?' asked Rocha.

'Yes, I knew it very well. It was the Brú na Bóinne and, what is even stranger, I seemed to be handing something to this terrified little boy. I couldn't get a grasp of the vision but it freaked me out a little.'

'You say this was the first time you have experienced this sort of vision?'

'No. I had a similar experience when I went to Tara for the first time and in my dreams before Arthur was murdered but that was just me own my own. It's never happened through touch before.'

'Interesting.'

Rocha Moone got up from her seat and walked to the kitchen and switched on the kettle. 'You can take the girl out of Ireland,' she shouted over to Lola, 'but you can't take Ireland out of the girl. A wee cup of tea makes everything better,' she added. 'You know, Lola, you've done a lot of travelling today, you need to get some rest. This city can drain you very quickly if you don't know how to protect yourself.'

'I can feel it,' said Lola. 'I can feel its enmity toward me. Like the city is hostile to my arrival. That sounds a bit mental, doesn't it?'

Rocha came back from the kitchen with something steaming in a cup and handed it to her before sitting in the seat opposite, so she was looking right at Lola.

'It isn't mental, as you put it. That is the sort of intuition that will keep you safe, my love. Carl Stein owns this city.' The name stunned Lola. It had been so long since anyone had actually said his name out loud. Aíbgréne and Celeste had always just alluded to him, so she was taken by surprise at Rocha's nonchalance.

'You don't speak his name?' said Rocha tilting her back with a curt laugh. 'He's not Lord Voldemort, Lola. Mind you, he's not far off it! More handsome, perhaps. I'm not sure if my niece told you that he and his son, whom I believe you are well acquainted with...'

Colour rose to Lola's pale cheeks alerting Rocha to her shame that her dalliances with the son of darkness were common knowledge.

'Sorry, darling.' Rocha knelt forward placing her hand on Lola's knee. 'I didn't mean to embarrass you, honey,' she said, 'but I have a tendency to get right to the point.'

'Yes,' said Lola, 'and your great-niece is very much the same.'

'Yes I'm well versed on Aíbgréne's reluctance to your visit, but sometimes her love for you clouds her judgement. She does care deeply about you, Lola, you do understand that?'

'Yes, I know,' conceded Lola reluctantly. 'But she can be frustrating. She underestimates me. A lot!'

'Lola, we have all underestimated you. Celeste, Aíbgréne, Carl Stein have all underestimated you and I dare say you underestimate yourself. At one time or another we have all questioned Arthur's wisdom, but,' she smiled, 'you haven't half proven us all wrong!'

'Is that what I felt, when I came closer to the city? Carl Stein's magick?'

'That, amongst other things,' said Rocha in a matter of fact tone. 'This has been the epicentre of Hell Fire Club activity since the coming of the Dutch and English colonists way back in the 1600s. The Hell Fire Club has been known by many names, across many traditions. Their knowledge of the mysteries is as rich as the Order's but they have perverted and desecrated that wisdom to suit their own dominator agenda which has prevailed for the last seven millennia.'

Rocha paused before continuing. 'So those early colonists that stole the land from the indigenous Lenape natives, here in New York, brought with them their own brand of magick and ancient wisdom. They have been instrumental in building this city and indeed this country. It is no coincidence, Lola, that New York is a global financial centre. The entire global agenda of the Hell Fire Club is managed from a one-point-one kilometre strip that runs northwest to southeast across just eight city blocks. The effects of that small area are felt not only in America but in the far corners of the world.'

Lola remembered her drive through Wall Street earlier that day and how much power resided in that tiny area.

'Do you think he knows I'm here? Carl Stein, I mean, do you think he knows?'

'I would guess that he knows you are here. In fact, I'd be sure of it. He needs you, Lola. We have discovered that last winter, the night he abducted you. I believe that Carl Stein's powers cannot harm you, but up until that point he himself didn't even realise that.'

'But they can harm me,' said Lola. Her hand reached for her throat where she was sure she could feel him restrict her airway again.

'When I say harm, I mean kill you. I understand he left with the Cube, but I don't think he fully understands what the Cube is for.'

'I don't fully understand what it's for and I'm the one charged with bloody protecting it.' Lola rubbed her neck and stretched.

'What do you mean, Lola? Are you telling me that my niece hasn't explained any of this to you?' Rocha was indignant.

'Well in fairness to Celeste, she and I never really got the opportunity to spend a lot of time together, what with her being taken and held captive by Carl Stein and when we rescued her...'

Lola trailed off as the pain of remembrance choked her. 'When we finally got to her she was at death's door. After that it took all her strength to get well again and the time never seemed right.' Lola thought of how frail Celeste had become and she wondered if she'd managed to truly break free from Carl's magick, but she kept this to herself.

'It wasn't ideal, Lola, you're right. Are you sure you want to do this now? You seem awfully fatigued, my young charge.'

'I'm exhausted Rocha, but one thing I've learned over the past year is not to put off to tomorrow what you can do today. Too much has been left to tomorrow. Arthur put off telling me any of this. Yes,' acknowledged Lola, 'he may have drip fed me information on some subliminal level but what good has that done me? Celeste and I left each after the cremation with the intention of continuing our conversation the next day. I wouldn't speak to her again until four months later. No, Rocha,' said Lola adamantly, 'there's no time like the present.'

Rocha smiled. 'As you like.'

Rocha picked up where Lola's encounter with the Steins had ended. She was very well informed in all of Lola's affairs and this gave Lola an immense sense of security. She had a deepening sense of connection with Rocha and believed that she wouldn't hide any of the truth from her.

'Without the Oracle,' said Rocha taking a sip from her cup, 'we can't be exactly sure how the Cube, or more importantly its pieces, are to be used. However, the Order has always been of the opinion that once separated each part of the Cosmic Cube acts as a key that activates a certain global ley line.'

'A what?' The term sounded vaguely familiar to Lola but she wasn't completely confident that she understood what a ley line was.

'Some people, like me,' Rocha pointed her slender finger at herself dramatically, 'believe that the earth is a conscious living organism, that it has a brain, a heartbeat, arteries and a soul, just like we humans do. Those of my school of thought maintain that there are certain meridians that allow this energy to flow around the earth much in the same way that blood brings life to our bodies. We believe that this in turn, if looked after properly, has a positive effect on the consciousness of humanity but if it is disrupted and harmed it can cause disease and illness, like much of what you see in the world today.'

Then like the spark of a flame, Lola remembered something Aíbgréne had said during her wedding, the night they both sat on the Mound of the Hostages and looked out across the sacred soil and earth of Teamhair.

'Yes,' said Lola, enthused that she understood. 'Aíbgréne told me about these. Is there one of these energy arteries at Tara?'

'Yes, Lola, we believe that there is. The Order believes there are five primary goddess portals located at certain sacred sites across the globe and that the Cube is the key to controlling these. Their locations are unknown or long forgotten. That's why we need the Lost Oracle because it is believed that it plots their locations.'

'So these keys or portals,' asked Lola, 'what are they supposed to do?' 'Activate a cosmic accession and usher the return of the Goddess.'

'Oh, is that all,' laughed Lola. If she'd been told over a year ago that she would be sitting in New York with member of a secret order discussing cosmic accession she would never have believed it.

'They are there to return the light of the Dé Danann to this reality and overthrow the existing paradigm that has oppressed and enslaved us since the Dé Danann retreated. That is why we must find the Oracle before the Hell Fire Club. Like a silver thread, Lola, we walk that fine and delicate line between the light and the dark. They have left no stone unturned in their pursuit for the Oracle. It has come to my attention in recent months that extensive research is being carried out in various countries all over the world.'

'So what do we do?' asked Lola, raising her arms in exasperation. 'Where do we start to look for this Oracle? How can I compete with a machine with tentacles in every pond?'

'I know nothing for sure, Lola. It is my belief that you have a very strong connection to the Oracle. Celeste told me that you had a sudden change of heart about applying for the internship out here.'

'That's right. I wasn't really interested but I can't explain it, when I woke up the next morning, it seemed like the right thing to do. Like it was the only thing to do.'

'Exactly' said Rocha her hazel eyes full of meaning. 'Indeed, Lola, here you are. I believe that the book, or at least part of it, has been calling you. I think that is why you suddenly felt compelled to come to New York and put yourself in harm's way. Let's be honest, Lola, you know exactly what you face here. That is why you have taken Aíbgréne's advice so ill. You know she is right about the dangers you face and naturally you feel guilty, although compelled to do what has to be done. The Oracle wants you to find it. It needs you to find it. You are its raison d'être, its reason for being. Like a mother yearning for her child, she longs to behold you.'

'Are you saying you think that the Oracle could be here in New York?' Lola's eyebrows knitted together in disbelief. 'Surely if it was, Carl Stein would know it.'

'The only reason I think it is here,' said Rocha nonchalantly, 'is because, my dear, you are here. As for the Steins, I don't know if they will draw the same conclusions. Only time will tell.'

Although illuminating, the conversation had left Lola completely drained. Her throat was barbed and her body felt as though all the pulp had been squeezed out of it. Beyond the wide-arched windows flamingo clouds gathered in the blue and silver sky and Lola longed to wash and sleep.

'I think I'd better call home and let everyone know I've arrived safely.'

'You do that, honey, and then get yourself to bed for some well-deserved rest.'

Lola dragged herself out of the comfy seat and up the stairs; each step felt like a mountain to her tired legs.

'You know, Lola,' shouted Rocha after her, 'we all believe in you. You're not in this alone – you never have been.'

Lola could only muster a smile. After she came off the phone to her parents, her head crashed on the plush pillow.

~9~

The morning light that crept around the edges of the blackout blind, along with the drone of the air con, roused Lola from a heavy sleep. She didn't remember much after her head hit the pillow, only that the pillow had smelled of lavender. Pervading dread that she might have slept in made her reach for her phone to check the time, but it was still in her case downstairs.

She had intended to unpack and lay some clothes out for the morning, but exhaustion and the oppressive weight that continued to bear down on her since arriving in this strange city had forced her straight to bed.

The sound of clinking of cups and the hiss of the kettle reassured her as she stretched and reluctantly crawled from the opulence of her soft queen bed and walked out into the bright hallway.

Sunlight assaulted her eyes and she had to allow herself a moment to get orientated. The stairs were broad but they didn't have a handrail, so Lola took to them gingerly, her feet reaching out suspicious they might not find the next step.

'You're up early' greeted Rocha as she rolled up her yoga mat. 'I was letting you sleep on.' She went to attend to whatever concoction she had brewing on the gas hob. It smelt good, like lemon and mint.

'What time is it?' Lola asked. Her voice was thick with sleep and her legs and body still heavy from the night's rest.

'It's eight after six, honey.' It took Lola's brain a moment to process what eight after six meant. She realised she was going to have to do that a lot.

Eight minutes past six. She could have cried. Her body clock was clearly off the chart. According to the student code it was nothing short of a mortal sin to be up before 8am.

'You can go back to bed if you want and I'll call you in an hour or so,' said Rocha in response to Lola's upturned face.

'No,' said Lola, momentarily seduced by the prospect of another hour in that blissful bed. 'I'd better not, Rocha. I have to unpack and find something suitable to wear today. It's my first day and I don't want to go in looking like I did yesterday.'

'How about some breakfast then?' said Rocha handing her a cup of her lemony brew. 'That tastes great. What is it?' Lola asked, taking another sip.

'It's my own blend. There's a little bit of mint, some lemongrass, dandelion root and of course a little bit of magick!'

Lola laughed but she didn't doubt that there was. Whatever the ingredients, the tea helped to wake her up and clear her head for the first time since she had arrived in the city.

'So what are the plans today?'

'Well I think we are just being introduced to our mentors today. I forgot to tell you yesterday,' beamed Lola. 'You won't believe who I got as a mentor.'

'Who?' said Rocha, playing along.

'Isaac Kane. Unbelievable, isn't it?'

'That is impressive. He took a one of my classes when he was at Columbia,' smiled Rocha. 'That's my claim to fame,' she laughed taking another sip of her tea.

'We need to get all our passwords and security tags sorted as they'll be taking us on a walk about to help us get our bearings. Speaking of which,' said Lola, 'can I walk from here to the paper?'

'No, honey,' laughed Rocha, 'you'd be safer getting the subway. Your stop is on my way so we can travel together if you like.'

'That'd be great,' Lola was deeply grateful to Rocha for taking her in. It was the only reason her parents had allowed her to come.

'Rocha,' said Lola sincerely, 'I want to say thank you for everything, it means a great deal.'

'Lola, it is a pleasure to have you. I wouldn't have it any other way, honey. Besides, you're not a stranger! You and I go way back. You had better go and shower and organise what you want to wear, we want to beat the morning rush.'

The mouth of the subway gaped open, warm and stuffed with commuters. If this was beating the rush, Lola didn't want to see it when it was busy. She followed close behind Rocha, who walked energetically pointing out the various stops and lines, telling her which one she needed but it all sounded like double Dutch to Lola.

The temperature rose as they descended further underground and the fusty smell of roasted peanuts and rubber wafted through the air. Every now and then, Lola would feel the whoosh of the warm air rising as another train in some unseen platform arrived or departed.

The mist had descended on her again shrouding her thoughts and churning her stomach. The energy of the city was brash and coarse, needling and prodding at her mind and flesh.

Everyone was in a hurry and entirely disconnected, as though each person walked around in their own micro-universe. Battling towards the platform was exhausting and demoralising with each woman and man fighting for themselves. No one stepped out of your way, no one waited while you slowed down and they all seemed so angry. Perhaps if she'd to negotiate this circus every day that's exactly how she'd feel herself, reasoned Lola.

Waiting ten-deep on the platform, Lola stood rigid beside Rocha. As she looked around her a cloud hung in the air, a profusion of yellows, pinks, reds, greens, orange, greys, browns and blues. The crowd's auras had been sloshed together like some exotic cocktail. Lola's head began to feel light and beads of sweat settled on her forehead.

'Lola, are you okay? You've gone awfully pale – even for you,' said Rocha, clearly concerned.

'I think it's the crowds and the heat down here, I feel a bit claustrophobic.'

'Do you have your ring?'

Lola nodded and fished it out from under her black dress. She had tried to buy a complete wardrobe before she came out to the States. Her black court shoes were new and they were beginning to hurt her feet already. On the way to the tube stop she'd noticed women in dresses and suits with trainers or flats on, now she understood why.

'It's here,' said Lola, flashing the ring at Rocha.

'I think you're going to need to wear that on your finger, Lola, while in New York anyway.'

Lola felt another surge of warm air speed up the tunnel, declaring the imminent arrival of their train.

'Okay, Lola, this is us,' warned Rocha, grabbing her elbow. 'Now, you are only six stops away,' shouted Rocha as the crowd surged forward, spilling into the carriage.

'I doubt I could do this every day. If it's only two miles away, I think I might try and walk in the morning,' said Lola, holding on tightly to the upright pole.

'You're not in Ballyvalley anymore, honey,' said Rocha laughing. 'You'll get used to it.'

The train jerked forward and Lola counted the stops until the voice over the speaker announced that they were now approaching 42nd and Times Square. Rocha nodded that this was her stop.

'As soon as you come out of the station, your building is directly across the road. Have a wonderful day. You look the part anyway.' Rocha gave her a wink as the train door closed again and Lola was carried along with a river of people rising to street level.

Lola was delighted to be above ground again. She crossed the street and entered the New York Torch, feeling satisfied that she looked much better than she had the day before. This observation was confirmed when Gregg, the front of house, who was busy chatting up one of the deliverymen, interrupted his conversation to stop her, thinking she was an imposter.

'Excuse me. Miss. Miss.' Lola was close to the lift before she even realised that he was addressing her. 'You need to check in at reception before you proceed to the floors above,' he said his tone petulant and scolding.

Lola wheeled around to explain that she was an intern when he stepped back dramatically as if she was contagious.

'Is that you, Miss Paige?' said Gregg, placing his hand on his chest for added effect.

'Yes,' grinned Lola rolling her eyes. 'Now come on, I don't look that different from yesterday.'

'You wanna bet?' Gregg looked back across the lobby and raised his hands to some unseen effigy in the ceiling. 'Now look what you've done, coming in here looking all smart.'

'What?' said Lola, following his gaze.

'Grant has only gone and left, now I have to wait another whole week until he's back again.' He opened the lift for Lola, stepping aside to let her enter.

'Lucky escape for Grant then,' she said impishly as the doors closed.

Most of the morning was taken up with a tour of the news floors and the various section desks. They each got their own lift and building passes as well as a press pass for when they were allowed out on assignment. By the time they had all that completed it was time for lunch.

'Do you fancy headin' out to grab a bite, Lola?' Erin asked after Gene had dismissed them.

'Yeah, I'm clean starving!' Lola hadn't eaten since 6.30 that morning and her stomach was beginning to feel abandoned. 'I need trees and grass.'

'What? To eat?' joked Erin.

'No,' laughed Lola, 'to feel and breathe and see.'

'I know just the place.' When the girls had decided on their choice of lunch, Lola followed Erin to the bank of cabs that lay as if sleeping in the growing heat.

'Where are we going?'

'Bear with me, Lola,' said Erin bending forward to speak to the driver. 'Central Park, please.'

'Sure thing, kid,' said the cabbie as they got in.

Five minutes later the girls were in Central Park. Erin led Lola to Sheep Meadow, one of the vast forty-nine zones of the 843 acres of beautiful countryside that lay in the middle of Manhattan.

Refugees from the heat and dust of the city lay sprawled out like debris on the worn green grass. Sunbathers, picnickers and families flooded into the open space in search of the same thing that Lola was looking for.

'How come I never thought of this?' said Lola, kicking off her shoes and letting her sweaty feet sink in to the fine blades of grass.

'I thought you could be doing with a little taste of home,' laughed Erin airily. 'You missin' all that greenery, Lola!'

'Something like that,' said Lola craning her neck up towards the sky, thinking of home and the land. It was only with a little distance that she could understand what a deep connection she had with the earth. She focused on the ground beneath the soles of her feet.

'Oh my god, that feels divine,' she breathed. Standing on a real bit of earth energised and reinvigorated her. She could feel the life of the soil and grass, the towering oaks and maples and elms that surrounded the park move through the warm dirt where the soles of her feet, like sponges sucked it all in.

'So, Erin O Connell,' said Lola finally, once she was recharged. She sat back down beside her new friend. 'You're from Boston? Your name is more Irish than mine,' joked Lola as she unwrapped her sandwich.

'Yeah, you know the usual story, my great-grandfather was Irish he was from a place called Skibereen.'

'Yes, in County Cork!'

'We went there a few years ago, we did Cork and Kerry and went up to Dublin, but we didn't get time to visit Belfast.'

'That's a pity, maybe next time. Belfast is a great city. I know I'm biased but it has been through so much and yet it has managed to re-emerge, like a phoenix from the flames. So what university are you at in Boston?'

'BC. Boston College,' she explained. 'I'm majoring in photojournalism. How about you, Lola?'

'I go to Queen's University. It's in Belfast. I'm studying journalism with politics and a bit of English lit. So photography,' said Lola truly impressed, 'that is a real art form. I love all the National Geographic stuff, it's something else. A picture can speak a thousand words.'

'Yeah, I've been taking pictures for as long as I can remember. My dad did it as a hobby and I just followed him. I like all sorts really but I'd love to work for National Geographic or Time Magazine. Not much chance of that.'

'Why not?' asked Lola.

'Well there might not be any jobs, I mean at the National Geographic anyway. The Steins you see,' explained Erin, 'they've recently bought the magazine and their first move was to reduce the work force by one hundred and fifty. That's what Carl Stein does, he uses his money to buy a national treasure and then he goes about destroying it! But he is so goddam hot and so is his son,' laughed Erin as an aside.

'He's a piece of shit is what he is,' shot Lola without veiling the venom in her voice. 'You know him personally, Lola?' joked Erin, never suspecting that she would. 'That's one way to put it, I suppose.'

'You are shittin' me, Lola. You're telling me you know Carl freakin' Stein?' Lola just nodded her head already regretting her outburst. 'His son Alex, you ever meet him? He's betrothed to Olivia Van der Vart, apparently she is the ultimate bitch. She heads one of Daddy Stein's companies and has more balls than most of the men that work for her. Ruthless, they say. I would never have put her and Alex together,' continued Erin but Lola wasn't hearing her anymore.

'Lola, you okay?' Erin's words echoed through Lola's mind and she tried to pick apart what she was saying. That familiar knot gathered in her solar plexus again, throbbing and contracting. She forced the palm of her hands down into the grass hoping that it would help clear her head. Her brain plucked and twanged at the words betrothed since childhood.

'Look,' said Erin with her mouth full, pointing at the centre spread in her magazine. 'It's all in here.'

Lola looked down at the page with glassy eyes to see Alex smiling with his arm around the waste of a tall redhead. Their white smiles hurt her eyes, hurt her heart. Lola's fingers involuntarily reached out and traced over Alex's face. He looked different. Older. His hair wasn't lose and free anymore instead he wore it sleek and swept into a side shade and Lola

thought it made him look more like his father. His face was still a work of art but Lola no longer recognised the person behind it.

Her appetite had disappeared she set aside the sandwich she'd been eating, it felt like ash in her mouth. Lola took a drink of her water.

She often wondered how she would feel if she saw him again. Based on her reaction to a mere picture Lola thought that it would be better that she was never in that situation.

'It's time were getting back to the office,' she said, closing the magazine over and handing it back to Erin. Lola jumped to her feet and put her shoes back on. It stung as she forced her blistered feet back into her heels. Tomorrow she would definitely do flats.

If Erin was intrigued, she didn't show it. Instead she lifted Lola's waste up and deposited in the bin. Both women caught a cab back to the office in silence.

'I'm working tonight. I'm out on my first job,' said Erin as they stepped into the lift.

'Oh great! Where?'

'Some benefit thing apparently – the who's who of New York will be there,' she laughed.

'Listen, have a great night and don't stay out too late,' said Lola as they parted on the third floor.

Lola went back to her desk wishing she'd never alluded to knowing the Steins, then Erin would have had no need to show her that grotesque picture.

Lola got back to work, she was working the copy desk for now, talking notes from journalists reporting on courts and sifting through press releases, hoping to find her first story. To think that she had come all the way to New York to do more press releases depressed her.

So far she had pitched three different stories to Gene Rush. Apparently everything had to go through him first before they were brought to the section editors. Lola was sure that the mass buying of property in Harlem by Stein Corp would be newsworthy, she'd found a press release buried in the pile on her desk. It was from the Friends of Harlem Community Directive and they detailed their distress at the takeover of their community, which they said was forcing locals out.

Lola was excited that there was a good story in this but when she'd sent the email to Gene earlier that morning he came back straight away telling her that it wouldn't suit.

Eager to get her first break, she'd sent another proposal across, this one was about covering a research visit of a visiting academic and the Book of Kells at Columbia University. Lola thought that this would make a nice little feature, something light but interesting but as of yet she hadn't gotten a reply.

She clicked into her emails to check again, but still nothing. Hopeful, she continued sifting through the remainder of press releases that lay scattered around her desk.

'Afternoon, Irish.' Spinning round in her chair, Lola found Isaac Kane smiling down at her and she actually managed to speak to him this time without tripping over her words.

'Hello, Mr Kane.'

'Isaac. My name is Isaac. Mr Kane was my father.'

'So,' he said as he picked up the press release she had been looking at. 'Is this what you have been up to? No stories yet?'

'No,' sighed Lola. 'Sadly not. I've pitched a few ideas to Mr Rush but he said that they weren't strong enough, he said press releases were the drill for all interns, so hopefully something will come up.'

'Eugene told you that? Did he?' Suddenly Isaac Kane's smile evaporated from his face and Lola panicked, wondering what she'd said to darken his mood so abruptly. 'Did he indeed?' repeated Isaac, nodding his head and flexing his jaw. 'Come with me,' he said.

He was already at the lift when she reached him. He looked down at her bare feet, but made no comment. There was no way that she could put her shoes on again. They travelled three floors before getting out again. It was different world up here, so tranquil compared to the chaos of the bullpen below.

Each office was glass-fronted and looked out onto some part of the sprawling city below.

'What's wrong, Mr Kane? Have I done something wrong, sir?' Lola's voice cracked and she feared she might cry.

'You?' said Isaac still seething. 'No. Sit here, Irish.' Lola sat quietly on the chair as directed. She tried to force her shoes back onto her cramped and swollen feet as Isaac strode towards one of the many executive offices.

Lola didn't recognise the person he was speaking to. He looked to be in his early forties with silver hair and slightly red complexion. Isaac was growing more and more animated now while the other man, relaxed and not exactly intimidated leaned back in his chair and tried to reason with him. Their ease with each other gave Lola the impression that both men must have been well acquainted.

The lift bell signalled and Gene Rush strode out. His eyes narrowed at Lola as he glared at her on the way past. Lola wished the chair and grey walls around her could have swallowed her up. Could this day get any worse, she thought, a pink flush flowered her pale skin laying bare her embarrassment. Being so far from home made every tiny crack feel like a colossal fault line.

The politics of the Ballyvalley News had been a doddle compared to this. By now Lola understood that whatever it was that ignited Isaac was nothing to do with her and more to do with the obvious tension and acrimony that bubbled between him and Gene Rush.

Looking back towards the office Lola sank deeper into the chair when she saw that Isaac and Gene were now jowl to jowl with the silver-haired man having to intercede, as though it was a children's playground.

Managing to get them both to sit at each end of the office he looked back once to make sure that they both remained seated before opening the door and calling for Lola to come in.

Lola's feet burned as she walked the short distance on the carpet tiles.

'Ms Paige,' the man extended his hand to greet her, 'I'm Chris Auld and I'm the Director of News here at the Torch. It's very nice to meet you.'

Lola knew he didn't think that it was nice to meet her at all. Americans were great at playing the game, but she knew the truth because his aura and his eyes were saying something very different. They were saying, I don't need to be dealing with this bullshit. I shouldn't be mediating between two senior members of staff over an intern that is one of many.

Yet he smiled his politician's smile and offered her a seat, which she gladly took as another blister burst on her foot. She could feel the warm liquid spilling out of it.

Completely embarrassed and a tad confused, Lola didn't look at Isaac and she dared not look at Gene. Instead she looked at the news director who was pretending to be interested in her.

'So, Lola, you've been working on the print copy desk. Down in the bullpen?' Lola didn't think he wanted a reply so she just nodded her head. 'It's where we all started, well myself and Isaac anyway.' This comment wasn't lost on Gene, as Lola noticed him bristle. 'It's where us rookies and greenhorns learned our trade. Of course everything is changing and we need to be part of that change, Lola.'

Lola nodded again.

'Isaac has been telling me about some of your work and he is very impressed. So much so he wants to know why you haven't gone out on your first story yet.'

Gene, not entirely happy with where the conversation was going interjected at this point. 'When the interns come in, we reinforce the idea that they must find their own stories. It is not realistic to spoon-feed them. Everyone else has managed to get their first break, so why can't she?'

'Is this correct, Lola. You haven't gotten a story from those hundreds of press releases you've trawled through by now?' His smile was sympathetic but his colours distracted Lola from believing it.

'Well, Mr Auld, as I was explaining to Isaac, I have pitched a couple of my ideas to Mr Rush, but he felt that they weren't suitable for the paper,' explained Lola, her eyes solely focusing on the news director. 'I mean I understand that there may have been some that weren't appropriate but I genuinely felt that plight of the Friends of Harlem Community Directive would have been at least worth investigating but Mr Rush didn't seem to think so, so I took his advice and left it.'

Rush tried to interrupt but Chris silenced him, nodding at Lola to continue.

'I also read a release that the Book of Kells is currently at Columbia University and they say that the travelling professor is on the verge of making a ground-breaking discovery, but I'm waiting to hear back from Mr Rush on that one.'

Lola looked momentarily toward Isaac who was smiling a bright grin. Erin was right, he was gorgeous, if you were into older men that was, as Erin seemed to be.

Gene remained silent but Lola could feel the animosity stream from him like a laser beam.

The director's face darkened as he turned to him. 'I'm not aware, Eugene, of interns ever pitching stories to you first. You and I know they speak to their mentors. There has obviously been some confusion over this.'

He spoke with authority and no one, not Gene Rush or Isaac Kane, interrupted or challenged him. He turned to address Lola now.

'Perhaps it would be best, Lola, for you to spend some time with your mentor. After all, that is why I was very keen for Isaac to become involved in our intern scheme. He has a great wealth of experience in the field and it's about time that he gave something back.' He flicked a grin at his colleague. 'Of course, Lola, you will still be under the management of Gene and you will answer to him, when necessary.' This bone of compromise pleased Gene as he nodded his head in agreement.

'Okay, Mr Auld,' said Lola, still a touch confused about what had just happened. Gene nodded his goodbyes to the news director and left, and the atmosphere in the room lightened immediately.

'Isaac, you've gotta cut him some slack, the interns have always been his gig, you can't come in and start pissing all over that,' said Chris, speaking to Isaac like an old friend again and not his boss.

'Chris, you know his problem is with me, not Irish here and she's bearing the brunt of his petty bullshit. Not on my watch. She'll be answerable to me and me alone, you tell him what you like, but I'm not having her treated like that. And there he is, the rat, still up to his old tricks. The Harlem story Lola pitched,' spat Isaac. 'Have a look at this.'

Isaac shuffled Chris out from behind his computer and tapped on the keyboard. 'Now look at this,' he demanded.

Chris looked at the screen and shook his head. 'What can I say, Isaac? He joslted her out of a story. This is what happens.'

'Not on my watch it doesn't. Not on my watch. Come on, Irish, at least there's one story left for you to cover. You'll learn to keep your ideas and leads to yourself. It's the first rule of this dirty business, keep your own council.'

'What did he do with my story?' quizzed Lola breaking into a slow canter to keep up with Isaac.

'He gave it to that kid Bebencowsky that's interning in digital. His name is on the by-line instead of yours. There is a war being waged in this place and as you can see, digital fight dirty.'

'Thanks for that, Mr K... I mean Isaac.'

He waved it off and fell silent again. When the elevator opened, he said, 'I've to see a man about a dog, I'll speak to you later.'

Lola stepped out of the lift. 'Just one more piece of advice, Irish,' said Isaac. 'Wear flats tomorrow.' He laughed as the doors closed, depriving Lola of a comeback.

Feeling determined, Lola sat down at her desk and fished out the press release sent from Columbia University, hoping that she hadn't missed the opportunity.

As she read through it again and checked the event date she was delighted when she realised it was still three days away.

Lola rang the number and reserved her place. They asked if she'd be bringing a photographer and without a second thought she said yes. She'd ask Erin to come along; it would be good craic if nothing else.

~ 10 ~

Eight stops and she would be at the university. Lola fished out a piece of paper from her holdall. Rocha had drawn her a rough map for directions. The grid system still confused Lola. 535 West 114th Street. It was all gibberish to her and seemed overly complicated.

Isaac had told her to dress formally, so she did. She wore a black skater dress with heels and fixed her hair into a loose Dutch braid along the back of her head. She brought with her a small briefcase-come-handbag with her notepad and Dictaphone.

Butterflies frolicked and danced in the pit of Lola's stomach in anticipation of her first story for the New York Torch. The metro desk would only take about one hundred and fifty words, two hundred max, but this didn't make Lola any less excited or determined to be thorough. She knew she would pour over every letter, making sure it was just right.

The house style for newspapers in America was very different from home. Here they started every column with the location like a wire or telegram. She had diligently read numerous printed stories since she'd started at the Torch to help her try and adjust to their way of doing things.

Lola looked at the map above her head. One more stop and she'd be there. The train wasn't as busy as usual and it was nice for a change not to have to jostle and fight her way on and off the train.

Gene had kept her very busy the last few days on the copy desk and running errands. She hadn't seen Isaac, which had irritated her a bit. Especially after the fuss he'd made about her being answerable to him.

He had, however, been in contact via email to say he had been away for a few days researching a story he was working on. He'd wished her all the best for tonight.

Finally the train jerked to a halt. It was her stop. Lola welcomed the rush of the cool evening air around her face and body each time she emerged from the bowels of the stifling subterranean platform.

This part of New York was very different. There were more trees for a start and she liked that. As she crossed the road there were signs directing her to Columbia University; she consulted Rocha's hand drawn map and notes again. Rocha was working late and had promised to come along to the library after she was done.

The main campus was just a few blocks away. The map didn't make much sense at present but when she finally reached the quad Lola got her bearings.

Built around the central Low Memorial Library, Columbia comprised of six small courtyards and two main terraces. The upper terraces, Rocha had explained, contained classroom buildings, dormitories and her final destination – the Butler Library – that sat on the east wing of the quad.

The large classical renaissance building, with its rusticated granite base glittering in the falling dusk, dominated the space. The façade featured an arcade of columns and Lola could see different names inscribed along the side of the library and at the front.

She read the names in time with her steps as her heels echoed across the empty court-yard.

Homer, Herodotus, Sophocles, Plato, Aristotle, Demosthenes, Cicero, Milton, Shakespeare, Goethe and so it went on. Some she knew and some she didn't.

Arthur would have known them all. There weren't many women listed but then that was nothing new, she thought to herself as she entered the library via the second floor door.

She had managed to cram in a bit of research on the Butler Library which would help her set the mood for her piece.

As it turned out, Butler was home to a very impressive collection. The library housed over two million volumes and now it was to host one of the most priceless and famous books in the world – the Book of Kells.

Lola was ashamed that she had to come the whole way across the Atlantic Ocean to see one of her country's greatest and most celebrated treasures. She remembered that Arthur had an illustrated book on it somewhere amongst the vast collection in his own library back at Brook Mill Manor.

The desolate pangs of homesickness hollowed Lola for a moment when she remembered her sanctuary and being nestled between the books and Arthur's old rocking chair. She missed home more than she had anticipated but she was determined to only rarely allow herself the indulgence of thinking about it.

After climbing the steps to the impressive building, Lola turned left and found the library information office. The night guard on the desk checked her bag, press pass and invitation and directed her toward the main domed lobby.

Lola loved libraries. They held a quiet sacredness for her. Her head fell backwards as she gazed up at the imposing dome of the cathedral-like building and, as with everything in the city, it made her feel so small.

'Take a left and you'll come to the main staircase, Ms. Paige. Your destination is the Rare Books and Manuscripts Library located on the 6th floor, on the south side. There are signs directing you. Have a good evening, ma'am.'

Lola checked her wrist watch. It was almost eight and the event would soon begin. She looked to the left and started her journey up the stairs eventually emerging into a long hall that was furnished in light wood and was brightly lit. Along the side of the walls were glass-fronted display cabinets and the room had a softness about it as the reception guests mingled and talked, drinking from champagne flutes and sampling the bites that were offered by waiters and waitresses on silver platters.

A well-dressed woman approached Lola, smiling the uniform smile that every receptionist and host in New York seemed to wear.

'Hi there. Welcome to tonight's event. Can I take your name please?' she said.

'Lola Paige, I'm from the New York Torch.' Lola's proud smile couldn't hide how good that sounded to her ears. Even the hostess seemed duly impressed.

'Oh fantastic,' she declared. 'We weren't sure if they would send anyone. Thank you so much for coming. The library curator will give a short introductory speech and then our patron will say a few words and that will be followed by the main presentation from our guest of honour, Professor Manus Moriarty. He's from Ireland like you,' she beamed.

'Will I get a chance to speak to them individually after?' Lola asked.

'Oh of course. Please have a look around and be sure to try the canapés, they're delightful.'

Lola smiled back and looked about the room of strangers nervously, hoping that Erin would have already made it there. In the meantime, she tried to look like she belonged at dimly lit receptions where they served champagne and canapés and discussed antiquity.

Her face was flushed and a light sweat settled on her head and she suddenly felt a little on edge. The ring was alert and ready as if it might be needed. It was always a step ahead, anticipating Lola's trepidation even before her brain or gut did. Lola put it down to nerves, this was her first story and she wanted to do it well.

'Smile,' said a voice from behind her. Lola turned to find a lens in her face and was blinded by the bright flash of Erin's camera.

'I don't think we'll use that one,' said Erin scolding her. 'Let me try again. Now this time, Lola, smile!'

Lola was about to protest but she thought better of it and did as Erin asked. 'Good girl, now that wasn't so bad, was it?'

'Put that away a minute.' Lola lifted a glass of champagne off a passing tray and necked it. This didn't seem to help her nerves any.

'Go easy, Lola, you don't want to be getting loaded on your first job,' laughed Erin. 'I thought you said you didn't drink?'

'I don't... Well not really,' said Lola absently as she looked about the room. The butterflies were at it again, their wings beating and flapping beneath her rib cage. Since she'd entered the room she could hear a soft melodious voice, sweet and soulful. So very faint was the tune it demanded her attention.

'That music is lovely. Where are they playing it?' Lola asked, her eyes searching for the source of the heavenly melody.

'What music, Lola?' said Erin, her eyes widening in bewilderment.

'Can you not hear that?'

'No.' Erin laughed. 'I've been all around the room and there's definitely no one playing music.'

'Oh,' said Lola, looking up at the ceiling. 'It must be piped through or something.'

'Are you alright, Lola? You seem a bit on edge.'

'Can you not hear that? Seriously?' Lola was beginning to worry herself now, as she looked about and everyone else was oblivious to the soft lullaby that strummed and swayed in her ears.

'Hear what, Lola?'

'It's like singing. A women singing?'

'No,' said Erin again. 'I can't hear anything. Listen, I need to go and mingle and take a few more pictures. Are you sure you're gonna be alright? You look kinda pale, Lola. I mean paler than usual.'

'No, no, I'm fine, you go do your camera thing. Is the book on show?'

'Yeah. Look there, down at the back.' Erin pointed to a glass case at the bottom of the room.

Lola politely excused herself through the crowd until she came to where the book lay open, encased in glass alone and unattended. Lola wasn't sure why she had made this observation but an anxiety knotted in her as she broke free from the others. The soft humming was clearer now but despite searching the alcoves and ceiling Lola couldn't pinpoint from where the sounds originated.

If she hadn't known better she would have believed that it was emanating from the book itself. The notion settled in Lola's mind and took root as she stood pensively gazing into the glass cabinet.

Daring to step closer, her eyes fell tenderly on to the brightly ornamented pages and the music grew louder like a rising wave until it completely filled her so that she could no longer hear the chatter of the other guests or the clinking of glasses.

Lola's ring recognised this book just like it had recognised the Lía Fáil all those months ago at Teamhair and, as before, Lola struggled to let that ancient part of her take over and connect with the book.

Lola became woozy. The music, like an opiate, lulled her into a stupor and she couldn't fight it. She didn't want to fight it. As she continued to gaze down at the text, fine golden forms burned through the thick black monastic ink rising off the page and evaporating before her inquisitorial eyes. Lines and slashes, symbols that she – Lola – didn't comprehend, but she knew Brigid, the ancient and sacred part of her, understood fully.

'She is a thing of great beauty, isn't she?'

Snapped from her reverie, Lola tore her reluctant eyes from the book, which had now been returned to its former self. Looking to the side, she smiled at the familiar face.

'I believe we've met already,' said the red-haired man. He was clean-shaven and dressed in a fine black suit and he looked much younger than when she'd seen him last at the boarding gate in Dublin airport.

'I'm Professor Manus Moriarty,' the gentleman extended his hand.

Lola hesitated fearing another flashback.

But this time it was fine. 'I didn't catch your name.'

'Sorry, Professor Moriarty. My name is Lola Paige.'

'Well, Lola, what has you here in New York and how did you end up at tonight's event?'

'I'm actually doing an internship with the New York Torch. This is my first story. Well my first story for them,' added Lola, trying not to sound like an amateur.

'Excellent, what a great opportunity. So how are you settling in? I don't know about you, Lola, but all these yanks with their 3.5 magnitude smiles, make me a touch uneasy,' said the professor with a grin. Lola laughed along, glad that she wasn't the only one who felt that way.

'Yeah, it's certainly a bit different than home,' said Lola. 'Trees. That's what I miss most,' she laughed again. 'I'd love to see green fields below these skyscrapers and some trees.'

'You may take yourself to Central Park, there are plenty of trees and grass there.'

'Yeah, I've been. It's lovely,' nodded Lola in acknowledgement. 'So have you come over with the book?' said Lola. She could tell from the tender way Moriarty looked at the book and how he lingered around its glass tomb that he was deeply connected to it.

His colours were more settled tonight Lola noticed. Each time Moriarty looked down at the book there was an explosion of pink and peach. Lola knew then that he wasn't only connected to the book but he loved it. She'd often seen the same colours when a mother or father was with their child. It was a thing of great beauty.

'Yes. I have dedicated my life's work to this book and that's what has me over here,' said the professor. 'I won't lie, Lola,' he added, more serious now, 'it took a lot to get me here. It was a huge risk to take something so old across the Atlantic, but our patrons made me an offer I couldn't refuse.'

'An offer you couldn't refuse? That sounds quite menacing,' Lola smiled.

'Yes, that is certainly how it felt at the time but they have been very kind to donate to my university and specifically to invest in my research and work. I take it you're a student yourself, Lola?'

'Yes, I go to Queen's in Belfast.'

'Well Trinity is no different. The cuts to education and university budgets mean that it's impossible for any research to be conducted without the help of external parties now. It's not something I or any other academic is overly comfortable with but what choice do we have?'

Lola realised these were the concerns and worries that had sparked the grey in his aura the first time she'd seen Moriarty. It must have been difficult for researchers of any kind to stick to their principles and keep outside influences from interfering in their work. She supposed that for men and women like the professor it was about compromise, they had to look at the bigger picture.

'I hope you're not recording any of this,' he laughed.

'No, strictly off the record, Professor Moriarty. So who are they? Who are your patrons?' asked Lola, intrigued.

Just as he was about to answer, a glass clinked calling the crowd to attention and the professor was beckoned to the front of the room.

'Sorry, Lola. Duty calls.'

Lola stayed with the book at the back, as he made his way to the front of the room, where a brunette waited for him. Silence fell as they all turned to face the small podium and the lady speaking into the microphone.

'First of all I would like to thank you all for coming to the Butler Library tonight and I hope you have enjoyed perusing the various collections and of course the fabulous piece of antiquity on display at the back of the room, the very reason we are all here tonight. For those of you that don't know me, my name is Vivian du Vaul and I am the curator at this fine library.

'I would like to take this opportunity to welcome my Irish colleague to Columbia University, and say what an honour it is to have him conduct the last of his research here at the Butler Library.

'But first of all it gives me great pleasure to introduce a gentleman that you will all know from the papers and magazines but he is someone who has been a wonderful and vital patron to Butler and now he has extended that philanthropy across the Atlantic to Trinity College Dublin. Without further ado, I would like you all to put your hands together and give a warm welcome to Mr Alex Stein.'

Lola stumbled back hitting the glass bookcase as his name hit her like a slap to the face. Her eyes desperately searched for the refuge of the nearest exit but her feet wouldn't obey.

Alex Stein took the microphone. Dressed in a navy suit and tie he looked every bit the vision. Lola's knees buckled and the room rotated around her, her hands grasped out trying to gain purchase on anything that might keep her upright but there was nothing to hold on to. A waitress passed with a full tray of champagne glasses.

Lola had only intended to steady herself but as reached out she pulled the tray and the waitress with her.

When she woke on the wooden floor, dressed in chards of broken glass and expensive champagne, Erin was gently tapping her face. Someone's knees acted as a pillow, cradling her head but she couldn't see who it was. Her legs and hands had tiny scrapes and cuts all over and some were bleeding freely.

'Bring some water,' said the voice holding her head up. Lola reacted as though she had been electrocuted, she rose like a shot, and sat bolt upright while Erin tried to reason with her. She just wanted to get out of there away from the prying eyes, away from the book away from him.

'Lola,' said Alex, his voice thick with concern. 'Please sit back down, let the first aider get those cuts cleaned up.' He stepped towards her.

'Don't touch me!' said Lola in protest. She shouted louder than she had meant to. Erin, where was Erin. Her friend had come back with a bottle of water.

'Please, Erin, please just get me out of here.'

'Okay, Lola.' Erin turned to the curious on-lookers. 'I think she just needs a bit of air.' Lifting her bag and camera she took Lola by the arm and led her out of the room. She didn't speak until she got into the lift.

Lola lay slumped up against the wall of the elevator, she felt like she was going to vomit as her vision sloshed from side to side. Erin was speaking but she couldn't quite latch on to her words. She was saying something about the champagne. Did she think she was drunk? Everyone else in the room must have thought the same thing. She was sure to be sent home now! Gene Rush would be all over this.

It seemed to take the elevator door years to open. Lola lunged forward towards the exit and the darkened lobby. She needed to get out. Busting through the doors she spewed right on the steps. Erin rubbed her back sympathetically. In her peripheral view she could see a pair of purple shoes running up the steps towards them.

'Lola! What happened?'

Lola slid down the back of one of the large stone columns. It was cool on her burning face. Erin handed her the bottle of water. She took a tiny sip and tried to steady her head, which was still spinning like a carousel.

The purple shoes belonged to Rocha. Erin was filling her in.

'She only had one glass of champagne,' she was saying. 'Unless, she had more when I was off taking my pictures. She was kinda acting weird, saying she could hear music or something. I walked about, but there was definitely no music playing.'

'Where exactly was she when this happened?' said Rocha. Her voice was urgent. 'In the room,' said Erin.

'No, darling. I mean where in the room?' Erin couldn't see how this was at all relevant but she answered the question anyway.

'At the back, beside the glass book case.' Rocha nodded her head, as if it all suddenly made sense.

'Did anyone else she what happened?'

'No. I don't think so, only the waitress. We were all facing the front of the room. The library curator was introducing Alex Stein and he was about to speak when we heard all the glass breaking at the back of the room. When I got back there, Lola was lying unconscious. She'd pulled the waitress and the tray of glasses down with her. That explains all the cuts.'

Erin pointed to the various crimson slashes on Lola's pale legs and arms.

'That's when Mr Stein came to the back of the room. He said he knew first aid. He was helping me when she came round. He tried to help her up but she didn't seem to want him near her. I know they have previous, Lola didn't go into the details, but the way she spoke to him, he must've really pissed her off.'

'You could say that, Erin,' said Rocha.

'Anyway, Ms Moone, she was so embarrassed and she just wanted out of there. I think she got up too soon.'

Rocha knelt beside Lola and felt her face. Although her complexion was pallid, her face felt like a furnace. Taking off her amethyst necklace, she placed it around Lola's neck. It felt so heavy. Lola felt the water bottle being thrust to her mouth again.

'Drink this, honey, you need fluids.' Her vision had steadied and now there was only one Erin and one Rocha.

'I feel like shit!' said Lola. She tried to get up, but her legs were like jelly.

'No you don't,' said Rocha reaching out and pushing her against the pillar again. 'Take it easy. You need to get your equilibrium. Erin, come help.'

Erin took one arm, while Rocha took the other, helping Lola to her feet. Lola's head felt like it had been cracked opened but the sickness had gone. She didn't open her eyes; instead she let the two ladies guide her towards the line of waiting taxis.

'Rocha, I'd feel a lot better if I came along with you,' said Erin. 'I know it's late but I'd like to stay with Lola if that's okay?' Rocha was happy to oblige and both she and Erin carried Lola towards the waiting cabs.

'At least tomorrow is Saturday, Lola, so you don't have to get up,' said Erin, trying to lighten the mood. But for Lola it had all been one monumental disaster, she was there representing the New York Torch and she had to be escorted out of the room. Humiliated didn't cover it. Lola tried not to think about it for now concentrating instead on the cool breeze flowing in through the open window.

If all else was lost tonight, as least she knew for sure that Rocha's theory was correct. Her fear now was that so too did Alex Stein.

Everyone else in that room probably suspected that she had drunk too much, but not him, he would know the truth.

~ 11 ~

Lola stretched to lift her new work phone. She'd no idea how long it had been ringing. Her blood turned to ice in her veins when she saw Gene Rush's name flash on the screen. 'Hello?' said Lola, her eyes squeezed closed as she waited for the onslaught to begin.

'I didn't wake you, did I?' said Gene Rush, his voice a slow burning hiss. 'You get yourself out of bed, take whatever painkillers you need to cure your hangover, and you get your ass in to this office. NOW! Is that clear?'

Lola forced the lump in her throat back down, managing to muster a feeble 'Yes' before erupting out of bed.

This was it. He had been waiting for his chance and now he had it. She was out. Lola doubted she would even get a chance to explain her side of the story. Besides, what exactly was that? What could she say? He clearly thought she had been drunk on the job.

Lola's hands shook as she fumbled hopelessly trying to dress herself as quickly as she could. Throwing on a pair of jeans, a long-sleeved t-shirt and a pair of trainers, she quickly brushed her teeth and washed her face. The humiliation sank like lead in her gut almost incapacitating her.

Rocha was on the phone when she came down the stairs. There was no sign of Erin she must have left before Lola woke up.

'Lola, why are you up? You need to get some rest.'

'I got a call from work, they heard about last night and they've summonsed me in.'

'Listen, my dear, I'll call you later. Okay. Bye.' Rocha hung up the phone and came towards Lola.

'What do you mean they have summonsed you in?' she said, her hand rising to hip in indignation. 'Who has summonsed you in?' demanded Rocha growing more animated. 'That ass Gene Rush?'

'The very one,' said Lola, the mortification stabbing at her again. 'He's going to sack me, Rocha, and the smug prick will enjoy every second of it. Out on my first story and I make a mess of it. He thinks I was drunk, you know.' Lola was growing more and more irate now.

'Wait,' offered Rocha slipping out of her house mules, 'let me get my shoes and I'll come with you. I'll explain what really happened.'

'Rocha, please,' said Lola, the resignation at her fate evident in her dull tone. 'What are you going to tell him? Oh hi, Mr Rush, Lola wasn't intoxicated last night she just happens to be an ancient Goddess reborn and from time to time when the two consciousness unite she loses all control of her senses. Last night she heard a book signing to her and this made her faint.'

Lola raised her eyes to the ceiling in frustration. 'He'd call for the straightjackets. For both of us!'

'Lola, pet,' Rocha spoke in a calm, soothing tone. 'This can be resolved. Besides,' she said wiping a few stray tears that had escaped Lola's eyes, 'you don't know what the outcome will be. Let me at least come with you, I can wait downstairs while you meet with him.'

Lola nodded and walked to the door waiting for Rocha to follow.

Both women sat in silence for the entire train journey. Rocha took a seat in the lobby while Lola made the short journey to the newsroom above.

As she crossed the open space, which was full of weekend staff, she could see Gene Rush waiting in one of the side offices for her.

His eyes narrowed in their usual shrivelling way and Lola could see that the aggression that was ever lurking in his blunt features was ready to leap into full view as soon as she walked into the room. This is going to be a Diplock court, thought Lola.

True to form he pounced as soon as she closed the door behind her. His theatrics were not as much for her benefit as they were for the prying eyes of the entire newsroom. It was not good enough that she would be fired, Lola's humiliation would not be complete until Gene Rush paraded before the village pillory and flogged her in front of veiled spectators.

Lola stood in the tide of the onslaught as wave after wave of accusation crashed over her. She was beginning to lose track now. She got the gist of what he was saying.

'Never in the history of this fine establishment and newspaper has any intern ever taken such liberties or brought the paper into disrepute.' Finally, there was a wide enough gap in his ensuing diatribe that allowed Lola to squeeze in an objection. She was at the point now where things couldn't get any worse for her and she'd never have forgiven herself for not offering some words in self-defence.

Just as she was about to plead her case, the door swung open as if it was about be torn from its hinges and in stormed Isaac Kane loaded like a gun and ready for battle. As welcome a sight as it was, Lola was capable of fighting her own corner. She needed to stand up for herself, especially on this count.

'Where do you get off calling her in like this, to some third-rate court martial?' he shot at Gene Rush. But before either man had the chance to go at it again Lola interjected.

'Isaac, please, I can handle this.'

'Okay, Irish, you explain.' He took a seat in the corner. Lola could feel the eyes of the world on her. Walking around the room she closed all the blinds before she started. This seemed to amuse Isaac.

'Mr Rush, first of all I would like to say I am extremely sorry for what happened last night but I feel your reaction is completely disproportionate to my perceived crime. You said that I have brought the paper and the interns into disrepute but I totally refute that.' Gene Rush was about to interrupt but Lola lifted her hand to hush him. 'Let me finish,' she said coolly.

'You claim that I was intoxicated on the job. I would like to inform you, Mr Rush, that I don't drink. I took a glass of champagne, one bloody glass to settle my nerves. It was my first story and I wanted to get it right, because if I didn't, I knew you would be on my back.' Gene Rush raised his eyebrow as if to dismiss her.

'You must be the only Irish person that doesn't drink. Isn't that a crime against your nation or something?' He looked around the room but neither Lola nor Isaac gave any credence to the low jibe.

'Maybe if you left New York once in a while, Mr Rush, you might be less inclined to make such ignorant statements,' shot back Lola. She could see he was growing more and more impatient with her.

'Anyway. I wasn't drunk. I wasn't anywhere close to drunk. I don't know how or why but I fainted. All I remember is feeling dizzy and reaching out to hold on to something or someone and the next thing I remember was being taken out of the room by Erin.'

'I have it on good authority that you were drunk, Ms Paige.' At this point Isaac was up in arms again and Lola was happy to let him continue. Gene Rush had no interest in what she had to say, it didn't suit his agenda, she could see that she was getting nowhere.

'How exactly did you find out about this, Eugene? Have you been checking up on Irish here or did the university call to make a formal complaint?'

'I have it on good authority, that's all you need to know.'

'Are you kidding me, Eugene?' Isaac twisted each syllable into Rush like a dagger. 'Answer the question,' demanded Isaac, 'was there a formal complaint?'

Gene answered reluctantly. 'Not as such but a source who was there called.'

'And what did this so-called source say?' continued Isaac as if he was cross-examining a suspect in court.

'The gentleman in question called to say that he was concerned about the journalist who was at last night's event. He said she seemed quite drunk and fell cutting herself, but she left before anyone could help her.'

'Are you having a laugh?' said Lola, feeling her temper erupt. 'This source wouldn't happen to be Alex Stein by any chance?' Her emerald eyes glistened and sparked boring into Gene Rush who uncomfortably squirmed back into his chair.

'That piece of shit,' said Lola, almost to herself.

'You know Alex Stein, Irish?' said Isaac, clearly struggling to find a connection.

'Oh I know him all right. This is a low blow. Trying to get me fired.' Lola was talking more to herself than anyone else. Her temper had betrayed her and again she had said too much.

'Why would Alex Stein want to get you fired, Lola? What are you to someone like Alex Stein?' asked Rush, clearly as confused about the connection as Isaac.

'Nothing, Mr Rush, I'm nothing to him,' said Lola softly. 'He's lying. For what it's worth, Mr Rush, he's lying.'

'He's lying. Seriously? What reason would Mr Stein, who, let me add, is a very generous patron to the Butler Library and whose father owns a stake in this newspaper, have to lie? He was protecting the paper and was genuinely concerned about you.'

'Carl Stein, owns this paper?' Lola slumped down into a seat as if she'd been pushed. Isaac handed her a glass of water.

'Here, Irish, drink this. You look like your about to faint again. For the record,' he threw Gene Rush an incendiary look, 'Carl Stein would like to own this paper but at the moment he is only a stakeholder. Long may that last,' he added.

'Ask anyone else who was there, Mr Rush, ask Erin. She can tell you that I wasn't drunk. I know that's perhaps how it looked but I fainted, that's all.'

'That's enough, Lola. You have explained yourself well enough.' Isaac stood up and opened the door, beckoning her to follow after him.

'Eugene knows the procedure for conducting enquiries into gross misconduct and he has spat in the face of every one. This is over, Eugene, or I'll have your ass in front of the disciplinary committee.'

Lola and Isaac left the room.

'You should never have come here today, Lola. Why didn't you call me the minute you spoke to him? Didn't you read the misconduct procedure in your pack?'

'Seriously, Isaac.' Lola rolled her eyes. Isaac laughed, shaking his head. He was beautiful when he smiled, less serious and intense looking.

Lola knew that in the past few years those eyes, like deep pools of jet, had seen some horrors.

'You are something else, Irish, you really are. You spoke well in there today but I'm more interested in how you know the Steins and why you think the Prince of Manhattan wants you out of this paper.'

'The Prince of Manhattan? Is that what you call him?'

'That's what he calls himself,' Isaac flashed his disarming smile again. 'So how do you know him? Stop deflecting the question, Irish.'

'It's a long story. A long and complicated one Mr... I mean Isaac.'

'Okay, okay. Maybe not today, but you will tell me some day.' Lola nodded her head in agreement.

'Isaac, I need a favour.'

'Another favour?'

'Yes,' laughed Lola gingerly. 'I need to get in to see that book again and to talk to Professor Moriarty.'

'You want to go back for more?'

'I want to finish the story. I need to see that book again.'

'Okay, I'll see what I can do. It's time I put you to work, Lola. I need a little research done; it's something I've been working on. I can't say too much to be honest, not yet. It goes without saying that anything you find and anything we discuss, it is exactly that. Between us.'

'Of course, Isaac,' said Lola, her brow furrowing in offence.

'I had to make sure,' said Isaac in response, 'as long as we understand each other. I'm heading back to my office. Get you on home and I'll meet you on Monday morning in the Bullpen. We're going out. And make sure you wear comfortable shoes.'

'Where are we going?'

'Harlem,' said Isaac as the lift door closed again.

Rocha was sitting patiently in the lobby, when Lola returned.

'Well,' she said as she rushed toward her. 'How'd it go honey? Did Isaac get there in time?'

'How'd you know about Isaac?' asked Lola suspiciously.

'Well I called him. I knew he was your mentor and I thought I'd try his desk and lucky for you he was in his office.'

Lola glared at Rocha defiantly.

'What?' smirked Rocha. 'You could just say thanks.'

'Well, the good news is that I still have a job – for now anyway,' said Lola as she walked out into the street.

The amber mid-morning light felt delicious at it rested on Lola's tired face. The warmth moved across her checks and neck down on her body evaporating all traces of tension and rigidity.

'It turns out,' continued Lola as they walked, 'that Alex Stein called the paper, feigning concern about the young intern who collapsed last night.' Lola was furious again. 'He led Rush to believe that I was inebriated and had collapsed in a drunken stupor. Can you believe it, Rocha?'

Lola scolded herself again, why was she continually surprised by Alex Stein's vile nature. It was who and what he was after all.

Lola didn't give Rocha time to reply; on she went, venting her annoyance.

'I mean of course you can believe it, we both can. Rocha, did you know that Carl Stein is a stakeholder in the New York Torch?'

Rocha shook her head. 'That I didn't know. It must be a recent development.'

'Isaac said that he has been trying to buy the paper for a long time, but thankfully there has been a lot of resistance.'

'I dare say that it's only a matter of time, Lola, before he gets his way.'

Something had been troubling Lola since she had heard that piece of information. It seemed ridiculous, but then there were so many facets of her life that seemed ridiculous and it didn't make them any less true.

'Rocha,' Lola reached out and touched her arm, stopping her in her stride. 'Carl Stein is a new stakeholder, and this is the first year that they have opened their intern program to an international student. I mean I'm as committed to journalism as anyone but I'm sure there were many interns as capable if not more so than me, but I was selected. Out of thirty-two thousand applicants, I was selected. Don't you think that seems a bit strange,' said Lola, 'too much of a coincidence?'

The look on Rocha's face seemed enough to confirm Lola's thoughts. She felt like a lab rat in a large wheel. Could all this have been engineered by Carl Stein?

The answer was of course it could. Chess 101, know your opponent.

But what should she do? Get on the next plane to Ireland and give up on the Lost Oracle and Cosmic Cube, or should she play Carl Stein at his own game?

'Lola, let's get something to eat. We all think better on a full stomach,' said Rocha leading her into a nearby diner.

~ 12 ~

Lola's mind raced through all the probable and improbable scenarios trying to connect the dots. She kept glancing at the stairs waiting for Rocha to come down. Rocha had been on the phone in her bedroom for over forty-five minutes now and Lola was beginning to get a little worried.

When she finally emerged down the stairs and joined Lola in the living room her ashen face did nothing to alleviate Lola's trepidation.

'That was Celeste on the phone,' said Rocha as she slumped down onto the couch.

'What is it?' Lola asked panicking. 'Is she okay? And Aíbgréne?'

Rocha waved her hand. 'No, no, my dear, they're just fine. It's Markus, Lola. It seems he has taken his own life. Celeste says the toxicology report cites high levels of coniine in the blood stream.'

'Hemlock,' said Lola in disbelief. 'Just like Arthur. They finally got to Markus too.'

'Well that's the shocking thing, dear. Police are calling it a suicide but we both know that this has the Hell Fire Club written all over it,' said Rocha with authority. 'It's come to light that they may have gotten to him quite some time ago. My niece, she's an amazing woman really, and has suspected as much for some time. She said that something about Arthur's death and her own abduction had troubled her greatly. It was something rather simple, innocuous almost.'

'What do you mean?' Lola asked. 'He's been dead a while?'

But no sooner were the words out of her mouth, when the realisation that Markus had gone rogue hit Lola. It all made perfect sense.

This was another play on the large chessboard that she had been blindly stumbling around since Arthur's murder.

'What was it that made her suspicious?' said Lola. She sank back into the sofa drained by the news.

'Well in the end Markus admitted it to her, gave himself up and for some months he had been working as a double agent but there were a number of things,' said Rocha as she leaned forward in her seat, her eyes clear and urgent. 'Including Arthur's last night in ....'

'Well we know that Bryce Neil was there the night Arthur died, that he was responsible.'

'Yes he was, Lola, but as Celeste said there was a third chair and a glass of peppermint schnapps, which lay untouched. Celeste said Arthur never drank peppermint schnapps but Markus did and then there was the small matter of when he arrived. He made her believe that he had just arrived the day of Arthur's funeral but when she left with him after the church service – I believe he spoke to you beforehand,' Lola nodded in agreement, trying to remember their conversation. Nothing seemed to stand out well not now. Of course it all seemed very strange and cryptic at the time. 'When Celeste was putting her things into the boot of his car,' continued Rocha laying the clues out one after the other, 'she happened to noticed two baggage tags on Markus's holdall. One was dated for that day which was the 21st June but the other a week earlier, which means he would have been in Ballyvalley when Arthur was poisoned.'

It didn't seem that implausible, thought Lola. He had been instrumental in supporting her trip to New York; he left immediately after the ceremony in the fort. The Hell Fire Club knew exactly where Celeste would be and when and everything they needed to know about Lola. It all made sense. Lola didn't know how she should feel. If he had betrayed her and the Order, he could certainly have betrayed Arthur.

'But,' said Lola, more in hope than belief, 'could all those things not be put down to supposition? Perhaps it was just a coincidence.'

'Well of course you are entirely right, my dear, that is why Celeste let her unease sleep, then a number of months ago she received a letter from Markus, confessing all.'

The tears that Lola had been holding back finally broke free from her eyes. She wasn't exactly sure what or who they were for but she let them come regardless.

She was drowning in the depths of subterfuge and deceit that engulfed her on every side and she berated herself for not putting the pieces of this horrible jigsaw together sooner.

Lola's inner voice mocked and taunted her, at 'growth' it scoffed, 'newfound intuition and wisdom' it laughed at her. You were never in control, it said, you will always be nothing more than a pawn in Carl Stein's game.

So what was his game? What was it he wanted and why was she here? Lola demanded herself. Rocha may still have been right about the book, perhaps its call was what had muted all other concerns. If the Steins were here then so too was the Cosmic Cube and she needed that and the Oracle.

'This hasn't been the best day for news, has it?' smiled Rocha, her light brown eyes heavy with empathy. 'I think I'll make us a cuppa. Perhaps that may take the edge off.'

'Where do we go from here, Rocha?' said Lola rubbing the stress form her temples. 'I mean should I just get on the next plane home? All this has obviously been set up by the Steins. I'm playing a game where there can only be one winner.'

'Weren't you always, Lola!' This was more of a statement from Rocha than a question and she was right.

'You have him scared, Lola. Can't you see that? Can't you see that everything you are and represent threatens the very heart of what the Hell Fire Club is and what it has built over millennia?'

This constant assertion that she was in some way a threat or had the Hell Fire Club running scared really grated on Lola. The notion seemed so utterly absurd. She didn't even have control over her own body and its reactions never mind a global network of sociopaths.

Lola reached for the blanket that lay over the back of the sofa, pulling it around her, hoping it would bring her some comfort. She would give anything to be back in the safety of Brook Mill Manor. She missed Arthur more than ever. It didn't seem to be getting any easier without him. Why hadn't he prepared her for any of this? Lola let the anger rise in her like fire; she was angry with Markus, with Arthur, with herself.

'Seriously, Rocha, how can I – one person – be and do all that?' she said through tears and gritted teeth.

'Why, Lola, do you think that the Hell Fire Club is exclusively male?'

'Because women aren't as smart?' Lola didn't want to play the game, what difference would it make to her situation. 'Because they hate women?'

'Not hate, Lola, so much as fear,' said Rocha. 'You must then ask yourself why they fear women so much. Why the re-emergence of the Dé Danann's light is fatal for them.'

'I'm not sure they do fear women,' argued Lola. 'They have no respect or regard for women, well not outside of their own sexual and ritual need for them, but I don't think they fear us.'

'Listen carefully, Lola.' Rocha handed her a cup of her homebrew before settling back into the seat. 'The story of the Goddess is intrinsic, not only to our story, but the entire construction of our society. The story of women, our governance and sovereignty over our own destiny, our own bodies even. Let me break it down.'

Lola laughed at the implication, as she dried her eyes.

'Sorry,' apologised Rocha. 'I don't mean to insinuate that you won't understand, I suppose I've been a lecturer for too long,' she smiled.

'No, please continue.'

'Our truth is prehistoric. What you are and what you embody is prehistoric. Prehistoric in that it was told and lived pre-his-story. Worship of the Goddess as the supreme creature goes back to the dawn of civilization, well before the last thirty to fifty centuries we call recorded history – a history that has been rewritten and manipulated by the ruling elite for all that time.'

Rocha sat on the edge of the seat. Her grey eyes glistened in the falling light, as the sun migrated from the southern window to the western side of the loft apartment.

Lola could see the compassion in her eyes and the knowledge; there was wisdom well beyond their years. That was another thought that had struck Lola as she sat looking back at her host, but she forced it to the back of her mind, concentrating instead on what Rocha was about to tell her.

This was the first time since Arthur's death she had anyone to school her. Rocha hid nothing and Lola liked that.

'Contrary to what we have been conditioned to think and believe about our own story, what we have been told by men for millennia, the archaeology in various sites all over the world confirms that we once worshiped the Goddess as the supreme giver of life.

'The female vulva was revered as a magical portal of life, endowed with the power to give life, to regenerate, to illuminate and transform. These early agrarian societies worshiped female sexuality, not in the base titillating way it is regarded today, but in a spiritual and sacred way. They worshiped life, not death, and as a result our societies looked and functioned in an entirely different way.

'This is all proof that this current dominator structure was forced upon us. Because it is a fallacy that we as humans were incapable of working in partnership with one another, evidence now shows that this partnership model is what has ensured our survival, our evolution.'

Lola shifted in her seat, almost spilling some tea over her jeans.

'Many years ago, Lola, I read Darwin's On the Origin of Species, a text that has been embraced by the scientific community with nothing short of religious fervour. This theory, we have been told, proves that to dominate is innate in each human, otherwise we would never have evolved into the species that we are today.'

'Survival of the fittest,' interjected Lola.

Rocha laughed. 'Indeed, Lola, survival of the fittest. And do you know what is so funny about that? Those words appear something like twice in the entire thesis but the words love and partnership appear over one hundred and fifty times. Isn't that amazing?'

'So what you're saying, Rocha, is that the Goddess and woman has been the victim of a massive re-mything process and as a result there have been profound political and societal implications.'

'Exactly, Lola!' declared Rocha, as though Lola had just solved some complicated conundrum.

'Of course the arguments and influences are complex things and the actual process has been a gradual one, but no matter how the church or some early Hebrew sects tried, in every religion and tradition from east to west, there are still traces of the Goddess.

'She could not be suppressed because the people's faith in her and connection to her was just too strong. So much so that we find her in the strangest of places. Look at our father church, for example, the reverence for "Our Lady", she is the Alma Mater, the "Queen of Heaven", these are by no means new phrases, these terms are ancient words once used to describe the Goddess.'

'Surely you can't just blame the church for sexism, Rocha. I know they have done a great deal to damage the image of women and sex in general but surely the wheels were well in motion before the Catholic Church was formed.'

'You're not wrong, Lola. Early Christianity had its issues but it was really with Saint Paul and later Augustine that the Christian idea that the human body – namely the body of a woman – was corrupt, even demonic.'

'But how did these men go about dismantling and discrediting something that had clear hold in the spiritual lives of most societies? This didn't happened overnight.'

'Of course not, it was a gradual process, Lola. Imagine a bed of rock, or a cliff face. On that cliff face you can see layer after layer, each secure, stable and solid. That is how it happened. When nomadic tribes from the north began to venture further south into the Fertile Crescent and old Europe, they brought with them their thunder gods and gods of war and their model of domination.'

'Why didn't they worship the Goddess? Why was their model different?' asked Lola, every bit the inquisitive student. 'Based on my own past and my own research there is vast evidence to show that Goddess worship was found in not just Ireland but from southern Iraq to France, to the Americas, all social structures growing and developing simultaneously.'

'That is an excellent question, young lady. The truth is we are not sure but some geographers believe that environment played a huge role in how they viewed the order of the universe and worshiped.'

Lola felt pieces of information that Rocha was giving her coming together in her mind to create a bigger picture. 'These Kurgans, who were meant to have originated in what is now Russia, were the original Aryan race and – another little fact Arthur once told me – the main families in the Hell Fire Club can trace their blood lines back to them. In their world, which was exposed and cold, it was a matter of survival at all costs, their male deities were revered as giving life and when they ravaged and looted old Europe and finally settled there they brought their dominator model with them and thus it was the beginning of the end of the Goddess in her original form. But where the Goddess could not be suppressed the age old political tool of co-option was administered,' explained Rocha.

'So that means they kept some elements of the myth or story and mixed it with their own. I suppose like they have done in Ireland with me, or I mean Brigid. She was once the Goddess but was co-opted as a saint after the introduction of Christianity.'

'Exactly, Lola, exactly.' Rocha was growing more animated now.

She bounced off her seat and went to one of her many bookshelves. Her nimble fingers traced the spines until she found what she was looking for. She came back with two books and threw them onto the seat beside Lola.

'Open the first one. Chapter one of the King James Bible and read the second line.'

'Let him kiss me with the kisses of his mouth: for thy love is better than wine,' Lola read.

'Now line thirteen.'

Lola proceeded as instructed.

'A bundle of Myrrh is my well-beloved unto me; he shall lie all night betwixt my breasts.'

'Now find chapter two verse twelve,' instructed Rocha. Lola nodded and flipped over the tissue thin page looking for the passage, then read it out loud again.

'The flowers appear on the earth; the time of the singing of birds is come.'

'Now chapter seven verse two.'

'My navel is like a round goblet, which wanteth not liquor: thy belly is like an heap of wheat set about with lilies.'

'You may ask, Lola, what an erotic poem is doing in the bible and the King James version no less. Biblical scholars would argue this is a lament or love song for Yahweh, but nowhere is he mentioned in the text. Just from the extracts above, you can see that the Song of Songs celebrates the Goddess, the female body and the union between man and woman. We also know from biblical scholars that the Old Testament has been heavily edited over the years by priest after priestly writer, each fashioning it to suit their own school of thought.

'Recent studies have found a link between the Sumerian Hymns to the Goddess Inanna and the Song of Songs. This is a perfect example of co-option.'

Lola was totally engrossed now. She'd never really thought about her history as a woman and the journey that womankind had endured, from freedom and reverence to slavery and back to the fight for freedom again.

She didn't know why but she felt better now. She felt stronger, like she was somehow fighting for every woman who had been robbed of her true divinity, her true understanding of just how powerful she was. And she fully understood why it had benefited the dominator model to keep womankind on her knees.

Carl Stein may have set the board, he may be even dictating the game but she had the power of every woman since before Eve running through her blood. He may have the blood of the Kurgan, but she had the blood of the Goddess.

~ 13 ~

Lola fixed her pencil dress; it had been riding up her legs on the walk in. She'd come prepared today, no heels just flats, and she felt like a new woman. Rocha had advised her to take a coat, as the weather reports forecast rain for later in the day, so she lifted her mac on the way out reluctantly.

The sun was shining and the streets of New York were still sultry with the mirage-grey heat hovering over the city. Rain would be a welcome treat, thought Lola. Despite her lightness and the pleasant feel of the sun on her bare legs Lola could still feel the frosty stare of the city's iron eyes as they observed her every move. She checked that her ring was secure on her finger.

Isaac was at his desk and he got up to greet Lola as she came through his office door.

'Irish,' he smiled at her, 'right on time. Have you got a coat, notebook, pen? You know, the things you need as a journalist.' Lola rolled her eyes.

'Just checking,' he said.

'You seem in awfully good form today, Isaac,' commented Lola as they left the building. 'Is it the thought of having such a capable intern that excites you?'

'Hardly, Irish.' Lola pretended to be indignant. 'We have a change of plan,' he shot her that diamond smile. 'Harlem will have to wait for another day. Today I have finally got an audience with an old friend of yours. I've been tryin' to get a sit down with this sonuvabitch for a helluva long time Irish so you can imagine my surprise when I got a call to the office on Saturday to say that Carl Stein had a slot available, but only on the condition that I bring a certain intern with me.'

He looked down at Lola, who was trying her best not to vomit on the path.

Lola thought that if she just looked ahead and pretended she hadn't heard him that he would let her off the hook.

'Irish, Irish!' He stopped now. Lola felt like a disobedient child as she picked a spot on the pavement and stared at it. Her mind was racing trying to pre-empt the questions that were about to come her way.

'Ms Paige.' This got Lola's attention and she looked up. His face wasn't harsh but it was stern. 'I didn't win four Pulitzer prizes because I let people avoid my questions. Persistence is the first rule of good journalism. That and always look for the truth from the ground up, rarely from the top down. Journalists...'

'"Are never real journalists if they are agents of power, no matter how they disguise that role. Real journalists are agents of the people",' said Lola, finishing the line for him. It had been part of his last Pulitzer acceptance speech. Lola knew it off by heart. 'What can I say, Isaac? I'm you biggest fan,' Lola gave him a sugary smile as if she wasn't being sincere.

'Flattery will get you everywhere, Irish, but not at the minute. I want an answer.'

'An answer to what? I met Carl Stein last summer in Ireland, when I was sort of seeing his son.'

Isaac raised his eyebrow. 'You were dating Alex Stein?' he laughed. 'You and the Prince of Manhattan?'

Lola started to walk again, picking up the pace. He was starting to irritate her now. 'Yes I know,' she shot at him, 'it's hilarious. Alex Stein. Do you think you're the first person to think that that's ridiculous? Alex Stein and Lola, now what would possess him?' mocked Lola on the defensive.

'Possess him! You mean what would possess you? I mean you're intelligent, you're kinda funny, and you're reasonably cute, for a white girl, I mean. What would you see in him?'

'Flattery will get you nowhere, Isaac. There is more to Alex Stein than meets the eye and a lot more to his father as well.' Lola wanted to change the subject. Besides she was about to see Carl Stein for the first time since he had taken her to the Temple at Newgrange and she needed to focus. 'Are we walking there?'

'You still haven't gotten your head around this city, Irish. No we're not walking, we'll get a bus at Port Authority.'

Lola dutifully followed him as he headed for 42nd Street. A bus was waiting. Isaac paid the dollar fifty for both of them before sitting down. Traffic was heavy in the city but there was air con on the bus so Lola was happy to sit and watch the crowds outside.

'We'll be getting off at Fulton Street and then it's just a short walk up Broadway from there,' said Isaac.

Lola had been staring out of the bus window so she wasn't really paying attention.

She watched the hundreds of people who were on their way to work or shopping or the countless other things that people could do in this city, none of which she had yet to experience.

It fascinated her how each of these bodies, who would be nothing more than a flash or a fleeting image before her eyes, owned their own troubles, thoughts, dreams, hopes. Each had their own story and according to their colours a complete and complex existence.

She was grateful that she was sitting on the bus, happy to be a spectator as the legions fought their way down pavements and across roads, negotiating lights and taxis, cars and cyclists.

Until now she hadn't really noticed the dance on the sidewalks. She had always been trying to navigate and find her own way, but now, as the bus crawled through the downtown traffic, from her vantage point it all looked like one big choreographed performance. Despite the perceived chaos, there was a beauty in the ebb and flow of all of those lives that touched for just seconds. It all worked.

The sky had deepened to a slate grey; its full belly threatened the rain that Rocha had foretold. The bus seemed to be moving more freely. Isaac nudged her out of her observation, tapping the stop bell before getting out of his seat.

'This is us, Irish.'

Lola pulled on her mac and tried to keep in stride with Isaac whose legs moved as though they were about ten feet longer than hers. Without warning he deviated into a café. The waitress knew him by name and threw him a flirtatious glance. 'Mr Kane, please follow me,' she said in her nasally New York accent.

'We can't do anything without breakfast. Have you eaten this morning, Irish?'

Lola shook her head as she looked down through the menus the waitress had just left them.

She didn't want to make eye contact with him in case he started quizzing her again. Lola couldn't remember the last thing she'd eaten. Everything tasted different here, so processed; even the bread and milk lasted for weeks, now that was just unnatural.

She thought about having eggs and toast. That was a safe bet; surely the eggs would be okay. The waitress came back with her green tea and Isaac's coffee and took their food order.

'So...' said Isaac, when the waitress had departed again. Lola could tell from the sharpened look in his dark eyes that round two of the interrogation was about to commence, but much to Lola's relief, it didn't come.

'So, Irish. As I said, I've been waiting for a long time to get this interview and I doubt I'll be getting another one any time soon, so I want to make the most of this opportunity. If at any time you want to interject or ask a question, please feel free. That's why you are here, that's why I decided to become a mentor. In fact I'll be disappointed if you don't.'

'Why've you had to wait so long? Does Carl Stein not give interviews? He seems to be everywhere, always in the papers so he must talk to some journalists. Maybe he just doesn't like you, Isaac!' said Lola flashing him a sheepish grin.

'Well there's that, then there's the fact that he was out of the country for a while, as you know.' He raised his eyebrow, nodding down at Lola.

'When he returned ... from Ireland – thanks to you I now know he was in Ireland – he was almost a recluse. He sent his son to everything on his behalf. It's only in the last month or so that he has come back on the grid or back to life. It was information lock down, no one seemed to be talking about it or know why.'

'So what is it exactly you want to talk to him about today? I mean what's the story?'

'Harlem, said Isaac. Lola immediately knew he was lying. Isaac's colours, normally vibrant reds and oranges, flashed with a touch of smoky black. That black was the lie or the veil. But for the simple fact that she could see beyond the screen, Lola would have bought the lie, he'd uttered it so seamlessly. 'I want to speak to him about Harlem, amongst other things,' Isaac repeated.

'I thought Bebencowsky had already covered that?' said Lola provoking him slightly.

'Are you serious? Eugene is so far up Carl Stein's ass he got Bebencowsky to write what Stein Corp wants.

Besides, Carl Stein has been hiding a very dark secret and I need to give him the right of reply.'

Isaac had Lola's attention now. 'You know about Carl Stein?'

'Damn right I know. He thinks he can hide what he really is behind a trillion dollar business and a fine suit and some cologne. I've been working on this for a short while and I'm convinced Stein is motivated by more than greed.'

'Is it connected to the Club?' asked Lola.

'Club? What are you talking about, Irish? What Club?' Isaac seemed genuinely confused. If Lola could have cut out her tongue right there and right then she would have and thrown it in the Hudson River.

'Nothing, I thought you were talking about something else. What did you mean?'

Isaac seemed to buy her excuse and began to explain what he had been working on.

'Well the building we are going to today is relatively new but it's now home to the oldest private investment banking company in America, Stein & Sons. Carl Stein's great-great- grandfather founded it back in 1818.

'Now not much is really known about how Stein's ancestors came upon their fortune. All we are told is that Great-granddaddy Stein made his fortune in the "textile" trade.'

'Textile trade? Does that mean the cotton trade, which in turn means the slave trade?'

'Very good, Irish.' Isaac was genuinely impressed, which made Lola feel very pleased with herself. His colours were clear so she knew that what he was telling her was the truth, or part of it anyway.

'I thought Carl Stein was from New Orleans or somewhere like that?'

'He was, Lola, but his people were from Alabama.'

'So that's it, that's your story? That he built his empire on slaves?' Lola hadn't intended to sound as disinterested as she did. 'Sorry, Isaac, what I mean to say is, do you really think anyone will care? This is America, this entire country, this entire culture was built on the blood and sweat of slaves of many colours and creeds. Actually, did you know the first slaves brought to this so-called "New World" weren't African, they were Irish?'

This amused Isaac Kane as he let out a blistering laugh shaking his head. 'I did not know that, Irish, but I will be sure to include it in my report.'

'You're just taking the piss now, so you are,' said Lola, stung by his jest.

This only made him laugh more. The waitress had come back during the exchange with their food. Lola ignored Isaac and started to eat. It tasted great. She hadn't realised just how hungry she was until then.

'Sorry, Sorry.' Lola didn't look up from her plate to acknowledge his apology. 'Come on, Irish. Anyway getting back to what I was saying. You are absolutely right, of course, that is not the only angle. Have you ever heard of the American Civil War?'

This was enough to send Lola over the edge. 'Are you for real?' she burst out, shaking her head.

'What?' said Isaac, holding his hands up. 'What have I said now?'

'Don't be so patronising, Isaac!'

'All I said was had you ever heard of the American Civil War, most Americans wouldn't have a clue.'

'Well in case you hadn't noticed, in case your skills of observation have deserted you, I'm not American, I'm Irish and I have heard of the American Civil War! Now that we've clarified that, would you like to continue?'

'Aren't you feisty? It didn't take you took long to find your voice. I think I prefer the awe- struck Lola, not this one.' He smiled that bright smile at her. She couldn't resist. 'So, tell me what you know about the American Civil War.'

'Seriously, Isaac, you're testing me now?' Lola was trying to buy herself some time, to allow her brain to locate the little she did know about the civil war. 'When Lincoln was elected as president on an anti-slavery ticket some of the southern states decided they didn't like this, naturally that is what their main income was based on – plantations, cotton, sugar cane – and they used slaves to produce this. Then there was a big fight and the Union won, well kind of.'

Isaac clapped his hands slowly and sarcastically. 'Well that was illuminating.'

'Well, it's the gist of it. So you were saying?' said Lola motioning for him to get on with the conversation.

'The civil war started in 1861 about a year after Lincoln was elected, as you rightly said on an abolitionist ticket. The war would rage for another four years, finally ending in 1865.

'Now the southern states were wealthy but they weren't that wealthy, so I asked myself, every war is funded by someone or something so who ensured that the Confederates could fight for four years.

'Lola, if I've learned one thing during my time in war zones it's that someone somewhere is funding it and making a shit load of money doing that. As the old saying goes, there ain't no money in peace.'

'So are you saying you have found evidence to suggest that Carl Stein's ancestors bankrolled the Confederates during the Civil War?'

'Not only that, but through their private investment bank here in New York they have cleaned slave money, and money used to fund countless wars and coups since.'

'You have evidence to prove all of this?'

'Not all of it, but I want to speak to him face to face, throw some of this at him just to see his reaction.'

'He's cold, he's calculating, he's shrewd, Isaac. He plays games like this just for fun, not to mention he is very powerful with friends in very powerful places. Oh and then there is the small matter of him being a stakeholder in the paper you want to print this story in. Good luck.'

'You think I can't handle a snake like Carl Stein?' Lola had touched a nerve.

'That's not what I'm saying. We all know what a great and celebrated journalist you are but I know this man. He is an abomination and he does not fight fair. All I'm saying is that you need to be careful.'

'How do you know so much about him, Irish?' asked Isaac, still annoyed. 'And what is it that you're not telling me?'

Where could she start? Isaac Kane would never be privy to the truth about her or how she knew all this about Carl Stein. She was tempted to give herself up in her desperation to share this burden with someone else. What a team she and Isaac would make unearthing and exposing all the ills of this sick world and society they lived in. Like Sherlock and Watson. Although, she would definitely have to be Sherlock, what with her powers of deduction.

'I don't know anything much about him but I have sat down to dinner with him and played chess with him. Speaking eye to eye can tell you a lot about a person, Isaac. Call it female intuition.'

Lola lifted her coat and got up to pay the bill. She tipped the waitress and waited outside the door for Isaac.

'I could have got that, Irish.'

'This is the twenty-first century. You paid for the bus, I paid for breakfast. Seems fair. Where to now?'

'Straight ahead, up Broadway. So you play chess?'

'Yes' smiled Lola in an attempt to lighten the mood. 'Not very well, but I play.'

'Did you beat him?'

'Who?'

'Carl Stein, did you beat him. At chess.'

'Oh, said Lola relieved. 'Yeah that time I did.'

Thick shards of rain began to fall and to slap the pavement. Lola buttoned up her mac. She didn't care if she got wet, she was grateful for something other than the oppressive heat and dust of this city.

She and Isaac danced their way through the orchestra of bodies that were all trying to avoid the rain that was starting to pelt down now. Even the rain was big and aggressive. It descended in large glass globs, smashing off the pavement and soaking Lola's bare legs.

'We're almost there, Lola,' said Isaac. Until that point Lola had felt great. Her head was clear and now her stomach was full. She had been enjoying the rain. Then she noticed the rain had turned red as scarlet drops hit the warm pavement, spreading out like oil.

Lola shook her head to try and clear her vision, which was becoming blurred. She called out for Isaac.

'Irish. Irish!' His voice sounded panicked but it hit Lola's ears as though he was speaking in slow motion.

As Lola fell into his arms she saw it, a large red cube and a building that must have been over fifty floors high shooting out of the concrete. Its glistening black frame with gold trimming and tinted glass added to the menacing impression. All around the imposing steel hung Carl Stein's magick like a fine and deadly gauze.

'The building, the cube,' she tried to warn Isaac, but he didn't understand. Instead he dragged her through the building's golden revolving door and into the lobby.

A sharp pain seized Lola, making her cry out in anguish.

'What is it? Lola, Lola.'

'This building, you need to get me out of here.' Isaac leaned in so he could hear her whisper.

Lola's skin and insides burned. It felt as though her internal organs were being fried. He was testing her. It was so unexpected that she'd had no time to prepare and the ring seemed impotent. This was strong. Stronger than her, stronger than anything she had ever faced.

'Get me out of here, Isaac, I need out. Now.'

Then she was out in the open, this helped a bit but not much. Although her head was light she could see a refuge like a beacon across the road. It was faint at first, but her eyes knew exactly what they were looking for. It was the same as the thin veil that protected Brook Mill Manor.

'Across the road, Isaac, to the trees.' Lola's nose was still bleeding. She was sure Carl Stein was watching her from one of those opaque glass windows as she retreated across the road to the park.

Two ladies came to Isaac's aid and helped him get Lola to a nearby seat. 'Your interview,' rasped Lola. 'Go. I'll be okay here.'

Lola could see the pull for him. He'd waited so long to get this interview but he didn't want to leave her in this semi-conscious state.

'I'll be fine, now go.' Lola waved him away.

'She'll be just fine here, sir, we'll look after her until you come back.'

'Are you sure, Lola?'

'Go, go,' she insisted with a wave of her hand. 'I'm feeling better already.' Reluctantly, Isaac left, crossing the road and disappearing in to Stein & Sons.

Lola closed her eyes and fell back into the chair. 'Go get Prospero, Edel,' she heard one of the women say. 'I think he might be able to stop the blood.'

~ 14 ~

From behind her closed eyes Lola finally came around relieved that her insides were alkaline and calm now that she was beyond the grasp of the Stein building. A feathery lightness buoyed her body and the nausea and pain that had stabbed at her just moments ago receded back behind the veil that protected the park.

Lola had no concept of what time it was nor how long she'd been unconscious; it felt like moments but she couldn't be sure.

He had planned the whole thing. All of it. She screamed at herself. How could I have been so stupid? She let her eyes remain shut yet to be convinced that her head had stopped spinning. She was playing catch up all the time. Nothing was working. This city had her and the little power that she had at her disposal in shackles.

Now that she was free from the crippling pain, Lola observed how disconnected from the ring she was and as a result disconnected from her intuition and her own power. All her strength seemed to be spent on keeping the spectre that followed her and bore down on her day by day at bay.

Lola finally permitted her eyes to open, but her vision was still blurred, as though she was underwater.

'Arthur, is that you?' The grey hair and beard, none of which was in focus, made Lola ask the question aloud. But when the voice that owned the mass of grey spoke, she had her answer.

'I'm not too sure who Arthur is but he must be a dapper looking guy if you're confusing him with me.' The accent was American and his voice was low and gravelly, like he smoked too many cigarettes. 'I'm Prospero.' Lola could see his face widen into a broad smile but it was all still somewhat of a blur. 'Welcome to Liberty Park,' said the man placing the back of his hand on her forehead and cheeks.

Lola rubbed her eyes, clearing her vision. It wasn't Arthur's voice and now she could see that it wasn't his face either. A dullness hit her heart. What was I thinking? That he had just materialised back from the dead? A spurt of anger twisted in Lola's chest and water gathered in her eyes. She swallowed it back but it stuck in her throat like dry bread.

When Lola's eyes finally found their focus, she realised that the face of the man who'd greeted her was no less kind than Arthur's, he even shared his golden brown eyes.

They reminded Lola of a lion's eyes and when you looked at them a sun always seemed to be rising or setting, such was the flux of colours.

But where Arthur had been soft and round at the edges, Prospero was tall and angular, lean as a knife. His salt and pepper hair fell on to his narrow shoulders in thick grey tangles from underneath a baseball cap. His beard, a perfect match, reached his collar bone, settling in a sharp point.

If he was a dog, Lola thought, he would have been an Irish wolfhound. Behind Prospero's silken beard lay a well lived-in face. It had the texture and colour of someone who was accustomed to sleeping outside in all conditions. Like a scarred cliff front, it had been hardened by the wind and rain, by the sun and snow alike, yet it had an aesthetic beauty, thought Lola. Despite its rough and creviced exterior, it was a kind face, a face that exuded warmth and wisdom in equal measure.

Prospero was wearing a worn tie-died t-shirt with swirls of lavender, magenta and cobalt blue. Lola couldn't catch his aura's colours and she supposed she was still reeling from her brief but terrifying encounter with Carl Stein's magick.

He wore socks with sandals, noted Lola, and a pang of affection rippled through her; the combination gave him an edge of vulnerability.

His dusty American lilt sounded like time itself, coarse but gentle and brimming with an understated confidence or knowing. Lola moved to get up.

'No no. Not yet, young lady,' admonished her makeshift doctor. 'You lost quite a bit of blood, that was quite a nosebleed you had. Do you get them often?'

'No not really. This is the first time that it's happened here.' She looked toward the Stein building again. A rancid and menacing mist still clung to it coiling itself around the building like a snake, taunting her, but she knew it couldn't harm her here.

Lola felt safe.

The man called Prospero followed her gaze as if he too could detect it but he didn't offer any comment.

'Was I out long?' asked Lola. It had only felt like seconds since Isaac had left her.

'You were out for a while but that bleed took it out of you. You'll be fine now,' said Prospero.

The rain was coming down in earnest now, splashing off the hot pavement. The smattering of saplings that were planted in the concrete park seemed to rejoice and Lola had the urge to reach out and touch them.

The lady who had first come to her aid shook the rainwater off the blue tarpaulin that sheltered them, letting it drain into a water harvester that was attached to the side of the makeshift tent.

Lola read the sign, it said Medical Tent in thick green paint. Even though she was in the financial epicentre of New York, she seemed to be lying in some kind of commune.

'Thanks for all your help. I'm not sure what came over me,' lied Lola.

'You came from the Stein building,' said Prospero, his eyes moving tenderly over her face. 'Do you remember that?' he asked.

She nodded. 'Thank you for helping me, sir.'

Prospero smiled and stretched out his hand. It was surprisingly soft to the touch. 'Around here they don't call me sir, they call me Prospero, on account of the long beard and the staff.' He nodded to a long piece of oak that had been fashioned into a staff. The wood had been worn shiny and it was decorated with various carvings.

'Edel here tells me that you're Lola.' A lady with cropped, multi-coloured hair and a long hemp dress smiled her introduction.

Lola acknowledged the women who had kindly come to her aid. Lola thanked her for her help.

Prospero turned to her again and repeated his earlier question. 'Edel says you came from the Stein building, over the road. Do you work there, Lola?'

Lola shifted and sat up, she was still a bit disorientated and weak.

'No, I'm interning with the New York Torch. I was accompanying my mentor to an interview. He'd gotten himself a rare audience with the owner of that building.'

'The one and only Carl Stein,' laughed the old man. 'We are well acquainted with Mr Stein here in Liberty Plaza, Lola. That ass has been trying to have us evicted from this square since our protest first began. He doesn't approve of our message.'

Lola looked around the small park for the first time, realising that she was sitting in the heart of the Occupy Movement camp.

She'd read numerous articles on the protest but it looked so different in real life. It was like the story Aíbgréne had once told her about the Agora of Alexandria where her favourite philosopher and mathematician Hypatia taught. She could see it all now, the small pockets of people dispersed around the square in deep discussion or handing out food and supplies.

'It feels good here,' said Lola. For the first time since she had arrived in the city her head didn't feel like it was going to crack open and her shoulders no longer carried their heavy load.

Lola slid down from the treatment bed and walked barefoot to the nearest tree. At the base of the thin silver trunk was a small little tuft of earth and grass. The leaves of the tree turned their unfurled faces up towards the falling rain as it continued to tap on the umbrella of green that fanned out above Lola's head.

Every now and then, bowing under the weight of the water, the leaves would spill their cargo onto Lola's forehead, cleansing her and reigniting her senses.

Lola blissfully closed her eyes and sucked in the smell of the bark, of the soil and the sweet scent of the rain as it fell on the warm patch of earth beneath her feet.

'Petrichor,' said Prospero. Lola looked at the old man who now stood beside her, staff in hand, looking every inch the Shakespearean sorcerer. There was a small dog at his feet, looking up as if waiting for some instruction.

'What you're smelling is the petrichor rising off the warm earth and leaves. The nicest scent on this earth.'

'That's the word for that sweet smell?' smiled Lola, genuinely interested. Another word came to her mind. She knew it wasn't hers mostly because it was in Irish and that usually meant that the memory belonged to Brigid, but then she was Brigid, so perhaps it was hers after all, she thought before saying it out loud.

'Tenalach,' she said softly, giving life to the word.

'The ability to hear the earth sing,' said Prospero. 'Tenalach is a beautiful word, from the Gaelige, the language of your tribe?'

'Yes,' said Lola, a ruffle of confused appreciation spreading over her rain-damp face. 'That's right!'

The little golden mongrel at his feet was growing impatient.

'Yes, Hermes,' he said kneeling down to ruffle the dog's ears. 'I know you are there. Let me see what you have for me, boy.'

Prospero petted the little dog before lifting a tiny rolled up note from underneath the dog's collar.

Moving away from Lola to a safe distance he unrolled the small piece of paper between his fingers. Lola watched with interest as Prospero's eyes scanned the few lines that were written in haste. She couldn't see what it was that he was reading but it brought a smile to his face.

The old man took a fountain pen from the pocket of his shorts, turned the note and scribbled his reply.

Prospero smiled warmly at Lola as he rolled up the message placing it back in the tiny opening in Hermes's collar.

'On you go, boy,' he commanded and, immediately obeying his master, the dog took off across the square. After a few seconds, Lola's eyes lost him.

'He carries messages? That's why you call him Hermes?' Lola thought this was the best thing she'd ever seen. 'Well it seems you both live up to your names then.'

'Irish.' Lola turned to see Isaac Kane with a thunderous expression striding towards them. 'I take it the interview didn't go well,' said Lola warily.

'It didn't!' said Isaac seething. 'That sonovabitch had me sitting in the lobby for over an hour, only to have his assistant come out and tell me something had come up and he'd have to reschedule.' Isaac shook his head and bit the underside of lip, trying to calm himself.

If Lola had been in any doubt that this had all been part of the plan, Isaac's tirade confirmed it.

Carl Stein had staged the entire thing. To test her, she supposed. He had no idea how she'd been dealing with all that the city had thrown at her but now he knew. He knew how vulnerable she really was and so too did Lola. This was his way of showing her who was really in control. But, undaunted, Lola would use it.

'I'm sorry, Isaac, I should have known.'

'What? What do you mean, Irish? This has got nothing to do with you. Like I said, that sewer rat and I go way back.'

'Isaac, this is Prospero,' said Lola introducing the two. 'He's been looking after me.' Lola motioned toward the old man.

'Good to meet you, sir,' said Isaac offering his hand. 'You've a great set up here.'

'The feeling is mutual, Mr Kane. I have to say I'm a big fan of your work. Is this the first time you've been to Liberty Plaza?'

The sting in the question wasn't lost on any of the party. Lola knew Isaac had been off reporting in the Middle East, trying to expose the futility of war, but his paper, like the majority of the mainstream media, failed to give any coverage to those in Liberty Plaza or talk about what they were trying to achieve through their peaceful protests.

'What can I say, Prospero?' said Lola trying to discharge the growing tension. 'The fourth estate is dead.'

This made the old man laugh. 'I think you could be right, Lola, but I can't be too hard on the New York Torch, after all it's kept me warm many a winter's night.'

'We had better get going, Irish,' said Isaac. Lola could sense his discomfort. 'Prospero, thanks a million for your help today.'

'You are very welcome, young lady. I think this belongs to you.' Lola looked down as the old man opened the palm of his hand to reveal her ring lying inside.

'Where did you get that?' said Lola snatching it from his open palm.

'It must have fallen off your finger, it seems a bit big for you.'

Lola urgently pushed Arthur's signet ring back onto her index finger.

'Take care, Lola,' said Prospero, lifting his staff and tipping his cap 'Any more nose bleeds you know where to find me.'

The rain continued to beat off the concrete as Lola and Isaac retreated to the shelter of a nearby cab. They rode back to the newsroom in silence. Isaac left Lola without a word at the bullpen, retreating in deep thought. He banished the noisy newsroom from his office, closing the door and the privacy blinds.

Lola had the idea on the way back. If no one was covering the Liberty Park sit-in, why didn't she? It was topical and Prospero was a fantastic character. She'd run with it and give it up to the metro editor. If she liked it she could use it; if not, well that was no loss either.

Switching on her computer she had four emails from Erin, each one more urgent than the last. Lola emailed her friend to let her know she was back in the office. She'd hardly pressed the send button when there she was beaming from ear to ear, waving a golden envelope in her hand.

'What? You won the lotto and you're coming to take me away from all this,' smiled Lola.

'Even better than the lotto. I've got a press pass for the Stein's Annual Charity Masquerade Ball.'

'The what?' asked Lola, trying to dampen her interest. Already the cogs of some scheme or plan were turning in the dark recesses of her mind.

'Every year Carl Stein opens his penthouse to a carefully selected few hundred of the great New York public and they give out these golden tickets. The Torch gets a few every year and Alfie can't be bothered going so he's sending me.'

If Isaac Kane was Lola's idol then Alfie Broadchurch was Erin's. He was photography's equivalent to Isaac Kane. Only Alfie, now is his late sixties, didn't court the bright lights and recognition like Isaac did, but he was a legend in the photography world.

'Look,' said Erin, fanning the opulent piece of card out in front of her grinning face but wishing Lola could share her enthusiasm. 'I get to work this party. These parties are legendary. No one knows who anyone is, it's all very mysterious because you have to wear a mask.'

Lola raised her eyebrows. 'A masquerade ball? Seriously, Erin, what is it, some sort of orgy?' All the while her mind was toiling wondering why. Why Carl Stein did this? There was sure to be an ulterior motive.

Then the opening struck Lola, an opportunity to roam undetected seemed too good to pass up, or was this another of his tricks? Lola mulled over it while Erin talked dresses and lenses.

'So how do you get these golden ticket things then?'

'You don't get them, Lola, they're given to you.'

'So who gives them to you?' asked Lola, the idea growing more resolute in her mind. 'There must be some sort of list somewhere. I mean they don't just pick people off the street to come or invite the ordinary Joe. Knowing the Steins, each of their guests must be handpicked.'

'Well, you're right in a sense. When it comes to the press; they probably have an idea of who they would like there. There are no names on them you just produce the ticket on the night so no one knows who you are.'

'I need one of those tickets, Erin. I can't have you going on your own now, can I?'

This made Erin even more excited. 'Just call up your lover boy and I'm sure he'll sort you out,' said Erin winking her eye at Lola.

Lola shook her head, rejecting the idea, even though she knew Erin was just joking. 'No, I'll need to get a ticket another way. Leave it with me. When is it again?'

'It's next Saturday night, the 4th of July, Independence Day. You better get a ticket, Lola, it'll be the hottest party in town.'

Lola sat pondering her next move for a few minutes before crossing the newsroom to Isaac's office.

Tapping the door gently, she waited for him to beckon her in.

'I'm busy,' said the voice within, 'go away.'

'Isaac, it's me, Lola,' she tried again.

The door swung open. Isaac had removed his tie and opened a few of his shirt buttons, his shirt sleeves were turned up to the elbows revealing his muscular forearms. He was even more attractive when he was in a stormy mood.

'I know it's you, that's why I told you to go away,' smiled Isaac. Lola paid him no mind and walked into the office and sat down.

Isaac closed the door but went about the room opening the blinds again. Lola gave him a cursory look.

'What, Irish,' he said, 'you can't be too careful these days. Besotted intern trying to make a name for themselves.'

Lola raised her hand signalling for him to stop talking. 'Firstly, don't flatter yourself,' she laughed. 'You're about ninety. Secondly, there are so many things wrong with that statement that I don't know where to begin. Believe it or not, the reason I have come over here is not to seduce you, Isaac, it's because I have a query.'

'I know, Irish, I'm just messing with you.' He smiled that dazzling smile and all thunder in his face broke away. Lola thought for a moment how best to approach the situation.

'So, what is this query you have for me?'

Lola looked about the office. His desk was very much like hers with paper and notes strewn all over it, but the rest of the space was neat and orderly. Pictures of what she could only guess where his neighbourhood and heroes lined the walls.

Malcolm X and Marcus Garvey where the only ones she recognised.

Isaac followed her gaze turning to the picture behind him. 'That's Malcolm X,' he said seriously.

Lola rolled her eyes in dismay. 'You are winding me up now, aren't you?'

'What? What did I say now?'

'I know who Malcolm bloody X is, Isaac,' said Lola, indignant.

'Yes, Irish, but do know who Malcolm X is?'

'Very funny, you're hilarious,' said Lola her face impassive and stern.

'Anyway he didn't have much time for people like you, Isaac, or should I say people in your profession.'

Isaac stared over his glasses at Lola. He must have needed them for reading, they made him look more distinguished but she knew he'd be too vain to wear them out and about.

'"If you're not careful the newspapers will have you hating the people who are being oppressed and loving the people who are doing the oppressing". He said that, that man up there, and how right he was. And another thing from that Plymouth Rock speech, even we Irish know the weight of Plymouth Rock.'

'Oh here we go again about the Irish slaves,' said Isaac. 'You are not actually trying to compare the chattel slavery of my ancestors and the subsequent institutional racism of this country to that of yours?'

'I'm not trying to compare, slavery is slavery, Isaac. What we share are the horrors of colonialism. Don't forget,' said Lola, the passion swelling and expanding in her breast, 'those signs in the shop windows and restaurants said: No Irish, No Blacks, No Dogs.'

'Did you come here to school me on Brother Malcolm here or is there something you want to know,' said Isaac shaking off her outburst.

'I wouldn't attempt to school you on Malcolm, but...'

'Lola,' warned Isaac. She could tell his patience was waning.

'Okay. This masked ball the Steins are organising, how do I get a ticket?'

'I'd thought all you'd have to do was just call your...'

'Very funny,' interjected Lola. 'How do I get one?'

'Why do you want to go to Chateau dans le Ciel in the first place?'

'Chateau dans le Ciel?'

'Yes, that's what that egomaniac calls his house. The House in the Sky, or something like that.'

Lola wasn't interested in where the house was or what Carl Stein named it, at the minute she just wanted to know how to get into it. The more the idea ripened in her mind the more it seemed a perfect plan.

There would be so many people there she would go unnoticed and the fact that each had to wear a mask was just perfect for her endeavours.

'I may be able to help you, Irish, but first I want to know why you are so keen to get into Carl Stein's home,' said Isaac, he was all journalist now poised and concentrated, 'when you pulled a nosebleed to get out of the last meeting?'

The last meeting, thought Lola. That didn't go so well. Then the thought struck her. If his magick was strong in his workplace what would it not be like at his home? She hadn't figured that into her master plan. Perhaps Rocha would help her or she could call Aíbgréne.

That wouldn't work either. Lola knew what her friend would say, so perhaps that wasn't the best option. All she needed was a small window to get in and get out. She would know if the Cube was there, she'd sense it. The ring would sense it.

Since her visit to Liberty Plaza, Lola was stronger. Neither headache nor nosebleed had assailed her and the city didn't seem as oppressive as it once had. She felt more of a connection with the ring, as it too seemed to grow with her.

Lola wasn't sure if it was all down to Rocha's necklace or the veil that she'd thought she'd seen around Liberty Plaza. She'd made the decision to go back again, just to see how it felt. For all she knew she could have imagined it, like she had imagined Arthur.

Isaac sat glaring at her waiting for an explanation.

'I thought it might be a good time to speak with Carl Stein about an interview or put some of your queries to him,' she lied. She was getting better at lying.

'You can't go marching into the man's house during a party and accost him, Lola.'

'I know that, Isaac, I'm not an idiot.'

'Well, I don't know about that,' he laughed at his own joke but Lola's face remained stoic. 'You certainly like to make a scene when you're out on assignment.'

'Those were a one off,' said Lola blushing, she felt genuinely embarrassed by the whole affair.

'Listen I can't make any promises but I'll see what I can do, now if that's all I'll see you tomorrow morning. We are off to Harlem. I'm sure all the brothers up there will be delighted to hear what you have to tell them about Malcolm and Irish slavery.'

'Thanks, Isaac, I really appreciate it.' Lola got up from her chair and headed for the door.

'For the record, Irish, I'm forty-six, not ninety!'

Lola laughed. 'Aah, I didn't hurt your feelings, did I? Forty-six, may as well be ninety to me.'

Lola closed the door tightly behind her. She would clock out early and make a detour to Liberty Plaza on her way home.

~ 15 ~

The rain had stopped and New York was born anew. She was too tired to try and get her bearings and she liked to be above ground so instead of getting the tube or taking the bus Lola hailed down a taxi.

The first few rushed by at lightning speed, like everything in this city. Everyone was in a hurry or had some place to be.

Finally a taxi indicated and pulled over to the pavement. As she was about to open the door of the cab, a man in a business suit and brief case got into the backseat and continued to talk on his phone before closing the door. Lola stood aghast as the taxi pulled out into the stream of traffic.

Lola shouted obscenities at the back of the car but no one cared. This was a new low, even for this city, she thought as she stomped towards the bus terminal.

Indignant, she didn't turn around when she heard the horn sounding in a car that seemed to be slowing beside her. It persisted but Lola looked straight ahead at the entrance to Port Authority pretending she didn't hear.

'Yo, Dorothy, you need a lift?'

Lola recognised the voice. It was Tommy Maloney, the driver who'd picked her up from the airport. He was laughing as she turned around.

'Bad day at the office, Dorothy?' Lola smiled and walked over to his car.

'Can you believe that asshole? What a dick,' said Lola, still bristling in anger.

'Where you going? I'll give you a lift,' smiled Tommy amicably.

'I couldn't afford your rates, Tommy. I'll get the bus.'

'Listen, I'm off now, I'm on my way home. Where you for?'

'Liberty Plaza.'

'Then Liberty Plaza it is, Dorothy.'

Lola slipped into the front seat beside Tommy, who by all accounts had witnessed her entire ordeal.

'The look on your face,' he said. 'Priceless. This is the big city, my friend, it's mean and every dog out there is out for themselves. Next time, you head dive into that cab!' This made him laugh even more.

'She was right, you know.'

'Who?' said Tommy confused.

'Dorothy.'

This only set him off again, this time Lola couldn't resist and she joined in. 'There ain't no place like home,' said Lola, mimicking his accent.

'These city folks, Lola, they got shit for manners. What're you gonna do?'

'Teach them some,' said Lola still feeling aggrieved.

'Is that why you're off to Liberty Plaza then?' said Tommy with a grin. 'How come your fancy paper don't write nothin about those people? Huh? And the great work they're doing. I go there you know on my lunch breaks, pick up a coffee and some knowledge. There's this old man living down there, goes by the name of Prospero. God, I could listen to that old guy all day. He just has this presence about him, you know? He's a mean chess player too, whips my ass every time.'

'You know Prospero?' said Lola.

'Do I know him? How'd you know him?'

'I don't,' said Lola. 'I met him today, would you believe? I took a bad nosebleed and he helped out.'

'Yeah that man is something else. Knows something about everything he does. Did you see that little dog of his?'

'Hermes?

'Yeah, Hermes, that's right. Cute little guy. I see that little fella round by Saint Patrick's Cathedral all the time.'

'So what do you know about Prospero, Tommy?'

'Not much.' Lola would have been inclined to believe Tommy but there was a slight deviation in his colours as flashes of jet pin-pricked his orange and yellows. Lola wondered why he would lie about Prospero. 'I play chess with the guy at least once a week, for the last year, and I can honestly say I really don't know much.' Again a spark of jet punctured Tommy's aura.

Lola watched more intently as he spoke. 'I know he comes from the west somewhere. I can't place his accent. I heard he used to be a teacher and fell on hard times, like so many people since the crash. He sleeps rough, like all the other protesters but he has brought structure and something very special to Liberty Plaza. I mean, you've met the guy,' said Tommy, 'you know what I'm talking about.'

Lola knew exactly what Tommy was talking about, although like him she found it hard to articulate. There was a calmness and decency about Prospero and Lola had no doubt that a little mystery helped his persona too.

'He gives the place serenity,' said Tommy. Lola could see he was telling the truth again.

'When you step into Liberty Plaza, even though you are in the heart of New York and right in the middle of the vipers' den,' Tommy was growing more animated now, 'surrounded by banksters and all those other white-collar rouges, it feels like you're someplace else.'

'It's like a sacred space,' said Lola.

'Exactly, Dorothy, a sacred space, that's what it's like.'

'You do know my name isn't Dorothy, Tommy?' Lola was beginning to wonder. She supposed he did, just like Isaac knew it wasn't 'Irish'.

'Of course I do, Dorothy. It's Lola Paige, ain't it?'

'Well done, Tommy,' said Lola sarcastically, 'you remembered.'

'You happen to remind me of poor Dorothy and this certainly is the Land of Oz. Some crazy stuff goes down in this city.'

'So, you said you play chess, Tommy?'

'A little.' Lola could tell from the little smile that curled on the side of his mouth that he must have thought himself quite good.

'Well we must have a game sometime then.'

'You play, Miss Paige?'

'A little,' she smiled back. This made him laugh again. 'The old guy...' Tommy Maloney broke off mid-sentence as if someone had just chopped off his tongue.

'What's that, Tommy?' asked Lola surveying the grey that came flooding into his aura. 'I was saying,' recovered Tommy, laughing a touch nervously, 'you are a one-off.'

It wasn't so much what Tommy Maloney said that plucked Lola's interest but more the way he said it.

There was a hint of familiarity in his tone but before she could examine him further, Tommy pulled up outside the Stein building just across from Liberty Plaza.

Lola surveyed the building again until she detected what she was looking for. It wasn't as obvious as it had been earlier that day and so far her body hadn't experienced its ill effects.

Lola ran her thumb over the ring on her index finger and took a deep breath before getting out of the car ready for the onslaught. It didn't come.

'Thanks, Tommy, you're a life saver,' said Lola eager to get across the street to the relative safety of the plaza.

'Anytime, Dorothy, and tell old Prospero I was askin. We'll get that game soon.'

Lola closed the car door and a tapped the roof of the car in acknowledgement. She crossed the road and wove her way through the camp at Liberty Plaza.

People here actually stepped out of your way and smiled, some even greeted her like a human being and said hello.

Lola's eyes searched for the veil. It was hard to see and at first she thought she'd dreamt the whole thing but as the falling sun was eclipsed by the hostile structure of the Stein building her eyes caught a tiny silver thread of it. It was there. Even if she couldn't see it she could certainly feel it.

The contrast between this small space and the wider city that circled like a battlement around it was like day and night.

Here there was gentleness and a sense of community that permeated casting a silver nimbus on the air around the camp. It felt like home.

Some groups were in conversation, some talked and debated over a large grill. Everyone began to queue ready for their meal. The homeless mingled with protesters and no one batted an eyelid. They sat side by side discussing the day's events or news.

Hermes found her first. The little terrier stuck to her heels summonsing her to follow him with a loud bark. She didn't argue, instead she followed the little dog through the crowds, watching in amusement as he was greeted and treated along the way. They all knew him by name. Hermes sauntered ahead, his nose proudly in the air sniffing out their final destination.

They came to a halt at a large cardboard box; it was so large that Lola could have walked inside standing. Clear sheets of plastic were wrapped around the outside and there was a bundle of blankets folded neatly in the corner beside a chair and desk. Hermes's bed lay beside his feeding bowls; papers and other news items lay neatly stacked.

Nothing was wasted here; everything was put to good use around the entire site. Lola marvelled at how what most people would call junk could be utilised to make life more comfortable for the protesters.

Prospero sat reading the Torch on a chair whose entrails bulged out of its worn seams. Lola thought it suited him. His face and torso were concealed behind the broadsheet. Sensing he had company, Prospero folded down the side of the paper to see who it was.

'Lola,' he smiled. 'I wasn't expecting you back this soon.'

'Hi, Prospero, I couldn't stay away.'

'Well you are most welcome, Ms Paige.'

Prospero neatly folded his paper and laid it at the foot of his chair. Lifting his staff, he beckoned Lola to follow him. 'You eaten yet, Lola?'

'Not yet but that smell isn't half encouraging.'

'Come on with me and we'll get you a bite to eat and then you can tell me what has brought you back down here.'

As they approached the grill or as the sign suggested 'Liberty Kitchen,' the hungry branched out into varying lines.

'Meat eaters are at the end, Lola, pescatarians next, then vegetarians and then vegans. We cater for all folk here, so pick a line according to your preference or perhaps you're like me and like a bit of everything,' said Prospero as he edged up the line.

'I'll follow your lead,' said Lola amiably. 'Tell me,' she asked, 'where does all the food come from?'

'It would surprise you, Lola. The kindness of people. What we can grow here, we grow, like our vegetables and so on. Some of the vendors around here are good enough to give us anything that is left after their day's work and then we have anonymous donors.

'One very generous one in particular. We don't know who they are, what they do, but they ensure that we have enough food, medical supplies, and blankets, water. The city won't allow us to have tents, so we have to make do with what we can find. It's okay in the summer but the winter is a different story.'

'So New York isn't so mean after all,' said Lola flippantly.

'This city feels mean to you, Lola?'

'That's an understatement,' again Lola's mouth engaged before her brain.

'How so?'

'It's nothing really, it's just very different from Ballyvalley and Ireland as a whole, that's all.'

'It's a harsh energy at the best of times. If you're at all tuned in, it's much worse.'

Lola didn't quite know how to respond to this candidness. She wasn't sure if Prospero was insinuating what she thought he might be. Her eyes instinctively searched for his colours but they came up short.

Lola was hesitant but the veil convinced her that all was well with this man. She'd seen it twice now and she certainly felt it. Someone must have put it there after all. Maybe Prospero lived up to his name in more than just looks.

Still, thought Lola, she wasn't going to risk articulating her suspicions, especially when she couldn't see him. And yet she wanted to trust her gut.

She refused to let fear conquer her. Lola refused to accept what all humans were being told at every turn: you are bad, you are predisposed to harm, to violence, to hurt. Beat or be beaten.

This place was evidence of basic human decency. Listening to others, helping others, respecting others, even if you didn't always agree.

'So what brought you here, Prospero?'

'How long do you have, Lola?' he smiled, still giving nothing of himself away. 'I'm here for a number of reasons. The sense of community, for one. The gentle non-violent way in which political ideas and theories are exchanged. Being around people who see the truth, who see beyond the veil that's held up by the men who run this city is very uplifting. Men who profit from misery and sell the lie of "us and them". They own the media, the corporations, the economy, and our minds.

'Society has been seduced by their dark arts, men and women who have contorted and desecrated ancient wisdom as a form of control. But look around you, Lola, look around you at this little island of hope. Not everyone is still asleep. Day by day, hour by hour more and more people are rousing from their slumber, as She too begins to rise.'

'You say these people have desecrated ancient wisdom. What exactly do you mean by that?' Lola tried to keep her voice steady to give the impression that she knew nothing of these ideas and themes.

'Look across the street at that monstrosity.' Prospero pointed at Stein Corp. 'Look at the symbol on the building, beside the name.'

Lola didn't have to look, she knew what their symbol was, she'd seen it, she'd felt it and she had experienced it in action.

'The owl,' said Lola, offering no more than that.

'Yes an owl, a creature of the night but this is an ancient symbol of the Goddess and of wisdom in a time of darkness. The owl was the seer of souls, the guardian of the dark, but it has been contorted and used to represent something entirely different now. That is only one of many examples I could give you, Miss Paige.'

'So how exactly does Carl Stein use this symbol? I mean if that's what it truly represents, the Goddess energy, isn't it quite counterproductive to their agenda?'

Prospero stood looking at Lola now, she could tell he was trying to figure her out, she could tell he was unsure of her.

'That's a very pertinent question, Miss Paige. But first you must tell me, what do you know of Carl Stein's agenda?'

Lola recoiled. 'Nothing. Nothing. I don't know the man at all. I never got to meet him today. I ended up lying here if you remember,' said Lola. She may have overdone it a touch.

Prospero's eyes narrowed. 'The lady doth protest too much.' Lola smiled weakly.

The woman behind the grill interrupted them. Lola held out her plate and thanked for the noodles and fish.

They both found a little ledge to sit and eat.

'So how are you so well acquainted with Carl Stein, Prospero?'

'He's been down here a few times. We haven't seen much of him the past year. He's been trying to have us thrown out of the park, but the park is privately owned so he's having some difficulty.'

'So whoever owns the park is allowing you all to stay here?'

'It would seem so.'

'Do you know this secret saviour?'

'No,' laughed Prospero, 'we don't but I'm sure in time they will be revealed.' Lola could tell the old man was being cautious and decided on a less direct tactic.

'I got a lift here tonight from Tommy Maloney,' said Lola deciding it was best to steer the conversation away from Carl Stein. 'He says he knows you.'

'Tommy, yes I know Tommy,' nodded Prospero. 'Tommy's one of the good guys.'

His choice of words again interested Lola but before she could probe any further a disturbance broke out on the edge of the park.

Lola followed Prospero as the crowd split and parted before him, like he was some demi-god.

A row of policemen in riot gear stood spread out in a thin noose around the camp. One protester lay broken on the floor, blood spilled from his head onto the grey pavement. As others tried to intervene they too were beaten. The protesters stood in a line, arms entwined holding fast, trying to prevent the insurgents from entering their site.

Prospero made his way to the front line. The human chain opened to let him and Lola through before locking again. Prospero confronted one of the police officers who appeared to be in charge. From their exchange, Lola got the impression that they were familiar with one another.

'This is private property and what you're doing is illegal,' said Prospero without so much as a hint of aggression in his voice.

'Move back, sir,' commanded the police officer. 'I order you to move back now,' he shouted into the old man's face. But Prospero did not back down; instead he seemed to grow taller. His refusal to wither unnerved the commanding officer and he rested his hand on the hilt of his pistol. Unmoved by the subtle threat Prospero stood his ground.

'Officer, I demand to know why you have assaulted this innocent man and woman,' said Prospero, pointing his staff to the injured party.

'Move back, sir, now. Or I will be forced to use restraint.' He stepped towards Prospero pushing his chest and the old man fell back.

At that point Lola could not explain what took hold of her. A wrath burned in her at the injustice of what she had seen. Her heartbeat pulsed loudly and the ring fell into rhythm until all she could hear was a thrum thrum thrum in her ears.

Lola helped Prospero to his feet, jerking in front of him to protect him from the blow the police officer was about to land on his head.

In self-defence, Lola raised her hands to protect them both from the impact. It was instant; a nanosecond so fast that she was sure that no one could have seen it. There was a blue flash and then the entire line of policemen lay in a disorientated heap.

The protesters weren't looking at her, no one suspected that she had anything to do with it; they stood dumbstruck as the police offers writhed and struggled to get to their feet.

Lola's body began to shake as Prospero escorted her away from the front line.

'Was that you, Lola? Did you do that?' his voice was no longer measured, Lola could hear panic and fear rise in it.

'Do what? What are you talking about?' Lola's knees felt like jelly.

'We need to get you out of here. Follow me,' said Prospero with urgency.

Lola followed him as he led her to the opposite end of the park and a line of taxis. He opened the door and ushered her in.

'You shouldn't have come here tonight, Lola, it's not safe.'

'Safe? It's the only safe place in the city,' Lola spat back, not entirely sure why she was angry with Prospero. She felt as though she had let him down or disappointed him. 'What have I done? Those policemen beat innocent men and women, that can't go unreported.'

Prospero ignored her last statement and spoke to the driver. 'Eddie take this lady home please.' He turned to her again. 'Leave it a few days, Lola, and come back then, we'll talk then.'

'They can't just get away with that,' she protested but Prospero closed the cab door and returned to the camp.

By now, the police were entering the camp knocking down anyone and anything that got in their way. White smoke crawled through the park as protesters tried desperately to cover their faces. Lola lifted her phone and began to take pictures from the cab window.

'Stop,' she ordered the driver. 'I need to get out, I want to video this.' Lola struggled with her phone but the driver wouldn't stop.

'Excuse me, sir,' said Lola, more forcefully now. 'I said I want to get out. Could you stop the car, please?'

'Mr Prospero said home, ma'am, so home it is.'

'You can't keep me here against my will!'

'Please, ma'am, sit back down. Listen to what the old man tells you. Now where to?' Lola sat back in the seat and rolled up the car window. 'Twenty-one Princes Street,' she muttered.

Some of the tear gas had penetrated the cab and assaulted her eyes and throat. Tears began to leak from her eyes. They stung her cheeks and her eye ducts as they poured out. Lola's body trembled with fear and outrage in equal measure. What had she done? She'd lost control but they were about to beat her and an old man. Prospero would not have survived that blow to the head, surely she'd saved his life, so why was he so angry with her?

Lola was assailed as she staggered through the door in a daze, her eyes vacant as if she was staring at some unseen object in the distance.

'Lola Paige, where have you been?' said Rocha rounding on her. 'I've been a worried sick about you.'

Lola could not even get the words out, she slumped onto the sofa but the panic in Rocha's face was real forcing Lola to offer some explanation.

'I'm fine, Rocha, I'm fine.'

'You don't look fine and you sure as hell don't smell fine. What is that?'

'It's tear gas.'

'Tear gas! Where were you, Lola?'

Lola told Rocha about what had happened in the camp and how she had just been trying to help Prospero.

'When that Police officer went to strike Prospero, I just lost it, Rocha. I messed up.'

'Messed up, how exactly did they get messed up, Lola? What did you do?'

'I didn't do anything, Rocha, well not intentionally. It's the ring. Sometimes she protects me and that's what she did. If that baton had connected with Prospero's head it would have killed him.'

'Lola.' Rocha was stern now. 'What exactly happened?'

'Well, as he was about to strike, the ring omitted this blue pulse, like it does sometimes, it sends out this ripple, but this ripple was really strong and it knocked down all the police officers.'

'Did anyone witness this?'

'It happened so fast, no one would have seen or heard. Only me, and maybe...'

'Maybe who, Lola? Maybe who?'

'The old man,' said Lola, the fatigue was hitting her limb by limb now. 'He asked me did I do that to the police officers. I told him I didn't know what he was talking about. So he put me in a taxi and sent me home. Then as we were driving off the police were coming through the camp with tear gas beating people and wrecking the place. I tried to get out to picture it or video it but the driver wouldn't stop.'

'Thank the Goddess he wouldn't stop.'

'Rocha, I'm fine,' said Lola the irritation slipping out. 'No one saw me. Anyway someone down there knows magick.'

'How do you mean?'

'Well there's a protective veil over the site. The only other one I've seen was at Brook Mill Manor. That one was very strong. But it's there. I saw it twice today and I felt it.'

'What were you doing there anyway?'

Lola explained to Rocha about the assignment, about the interview with Carl Stein, what had happened on the approach to the building and how she ended up in Liberty Plaza.

'You think Carl Stein planned all this?' Lola watched as Rocha sat down her face became pallid and drawn. Lola understood how responsible Rocha felt for her safety while she was staying in New York. She had made a promise to Celeste to take care of her, but this was not Rocha's fault this was the sum total of Lola's reality now.

'Your life has changed beyond measure, Lola,' said Rocha apologetically, 'and I wanted to give you the space to find your feet, to have as normal a life as possible while you are here. I underestimated how strong your powers are. Me, I've been in this city so long I've built up an immunity to the Hell Fire Club's presence but I had forgotten what it was like for me when I first arrived here. Like you, I too struggled but it has grown even more volatile.'

Lola didn't require Rocha to articulate her concerns she could see the grey growing in Rocha's apple green aura.

'Rocha', said Lola, 'let's be straight here, none of this is your fault or your doing. This is reality for me now and no one, not you not Celeste, not anyone can shelter me from that but you are right it is stronger. I couldn't be sure at first. The magick was like nothing I've faced before. Even the night we rescued Celeste Aíbgréne was more affected by it than me,' explained Lola.

'This was a whole new level. It was so strong, Rocha, I could actually see it manifest itself like a fog hanging around the building. It breathed and flexed like he was controlling it. Like it was an extension of him. I took the nosebleed three blocks away, that's how badly it affected me. It felt as though he was watching me, my every move. He never gave Isaac the interview. Kept him waiting for over an hour and then made some excuse. Isaac was livid when he came back to get me. Then I knew.'

'His powers have grown exponentially. I can feel it myself, Lola. This is a very worrying development.'

'I thought his strength lay in this city. Being here is what makes him stronger?'

'No, it's more than that. I can feel it myself. Something is not right.'

'It might be nothing, Rocha,' said Lola as she moved to the edge of

119

the sofa. 'But when I went back tonight, I could barely see it around the building and the magick didn't feel that strong, in fact I could barely feel it at all. I feel like someone has recharged my body, the ring seems stronger than before.'

'Lola, you need to get this notion that the ring and you are separate out of your mind. You are what controls the ring. It does not control you. Therefore you need to learn how to act responsibly. You clearly have no control over the immense power that lies within you.' Rocha's words matched her colours now. She didn't hold back as she paced up and down.

'I suppose it's not your fault,' she said more to herself than to Lola. 'No one has ever taught you how to control it.'

'Control it? Don't you think you're over reacting a little, Rocha? It's not like I went full-scale Carrie on them.'

'Lola,' urged Rocha. 'Darling,' she said, her tone was softer now. 'I don't think you appreciate how serious this is. We don't know exactly how strong you are yet. We don't really know how much of her has awakened in your subconscious or conscious mind.'

Lola sat in silence unarmed by Rocha's candidness.

She couldn't deny that she felt scared and that Rocha was right, she felt in no way in control. She had believed until now that the ring worked of its own volition, only to discover that she was responsible for its actions, even if she wasn't fully conscious of the fact.

It did make sense. Whenever she was in sheer need, whenever she was faced with a fight or flight scenario, the ring kicked in. Lola thought about all the times that it had activated. The first time, it seemed like eons ago, but that summer night in Belfast when that young man had followed her to Mystic Moone. It was Brigid who had been alerted to the danger. The same thing happened when she saved Celeste. When she'd been drugged by Alex, they were able to take the ring from her – she should have realised then that without her the ring didn't work.

All the while she had been waiting on the ring to do something but it had been waiting on her, waiting on her command. Tonight she had made an emotional reaction and the ring responded accordingly. She wanted to flatten that police officer and that's exactly what she did.

Lola looked down at the granite ring on her porcelain finger. It was only a ring, Arthur's ring. That's what made it special to her mostly, that it had belonged to him, that he had worn it. It made her feel closer to him.

She slid it off her finger and held it up.

She marvelled at how the granite could be a conduit for such strength. It was so unassuming, the little triple spiral carved into it was perfect, but it wasn't ornate it wasn't ostentatious; it gave no indication at all of what magick lay within.

'What's happening to me, Rocha? What am I doing here? How did I get here? I'm stumbling around this city blind. Blind to what I face and clearly blind to what I am. And for what?'

'For what?' answered Rocha after a while. 'I'm afraid that's not so easy to answer, Lola. The reasons run deep, like your story, old as time itself. The Goddess rises in you and the only advice I can offer you, my darling girl, is don't fight it and don't doubt it. You must trust it and then and only then will you be able to harness it. She rises and you must rise with her.'

'But I can't fight him, he's too strong. Rocha, I can't even see the playing field never mind navigate it, never mind own it.'

'Tonight changes everything. Something has altered in you, Lola. Perhaps it's the book that strengthens you; perhaps it's the Cube. I don't know, but manifesting your magick in such a physically powerful way, even you must recognise that something is afoot.'

'It's not the first time that this has happened.'

'Have you ever taken down as many people before?'

Lola thought about it for a minute, the most was about fifteen people, the night they rescued Celeste from Mussenden Temple. Tonight there had been at least forty police officers in that line.

'No,' she answered. 'I need to get back to see that book, Rocha. You work at the university, could you fix this for me?'

'I would like to examine it with you. I'll see what I can do. I had planned on being out of town this weekend – I'm not one for the 4th of July celebrations – but in light of recent events, it's perhaps best to stay with you.'

Lola hadn't told Rocha about her plan. She knew that she would be opposed to it. If she was out of town that would make life a lot easier for her.

'Rocha, don't be silly. I'll be fine. You don't need to change your plans. Besides,' smiled Lola impishly, 'who's going to mess with me?'

'That's what I'm afraid of, young lady. Have you any plans, for the weekend?'

'Yes,' said Lola. 'I think a few of us interns are going out for drinks.'

It wasn't really a lie, reasoned Lola.

'Good, you need to try and enjoy your time here and act like a young adult from time to time. God knows you carry a great burden and you deserve a reprieve every now and then.'

Reprieve indeed, thought Lola. But first she had to get her hands on one of those golden tickets.

~ 16 ~

The newsroom was unusually quiet when Lola arrived to work on Tuesday morning. There must be a news meeting upstairs, she thought as she settled into her desk. She had started writing up a report on the events in Liberty Plaza and wanted to upload the little pictures and footage that she had there.

Lola made her way over to Isaac's office. Half the newsroom seemed to be crouched around a few computer screens. No one noticed her. Whatever they were watching it had their full attention.

Isaac was standing with one of the groups. 'What's all this?' asked Lola, nudging in close enough to smell his aftershave. It smelled floral yet musky with woody notes.

'Have you not seen this?' said Isaac, his eyes locked on the monitor.

Isaac stepped out of her way so she had a clear view of the screen. The video showed the previous night's scenes from Liberty Plaza.

'I was there, I saw it first-hand,' said Lola. Some of the other reporters looked around, curious now, suddenly interested.

Isaac guided her by the elbow into his office and closed the door. 'You were there?'

'Yeah, I've written up some copy and I have some pictures to go with it. It was awful, Isaac. What those police men did to those innocent people.'

'What the police did! Lola have you been on social media at all today? That footage you saw out there went viral last night and it didn't show any protesters being assaulted. It showed...' Isaac broke off. 'Hell, I don't know what it showed. I've been in warzones and I have never seen anything like that.'

'What do you mean?' Lola's blood ran cold. She reached for the nearest seat and fell into it.

Isaac logged into his computer and turned the screen around so she could see it. The footage was quite grainy; it looked as though it had been taken from a security camera high up on a building.

The video showed the backs of the police standing in a long line, facing off against rows of protesters. One of the police officers could be seen stepping forward but his body obscured the view of the two figures in front of him.

Lola knew that it was Prospero and that she was beside him. Then the screen was lit up by a lightning blue flash which was captured by the camera as the windows of the office block shook from the force.

The camera momentarily cut out and when it came online again each of the policemen were on the ground. Lola watched herself being led away from the scene by Prospero.

A blinding panic rose in Lola, not because she could be identified in the footage but if she was correct and the video had been shot from the Stein Corp building, and that meant Carl Stein had seen her little display.

Isaac replayed it again and again, pausing it for a second here and there. Lola sat rigid in her seat. Now she understood why Prospero had gotten her out of there straight away.

She could tell that Isaac was onto something the way he looked at the screen and then at her.

'What that footage doesn't show you is the two assaults that took place before the video starts or the assault that was about to take place before that blue thing happened,' said Lola trying her best to sound unperturbed. 'That footage must have come from the Stein building, based on the viewpoint,' she argued, 'and Stein has been trying to have the protesters evicted for ages. He's been behind the systematic intimidation of the movement since they arrived in Liberty Plaza. How do you know this isn't some hoax?'

Isaac looked at Lola. 'Lola, over forty police officers were thrown to the ground. Their testimony, not to mention various eyes witness accounts, say that some device was used by the protesters and you're coming to me with some conspiracy theory?'

'Device? Don't be so silly, Isaac. What do you mean device? They are peaceful people, they aren't even aloud to erect tents for god's sake never mind harbour futuristic weaponry.'

'How else can you explain what happened then? The police department, the mayor's office, every news station in the city is all over this. They have arrested the old man in the picture. That guy you introduced me to, what was that whack-job's name?'

'Prospero!' shouted Lola, jumping to her feet in agitation. 'They've arrested him? For what? I was there. I know what happened. He did nothing wrong!'

'Keep your voice down, Irish,' said Isaac. He leaned over the desk now and spoke in hushed tones. 'I know that was you with the old man in that footage, Lola. I have no idea what took you back down there but this Lois Lane bullshit has got to stop. Either you are very unlucky or trouble seems to seek you out. That was some serious shit down there and the city of New York will not take it lightly.'

'Are you seriously saying what I think you are, Isaac?' The wind was sucked from Lola's sails. 'You of all people should know the value of real journalism, isn't that why they gave you those awards?' said Lola, her voice almost cracking. 'You have a brass neck,' she seethed in disgust. 'Those people at that camp in Liberty Plaza, who lie in cardboard boxes, who endure the worst this city can throw at them and the worst that Carl Stein's money and power can throw at them, they do it for you, Isaac, and everyone like you. They are taking a stand against the tyranny that is rising and rising, a tyranny that the media and most of America are blind to. Yes it's easy to marginalise them and call them whack-jobs, if that's what helps you sleep at night. Isn't it an indictment of real journalism that my role model should be Lois Lane, a fictional character?'

Lola got off her seat and walked out of the office, leaving the door gaping open behind her. She returned to her desk and began typing ferociously on the keyboard.

Suddenly Isaac's office door was flung wide open and she could see him come raging across the newsroom.

She could tell by his expression that she'd crossed the line even if what she had said was true. Everyone of course had returned to their desks by now, so they had a front row seat, all that was missing was the popcorn.

'Who do you think you are? You will learn to show some respect, Miss Paige!'

125

Lola's face flushed. She could feel the anger and embarrassment rise in her like a hurricane. All it would take was one thought, one flick of her wrist and Isaac Kane would be lying on the other side of the newsroom. She took a deep breath to settle herself.

'I have been a journalist for over twenty years and reported from some of the worst warzones on this planet and you give me that, in there.' He pointed to his empty office in reference to their heated exchange.

'Really, Mr Kane, you want to do this here?' said Lola, surprised by her own restraint. This seemed to stop him momentarily. He nodded for her to follow him out of the newsroom. They were now out of earshot but still the rest of the bullpen and journalists could see their exchange.

They pretended not to be watching but Lola could feel their eyes on her back. Lola guessed that this display was more for Isaac's benefit than hers.

'You were the one who insulted me, Isaac. I apologise if I have offended you, but I was only holding you up to your own self-professed standards. I was there; I have pictures of police entering the site, with tear gas, and batons. Wrecking all in their path. These are not terrorists; they are middle-aged men and women exchanging ideas. I thought this was a free country, Isaac? If you had spent any time at all in that camp you'd know that.'

Isaac had calmed down now; he was back to his normal cool self.

'I'm a senior journalist with years of experience. You, Lola, are a greenhorn. You need to remember that,' he said. 'You could have gotten yourself hurt.'

'Are you done? Am I dismissed or would you like to keep me in the village pillory for a little longer?'

'Look, Irish,' and there he was, the Isaac she had respected and idolised, the one who had fought her corner and stuck up for her. He was back again but it was too late for Lola. 'I'm only looking out for you, that's all. You're young and eager and sometimes that can get you mixing with the wrong kind of people.'

Lola could have raised another fifty objections to his condescension but she turned and walked away. Gene Rush passed her halfway across the news floor. His face contorted in what was his attempt at a smile.

'Trouble in paradise, Miss Paige?' Lola ignored him and returned to her desk. She finished the rest of her story, uploaded the pictures and sent it through to the metro desk editor.

She didn't rouse when her desk phone rang; it was usually for someone else. One of the journalists, shouted for her, 'Hey, Greenhorn! It's for you. What am I? Your secretary?' Lola fought back the tears; she knew she would have to toughen up if she was ever going to survive in this place. She couldn't take it all personally. She picked up the phone, delighted to hear Rocha's voice on the other end.

'Have you seen the news, Lola?'

'No,' replied Lola, sullenly. 'I've just heard this morning. Where did you see it?'

'On Twitter, where I get all my news.' This made Lola smile.

'The footage was very grainy, you can't see much, Rocha. It's not ideal I know but you wouldn't know it was me.'

'Lucky for you, you are right but do you understand now why you must be careful?'

'Please, Rocha,' pleaded Lola. 'I've had it already from Isaac for being there in the first place. I can't take another lecture. Besides I'd prefer not to talk about it over the phone. We can talk later.'

'Yes, that's actually what I was calling for. I've spoken to the curator at the Butler and she has very kindly granted us access to the book. Vivian is an old student of mine. Professor Moriarty will be there as well, so you can get your story after all. They have said strictly no photos.'

'That's great, Rocha, thank you so much. When?'

'This afternoon, around three.' Lola looked at the clock on her screen, it was almost one now. 'Yes, that should be fine, will I meet you at the library?'

'Yes, I'll be waiting for you outside.' Lola thanked Rocha again and hung up the phone. Her stomach lurched; she could do with some fresh air and something to eat.

She texted Erin to see if she was around on her way out of the office. Just as she was leaving the lift she got a reply. They arranged to meet at a nearby deli.

'You got a ticket for Saturday night yet?' Lola had completely forgotten about the Stein party.

Isaac was supposed to get her a ticket but he hadn't mentioned it. She doubted he would now.

'No not yet,' said Lola. 'I don't think I will at this late stage to be honest, Erin.'

'Well maybe we can meet after then. We can go out for a few drinks?'

'Yeah, why not. Rocha is out of town this weekend so it would be g to get out and about, actually see what New York has to offer.'

'Yeah, it'll be good for you to let your hair down a bit, get out of that bullpen. You okay, Lola? You seem a little frazzled.'

Lola didn't want to trawl through everything again, so she muttered something about the heat and being tired. Erin didn't push it. She was happy to talk about her assignments and Lola was happy to listen until it was time to return to the newsroom.

The pair parted with a hug at the lifts as they each went their separate ways. Lola was thankful to have Erin. She was great fun and good company. She really missed her girls back home and she missed talking to Aíbgréne.

She would have to phone her at some stage. She was sure that Rocha had been keeping her and Celeste informed anyway but the longer she left it the more difficult it would be. It wasn't that she had been avoiding the call, it was just that she seemed so preoccupied and busy all the time and when she came home in the evenings all she wanted to do was wash and sleep. City life wasn't glamorous at all. She missed the familiarity of Ballyvalley, the smallness. That's why she was drawn to Liberty Park; it offered her a little taste of home.

The thought reminded Lola that she would call on her way back from Columbia. She was worried about Prospero and she felt responsible for what had befallen the protesters.

Back at her computer Lola checked her inbox to see if Maria, the metro editor, had responded. She felt a touch dejected that there was nothing. Gene Rush and Isaac had been in conversation for over five minutes now, Lola observed from behind her monitor. It surprised her that they seemed capable of being civil to one another. Then she thought they might be talking about her.

It was almost two fifteen now and she would have to be leaving if she didn't want to be late. She had to report all movements to Gene and she had considered emailing him but decided against it. She didn't want to give cause for reproach. Lola took another glance from behind her screen, they were still talking. She shut down her computer and lifted her things approaching the office gingerly. She tapped on the door and entered. She avoided looking at Isaac; she was still sore with him.

'Mr Rush, I have an interview at Columbia, so I'll be leaving the office now.' Surprisingly there was no snide commentary from Gene Rush, he nodded his head.

Lola left the New York Torch and waved down a cab. She took a precautionary look behind her to make sure no one was going to steal it and quickly jumped in.

'Where to, ma'am?'

'Columbia University please,' said Lola. This was going to be an interesting interview she thought as she closed her eyes and let her head fall back on the seat.

~ 17 ~

As promised, Rocha was waiting outside the main building. The sun streamed down on the large glass doors and Lola wished she could stay in its warm gaze for a little longer.

The air con hit her bare legs like a blast of ice when she entered the cool foyer. Reaching into her bag she pulled out a light cotton cardigan. It was like an accordion but she felt so cold that she didn't care how wrinkled it looked.

This time they took the lift. Rocha punched a code into the security buttons and they dropped down to the basement level of the library.

The elevator door opened up on to a dimly lit corridor, which made the beige tiles and walls glow a sickly yellow. It reminded Lola of a war bunker she had seen in some documentary once.

The women passed numerous brown wooden doors. Rocha pointed them out as they went.

'Everything,' said Rocha, bobbing her head at the various doors, 'the university acquires for the library is brought down here first. They examine them and repair them if needed. Actually the repairs are ongoing. Where we're going now,' she said smiling back at Lola, 'is a brand new facility paid for by patrons of the Butler Library. One you are already acquainted with.'

'Alex,' said Lola. His name sounded odd now that it floated in the air and hung thick and awkward in the narrow corridor between them.

Rocha offered no reply, instead she kept a steady pace until they reached yet another non- descript brown door.

'This is us, Lola.' Rocha pressed the buzzer.

A lady's voice seeped through the speaker. 'How may I help you?'

'Hello, Rocha Moone, I'm here to see Vivian.'

'Professor Moone, please come in.' Rocha smiled into the camera and waited for the door to open.

In stark contrast with the dim corridor, this large open room was bathed in natural light but there didn't seem to be any windows. Rows of workstations lined the perimeter of the room and each had someone working at it. Lola watched as the men and women sat deeply engrossed in their tasks.

Some leant over magnifying lamps, scrutinising book spines, others seemed to be sowing and mending. The space was fresh and open with a communal area in the middle. Off to the side lay a small portion of the room that had been boxed off with low-level partitioning. This was like a mini warren, with tools and books scattered everywhere.

'Rocha,' said Vivian du Vaul as she rushed to meet them. 'How great to see you.' She pulled Rocha into a warm embrace. 'It's been too long,' she said smiling.

The library curator had her long chestnut hair fixed in a neat plait and was wearing lose jeans and a long sleeve t-shirt, making her look more youthful than Lola had remembered from when they last met.

'What an amazing facility you have here,' said Rocha, taking in the preservation lab. 'I really appreciate you giving us this opportunity.' Rocha turned to introduce Lola. 'Vivian, this is Lola Paige.' Lola smiled and held out her hand.

'Lovely to meet you, Ms Du Vaul, and thank you very much,' she said sheepishly.

'So, Lola, Rocha informs me that you're interning with the New York Torch, very impressive. The larger papers never really pay us or the great work we do here much attention, so thank you very much for coming along.'

'You're very welcome. I had planned to cover this the night I was last here but...' Lola trailed assailed by her embarrassment.

'The poor girl was mortified,' laughed Rocha. 'Everyone must have thought that she was the worse for drink. It was absolute fatigue. Silly girl had eaten nothing all day and add to that exhaustion and the nervousness about her first big story and this is what happens.'

Rocha squeezed Lola's hand. Lola reciprocated. She was grateful for the help.

'Now,' declared Rocha, in full control of the situation. 'Tell us all about this place. What a marvellous addition to the library. The last time I was down here, many moons ago, it was just that corner over there for the binders and a few old x-ray machines.'

Lola retrieved her Dictaphone from her bag. 'Do you mind if I use this, Ms du Vaul?' she asked.

'Not at all, Lola. But one thing I will ask of you, is our main patron – Mr Stein – would prefer if his name were to stay out of the papers. He wouldn't want anyone to think there was a cultural conscience under that playboy exterior,' she laughed. Lola smiled politely.

'So along the side here you can see various work benches,' said the curator as she walked them around the room.

'These are the wonderful people who ensure that the books in all our collections upstairs remain in a stable condition. The lighting in the room is powered by natural light bulbs, the temperature, which is controlled by the large fume you can see at the corner of the room, is set to create the optimum conditions for paper. The door beyond that is where certain documents can be washed with a special ionised water system.'

'Do you handle all documents in here, Ms Du Vaul?'

'No. No. This is paper and book repairs. As I said the humidity in this room would not be appropriate for say more organic materials, like the book you have come to visit today.'

'Is that because it's written on vellum?' asked Lola.

'Exactly.' They walked a little further.

'These are the binders,' she pointed towards a woman who was working on the spine of a yellowed book. The worker lifted her head and waved the white bone folder in their direction in acknowledgement.

'Simone is working on a seventeenth-century leather binding to reinforce the front hinge on the book.'

'Has Mr Stein provided you with all of this?'

Vivian nodded her head vigorously. That and a great deal more, Ms Paige. He has not only given us this wonderful working environment but he is providing us with the very latest in preservation science technology. With that I think I should hand you over to our resident expert. She has worked on a few of Alex's father's private projects. We are so very lucky to have her and her expertise.'

A short woman came towards them in a white lab coat smiling. She looked to be in her late forties, with dirty blonde hair that fell in loose curls styled neatly to her chin. She had all the clinical air of someone entirely at home in this kind of environment.

'Ladies, this is the wonderful Susie Delaney,' said Vivian. 'I will be leaving you in her very capable hands. I'm afraid I have a dinner to attend and I need to go and get ready.' Rocha and Vivian embraced goodbyes, leaving Lola to talk to their new host.

'Could I just ask you to give me your name and your role here at the preservation department, please?' asked Lola, pointing her Dictaphone under Susie's mouth.

'Of course. My name is Susie Delaney and I am the lead preservation and imaging scientist at the facility here.'

'Vivian mentioned that you have worked for the Steins before. What kind of projects did you work on?'

The lady gave Lola a furtive look, Lola could tell there was an element of suspicion in her eyes but she answered.

'Well it was just a consulting role based on Mr Stein's substantive private collection, we used some of the new technology, now at our disposal here, to investigate how to stop the items from deteriorating.' By now Rocha had joined them again.

'Mr Stein, I mean Carl Stein, initially contacted me through a mutual friend who worked for National Geographic. They had partially funded a project that I was working on with another scientist.'

'Yes!' exclaimed Rocha. 'I watched that programme. I thought I knew your face from somewhere. Professor Delaney, what a pleasure it is to meet you.' Lola listened to the exchange like a spectator, having no previous knowledge of Susie Delaney or her work.

'You were part of a team trying to uncover a lost Leonardo behind Giorgio Vasari's battle scene, in Palazzo Vecchio in Florence! That was just fascinating. The work was ground breaking.'

'Yes it was and frustrating as well,' said Susie with a curt smile. 'I was honoured when Seracini contacted me to help out. As I was saying to Lola, Carl Stein was involved in National Geographic and I did some private work for him as a result. His son later contacted me and offered me this opportunity and I couldn't resist. Alex was very keen to build a state of the art facility here at the Butler, a centre of excellence so to speak. A place solely dedicated to preservation science that everyone could use and that would further the pioneering art of preservation technology.'

'What kind of technology?' said Lola trying hard to give of an air of professionalism.

'For the first time, we here at Columbia and at Butler have a rare opportunity to test and use the latest Synchrotron techniques. Unfortunately these require small samples to be taken from the books or paintings but for items such as the Book of Kells, as it is a priceless piece of antiquity, we would not be recommending this approach.' Susie's face broadened out into a warm laugh.

'Synchrotron?' said Lola furrowing her eyebrows with bemusement. 'Perhaps, Professor Delaney, you could dumb that down a bit? I wish I had your intellect but I don't, so perhaps you could explain it to me like I'm me,' she laughed.

Lola's candidness seemed to soften the scientist's starchy edges and Lola could see that she was beginning to relax a little. Lola could speak to people on every level and if she didn't understand she was never embarrassed to ask. Arthur had taught her that. 'There is no such thing as a silly question if you don't know the answer,' he'd say. She never stopped asking after that.

'Yes,' said Susie, nodding her head magnanimously. 'Sorry. I'm so used to talking in jargon all day long. As you can probably tell I spend a lot of time down here talking to books.'

'As long as they aren't taking back,' smiled Lola. She was sure that she was the only person crazy enough to hear books singing.

'Well synchrotron in this capacity offers us the ability to use hard-imaging x-rays, which are put through a specific crystalline beam line. This produces a series of images that enables us to see various hidden layers. We can also build a picture of what minerals, composites and molecules are present. This is non-invasive technology and can tell us a lot about provenance, how far an item has travelled, its organic remains, dyestuffs, pigments, and lithic material. I could go on.'

'So is that why the Book of Kells is here? To undergo these investigations?' 'Yes, exactly. Please, follow me.' Lola and Rocha followed Susie to the bottom of the room where they passed through another set of security doors.

'I'm afraid, Ms Paige, I will have to ask you leave your bags and Dictaphone outside. I will be more than happy to answer any questions you have when we come back out. Ladies,' she handed them each a white coat, gloves and foot covers. 'Can I ask you to take off your shoes and wear the slippers as well? This is a highly controlled environment and we rarely let outsiders in here. Manus is already inside.'

Lola and Rocha were happy to comply.

'The music is lovely, does it help you work better?' asked Lola absently. Rocha shot her a cautionary look, but it was too late.

'Music, Ms Paige, what music is that?' said Susie her eyes searching around the room for the sound.

'I'm probably hearing things,' stumbled Lola, giving a dismissive wave of her hand.

Lola give Rocha a furtive look but she gave nothing away as to whether she could hear the soft voice as well.

The bright white room was slick and sparse. The only items it housed were an oak table and a few office chairs scattered around its frame. The air in the room felt moist and a few degrees cooler than the exterior lab and Lola remembered that this was because the books stored in this section of the lab where made from organic materials.

Every minute detail had been taken care of. Upon entering the room, Lola could not dismiss the sound of the voice because as they drew closer to where the visiting professor sat it grew clearer and louder.

Moriarty was oblivious to their intrusion as he sat engrossed in the pages of the large folio that lay agape on the polished table.

'Manus, we have company,' said Susie, offering Lola and Rocha a seat.

Lola was delighted to be sitting down. She found her eyes transfixed on the brightly coloured pages. The musical voice was so vivid now she couldn't hear what the others were saying. The susurration sounded like wind sighing through the boughs of a tree or the crest of a wave as it exhaled onto the shore and she was in rapture. Lola tried everything to resist the urge to reach out and touch the pages that called to her. The room and chatter around her warped in and out of her auditory awareness.

She could hear the voice clearer than ever now and the song it sang was an old one. It spoke to the very soul of her being and that ancient woman that lay deep within her stirred.

It felt as though a longing had been sated deep within her and this confused Lola, she'd only just discovered the book and yet it was like she'd always known it. The tiny hairs on her arms stood erect like antenna in recognition of this primal bond urging her to reach out and physically connect with its fleshy pages.

The book emanated a tender pulse as if it too had a heartbeat. Lola could feel it and so too could her ring. A golden mist hovered above the document and in that moment Lola realised that Rocha was right – the book had been calling her all this time.

She couldn't resist it any longer; it was as though the book, like an anxious mother, needed to feel her touch. Then she did it, she removed the glove and reached out and gave the book what it had wanted, what it yearned for.

Lola's jade eyes rolled back in her head and her senses where immediately heightened. She could smell cold earth and stone; she could smell the sharp resin of the torches as their light licked the granite walls around them. She could feel the years of wisdom and power the book possessed. She could feel her own heartbeat, her breath and her thoughts as they rhythmically ticked in one grand symphony with the book's pulse.

In rapid motion, scene after scene unravelled behind Lola's curtained eyes. Yet, this inner sight did not belong to her or Brigid, it belonged to the folio itself. Lola, in a flash, saw the many hands that had held it, the many places that it lay concealed, those who had loved it and those who wished to harm it. She shared it all with Lola now.

This book had a voice and a song and now she was revealing tiny golden lines and slashes. Lola's right hand searched for the pencil and pad that she remembered seeing on the sparse table and with the inner sight of a prophet, she blindly copied down on the pad what was being shown to her.

Lola's eyes shot open again taking their time to orientate to their surroundings. The voice was gone and all she could hear now was the drone of the room's thermostat. As if with new vision, Lola starred down at the page she'd been writing on and dropped the pencil out of her right hand, it felt alien and wrong there. She gazed in confusion at the marks her non-writing hand had made on the notepad before lifting her head beseechingly to face the stunned silence around the room.

Surprisingly, it was Moriarty who rescued her this time as Rocha looked as confounded as Lola did.

'Susie,' he said as if they had witnessed nothing out of the ordinary, 'the results from the last x-ray, are they back yet?' Lola watched as the scientist's eyes darted around the room, appealing for confirmation that what she'd just seen had been real but no such assurance came so she turned back to Manus.

'Yes, Manus,' said Susie, her voice taut as her mind scrambled to process the scene. 'I'll... I'll go and check with the lab.'

Once she had scuttled out of the room, Manus Moriarty leaped to his feet snatching the piece of paper Lola had scrawled her etchings on.

'You feel her? You feel her too! You see it?' Tears began to gather around the edges of Moriarty's wide eyes.

'That first night, upstairs,' said Moriarty, rubbing his fingers over his forehead in vexation, 'I could see the effect the book had on you, it was the same look of recognition in your eyes that I'd once known in my own. For years I've thought that what I was doing was madness but now you have shown me that it's all been worthwhile, that I wasn't wrong.'

Moriarty knelt down in front of Lola taking her hand in his. His eyes searched her face in reverence as if she were some exotic vision.

'Please,' he begged, 'tell me everything you saw.' Moriarty's colours fell around him like a multi-coloured snowstorm. His colours told the truth and they matched his words and his expression but still Lola hesitated.

'I'm sorry, Professor,' said Lola flatly. 'I don't know what you're talking about.' But her rebuke was meek as she focused on his aura and the honesty she found there in the blue, indigo and vermillion.

'Lola.' Lola turned to the earnest voice. She'd almost forgotten that Rocha was there. 'It's okay,' said Rocha, her eyes full of reassurance. 'You can tell him, he's an old friend.'

Moriarty's confusion played out on his face as his eyes searched from Rocha to Lola trying to understand the words that their silent expressions were speaking. Moriarty, while thrilled with developments, still found it all a bit unsettling. He wiped his brow with the back of his hand, waiting for either woman to explain who they were and what had just happened. His eyes had rested on the lines and slashes that Lola had written. He recognised the lean forms from when she had shown them to him, all those years ago. A sense of vindication and relief rose in him while his scientific mind tried to challenge and contradict what his eyes had seen and his heart had known. But he wasn't alone, now there were others.

'Professor, how did this book come to be here?' asked Rocha urgently, her eyes darting to the door. 'Come on, Professor, quickly now. Why are you here?'

'Alex Stein,' managed Moriarty as he tried to organise and focus his thoughts.

'What about him?' Lola asked. 'Does he know about her?' She wasn't sure why she referred to the book as 'her', maybe it was because Moriarty had. 'Does he know what this book is?'

'What is it?' asked the professor philosophically, but Lola did share his pensive mood.

'We don't have time for this,' said Lola hearing Susie enter the key code to the room. Reaching across the table, she snatched the piece of paper out of Moriarty's hands and stuffed it down her bra.

'Well?' asked Moriarty with absolute composure when Susie joined them again. She was more composed now as if she'd convinced herself that it had all been in her head. The atmosphere in the room was charged and while Susie's colours subtly reacted to it there was nothing in her demeanour to indicate that she herself sensed the tension.

'There've been some developments but I think it would be best to have this conversation at a later date,' said Susie, her eyes motioning towards the company.

'This is off the record, Ms Paige,' said Moriarty, now restored back to his composed and scholarly self. His eyes flashed a warning at Lola. 'Is that okay?'

'Yes of course.' Lola was no longer on official duty and she was keen to hear any news about their research.

'Manus, I don't think...'

'Susie. Go ahead,' said Moriarty. 'What have you found?'

'Well, in all the tests that we've carried out to date nothing was revealed that you didn't already know about the document. However,' she hesitated again unwilling to speak so frankly in front of Rocha and Lola but coaxed on by Moriarty she continued, 'our latest tests are showing something significant to your cause, Manus. Up until now it was believed that the script was written on calf vellum. Our beam line technology has allowed us to have a more comprehensive look at the layers and we believe – but may I add we are at a very early stage – well, it looks like the material may not be calf vellum after all but that of the Megaloceros giganteus.'

Moriarty slid down on to the chair as if he'd been hit with a stun gun. Unlike Lola, he clearly understood what a profound development this was.

'The Irish Elk or Irish giant deer. They roamed Ireland over seven thousand years ago,' said Moriarty, running his fingers across his forehead, trying to order his thoughts. 'This is ground breaking, Susie,' he finally said.

Lola thought they had overstayed their welcome and decided it would be a good time to depart. She'd got what she had come for, a closer look at the book, and now she was sure that their suspicions had been right.

Lola got off her seat, the piece of paper she'd stuffed down her bra was digging into her breast and she shuffled her shoulders to try reposition it but it didn't work.

'Thank you for your time, Professor Delaney, you have been so kind. We will go and let you and Professor Moriarty have that chat.'

Lola shook the lady's hand and turned to Moriarty, 'Congratulations, Professor, and thank you for all the information. If you'd like to add anything you can contact me on the news desk at the New York Torch,' Lola give him a knowing nod. 'I'm sorry I don't have a card or anything but I'll be easy enough to find,' Lola added, but Moriarty seemed to be miles away, deep in thought.

As Lola turned to leave something stabbed at her heart, every part of her being seemed to scream and wail and she didn't want to leave the book behind. The book felt this tearing too. The butterflies that lay caged in Lola's chest sprang to life again, beating their airy wings against her breast.

With the vision still vivid in her mind and her connection still strong, Lola soothed the book and herself, explaining that she would be back soon.

Susie Delaney led them back through the preservation lab again where the workers methodically and lovingly restored the timeless volumes. Books were eternal objects, given the right care, thought Lola, and they could survive just about anything.

Despite everyone still working at the same pedestrian pace, the news about the book's vellum had already filtered through the laboratory. Lola detected a slight charge in the air. As the lab door slid closed behind them she caught a glimpse of Alex Stein emerging in a flurry from one of the side investigation rooms.

For a fleeting moment as their eyes locked, they exchanged a million unspoken words with one telling the other she is mine and I will have her.

Lola knew then that she wasn't the book's only admirer. She had to get Her out of there and she would need Moriarty's help.

She and Rocha didn't speak a word until they emerged from the basement and were back out in the warm embrace of the sun. The heat caressed Lola's cold skin and it felt like a tonic. Her mind was an explosion of thought, the Lost Oracle was here in New York and the Steins had full control of it.

Lola forced herself to remain calm. She would speak to Moriarty and, once she did, she was sure they would be able to secure the book.

'Well that was illuminating,' said Rocha, taking a seat on a nearby bench. Lola, exhausted, slumped down on to the wooden plinth beside her.

'Could you hear that in there, Rocha?' Lola hoped she had felt something.

'I couldn't hear anything but I could certainly feel it. The connection is much stronger with you, Lola, I could sense that alright,' said Rocha formulating her own thoughts.

'That is certainly the Lost Oracle.' Rocha laughed. 'And to think it has been at Trinity College all these years disguised as something else entirely, a Christian Gospel of all things. How clever!'

'I felt awful leaving her.' Tears began to crowd and gather in Lola's eyes. 'I can't explain the feeling, the love I felt towards her, the tenderness.'

'It's funny you should say that, Lola,' said Rocha. 'I could see a fine silver thread connecting the book and Moriarty and I could see one connecting to myself as well but when I looked at you it was a bright golden ribbon of light and it ran from the heart of the book to your sacral chakra,' Rocha touched Lola's navel. 'Right there,' she said, 'like an umbilical cord. Its energy seemed to be flowing into you and it was pulsing the whole time. It was quite beautiful,' marvelled Rocha, her eyes falling on Lola as if for the first time.

'The book clearly recognises you as its child, how very interesting,' she laughed.

'I hope we can trust Moriarty,' said Lola, still feeling a little unsure. 'His colours are good and it's obvious how much he loves the book. He's dedicated his entire life to it, she showed me.'

Lola summoned the image again. 'She showed me lots of things like how she revealed herself to him as a reward for his devotion and diligence. I think that's what's been driving him all these years. He thinks that something lies beneath the text and he's right but it's not what he thinks it is,' explained Lola as if she was suddenly an expert in the field. 'All the science in the world won't open up the book's true nature. Only the light of the Dé Danann can do that.'

'All that in just a few minutes, Lola,' said Rocha. 'Maybe you're the real deal after all,' she smiled, giving Lola a gentle poke in the ribs with her elbow.

'I can see that you're connected to this book too, Rocha, and back in the lab you told me that you and Moriarty were old friends, but by the look on his face, it was clear the man had never laid eyes on you before.'

'He hasn't,' smiled Rocha, in that characteristically all-knowing and patient way. 'Just like you and I, Lola, this is the first time we've met... In this lifetime.'

Rocha's words, like a key unpicking a lock opened up a recollection that had been buried deep in Lola's memory.

It was a remembrance of a recurring nightmare she'd had for an entire six months before Arthur had died. In light of everything that had transpired she now understood that it hadn't been a dream at all but an actual experience from her previous life.

In that time, now long forgotten, she was known as Brigid, or In Rúad Rofessa, the Red one of Great Knowledge.

Lola recalled the temple and the four Guardians that stood before her loyal and true. Trusted friends and teachers. Lola fought to remember their faces, searching for some similarities between the Manus and Rocha of today.

'I don't believe it,' said Lola, confounded by the revelation.

'Now there's a surprise,' laughed Rocha. 'You don't believe what?'

'I remember you,' said Lola, shaking her head in disbelief. 'In the temple before I died, I remember you and the others, the other Guardians.'

'Good,' said Rocha, laying her hand on Lola's. 'That means your connection is getting stronger, that you are getting stronger.'

'The memories started to come about six months before Arthur was murdered. At the time I couldn't understand it and I never told him about it and to be honest I'd forgotten all about it until today when you said that we'd known each other before.'

'What do you recall now, Lola?' asked Rocha, her eyes urging Lola to remember.

'Everything,' said Lola, it was all clear in her mind now. 'I remember running through the forest, someone was after me and I had the Cube and a sword, Solus I called it,' said Lola. Her body tingled and her head rang with excitement as the fragments of her ancient past began to piece together.

'I came to the temple, it was winter, the eve of the solstice and a light snow had begun to fall. The four of you were waiting inside for me.' Lola described the scene that reeled through her mind in vivid detail.

'I can still smell the earth and the stone. I gave you each a folio...' Lola paused for a moment.

'Rocha,' said Lola her expression full of revelation and wonder. 'I split a book into four pieces and gave each of you a piece. Do you think this could be the same book?'

141

'I don't think that it is the same book, Lola. I know by all that's in me that it is the very same book.'

'But how?' protested Lola, the left side of her brain trying to rationalise and reason.

'It's simple really,' smiled Rocha. 'Magick.' Lola shook her head and wondered how she still struggled to believe in magick.

'Did you see him?' asked Lola. They had a major problem on their hands, and neither time nor circumstances were on their side.

'That I did, my dear, and he saw you. That look in his eye makes me wonder if he is completely lost to us.' Lola didn't want to think like that. She needed to see Alex Stein as the enemy. He was the enemy.

'Susie Delaney, do you think she can be trusted? I mean she's technically employed by the Steins.'

'I don't know, Lola, the jury's out on that one. Besides we have other things to worry about at the moment.'

'Like this?' grinned Lola, producing the piece of paper she had stuffed down her bra. She smoothed it out and set it on the bench between them so they both could examine it.

'I've never seen anything like this, Rocha. It just looks like lines and slashes to me.'

'I have,' said Rocha, her peat-brown eyes examining the markings. 'It's an ancient form of writing that was used in Ireland called ogham. It was devised and used by the Order to conceal and protect the secrets of the House of Dé Danann. Eventually it made its way into scholarly use but it was still pretty obscure. I wonder if this is how she is choosing to communicate with us?'

'We're talking about a book here, Rocha, not a conscious being.'

'Still you try to rationalise, Lola.' Rocha made a plaintive hiss through her nose. 'Even after everything she has shown you, after everything you have experienced. Now I know why Arthur chose not to tell you. He understood that you would have to experience it to believe it, but I'm not sure even that is working.' Rocha widened her eyes and considered Lola for a moment.

But Lola didn't need convincing, she only longed for her life to be back to the way it once was, so every now and then she liked to check, just on the off chance that someone would tell her what she wanted to hear.

'We need to get ourselves an archeolexicologist.'

'What's that when it's at home? I need to start carrying a dictionary around with me.'

'I haven't heard that turn of phrase in a long time,' laughed Rocha. 'An archeolexicologist is someone who studies archaic languages. And luckily for us, Lola Paige, I know where we can find the best there is in the business. If he can't help us... we'll need to rely on you.'

'So let's pray he can,' said Lola.

'Exactly.'

As they made their way to the School of Archaeology, which lay across the vast quad, Lola began to feel anxious again, that fluttering bird in her chest had returned. Lola's eyes drew back toward the library and there they rested upon the very object that had been calling them.

He was standing outside the main entrance leaning casually against one of the large stone pillars, stone against perfect stone, watching her as she crossed the quad. Her stomach kinked as if it too remembered him. A pang of sadness assaulted Lola's heart again but this time she knew it had nothing to do with the book.

~ 18 ~

*A*lex's eyes surveyed the perfection in the buildings, their pillars and arches, the curves of the stone and angles that had been meticulously designed and constructed. He let his hand caress the deep undulations carved into the thick limestone column as he leaned against it watching Lola Paige.

He was still sore that their company hadn't managed to get the restoration contract for the building. There was a huge parting of the waves between Alex and his father when it came to preservation and architecture.

The Butler, he thought, although only a few decades old, was a thing of great beauty, just like the porcelain legs of Lola Paige that disappeared into the opposite building. Alex made a mental note to find out what department was housed there.

He was surprised when he'd learned that there was another Moone living and working in New York. He couldn't seem to escape them. They all had those same earthen eyes that wore the same look when they saw him. It was a look that said: you're worth saving, you have more of her in you than you realise. But they were all wrong. Alex immediately snatched the thought from his head. It served no purpose. Thinking of his mother served no good.

Of course they were wrong, the Moones. They seemed to hinge this delusion of his apparent redemption on one insane moment of weakness but Alex accepted that he was beyond redemption.

Alex often wondered if that's what had drawn him to architecture. Was it the control and the insatiable pursuit of perfection, a perfection that could be great and imbued in buildings but not in himself? The things he'd seen and the things that he'd done, no amount of philanthropy or the sporadic resurrection of his conscience could change that. Much to his father's annoyance, Alex had taken a step back from the Club's more ritualistic activities. This wasn't in protest against the faceless women whose lives were being cut short, his reasons were much more self-centred than that, at least that's what he told himself.

It was as though she was there with him, like she was in the chamber, looking down on him. He had never experienced what it was like to have a mother, the tenderness in her eyes, the unconditional love that he felt when she looked at him. He felt her in him and her presence around him from time to time.

No matter what his father had told him, no matter how many times he said that he had dreamed it, Alex knew that what he'd felt that night when they'd brought Lola Paige to the temple at Newgrange was real.

His eyes may very well have been shut and he may have been unconscious but the vividness of his experience lingered with him for too long for it to have been a figment of his imagination.

His mother wasn't the only woman he felt a stronger connection with since that night. Alex had felt Lola's presence down in the lab, even though they were in different rooms. He had sensed her light; even across the wide expanse of this sprawling city he could feel it. Like a human GPS Alex Stein was sure he would be able to pinpoint Lola Paige no matter the location, such was their intimate bond.

His mind wondered back to when that bond was consummated. To when they both lay naked and twisted in each other's bodies. He often thought about that rainy day by the sea in Ireland. He'd never felt more alive and more exposed than he had that day.

As he watched her in deep conversation, he couldn't quite access what it was that made him long for her or what glitch in his wiring that made him care for her.

All Alex cared about was that it hindered him. It made him weak. She had ruined his life, just as he would no doubt contribute to the ruination of hers.

When she had turned around before walking into the building to discover him watching her Alex knew that Lola felt the connection too and a wave of contentment ruffled through him.

She seemed different somehow. He wondered if it was because of her hair, which didn't fall down her back anymore, but was cut to just above her shoulders. No, that wasn't what made her seem different, he decided.

The innocence that had radiated from her when they first met was gone, but this did not dilute Lola Paige in any way. It was clear that her initiation into this alternative existence had only made her stronger.

In the darkness that seeped from every square inch of Manhattan, now controlled by his father and soon him, Lola Paige stood as tall as a lighthouse in the black of night. Her growth and power emanated from her in thick beams but her light, as powerful as it was, was also her greatest weakness. Alex understood that Lola would be dead before the snuffing of her flame was even registered and then maybe he would be able to get back to his old life.

He knew that Lola wasn't drunk that night at the Butler, despite what he had told Gene Rush. He had seen only what he could describe as a golden haze rise from her as she lay unconscious on the floor. He was sure she'd felt some connection with the book and that suddenly changed everything.

Initially, Alex had been sceptical when his source had pointed him towards the Book of Kells and Professor Moriarty's obscure 'Equinox Theory'.

When he first visited Trinity he was unconvinced that the Book of Kells could be a possible match for the Lost Oracle of the Túatha Dé Danann. Yet, the notion intrigued him. If true, it was nothing short of genius. How audacious to hide such a coveted magickal book in plain sight for centuries. But it all seemed too easy. The Hell Fire Club with all their resources had been searching for it for many years and come up empty handed.

He found the professor to be completely enamoured by the book and as a result he'd been quite uncooperative. His reluctance was another thing that piqued Alex's interest. He was genuinely surprised when he had received the call to say that Moriarty had agreed to bring the book to New York. Alex was delighted that Trinity's provost had done enough to convince him.

But since its arrival, Alex's access to it had been minimal. He'd to rely on Susie for most of his information. She'd been keeping him in the loop and on the rare occasion that the visiting professor allowed him access he had been unable to examine it properly. He knew that what they were looking for could not be revealed by science but only something more powerful and thus he was brought back to Lola Paige.

However, he needed the book in his territory and dangling the carrot of science and discovery was the best way to do that. Professor Moriarty did not disguise the fact that he didn't trust him. This amused Alex because he knew that the professor was right to mistrust his intentions. Despite this, or perhaps because of it, he found that he respected Manus Moriarty.

After all, this man had dedicated his entire life to this book and it wasn't the lure of money but the lure of discovery that had forced him over the Atlantic. Alex could tell that he loved it from the way he handled it and looked at it, the way he guarded it from the dangers of the world.

Yet, it wasn't until Lola showed an interest that he began to rethink his views – perhaps the old man had been correct all along. Alex knew that Lola would do the work for him, he just needed to sit back and let her. Unfortunately, she also understood now that he had a vested interest and she was able, unlike him, to gain access to it whenever she chose. Susie had told him that it was only a one-off but he knew Lola and he knew that she was on to something. He had seen it in her eyes as the lab door closed separating them once again. He'd seen that fire and defiance so many times before in those fierce green eyes and every time it stirred something unbidden in him. She was excited about this book and he wanted to know why.

Alex's cell phone vibrated in his pocket. He lifted it out and answered.

'Susie,' he smiled.

'Sorry, Mr Stein.'

'How many times do I have to tell you, Susie? Mr Stein is my father, please call me Alex.' Even though he couldn't see her, Alex could tell she was blushing.

'Alex,' she laughed. 'I couldn't get speaking to you earlier but we have just had a major breakthrough. Alex's stomach tightened.

'Yes,' he urged.

'Well some of the latest test results have come back and it appears that there are traces of something much, much older underneath the calf vellum.'

'Like what, Susie?'

'Megaloceros giganteus.' It was meaningless to Alex. 'English, Susie.'

'Yes, sorry. Irish Elk or the Giant Irish Deer to be more exact.'

'And why is this so significant, as you put it?'

This made the professor laugh. 'Because, Mr Stein ... Alex, these creatures have been extinct for over seven thousand years.' Alex was at a loss for words, his reserve temporarily abandoned him. Had he hit the jackpot? Had his source been right?

'Does anyone else know about this, Susie?' Alex's tone darkened.

'No, just Professor Moriarty.'

'Does she know about these findings?'

'Who?' replied Susie meekly.

'The reporter. Does she know about these findings?'

'Well yes, Professor Moriarty wouldn't...'

'Damn it, Susie!' spat Alex.

'Who else?' he demanded. 'Who else knows?'

'I don't like your tone, Mr Stein. The young reporter has given Manus and I her word that she will not discuss these findings until we are ready to publish and Rocha is a fellow academic, she will keep quiet no doubt. Good afternoon, Mr Stein.'

Alex threw back his head, running the palms of his hands over his face in frustration. He thought about calling Susie back to apologise, but he didn't.

Alex checked his watch. 'Damnit.' He was late.

Alex Stein summonsed a cab and slid into the back seat feeling agitated and drained.

Why had his life become so serious and so complicated, he asked himself. Lola bloody Paige is why, answered back his mind, taunting him.

'Where to, Mr Stein?' It was hard for him to go anywhere in this city without being recognised, but being recognised as a womaniser and playboy was preferable to people seeing him for what he truly was so he was happy to play the part.

'Downtown,' answered Alex. '7th precinct on Pitt and Delancey. If you could drop me off at the side entrance, I would appreciate it.'

The cab driver laughed. 'You in trouble again, Mr Stein? What is it this time?'

Alex forced a smile onto his perfect face. 'Speeding fines, they like to make an example every now and then and make me come down to the station.'

The covenant that he had entered into was an uneasy one. Many times he had considered backing out of it, yet still he remained tied and bound in a prison of his own making, a torture he endured on daily basis.

Alex stared blankly at the streets of New York. This concrete jungle would all be his someday. There was so much raw and rugged beauty to the city, its boroughs and its people. The cab pulled up a short distance from the police department. Alex paid the fare giving the driver a generous tip and entered the red-brick building via the side door. His source would be pleased with the information he was about to receive.

~ 19 ~

Lola took a picture of her byline in the metro section and folded up the paper. She wrote out a text and sent it to her dad's mobile and tweeted another for the girls at home. Her first byline for the New York Torch and she was brimming with pride.

Maria, the metro desk editor, had been really kind and given her much more coverage than she'd expected. She had even sent Lola over a cutting from the paper with a little note saying well done and a smiley face drawn on the pink post-it.

Thinking of these tiny touches made Lola's heart soar again and made trawling through endless press releases all worthwhile. It had been a strange week as she tried to juggle work at the Torch alongside her duties to the Order.

Most of her working week had been spent researching and filing copy for some of the other senior journalists in the bullpen. She had even run into Jodi a few times when the fashion editor had come down looking for Isaac.

Lola learned that they had been colleagues when Jodi had worked down in news. She couldn't imagine Jodi sitting in the bullpen with all the hacks, with their coffee-stained teeth and their nicotine-yellow fingertips.

Every evening after work, Lola stopped by Liberty Plaza in search for Prospero but he hadn't been back seen since his arrest. She felt responsible and had called every precinct in the mid-town area in search for him but came up short.

The camp was a rudderless ship without him there. The atmosphere had dampened and Lola could tell they were all concerned for his whereabouts too. It was clear why the police had targeted the old man; he was their lynchpin.

The day before, Rocha had sent an email through to her at work. Her colleague, the archeolexicologist, had come back with a rough translation of Lola's etchings, and what she'd written down left her more confused than before.

It read: 'My daughter, my light. The great even time will soon be upon us.'

Lola had mulled over the message for the last twenty-four hours trying to unlock its meaning. She guessed that she might be the daughter and the light but the great even time, that made no sense to Lola at all and Rocha had left the city reluctantly to spend the weekend with friends, so she would have to wait until she came back to shed any more light on the cryptic message.

The apartment felt bare without Rocha and so did the entire city, which looked like it had been tipped up and emptied out. Only a skeleton staff was in place in the Torch newsroom, everyone else was getting ready for the 4th of July celebrations, everyone accept for Lola.

Erin had agreed to stay with her at the apartment over the weekend but she had been out working so much that Lola may just as well have been on her own. The girls had agreed to meet at the works party later that night when Erin was done at the Steins'.

Lola couldn't help but feel a touch sorry for herself, it had been so long since she'd been out and because she was still only nineteen getting into clubs and bars in the city wasn't straight forward.

Lola looked across the news floor to where Isaac's office lay in darkness. Their little spat had put to rest any hope of securing a ticket for tonight's party at the Steins'. She'd done her utmost to avoid Isaac for most of the week, which wasn't too hard since he'd spent a good deal of it out on assignment and even though she was still sore with him, she was beginning to feel irritated by his absence – after all he was meant to be her mentor.

Then add to that Professor Moriarty, who was fast becoming another source of consternation for Lola. She had so many balls to juggle she was sure that she'd drop at least one of them.

Moriarty still hadn't made contact with her and she was getting more and more restless. She'd thought about visiting the library so many times and each time she had to check herself. Being a constant presence there could potentially jeopardise everything because she was sure that the Steins would be kept abreast of all the book's visitors. Alex knew too much already. It was now only a matter of who could get there first.

Tidying around her desk, Lola put her computer to sleep and headed out into the sunshine for some lunch. She'd made her own lunch because Rocha warned her that most of the delis around the office would be closed for the holiday.

She thought about going to Central Park again but instead Lola found a comfortable spot beside a tree in the small office garden that lay hidden in the centre of the building. As she sat eating her salad, Lola revelled in the light's warmth as it flowed down on her bare skin.

A delicate breeze filtered through the garden carrying with it the rich smell of Lola's coconut sunscreen. It was a factor fifty – for those with no melatonin, the image of her white skin made Lola laugh to herself.

Her body expanded with the breath of the sun as it rested on her face and limbs only to be interrupted by the sporadic breeze, which softly chased the heat away. The ebb and flow of the two coaxed Lola's eyes into a light sleep.

The muted shades of umber and yellow behind her closed lids made Lola think of Aíbgréne and she was reminded of how much she missed her friend.

Rocha spoke to her and Celeste on an almost daily basis, keeping them up to date with all the latest developments but Lola was still too cowardly to call herself. She'd been happy with Rocha's intermediary skills. Even though she spoke to her parents and the girls a few times a week, Lola still missed home terribly.

This world was so alien to her, the streets, the language and the food. Everything was shiny and hard. Tommy Maloney was right, she was like Dorothy and lately she'd have given anything for a pair of ruby slippers to get her home but her duty to the Order made sure that she did what she must and not what she wanted.

The Oracle had occupied so much of Lola's mental space that the angst and trepidation about how she was actually going to get her hands on the book stalked her thoughts day and night.

It would be impossible without the help of Moriarty, and sharing a connection with the book was entirely different than enticing him to conspire in its theft on his own. Lola had always maintained that the secrets of the Order were not hers to give away but it was vital that she convinced him to help so she would have to wrap a kernel of truth in whatever lie she decided to tell him.

Stretching off the relaxation, Lola got up depositing her waste into a nearby bin. She slipped on her flat pumps and headed back to the office.

Her phone beeped announcing the arrival of a message. It was from the girls, in their group chat. Each of them congratulating her on her first story – all three hundred words of it, smiled Lola to herself. Just as she was replying, another message came through, this time it was Erin, she had just picked up her dress for the party and it was beautiful.

Adjusting to the light inside the building, Lola put her phone on silent and slumped down at her desk. It took her a moment to realise that the large brown envelope in front of her had her name on it.

She looked around at the few others who sat in the bullpen but no one looked up so she opened it, pulling out a note that was stuck to a golden raffle ticket.

Irish, sorry if I was a touch heavy handed. I hope you'll forgive me and stop avoiding me. We have work to do.

Have a great night, Isaac. PS I realise you probably have nothing to wear, go to the sixth floor (the fashion department) and speak to Jodi. I believe you two have already met. She's expecting you.

Lola read and re-read the letter. Her initial response was to tell her mentor to shove it. It had taken him a week to come and speak to her, but she needed to find the Cube and this was the best place to start.

Lola packed up her things and headed for the lift. She hadn't been beyond the first three floors of the building before. Moments later, when she stepped out of the elevator into a contemporary reception space, she could have been in a different building altogether.

Large life-size pictures of models in the latest fashions hung on the gallery-white walls. All of the work booths were empty as they sat dormant in the darkness.

A central aisle ran up the middle of the room with booths on either side. At the top of the space lay three glass fronted offices, which ran across the back wall, they too where unoccupied and Lola was about to turn and leave when she heard music issuing from one of the doorways that lay to the side of the office. Lola followed the sound and tapped on the door.

'Hello?' said Lola, shouting hopefully over the din.

Suddenly the volume of the music reduced and Jodi emerged from behind a rail of clothes beckoning her in.

'Lola!' Jodi smiled at her from behind a pair of black thick-rimmed glasses. Even dressed in slacks and a lose jumper with her hair tied in a headscarf, Jodi was stunning and Lola couldn't drag her eyes from her cocoa skin. In the white light of the wardrobe room, which occupied a corner of the building, Lola could see Jodi more clearly. Her colours were rich carnelian and bronze with slight tones of mauve flashing in and out like a beacon and they made Lola like her instantly.

'Great to see you again, Lola,' said Jodi. 'Please come in.' She stepped back and her almond- shaped eyes, the colour of faded moss, opened as they considered Lola.

'Let me have a look at you. Well you sure look a lot better than when we first met. Isaac wasn't wrong, you're striking and those eyes and skin, like alabaster. You one helleuva white girl.'

Lola's face reddened at the compliment and she wasn't sure if it was because Isaac had said it or that Jodi agreed.

'You blushing girl?' laughed Jodi. 'You got a thing for Mr Kane?'

'Me? Isaac? No no. I mean he's good looking and all but I don't... you know, I don't...' Lola's apparent discomfort only made Jodi laugh even more.

'I'm just messin with you, little sister. That man is fine and he must like you a whole lot to make him come here to see me.'

'Now come on over here and let me have a look at you.' Lola stood feeling self-conscious as Jodi walked around her and eyed her up. 'What's your size, Lola?'

'Size eight, I think. It depends.' 'UK eight, that is?'

'Yes.'

'Your feet?'

'UK five,' answered Lola.

Jodi was a good five inches taller than Lola, even without heels, and she bent over her and lifted her hair up, muttering suggestions to herself.

'I love your bangs, they're so cute.'

Lola had already had this discussion with Erin so this time she understood her bangs to be her fringe. Americanisms, it was like having to learn a new language at times.

They had sidewalks instead of pavements, cabs instead of taxis, cell phones instead of mobiles, restrooms instead of toilets and just the other day when she'd asked Erin if she wanted an ice lolly, she hadn't a clue what Lola was talking about until she showed her. 'Oh, a popsicle, yeah sure,' she'd answered. It was the time thing that really challenged Lola. Everything was ten after this and fifteen after that and when Isaac ended an argument or made a point he'd say, 'That's it! Period.' Where Lola came from, a period was something she'd had each month since she was fourteen.

Jodi continued to busy about her, lifting and clipping her hair and backcombing it so hard that it brought tears to Lola's eyes.

'You've got that whole Hepburn thing going on,' said Jodi, as she dusted Lola's hair with a white powder that made it rigid. 'Yeah let's go with that,' she said disappearing into another room.

She emerged with two dresses and a bottle of hairspray. By the time she was finished, Lola could hardly breathe.

'That should do it,' said Jodi, reaching over and lifting the dresses she'd picked. Both were black and one was shorter than the other. Holding them up she scrutinised both, looking from Lola to each dress and back again. Finally she decided on the longer of the two. Lola felt like a spare part so she tried to make light conversation.

'So you work up here in fashion, Jodi. How long have you been here?' asked Lola, genuinely interested.

'I'm the editor of the bi-weekly lifestyle magazine. Isaac and I used to work in news together.

It's tough in the bullpen but I loved it down there, all I ever wanted was to be an investigative journalist.' Jodi's eyes darkened and her tone became hushed as if she was remembering some past hurt. Lola observed the grey as it invaded her colours and wondered what the root of it was. 'But when Isaac left to go off to Iraq for the first time, things changed for me. So when this job came up, I took it. I've been editor her for a few years now and I've grown to love it.'

Not wanting to seem too familiar, Lola didn't question her further.

'So,' said Jodi, her face brightening into a smile again, 'Isaac tells me you're for the Stein Fourth of July party tonight, Lola.'

'Yes,' said Lola, wondering if she had lost her senses. She hadn't given too much thought to her master plan but now that it was looming ever closer she was becoming more edgy.

'You're in for one hell of a party. Chateau dans le Ciel is something else. We did a fall fashion shoot there a couple of years ago. It was spectacular,' said Jodi examining the dress again. 'I've heard it's the after party's where it really goes down,' Jodi raised a perfectly sculpted eyebrow at Lola. 'So, little lady, if anyone invites you to the after party make sure to stay clear, you hear me?'

Lola nodded her head in obedience but her curiosity had been piqued. 'What have you heard, Jodi?' Lola tried to make it sound as though she was interested in the gossip more than the story.

'Let's just say some of the models we use for our shoots talk. The Steins own quite a lot of agencies in town. In fact I'd say Alex goes through at least ten a week.' Lola's stomach sank as she pictured Alex with ten women as beautiful as Jodi.

'Well it was something I worked on once but let's just say I've heard that Carl and Alex Stein like to share their playthings. White boys and money, the more perverse the better.' Jodi's face darkened and the grey came back and Lola knew for sure that she wasn't divulging all her misgivings. Lola made a mental note to ask her about it sometime. She suspected that there could be something useful in it.

By now, Jodi had styled her hair into a large bouffant, slicking her fringe over neatly to one side.

'Right, try on this dress, I think it will be perfect for you.'

Lola took the dress behind the curtain and slipped it on. She had to get Jodi to zip it up at the back for her. The dress had thin spaghetti straps and an eyelet top that cupped her breasts as if it was made specifically for her. It slipped over her hips and down to her calves, with a slit that almost came to her upper thigh. Lola kept self-consciously closing it over.

Jodi slapped her hand away each time she held the slit closed. 'Stop that, you need to show off those fabulous legs.'

'My legs are one thing but showing off my knickers is another.' This made Jodi laugh again. 'Are all Irish girls as hilarious as you?'

'Not all of them, but some maybe.'

'Seriously,' smiled Jodi, 'you can't see your knickers, not even close. Here put these on.'

Lola obediently slipped her feet into a pair of black court shoes. She felt as though she was being propelled forward, such was the gradient of the heel that she was sure she'd crash head first onto the floor.

'I'm never going to be able to wear these shoes, they're ridiculous. I can hardly stand in them never mind walk. You'd have to wheel me around the place,' protested Lola as she tried to regain her balance.

Jodi gave Lola a scolding look but Lola could see the tenderness in her face.

'They're Louboutins, they're meant to be ridiculous,' she said. 'Ridiculously beautiful.'

'I'm a journalist, Jodi, not a model, just in case it wasn't obvious enough,' smiled Lola. 'I couldn't handle those things, besides, they cost more than my plane ticket here.'

'Okay, what about these.' The next pair were similar or at least they seemed similar to Lola's uneducated eye.

'These will do fine.'

'Indeed,' laughed Jodi. 'I trust you can handle your own makeup?'

'Yes,' smiled Lola, 'I can just about do that much.'

'Good, because I've a business date with our friend Mr Kane and I don't want to keep him waiting too long.' This revelation annoyed Lola more than she liked. She thought of what an amazing couple the two of them would make. How gorgeous they would look naked together. Lola changed quickly and thanked Jodi for all her help.

'It's a pleasure, little lady. Please be careful tonight and do not accept an invite to Carl Stein's after party,' she laughed. 'Oh and have those back on Monday morning, dry cleaned.'

'No bother,' promised Lola as she made her way towards the lift again.

It was almost five o'clock. Fishing her phone from her bag she called Erin to tell her the good news. Erin was technically working so she had to be there earlier than Lola. They arranged to meet at the venue.

Lola rushed from the taxi and into the apartment block. She dumped her clothes and hoped that there would enough hot water to allow her to shave and wash.

It was after seven when her phone beeped with a text message from Erin and she was just about to leave the house for the party. Lola opened the picture of a tall blonde in a long red fitted dress with a golden Venetian facemask on.

Suddenly she remembered that it was a masquerade ball. How could she have forgotten that!

Panicking, Lola thought desperately about where she was going to get a mask. All of the shops were closed because of the holiday. Running out of ideas, she called Rocha on the off chance that she had something that would do.

Luckily Rocha was able to help. Lola hadn't planned on having to tell her about her little outing so she was caught off-guard when Rocha's quizzed her on where she was going.

'It's an office party. Apparently they do this every Fourth of July.'

'Great,' said Rocha. 'You need to get out and let your hair down. Go to the closet in my bedroom on the top shelf there is a large white box, in there you should find what you need.'

'Thanks, Rocha, you're a life saver.'

'Lola,' said Rocha, her tone was almost cautionary.

'Yes.'

'There is a silver one, the finest in my collection, it is decorated with fine white quartz crystals and comes up on the side like a half moon. It is decorated in tiny triple spirals. Wear that one,' said Rocha. 'Have a great night and stay safe, please. I'll see you when I get back.'

Lola did as she was told. When she located the white box there were lots of different masks. Wrapped separately was the one Rocha had recommended. It felt much lighter than Lola had anticipated but Rocha's description did not do it justice.

The silversmith work was so fine the carvings looked like thread and there were triple spirals and other Celtic forms carved into the mask which was embellished with fine quartz crystals so that it refracted and sparkled when the light hit it.

Lola could feel that it was special, there was magick in this mask and she was grateful because she might just need the extra bit of help.

Before she got out of the taxi, Lola paid the driver and slipped on her disguise which only covered half of her face. Photographers stood at either side of the carpet that had been laid across the grey pavement. Lola stepped from the taxi and onto the long scarlet tongue that lead to the mouth of the fine building. The flashing bulbs disorientated her, leaving her eyes a flurry of white and yellow spots when she stepped into the dimly lit hallway.

A queue had developed for the private lift that shuttled the guests up the staggering forty-one stories to the Penthouse above and Lola waited anxiously in line to get in. Up ahead two bulky men in black dinner suits stood guard at either end of the hallway scanning the tickets.

Retrieving hers from her bag, Lola froze when she recognised on of the Stein's security detail. The last time she'd seen him he was dragging her through the snow to the temple. Lola pretended she couldn't find her pass stepping into the other line discretely.

Finally it was her turn, and she tried to steady her hand as she held out the golden card to be scanned. With a nod of his head the door man permitted her to enter the packed lift.

'Ma'am,' Lola recognised the deep voice, it had an accent like her own; if she spoke she would be sure to give herself up. Turning with dread, she nodded her head in thanks when Derek handed her the lipstick that had fallen from her bag. She could see him scrutinise her a little closer as the lift door groaned shut.

~20~

The spacious hallway, which was decorated with chequered tiles and an exuberant golden console table and mirror, was alive with bodies as they made their way to the room beyond. Something disturbed the large crystal chandelier that hung overhead forcing it to tinkle its soft music.

Lola hadn't expected anything less than grandeur and opulence. If Carl Stein's library and dining room back at Chateau Bacchus had been a nod to Louis the XV, then this was an all- out homage. Every corner of the busy room screamed old money. A thick padded scarlet carpet lined the sweeping staircase that led to more rooms upstairs and anything that was stationary seemed to be plated in gold. It was all a bit vulgar to Lola.

Being rich was one thing but making sure everyone saw it was another. She already understood the type of man Carl Stein was and she knew that all this was an outer expression of how he viewed himself – as royalty.

Lola followed the group that she'd exited the lift with into a beautiful ballroom where small tables and chairs were placed neatly around a walnut dance floor. The floor shone like glass reflecting the muted mellow glow that spilled from the fanned lights around the room. Plush red curtains decorated the large windows that punctuated the wall space and at the eastern and western tips of the room the open veranda doors allowed the cool evening air to carry a profusion of perfumes in on its breeze. It was truly magical.

Looking up, Lola could see two staircases at either end of the room leading to a second tier of the ballroom, where the special guests got to sit. That's where Lola found Carl Stein in deep conversation with a young red-headed woman.

Her skin was as pale as Lola's but it seemed more refined and polished than hers; it was like marble against her silver dress. Even with a mask on, Lola could tell how striking she was. Lola's eyes continued to scan the balcony area, searching for a door but there was nothing obvious.

In an attempt to melt into the scene, Lola lifted one of the pink champagne flutes from a passing waiter. It smelled delicious but she was adamant that she wouldn't be sampling the goods tonight; the delicate glass of bubbly was strictly for show.

For the most part Lola felt fine, but since entering the ballroom she could feel her head start to throb so was determined to get in and out of the place as quickly as possible. She took another sniff of the champagne glass and her eyes watered as the fizz caught in her nostrils. A dull heaviness gathered around her temples and slight heat rose around her, Lola searched for one of the opened doors and excused herself through the crowd. Perhaps some air would help her focus.

The flash of a camera drew her eyes upwards again and she saw Erin happy at her work. She was taking a picture of the guests above. Most of the men wore black Scaramouche masks and Lola noted with interest how Carl Stein insisted on the redhead staying in for one of the shots. He and Alex were wearing their customary golden masks, setting them apart from the others. Lola realised that this was the New York chapter of the Hell Fire Club and she wished that she was strong enough to take them all out there and then. Instinctively, she adjusted her own mask hoping it would conceal the face below it for long enough to get the job done.

Lola emerged out onto a balcony happy to have the patio to herself. In the retreating light the city spread out below her feet and from up here the buildings weren't as daunting. The sky had turned a light pink embalming everything below with a gentleness.

To the right lay the wide expanse of Central Park and Lola let her eyes soak in the many verdant shades like it was the first time she'd seen trees and grass. To the left stood Manhattan and its colossal skyscrapers but tonight the city actually looked beautiful. Lola could see the order from above and she understood why Carl Stein had chosen this exact building.

It must certainly have been the best place from which to observe his kingdom.

Closing her eyes Lola shut out the city below and inhaled deeply, tuning into the ring and her own energy field. She could feel the quartz from the mask melt with her own vibrational field adding to her strength.

Lola focused on the Cube, she allowed herself to visualise the five crystalline shapes as they broke apart, calling on each one.

No sooner had Lola settled into her mind space when she was shown a set of stairs and a concealed door behind a red curtain. As she passed through the door she climbed a narrow set of steps leading to a service stairwell. At the top of the stairs she was directed to the door on the left and to the office within where a large golden antique bureau sat alone in the middle of the room accompanied only by a leather chair.

Lola's eyes were guided to a picture on the wall of Carl Stein standing beside an old man. The Cube was behind there. She couldn't see it but she could feel it.

Lola's eyes snapped open taking one last breath of the pure evening air, before she advanced all focus and determination into the ballroom. Just as before she let her eyes be her guide as they searched for the red curtain up above. Finally she found it but it was positioned right behind the table Carl Stein and Alex were sat at.

Great, thought Lola, right in the middle of the viper's pit. She would need a miracle to get up there never mind through the door undetected. Where was the Féth fíada of Manannán Mac Lir when you needed it? It would take the old Irish God's misty cloak for her to stand a chance.

As she stood pondering her next move, Lola's head began to hurt again. Every now and then she could see a camera flash go off as Erin went about her work. Various people came and introduced themselves to her; she just smiled and nodded, trying not to focus on the growing pain. Lola didn't want to give too much away and tried to remain as inconspicuous as she could.

Erin had the camera slung over her shoulder when Lola finally caught up with her. She was on her third glass of champagne.

'Is this some party, Lola, or what? You look fantastic by the way,' said Erin taking another drink from the glass. 'I wouldn't have recognised you at all. So how did you get a ticket?'

'Isaac,' shouted Lola over the music. 'He came through in the end.'

As they were talking Lola felt a cold hand tap her shoulder but the touch stabbed at her skin as though she'd been pricked by needles. Wincing, Lola turned abruptly and found herself face to face with Carl Stein's redhead. She looked like porcelain up close, but that was where the delicacy ended. Lola's headache was getting worse so she couldn't focus on the girl's colours. The top half of her face was concealed by the silver mask but there was an arrogance to it that Lola could sense just from the way she tilted her narrow chin upwards.

Lola could feel the heat of the girl's dun eyes as they travelled across her face down towards the ground.

'I love your Manolos,' said the redhead, her claret lips parting into a counterfeit smile. 'They're not even out in the shops yet, you have to tell me where you got them.' Her accent was American but it was clear of any geographical undertones and it had a honeyed ring to it that Lola didn't quite trust.

Lola had no idea what she was talking about until the woman pointed at her feet.

'Oh the shoes,' said Lola trying to soften her accent, 'a friend let me borrow them,' she beamed back at the girl.

'I wish I had a friend like that.'

'You do,' said Lola, nodding towards the balcony that overlooked the dance floor where Carl and now Alex sat in conversation.

Titling her head back, the women gave a shrill laugh and lit a cigarette. She inhaled a deep puff before blowing the smoke down into Lola's face.

'I'm no man's plaything, Miss... what did you say your name was?'

'I didn't,' smiled Lola back curtly.

'That accent,' said the redhead, slowly taking another draw. 'Where is that from?' Her tone tightened and for a split second Lola caught the murky red of her aura and it told Lola that she had rattled her.

Before the two could further their conversation a couple approached the woman, calling her by name.

'Olivia!' beamed the lady, 'you are just a vision. I hear congratulations are in order. Finally someone is going to make an honest man of Alex Stein.'

Erin guided Lola away by the arm. 'I know you and Alex had a thing. I was going to tell you myself that she was his fiancé,' said Erin, her voice full of sympathy for Lola. 'Olivia Van der Vart, she's from one of the oldest families in Manhattan. It's like an arranged marriage or something.'

Lola's ears felt like they had been filled with glue and she couldn't hear Erin. She needed air and a seat. The band was playing but Lola felt like she was floating above the entire scene. Panicking that she was having some sort of episode again, she looked around desperately for the toilets.

'Toilets, Erin, where are they?'

'I'll take you. Sorry, Lola, I didn't think you'd take this so badly. I thought you hated Alex Stein.'

'What?' said Lola, confused.

'Are you okay? You're not going to faint on me again are you? Here, drink this.'

Erin shoved a bottle of water under Lola's nose. She drank deeply then taking a deep breath seemed to recalibrate herself. She closed her eyes and tuned into the ring and made sure her auric shield was still working.

'Sorry about that, Erin. I felt lightheaded again. I haven't eaten much today and with all the rushing...'

'I don't know, Lola, every time you're in the same room as Alex Stein you seem to go all crazy.'

'I can assure you, Erin, this has nothing to do with Alex Stein,' lied Lola. 'I hear the band playing, let's go and enjoy ourselves,' smiled Lola, trying to reassure her friend.

Erin and Lola danced for a while as the guests began to pour into the ballroom. Alex and Carl had even abandoned their stations; the top floor was entirely empty now and this was Lola's chance to do what she'd come here to do.

'Erin,' she shouted over the music. 'I need you to do me a favour.'

'Yeah, whatever you need, Lola.'

'I need you to distract that security guy there. Long enough so that I can get up those stairs.'

'Why...?'

'I'll explain later but do you think you can help me out?'

'Leave it with me.'

Lola watched as Erin made her way over to the burly suit and began to talk to him. The conversation seemed to be going well. She started showing him her pictures on the camera and he wrote down something on a piece of paper for her. Lola looped around the edge of the dance floor and slipped up behind them. If she was caught she could just play dumb.

To her surprise she was up the stairs without so much as a backward glance. Lola made straight for the red curtain. Creeping behind it she turned the handle of the door. It was open, much to her relief. She stepped through and found herself at the foot of a dark stairwell, just like her vision had shown her. Rummaging in her clutch bag Lola found her mobile and used the torch on her phone to navigate her way.

Sure enough, as her inner-sight had predicted, it led directly into a study. The only light available was from the hall opposite as it slid in through the half opened door. Lola took off her shoes to help her move more freely. She had a strange feeling of déjà vu as she tried to locate the painting she'd been shown. There were a few on the wall and because the light was faint it took a while but she found it hanging close to the large bureau, where a number of files sat stacked neatly on the desk.

Lola peeled back the manila cover on the top file. Across the front page in thick red ink, it warned 'Top Secret'.

Naturally, Lola's interest was awakened. From what she could tell, the information looked like a series of numbers that might be co-ordinates. At the bottom of the page it said 'Operation Babylon, Codename Inanna'. Lola took a picture with her phone and slid open the file below.

A picture of a young Marine smiled out at her. He was staggeringly handsome and his dark skin was smooth and clean-shaven, his hair was cropped so short it almost looked like shadow on his round head. The file noted his name, rank, age and an address in Harlem. Lola was moved again to take another picture. There was no way she'd remember all the details. She read the name – Lemar Jenkins – and wondered why Carl Stein was interested in this young man.

A voice sounded in the hallway alerting Lola to the approaching footsteps. Frantically scanning the room for an exit, she decided that she wouldn't make it to the side door in time and threw herself under the bureau.

The soft military tread was almost at the foot of the door when Lola noticed her shoes lying just a few inches from the front of the study table. Without so much as breathing, Lola forced her arm underneath the desk. Her fingers groped blindly until they found the stiletto heels and whipped them to safety.

Covering her mouth in fear that her breathing would be heard, Lola listened and watched as the owner of the black shoes crunched around the room, sinking into the deep carpet pile. Squeezing her eyes shut, as if that would help, she prayed that the owner of the shoes would exit through the service door but slowly they stalked around the room coming to a halt in front of the bureau. Lola inhaled, her body was cramped and contorted underneath the desk.

'It's not here,' said the silvery voice. Lola forced back the gag that was knotting her throat. She would have to confront him. There was no escape, he had her cornered.

'It's not here,' repeated Alex. His voice was clear and pleasant, as though it was commonplace to find intruders in his private abode.

Lola, resigned, pushed the chair out and crawled out from underneath the desk on her hands and knees.

'That's the way I like to see you, Lola,' said Alex, casually tilting his head as he looked down at her.

Unperturbed Lola rose to her feet and slipped back into her heels. While her insides were volcanic her exterior was like ice. Standing upright she squared her shoulders and smoothed down her dress with the palm of her hands, matching Alex's certainty pound for pound.

His hold on her was crippling but he would never know that. Lola's eyes did not hide nor shrink from his and as she stood staring into the face of this effigy, who, like David was chiselled from the finest marble, the air crackled and hummed between them like an electric wire.

Lola remembered that she was still wearing her mask and although he had no physical disguise on Lola could see that Alex wore one to. His colours betrayed the apathy that he tried so hard to sell and the swell of carmines and blush pinks that enveloped him almost succeeded in disarming Lola. She knew that Alex was telling the truth about the Cube, the longer she stood in the room the less she could feel it. It had been there but it was gone.

'Where is it, Alex?' said Lola. Her voice sounded brittle as she struggled to prevent her own mask from slipping.

Alex moved around the desk, closer to her, forcing her to take a step backwards. Lola scrutinised his even face, but it gave nothing away. Had she not been able to see his colours, his only tell would have been his clenched fists – he did this when he was anxious or uncomfortable.

He took a step closer again but this time Lola didn't back away, she needed to stand firm, and she knew that he wouldn't hurt her. She knew that he would never get the chance. He lifted his hand towards her face and slipped off her mask.

'No need for masks among old friends, Lola.' Lola's stomach leaped and her insides burned as her name trickled off his tongue.

'You should take your own advice, Alex,' smiled Lola glibly. 'You wear that many masks it's hard to know what your true face is.'

Alex gave a mirthless laugh. 'And there she is, Lola Paige. For a moment, with that dress,' he ran his finger along the length of her strap and it felt like fire, 'I thought the New York Torch had made a lady out of you.'

'I'm no man's lady, Alex,' said Lola with a curt smile, 'but I'm certainly all woman.'

'I remember,' he said as he stepped in again. Lola could smell his woody cologne and feel his warm breath as it rested on her chest.

'Good,' she smiled, staring back into his polished-blue eyes. 'Hold on to that memory and enjoy it,' said Lola, praying he hadn't noticed her skin flush.

'You're different somehow,' said Alex as he surveyed her, trying to find out what it was. 'You cut your hair but it's not that. It's those eyes, they've lost their lustre, their sparkle. When Irish eyes are smiling,' he said half-singing half-speaking the song.

'My eyes have lost their lustre,' said Lola sarcastically. 'I wonder what could have contributed to that, Alex. Let me see, was it having someone I love murdered? Was it having someone I love kidnapped? Was it falling in love with a soulless piece of shit or perhaps it was being drugged, abducted and left for dead? You take your pick,' said Lola, her composure slowly slipping. 'You've changed as well, you know! I see you've grown quite fond of brill cream.' Lola ran her fingers through his greasy hair.

'That side shade, it makes you look older. No,' said Lola shaking her index finger in the air. 'I know what it is, Alex. I don't know why I never noticed it before but it makes you look more and more like your daddy, but,' she went on, 'I'm sure that's the entire point, to look and act and be just like your daddy. What a role model.'

Alex stiffened. It was subtle but it was enough for Lola to know that her assault had hit its target. However, as quickly as he had given himself away the calm and collected Alex was back.

'It has been a tough year for you, Lola, I don't deny that but coming to this city is only going to make that worse.'

'That sounds awfully like a threat, Alex, and I think we both know how well I respond to threats.'

'You are out of your depth, Lola. I saw your little display with those freaks at Liberty Plaza, it was quite impressive. You did much better than the first time you visited.'

'So now you're stalking me!'

'Ha,' Alex made a plaintive sound through his nose. 'Don't flatter yourself, Lola.' The rebuff stung but Lola smiled, batting it off.

'Anyway, I'll be missed down below. It's always a pleasure talking to you, Lola.'

Alex stepped in pulling her close to him. Lola didn't protest. The charade didn't fool her. Alex was as susceptible to her as she was to him.

'Mmmmm if only things were different.' He loosened his hold and Lola stepped back again. 'How did you know it was me?' she asked. 'How did you know I was here, tonight?'

This made him laugh again. 'Lola, those who shine from within don't need a spotlight.'

'Does he know I'm here?'

'I don't think so. You'd better go before he does.'

'I will get the Cube, Alex, it's only a matter of time.'

'As is your demise, Lola.' There was tenderness in his voice now, reminding her of the Alex she had once loved.

'Congratulations by the way,' said Lola, slipping on her mask again and heading towards the service door.

Alex looked at her confused. 'Congratulations?'

'On your engagement. And a redhead, no less. I'm impressed; you're not nearly as predictable as I thought, Alex.' Lola smiled and closed the door behind her. Whatever had been keeping her from breaking apart during their exchange had deserted her. She gingerly opened the door praying that the tables would still be empty, luckily they were. Fixing herself she descended the staircase. The security guard was about to approach her when she felt an arm slip around her waist.

'She's with me, Phil,' said Alex's commanding voice.

The security guard gave him a knowing nod. 'If you ever feel like sharing, Mr Stein, let me know.'

'I'd only share the best, this one isn't pedigree.' Alex laughed at his own joke and forced Lola forward as she was about to reply.

'Now, now, Lola, don't cause a scene. It's time for you to be a good girl and go home.'

Lola knew he was right. Her head was starting to throb again; being in this place was taking its toll on her. She hadn't noticed until now how bad it was, but she felt sore all over.

'Aren't you going to introduce me to your delightful friend, Alex? How rude.'

Alex squeezed Lola's arm involuntarily, as they both turned around to face his father. 'She's just leaving, Father,' said Alex, still clutching Lola's arm with an iron grip.

'Ms Paige, well aren't you a sight for sore eyes. You can't leave without giving the host a dance. Now, now, Alex, don't be so hasty to turn one of our guests out, especially an old friend like Lola here.'

Lola shrugged free. Smiling she took Carl Stein's arm and followed him to the centre of the floor. She could see flash after flash as various photographers took pictures, no doubt wondering who she was.

Carl Stein slid his hand around her waist, pulling her closer to him.

'How did you know it was me?' said Lola, her hand reaching up to make sure that her mask was still in place.

'A light like yours can't be hidden under a mask or a designer dress,' said Carl. 'Welcome to the underworld, Persephone,' he smiled.

'That must make you Hades,' replied Lola. 'But I don't think that's an accurate description and frankly it's a bit of an insult to poor Hades if you ask me,' said Lola with all the nonchalance she could muster.

Carl turned her around smiling his politician's smile at a nearby photographer. He pulled her closer still. 'How come, Miss Paige?' said Carl in his slow orotund voice.

'Well,' said Lola, she had to use all her strength to remain resolute. 'Even Hades was capable of love and you, Mr Stein, are capable of no such thing.'

Lola never allowed the smile to fall from her face. 'You disgust me. Think well of this dance, Mr Stein. It's the closest that you'll ever get to me.'

'I don't believe so but I am enjoying our little game. I must say, you have grown immensely but you are no match for me or this city, Ms Paige. Oh your little display at Liberty Plaza was a joy to watch, but that is nothing compared to what I will rain down on you. Am I to deduce that you came looking for something here tonight?'

'I will find it, Carl, and if that means going through you to get it so be it. You cannot harm me.'

His hands slid up along Lola's back onto her bare skin and she could feel him channel his toxic force field trying to prove her wrong. As she fought against it she could feel it tighten and slacken like an elastic band.

The camera bulbs continued to flash, as the song came to an end. The lady sang the last words and that was all that Lola could hear, her voice was like air itself, light and angelic.

'You are my sweetest downfall, I loved you first.' The singer stood up from the piano as the crowd applauded in great rapture. Ever the showman, Carl Stein released Lola to join in the chorus of approval.

Lola's eyes fell on Alex with his bride-to-be, he wore his golden Scaramouche mask again and the two looked like a vision of love and happiness. But again his colours told a different story; his pinks had been transformed to a slate grey.

'You see, Lola,' said Carl Stein leaning down to whisper in her ear. 'You see how happy he is, how perfect they are together. He will never be yours, you will never win him.'

Lola could see he was right but she knew that Carl doubted his son. She took a deep breath before turning to face the man who had destroyed her life and threatened everything she held dear.

Lola stepped forward looking deep into Carl Stein's frosty eyes. She so desperately wanted to wipe the smug look from his privileged face even if the only way she could do it was to tell a lie.

'I don't need to win him, Mr Stein,' said Lola, returning his syrupy smile, 'You see I don't have to win him,' she glanced over at Alex, 'because I already have.'

An uneasy grin curled on his face and Lola felt satisfied that'd she'd hit a nerve.

Her body ached all over and she could feel the first drops of blood gather in her nasal passage. It was time for her to leave and she needed to move fast. 'Oh and stop hiding from Isaac Kane and give the man an interview,' scowled Lola, in a parting hit at Carl Stein.

Erin was in the middle of a group picture when Lola grabbed her by the arm and led her to the lift. Lola pulled a handkerchief out of a man's suit pocket and stepped into the lift before he had time to react.

'Lola,' laughed Erin 'Where's the fire?'

Lola talked as she held the silk material to her nose, trying to stem the bleed. 'It's after party time and I need a drink.'

'Let's go then, my little Irish leprechaun. It's time you let yourself go, I was beginning to think you were going on for the nunnery. I hope Danny's here tonight. Oh my God, that man is so hot I get wet just thinking about him.'

'Erin!' frowned Lola, slapping her bum,' too much information.' The concierge outside the hotel hailed them a taxi.

'Where are we going, Erin?'

'Oh yeah, 47th Street please, Lanagan's bar.'

'We're going to the Baarh,' mocked Lola.

'No wur goin to the bur,' laughed Erin, trying to replicate her Northern Irish accent.

'That wasn't even close,' said Lola, feeling lighter already.

'Tell me again, Lola, what is it you call sneakers?'

'Guddies.'

'Ha. Guddies, that's hilarious. Guddies.'

'I got some great shots of you dancing with daddy Stein, I'll have to look at them later.'

Lola took the hanky from her nose and tilted her head back. 'Has it stopped bleeding, Erin?' Erin inspected her nose for a second.

'Yeah, it's stopped.'

Lola allowed her head to fall back on to the seat. She felt exhausted. Fireworks reflected off the high-rises as they passed through downtown Manhattan. Lola hoped Isaac had made it to the after party; her expedition into enemy territory had yielded some very interesting intel.

~21~

Lanagan's Bar was jumping when Lola and Erin arrived. Apparently it was just a few blocks away from the Torch and had been a favourite haunt of its journalists and employees for years.

It was just after midnight and the fourth of July celebrations were well underway. Lola and Erin fought through the throng to the back of the bar where the band was playing. The small semi-circular stage was dressed in faded velvet curtains that must have been blood red at one time.

The rest of the furniture in the bar was upholstered in the same jaded velvet whose fabric housed years of cigarette smoke, spills and ash burns. Some revellers were swaying to the rhythm and blues band while others jostled for position at the busy bar, which was obscured by the thirsty, searching for more drink.

The girls were over dressed and this was confirmed by the way Gene Rush's eyes almost popped from his head when he saw them making their way through the crowd.

'Lola,' he managed, all the while staring at her breasts.

Lola shot him a caustic look and walked on, her eyes scanning the faces for Isaac. As the crowd thinned out towards the back of the bar, she found him sitting in one of the half-moon booths in deep conversation with Chris Auld.

The sex appeal poured from Isaac Kane. His face was furrowed in consternation and the sleeves of his crisp white shirt were rolled up to the elbows.

Without invitation and still light-headed from the nose bleed, Lola slumped down into the seat beside him. Boldly she lifted his glass of bourbon and knocked it back in one swoop before setting the empty class back on the table.

Isaac, cut off in mid-sentence, looked at the glass and then back at Lola. 'You feeling okay, Irish?' he asked raising an eyebrow.

'Feeling great, Isaac.' Lola's body relaxed and a warm contentment rippled through her as the liquid swirled in her stomach. She leapt off the seat and made directly for the bar, worming her way in.

'Greenhorn, would you look at you!'

Bill Ogle sat opposite Lola in the bullpen and had only ever spoken to her on the rare occasion he answered a call that was for her. His skin was the colour of ash and the few strands of hair he still possessed he wore slicked back off his pock-marked face. His fingertips looked as though they had been dipped in iodine, they bore the hallmark of years of excessive smoking.

Bill was a dinosaur who thought copy should still be typed on a typewriter and that women should only be present in a newsroom to serve coffee or to clean out his wastepaper bin.

Lola thought Bill was a dick. The other men in the bullpen treated her with an affable disinterest but Bill Ogle was a bit more hostile. He was a passive aggressive, disparaging in his gaze and of her right to be there.

Lola took a step back as Bill bore down on her but the bar was so crowed there was no place to go. His breath smelled of alcohol and cigarettes and Lola was sure if she lit a flame under it he would ignite in a torrent of fire.

His hands began to wonder over her waistline.

'Look at you, greenhorn,' he slurred again. 'Dressing like that could get you into trouble.' His words were a spray of spit and gin as they fell on Lola's face.

'What did you just say to me?' Lola demanded, her face twisted in disgust. Her temper started to awaken and the ring was ready for the fight.

One flick of her wrist and old Bill the dinosaur would be lying in a pool of his own urine. The thought seduced her but she took a deep breath and centred herself. She couldn't afford any more lapses in control.

'Greenhorn, I'm just saying, women these days running around half dressed are asking for trouble,' said Bill swaying, as if in time to the music.

Bill's misogyny didn't surprise or shock Lola. Journalism, and the world in general, was full of it, and while she abhorred Bill's sentiments some part of her respected his honesty.

Bill Ogle wore his ignorance like a badge of honour so you always knew where you stood with old Bill. It was the men, thought Lola, who had learned how to hide their misogyny behind a smile or a silver tongue. They were the ones you had to worry about. The Carl Steins of this world, whose one-hundred-watt smile distracted you while he drove the knife into your back.

'Firstly, Bill,' said Lola, violently swiping his hand from around her waist, 'the only thing green around here are your teeth. Secondly, you speak to me like that again or even think of spouting that misogynistic bullshit in my presence again, I'll rip that filthy tongue out of your mouth. How about that?' she smiled.

Bill didn't take too kindly to Lola's rebuff because in Bill's world, women should be seen and not heard and women should honour their superiors. In a drunken stumble, his long bony fingers grasped hold of Lola's arm. Squeezing it tight, his long nails punctured her skin. Lola was momentarily taken back by his strength.

'Who do you think you're talkin to, ya dumb Paddy?' he seethed. 'I was a staff journalist at this paper before you were even a sparkle in your daddy's eyes.'

Lola's body shook as though she would explode. By now they had a bit of an audience, but no one intervened. Lola prayed they would but not for her, for poor old Bill.

'Bill, you have ten seconds to get your nicotine stained hands off me,' Lola warned, but he only dug his nails in deeper to her arm. Lola didn't know how long she would be able to hold back the surge that was rising inside of her.

'You heard her, Bill, get your hands off her. Now.' Lola had heard Isaac angry before but she had never heard him this angry. The old reporter let go of her arm but he never let his gaze drop.

'Here's your hero, the house...' before he could utter another word Bill was laying on the floor writhing in pain. Hot red liquid flowed from his sharp nose, which now lay across his face at an irregular angle.

Lola felt as though her hand had been shattered into tiny pieces. A loud cheer went up around the bar. Lola turned to the bartender and ordered four shots and a glass of ice.

'Looks like old Bill not only hates women, he doesn't like black people either,' said Lola. Grabbing some of the ice out of the glass, she rested her tender knuckles on it. Using her good hand she downed the shots that were laid in a neat row on the counter. The fourth was plucked from her lips before she could finish it off.

'Hey,' said Lola in protest. She could feel the alcohol as it hit her knees, making them feel loose and tingly.

'Hey nothing, you owe me one, Irish,' Isaac Kane smiled that smile; the one Jodi had been lamenting earlier. Lola's head was light and suddenly she felt happy and carefree again.

'Bartender, another round,' she shouted, but Isaac interjected.

'Joey, a pint of water with ice and lemon for the lady and a bourbon neat for me.'

'Hi.'

'I thought you didn't drink, Irish. You've had enough.'

Lola stuck her tongue out at Isaac.

'You're so bossy,' she mocked. 'Look at me I'm Isaac Kane. I'm sexy and smart and successful. I've won a million Pulitzer prizes. Blah blah blah.'

Isaac stood staring at Lola. 'You finished, Irish? That you done?'

He led her by the elbow as if she was a naughty child to the booth that he had been sitting at.

'Take a seat and drink your water and shut that mouth for ten minutes.'

Lola was about to launch off on one again but the room was swirling a full three-sixty degrees now and she was so busy trying to steady her head that she had forgotten what it was she was going to say.

Lola took a long gulp of water and allowed her eyes to close. It helped, there wasn't as much movement in the blackness behind her eyes.

The hum of voices and smell of perfume and sweat seemed to float over her until she couldn't hear them anymore. When Lola woke, the band was gone, as were most of the revelers.

The jukebox was playing and a woman's voice oozed out over the bar. She looked for the clock on the wall, it was 3.30 am, she must have been out for the count for over two hours. Her fist still ached; she flexed it suddenly remembering why it hurt.

Lola's head felt like someone was trying to crack their way out of her skull with a lump hammer. Isaac was still deep in conversation, this time it seemed to be about jazz. Isaac loved jazz.

His office had a record player and shelves and shelves of vinyl and he played music all the time so Lola recognised the voice of the lady singing.

Isaac would play her records at the office from time to time, she couldn't remember her name but her voice was a thing of great beauty. It was deep and soulful and when she sang you believed her like she was speaking some eternal truth.

She was warning Mr Backlash now, telling him that if he didn't stop treating her people like 'second-class fools' there'd be trouble. The piano was upbeat, like the guitar, but it was full of attitude and self-assertion.

The lyrics made Lola think of home and all that her tiny little part of the world had come through. She thought of the Hell Fire Club and how relevant the song still was today.

'Joey the Lips said jazz is intellectual music; he said it's anti-people. Abstract, cold and emotionless.' Lola had no idea what made her think of The Commitments, but she thought it was hilarious. Isaac looked down at her confused.

'Joey says jazz is musical wanking.' This really set her off now as she fell into kinks of laughter at her own joke.

'Joey says soul is socialism, soul is community, it's democratic, anyone can play it. Now that woman there can sing, she can touch your soul.'

Lola didn't know whether she was swaying to the music or the room was swaying to her. She suspected that she might still be drunk.

'What is that? Blues?' she asked, bright and interested in the siren calling her from the jukebox.

Chris Auld, the head of news, was laughing now, while Isaac was trying to find something to say. 'You're a Roddy Doyle fan, Lola?' Chris laughed, letting her know that he got her reference.

'Not overly,' said Lola in a lofty manner as if she were highly educated in these things, 'but Joey the Lips speaks the truth. What do you think, Chris?'

'Who the hell is Joey the Lips?' said Isaac, injured that he didn't share the joke. 'Clearly some fool that knows nothing about music,' he added, clenching his jaw in irritation.

'God forgive you, Isaac Kane, Joey is music, he lives it, he breathes it, he spreads its gospel,' said Lola enjoying herself.

'It's true,' agreed Chris joining in.

'You're clearly still drunk, Irish,' Isaac shook his head and took a sip of his bourbon.

'Now this is music, Isaac. Who is that singing? Her voice.' Lola began to sing with the chorus now. 'Mr Backlash, Mr Backlash, I'm gonna leave you with the backlash blues.'

'Oh you like Nina,' he said defensively. 'I thought jazz was... what did you call it? Anti- people? Well Nina Simone there,' Isaac nodded to the jukebox, 'just happens to be one of the greatest jazz musicians of all time.'

'That doesn't sound too jazzy to me, Isaac. It sounds more like the blues,' said Lola still moving to the song as it ended.

'Well,' said Isaac, finally smiling, 'she just happens to be singing the blues there.'

The jukebox clicked and it was Nina again. This time it did have that raw jazz sound, the tinkling piano, the mournful saxophone. From the opening line the need in Nina's voice was immediately conveyed and it made Lola want to dance.

She stood up and put her hand out to Isaac, she knew what she was doing but she could just blame the shots tomorrow. Suddenly Isaac seemed quite awkward.

'It's time for you to go home, Irish,' he laughed trying to disguise his unease.

'One dance, Isaac, listen to that voice, that song,' pleaded Lola. 'It was made to dance to. Then I'll go home.'

'That song wasn't made for dancing, Irish,' said Isaac as he took her hand and led her out onto the empty dance floor.

Isaac took her in his arms, slipping his knowing hands around her waist. Lola moved closer to him and let him lead the way, swaying methodically to the song. This time Nina wanted some sugar in her bowl, some steam on her clothes.

Isaac's eyes never left Lola's making her blush a little. He lifted his arm and turned her slowly around, spinning her out and back. Soon they moved in unison, feeling and anticipating the other's gentle moves.

'Not bad for a white girl,' he smiled as he pulled her close again. Lola could see how easy it would be to fall helplessly in lust with Isaac Kane. He didn't even have to try, it was all just there, strength, gentleness, intelligence and arrogance all in equal measure.

'I'm not white, Isaac,' said Lola indignantly, 'I'm Irish.' This made him laugh.

'You've always got an answer, Irish. That mouth will get you in trouble someday.'

'I think we both know I'm a bit late for that lecture, Isaac. Besides, you're one to talk.'

Lola was rocking close again, she could smell his aftershave and see the pulse of his jugular vein underneath the open collar of his shirt. She was starting to feel more like herself.

'So we friends again?' said Isaac, looking at her with an impish relish.

'Thanks for the ticket and the outfit,' said Lola seriously. 'I suppose we can be friends again. That reminds me by the way, I found something I wanted to talk to you about.'

'Not tonight, Lola,' smiled Isaac softly. 'You've had a long night, we can talk about it tomorrow. You look stunning by the way,' he said as an aside.

Lola caught his gaze and for a second she liked what she saw in his eyes and all around him. As the song ended, they parted.

'Time for you to go home, Irish.' Lola nodded in agreement and lifted her bag. She said goodnight to Chris and left the bar.

Lola allowed her aching feet to rest on the cool pavement; it felt great as the tension drained from them and the blood began to flow freely once again.

She gave the cab driver her address.

Traffic was much lighter and it only took minutes to get to the apartment. Lola placed her shoes and bag on the floor, shoving her phone down the front of her dress while she fought with the stiff lock on the apartment door.

Finally it opened. Lola didn't feel tired anymore and she decided that she would drink some of Rocha's magic tea; it might help with any hangover that she would suffer in the morning, she thought. The kettle came to the boil and she let the tea stand for a while to infuse. Lola lifted her phone and saw five missed calls from Erin. Her friend had sent a message.

I've gone with Dan. I tried waking you but Isaac said he would look after you. See you tomorrow for all the goss. PS Remind me never to get in a fight with you! Poor Bill.

The thought made Lola cringe, she had assaulted an old man, even if he was a sexist, racist drunk, she should never have resorted to physical violence. Gene Rush would no doubt have something to say about it.

Lola put the thought to the back of her mind and took a sip of the tea infusion. It tasted great. She was just about to sit down when the door knocked. Erin had planned on staying with her tonight so for an instant she thought it might be her fellow intern. Lola had the door open before she even realised how dangerous it was not to check who it was first.

When she saw who was standing there she tried to slam the door shut, but Alex wedged his foot in the doorway preventing her from closing it.

'Lola, I only want to talk. I just needed to see you.' There was a pleading in his voice that momentarily distracted Lola, which gave him the opportunity to slide his shoulder and leg into the narrow opening.

'You shouldn't be here, Alex,' warned Lola. 'Please. I don't want to hurt you.' Lola's ring seemed to be sleeping but she understood that she was in full control; it had not stirred because she had not bid it to.

'You might want these.' Alex handed in her shoes and bag through the gap in the door. Lola opened it fully and permitted him to enter.

'You've five minutes, Alex.'

Alex stood in the doorway; he wasn't sure why he'd come. Why he'd waited nearly three hours for Lola to arrive home.

'I needed to see you. I wanted to see you.'

Lola was trying her best to be firm, to not crumble. It was easier when she didn't make eye contact.

'How did you know where I lived and how did you know that I was in by the way?' Lola was genuinely annoyed now she didn't have to pretend.

'You know how, Lola. We've been keeping a very close on eye you since you arrived.'

'Of course you have. This is all part of daddy's game, isn't it?'

'Yes.' Alex's honesty surprised her. 'You don't stand a chance against him or this city and it's only a matter of time before you meet your end.'

'Get out. Get out now,' screamed Lola. She'd had enough; besides, it was too painful to be in the same room as Alex Stein, it tormented her.

Alex stepped towards her, he reached out to touch her but changed his mind and let his hands fall awkwardly by his sides.

'Please, Lola, just listen to me,' said Alex clenching and unclenching his fists. 'Go home and forget about all of this. You owe Arthur nothing, you've almost given your life once for his Order and what has he done for you, only left you here alone and exposed.'

Lola reached forward and landed the palm of her hand with a clean thwack on Alex's cheek. He barely flinched.

She didn't realise it but tears were leaking from her eyes. 'How dare you speak his name. How dare you presume to lecture me, you the one single person who has destroyed my life. It's not Arthur that has thrown my life into peril, you and that piece of shit you call a father are responsible for that.'

'I saved your life,' said Alex, his tone growing more contemptuous. 'What a lapse in judgment that proved to be,' he said rubbing his jaw. 'Everything I have taken from you, Lola, you have taken from me in equal measure. I may have destroyed your world, but you have obliterated mine.'

'I haven't even come close to obliterating it, Alex,' fired Lola, 'but you mark my words, I will, even if it kills me. The line has been drawn and you better decide what side you are on.'

'I think it's clear the side I have chosen, Lola,' said Alex calmly, almost tenderly.

'Well then,' said Lola opening the door. 'It's time you went running back to daddy like a good little boy.'

Alex closed his eyes trying to compose himself. This had not gone to plan, but then nothing did where she was concerned. Lola Paige knew all his soft targets and she assaulted them with callous proficiency.

She had the ability to infuriate him, to unman him. Her heart lay on her sleeve red and pulsing and the unabashed honestly that erupted from her beautiful mouth only made him love her even more.

Alex closed the door. 'Lola,' he said taking a deep breath to steady himself. 'That's not why I came here. I didn't come her to argue with you. I came here to...'

'To what, Alex?' said Lola, growing more and more irate. 'To torture me a little more? To confuse me a little more? Please tell me why you've come because I'm exhausted trying to figure you out. Whatever conflict you feel, whatever struggle you grapple with it's nothing compared to what I have gone through this past year. Do you know what it's like to have your world turned inside out and upside down? To have one of the greatest people you have ever known, the kindest most humane person murdered in cold blood. Then, are you ready?' said Lola, 'Here's the sickest part, as if all that isn't enough, to then find out that you're in love with the very person who was complicit in that murder, that every time you see him, your heart aches and your stomach knots because you love him when you desperately want to despise him.'

'Yes,' said Alex coolly. 'I do.'

'What part can you empathise with?' mocked Lola. 'As if you were capable of experiencing anything as human as empathy. You saved my life, Alex, a life you put in danger. Do you want a thank you? Should I be falling on my knees like every other woman in this city and washing your feet with my tears?'

'I should go,' said Alex turning to leave. 'I shouldn't have come.'

'What were you thinking?' Lola turned her back and rested her hands on the island in the kitchen. She waited for the door to open and she felt happy when it didn't. She could feel him there just inches behind her, still and silent like an icon.

Lola could hear all the words that he wanted to speak moving around inside him. She knew that she unarmed him but he always managed to keep his mask in place, he rarely permitted it to slip. What mask was he wearing now, she wondered.

Lola didn't flinch when she felt his hand rest on her shoulder. Her body registered the touch before it happened, part of her welcomed it, all of her welcomed it. She had missed it, craved it like the opiate it was.

Lola turned to look this self-professed god in the eye not scared at what she would find there.

This time she hadn't the luxury of ignorance; she could see Alex Stein in all his horrific beauty.

No words were required now that their bodies were engaged in a veracious dialogue. The electricity that ignited between the two hung and hummed in the thread of light that separated their bodies.

Lola ran her fingertips across Alex's eyebrow, trying to iron out the furrows on his forehead. She cupped his face in her hands and reached up and laid a soulful kiss on his lips. Lola didn't care if he didn't reciprocate, she had decided that it was what she wanted to do and so she did it.

But Alex immediately responded as his lips found hers once again. Lola pulled his jacket off, followed by his shirt. She ran her fingertips down his exposed chest until she came to the little white scar that marked where his heart lay. It felt cold and rough to the touch, one tiny mark that spoke a million words. Lola kissed it gently, allowing her tongue to skim across it.

'Thank you,' she whispered to the tiny piece of dead tissue.

When her eyes met Alex's she knew this is what he had come for and for tonight she would give him his wish. After all it was hers too. She wasn't a novice at this anymore, this time Lola didn't feel any of the uncertainly or fear, she felt fully in control of her emotions and her desires.

Alex's skilled hands found the zip of her dress, loosening it he gently pealed the dress from her skin and let it fall to the floor. Lola stood bare covered only by her fine underwear but she didn't feel self-conscious or embarrassed, she embraced her nakedness with honour and pride. After all she had the spirit of every woman running through her veins.

She beckoned Alex closer as he seemed unsure and helped him remove his trousers. Every kiss, every touch, every subtle movement was slow and methodical making the exchange highly intense. They didn't want to miss one moment of it.

Lola took Alex by the hand and led him up the freestanding stairs and into her bedroom, now fully awake.

~22~

Alex rinsed the shampoo from Lola's hair and watched as the white foam swam down her back, disappearing over her bum. He'd never experienced such intense sexual pleasure with any other woman, not the way it was with Lola, not even back when he'd partaken in the rituals of the Club. He felt like he had been born anew.

He was exhausted and exhilarated simultaneously. Something had changed in Lola, not that he should have been surprised.

Her eyes of jade still felt like lasers cutting right through him and while he could see them cloud from time to time with the weight of expectation that had been laid on her narrow shoulders, the growth in her was also reflected in their fire. There was a majesty and surety in those deep lakes of green. Lola now carried the flame of her light erect and proud which unsettled him for various reasons.

Her energy and power were still quite raw but Alex could see that Lola was beginning to understand it, to control it.

'I'd the strangest dream last night,' said Lola as the last of the suds were rinsed from her hair and body.

'Dream,' said Alex with a smirk. 'Do you not have to fall asleep before you can dream?' Lola laughed, reaching up to kiss him again. She turned the shower faucet all the way around to cold and stepped out leaving Alex cursing her.

'That'll cool you down, Mr Stein,' said Lola as she wrapped herself in a flannel towel.

'Now, now don't be too hasty,' said Alex as he tried to reach for her. Lola nimbly slipped out of his reach.

'Your dream,' he said. 'What was it about?'

'I dreamed Aíbgréne was in the room. Just in the corner, but then when I looked again she was gone.' Alex dried himself off, Lola noticed him momentarily brace.

'What, Alex, what is it?' He wouldn't look at her; he just continued to dry himself off. '

Alex!'

'That might not have been a dream.' Lola stopped in her tracks.

'What do you mean, Alex?'

'She may have been there,' he said concentrating on drying his legs, 'there in the corner of the bedroom. I saw her as well. Does the Moone girl do that a lot? It's a bit creepy.'

'The Moone girl? You mean Aíbgréne? Your cousin.'

Lola felt sick. If he was right, that meant that Aíbgréne had seen Alex in bed with her.

'You need to leave, Alex. You have to go,' said Lola in panic. Lola had been procrastinating when it came to calling Aíbgréne; this only made it even more difficult. How was she going to explain this to her, caught red handed with her nemesis. This would validate all Aíbgréne's concerns.

'Lola,' said Alex trying to calm her down.

'Lola nothing, Alex. This was a one off, let's not pretend that last night, or this morning or any of this is going to change anything between us.' The atmosphere freshened between the two. 'Like you said, you've chosen what side of the line you want to stand on and so have I. What I feel or what I think I feel for you can't and won't change that and don't pretend it's any different for you.'

'So now you can read my mind?'

'No, Alex, I can't read your mind but I can read your eyes, your body, your words, your deeds.'

Alex went about gathering up his clothes from the stairs, to the living room until the trail ended in the kitchen. He finished dressing. His forehead wrinkled in deep furrows, clearly confused by the sudden drop in temperature between the two of them.

'So am I to go now?'

'You'd have had to go sometime, Alex,' said Lola, the sharp edge of her tone blunted.

'Take care,' said Alex as he turned to leave.

'Yeah, I'll be fine if your dad stops trying to kill me.' Lola regretted the words as soon as they left her tongue. Despite everything that had passed between them she didn't want to sully what they had just shared.

'He won't ever stop trying to do that, Lola,' said Alex evenly. 'Well not until he gets what he needs.'

'He already has one thing belonging to me but he won't have it for long.'

'What your searching for is long gone, Lola. I was actually surprised that you could detect it at all. Your powers have grown but it's not enough.'

'Where is it now, Alex?' Lola knew that she wouldn't get an answer but she asked the question anyway.

'I'll tell you that if you tell me what your interest in the Book of Kells is.'

'The Book of Kells?' said Lola in a half laugh. 'My only interest was to cover a story for the paper. I thought that would have been evident by now. Why?' she asked turning the question around. 'What's your interest in it?'

The confusion flashed in Alex's eyes just long enough to let her know that she'd sold the double bluff. Alex laughed but Lola could see the uncertainty on his face.

'Whatever, Lola.' Alex turned and opened the door. Before he left he turned back towards her, his eyes softened. 'Please think about what I said, Lola. About leaving this city.'

Lola was about to launch into another tirade but she stopped herself, instead she stood on tiptoes and kissed him on his open mouth. One more wouldn't hurt, she thought.

'I wish all the love I have in my heart for you, Alex, was enough to liberate you from your self-imposed prison.'

'Love,' said Alex. The word stuck in his throat as her honesty caught him short as it always did. 'Love is a laser quest, Lola,' he grinned.

'Yes,' said Lola gently, 'and I'm not being honest by pretending you were just some lover.'

Alex laughed at the reply and played along. 'Is this one of those games you're gonna lose, but you want to play it just in case?'

'You know what they say,' said Lola, 'suck it and see, you'll never know.'

'Be cruel to me 'cause I'm a fool for you,' said Alex the warmth returning between them once again.

'You're a fool for no one, Alex Stein, but you play the part well.'

'That's not true, Lola, you know I'd probably still adore you with your hands around my neck, or I did last time I checked.'

He stepped in closer to Lola again, pulling her next to him. It was her turn now to think of a retort. Her mind raced through their favourite band's lyrics, trying to choose something that would be apt. Then she had it.

'Am I to call off the search for your soul or maybe I should just put it on hold again,' replied Lola.

'I'm pinned down by the dark, Lola,' said Alex. There was a deepening sense of sorrow in his words.

'Well,' quipped Lola trying to lighten the mood, 'you just need to remember that all those other girls are just post-mix lemonade.'

'I think we're going to run out of Arctic Monkey lyrics,' said Alex bringing an end to their exchange.

There was shuffling behind them and Erin excused herself, greeting Alex as she walked past him. If the sight of Alex Stein with Lola surprised Erin she gave no indication as she took a seat on the settee.

'Lola,' said Alex, 'you are my sweetest downfall.'

Lola closed the door, shutting her eyes she leaned up against it to gain her equilibrium. She searched for the lyric but came up short, it wasn't one of Alex Turner's.

'Lola Paige, you dirty dog!' laughed Erin, jumping from the seat and throwing her arms around Lola. 'I'm just glad that one of us got lucky last night.'

Lola was so caught unawares she didn't know how much Erin had seen or heard.

'I'm so sorry, Erin. I had way too much to drink when we got to the bar. I'm sorry you had to leave on your own, some date I am.'

'Oh, I was fine, Lola. Besides, I didn't leave on my own,' said Erin sheepishly. 'Oh Dan,' smiled Lola delighted for the reprieve.

'Oh Dan indeed. That piece of shit is married you know? Can you believe it? Married with a kid. He took his wedding ring off.'

'How did you find out then?'

'Well we were, you know... about to get down to business. We had gone back to my place and I asked him if he had any protection. He pulled his wallet out of his pocket and what fell out only his freakin' weddin' ring. You'll never guess what he did; he just picked it up and put it back in his pocket, like it was nothin'. He opens his wallet to get the johnny out and that's when I see the picture of his kid. I lifted his trousers, his shirt and shoes and threw them out my door and that rat with them.'

'Dirty Dan,' said Lola, trying to be serious. 'You're a good girl, Erin,' she said giving her a motherly pat on the back.

'Which is more than I can say for you. Alex Stein,' she elongated the way she said his name, pouring over each syllable adding extra emphasis. 'That is one fine human being. If he had a ring on that figure and ten children at home, I wouldn't think twice,' she laughed.

Lola could feel her face betray her again as it turned crimson. 'Nothing happened,' she stumbled so clumsily over the denial that it sounded heavy and industrial as it fell from her mouth.

'You are too cute, Lola. I mean you can't even lie, the truth is written all over your face. Plus I can smell the sex in here and it should be bottled and sold in Macy's.' Erin thought this was hilarious as she burst into her high-pitched laugh.

'Anyway, your secret's safe with me,' she said crossing her heart with her fingers and blessing herself. 'My lips are sealed.'

'Thanks, Erin,' said Lola relieved. 'It was a one off. It's complicated between me and Alex.'

'I actually came over to show you these.' Erin produced her camera from out of her bag and switched it on. She called Lola over to sit beside her. 'Have a look at this.'

Erin flicked through the pictures of the revellers at Carl Stein's party until she came to a series of images of Lola dancing with the host.

'At first I didn't notice anything but then as I flicked through the pictures it got clearer and clearer.'

Lola was unsure what it was that the camera had captured. Her mind raced, clamouring through the events of the previous night, but nothing stood out, well nothing stood out apart from her assaulting a senior staff member and drinking way too much alcohol.

As the stream of images sailed past her eyes Lola noticed the golden elliptical plate as it expanded around her, bleeding in threads into something opaque that pushed and distorted the liquid light.

Carl Stein had clearly been trying to assail her as they danced, testing and pushing her. She sat motionless, unsure how to explain it, uncertain if it would be at all helpful to her cause to offer any explanation.

Lola had never seen her own aura before and it captivated her. Her light was a thing of great beauty as it spread around her like a mantle made from some balmy vapour. She wondered if this was what Alex and Carl Stein saw when they looked at her. Was this why she was so conspicuous in the city?

'What caused that?' asked Lola, her voice as dispassionate as she could manage.

'Well, Lola, I'm going to say something and I hope you don't think that I'm bonkers, but I think it's your aura.'

Lola had just taken a sip of water from the bottle and almost spat it out all over the place; some even came out her noise.

'My what?' said Lola wiping her mouth.

'I know it sounds crazy, but I really believe it all that stuff. My gramma lived in Salem and I spent a lot of time with her you know during the holidays. She was mad into all that stuff. I've pictured it in plants and things but this is the first time I've captured it in a human.'

'It must be a trick of the light or glare or something,' offered Lola. 'You're a photographer this kind of thing must happen all the time.' But Lola's smile was uneasy.

'I shouldn't have said anything,' said Erin embarrassed now. 'You must think I'm some sort of freak.'

'Erin,' said Lola giving her hand a reassuring squeeze, 'don't be silly. Of course I don't. If you say it's an aura, whatever that is, I will take your word for it.'

Sated by Lola's encouragement, Erin was animated once again. 'I've never seen anything like this, Lola. It's beautiful, I couldn't even Photoshop this in. I want to take another picture of you, just to see.'

'You know I hate pictures of me, Erin. Maybe later. What about the others? Did they turn out okay?'

'Yeah they're great; we'll get something out of them. It was some party wasn't it?'

'Yeah, some house. Nothing that I wouldn't expect from Carl Stein,' answered Lola vacantly. She could tell that Erin was intrigued and although her friend never pried too much Lola felt guilty that she couldn't offer her some sort of explanation or confide in her what an amazing thing she had captured on her camera.

'Would you like a coffee?'

'No, Lola, I'm going to head into the office for a while to file these pictures and write up some copy. Erin got up and walked to the door. She hugged Lola. 'I'll see you in the morning.'

'See you in the morning, Erin.' Lola fell onto the couch, exhausted. If there one thing she hated as much as Carl Stein it was deceiving people. She checked the clock and tried to calculate what time it would be at home.

She'd have to call Aíbgréne, there was no way she could put it off any longer. Lola lifted her phone and dialled her friend's number. The phone rang and rang and for a moment Lola thought she'd gotten a reprieve but just as she was about to hang up Aíbgréne answered. She sounded groggy with sleep.

'Lola. Lola, is everything okay?' she asked, her voice suddenly alert.

'I'm fine, Aíbgréne, it's so good to hear your voice.' Lola really meant it. It felt like years since she'd spoken to her friend, the only friend that she could share any of this madness with. 'How have you been?' asked Lola tentatively. 'How's your mum and Daithí?'

'They're fine. I'm fine. I'd be a bit less stressed if you weren't sleeping with Alex Stein but hey, what can you do?' Aíbgréne's caustic rebuke, although anticipated, knocked the pulp from Lola.

The silence crackled and sizzled between them. Lola hadn't called her to fight or argue and her spirit was bleached and paled by the constant barrage of conflict, the conflict of love, the conflict of duty, the conflict between her and this city.

'I didn't call to fight with you, Aíbgréne. I called to...' Lola trailed off. Why had she called? To grovel and explain herself? To plead for pardon?

'Why did you call, Lola? After all you've been in New York almost a month and this is the first time that you've bothered to reply to my voicemail. Did you know that Celeste has taken sick again? Or that she has been acting so strange,' accused Aíbgréne. 'No I don't suppose you did and now I understand why you've been so pre-occupied.'

'Celeste is sick?'

'Yes,' spat Aíbgréne, 'whatever that monster did to her, it's back again. We've tried everything.' Lola could hear the cracking in Aíbgréne's voice as Daithí comforted her at the other end of the line and Lola wished desperately that she was there with her instead of lying here in this hostile city.

'Have you tried...?'

Aíbgréne cut Lola off mid-sentence. 'Don't you think we've tried everything under the sun, Lola?' she snapped. 'Nothing is working. It's him, it's all him I know it and now to add to my load I discover you are in bed, literally, with Alex Stein.'

'It was a one off, Aíbgréne... It's not what you think. I know you have your plate full but you haven't been lighting up my phone calling me, have you? You couldn't even bother making it to the airport to see me off.'

'You seemed pretty familiar to me, Lola. I don't know what to say to you, other than you are playing with fire. Do you know the power you are giving away sleeping with Alex Stein?'

'What?'

'One of the many things you clearly don't know.' Lola could tell that Aíbgréne must have been at breaking point because she was acting so out of character.

'What do you mean giving my power away?' demanded Lola.

'Sexual energy is very potent, Lola; it is not to be trifled with, especially not when you're you! Every time you allow that man to come into your...' Aíbgréne paused for a moment trying to find the appropriate wording. 'Each time you allow him into your sacred space,' she said, 'he leaches energy from you, just like his father did to my aunt Aurora. Just like they did to that poor Jones girl and the countless others we don't know about. None of those girls have what you have, Lola. That is what he craves, not you, it's what he can gain from you. His looks and silver tongue are all part of his arsenal.'

The anger flew into Lola's breast like a pack of hounds until it escaped through her throat and flashed off her tongue.

'I'm so sick of you and your condescension,' she shouted down the phone. 'Perhaps if you hadn't been creeping about my bedroom like a ghoul in the middle of the night uninvited you might not have cause for concern. You act like you have all the answers, you know nothing, you couldn't save Celeste and you couldn't save yourself, you needed me for that! Don't ever forget that.'

Aíbgréne was about to reply when Daithí came on the phone.

'Lola, it's me,' said Daithí apologetically. 'Aíbgréne is under immense stress at the moment, she's hardly slept since Celeste has taken ill again. She worries about you. She couldn't cope if anything happened. I don't know what is going on with you, but I know you would never compromise the Order or yourself.'

The tears stung Lola's eyes as they forced their way out. She didn't know what to say.

'Daithí, take Celeste to the Manor. It's the only place you'll get her well again. Aíbgréne has everything she needs there. If Carl Stein has some hold on her, he won't be able to get to her there. I'll text my dad and let him know that you'll all be staying for a while. There's plenty of room. I'll call you in the next few days.'

Lola hung up the phone. Her chest rose and fell in heavy waves as Aíbgréne's harsh words stabbed at her – the truth hurt.

Why was she offended by Aíbgréne's assessment of the situation? After all she'd always known how much she hated Alex Stein. Why was she so indignant at the idea that Alex would be capable of the worst treachery? Of course he was, he had proven that before.

Lola needed a bath it was the only thing that would purge him from her body and thoughts. Her phone rang on and on as Aíbgréne's smiling face flashed on the screen but Lola didn't answer, she was too tired to argue or to hear any more home truths.

Lola didn't hear Rocha return or the rain that tapped on the windowpane of her skylight as she fell into a black sleep.

The streets of New York were refreshed and cleansed by the previous night's rain and the city was subdued as the mirage-grey streets wavered in the high morning sun. Lola had left early, even before Rocha had gotten out of bed. The morning commute wasn't filled with the normal dread for Lola because her mind was so preoccupied with other things.

She checked her phone for any correspondence. Her dad had texted. She opened up the message, relieved that Daithí had convinced Aíbgréne to go to the Manor. Lola wasn't sure why she had suggested it but she trusted that the decision was the right one.

She thought of how the gardens at Brook Mill Manor would look on a July morning like this, with the sun gently stirring the roses and sweet pea out from their dewy sleep. She envied Aíbgréne and Daithí because there was nothing more that she wanted than to be at home safe with her brothers and parents. She didn't often allow herself to indulge in these fancies of thought, it served no purpose other than to unsettle Lola. She was chained to her duty and her duty required her to be in this city for a little longer. She couldn't leave New York, not without the Cube and the book.

As she closed her eyes to better remember the book Lola could hear its melancholic call and it unsettled her, there was no way she could abandon it and go back to Ireland, she would never forgive herself if she did.

The train jerked to a sudden stop and Lola's eyes flashed open with a fresh idea. She looked at her phone again, this time she searched for the pictures she'd taken at the Steins' and when she found them she looked down at the young Marine. His face was stern but Lola could tell from the glint in his caramel eyes that under that stone exterior there was more than the picture revealed.

Lola read his details. Lemar Jenkins, special detail, Iraq. Then it gave his age and address. He didn't look much older than her, but according to his file he was twenty-five. Following the path laid out by her inner sight, Lola jumped off the train and exited the subway station. There was a row of yellow taxis waiting and without hesitating she got into the first one, holding her phone out in front of her.

'Hi, 3170 Broadway please,' instructed Lola settling into the cool leather.

The cabbie performed a swift double take. 'Thirty-one seventy,' he repeated after her. 'Yes,' smiled Lola, waiting for him to take off.

'You sure, ma'am?' Lola looked at the screen shot again in case she'd made a mistake. 'Yes, that's what it says here. Is there no such address?' asked Lola confused.

'There sure is such an address but not the type of address someone like you should be going to.' Lola had no idea what he was talking about and even though she didn't ask the driver why, he decided to enlighten her anyway as he merged into the stream of traffic heading uptown. 'The Grant House projects, that's where you're goin?'

'Yes I think so, if that's where this address leads me. I have a building number, what looks like a floor number and an apartment number.'

'There was a major raid there a few days ago, over a hundred kids arrested for gang related violence.'

'I'm sure I'll be grand,' said Lola trying to end the conversation.

'You're Irish?'

'Yes,' smiled Lola preoccupied about what she was going to say if this Lemar Jenkins was actually at home. Hi, I found your information when I was trespassing in someone's house. How are you today? That wasn't exactly going to cut it.

'A young girl, about your age,' continued the driver, 'she was shot dead there a few months back. Chased her down and shot her in cold blood. Had her whole life ahead of her, it's so sad.'

'That's awful,' said Lola absently, she hadn't meant to sound aloof or uninterested. The cabbie eyed her curiously in his rear mirror clearly wondering why this white girl was feeling so unperturbed about going to Harlem but Lola paid him no mind.

The taxi stopped and started at the various traffic lights; finally after fifteen minutes the car came to a halt in front of a row of colossal redbrick high rises. Lola looked at the floor number again. It said floor seventeen and she hoped the elevators would be working.

As soon as Lola paid the fare, the driver's wheels screeched and took off although she had barely managed to but both feet on the pavement. She looked around. The space was much more open than downtown, where the buildings seemed to lean in on you all the time.

The sky was becoming more overcast which compounded the intense humidity and the screech of a passing train filled the air as Lola craned her neck to take in the complex. A few metres to the right of Grant House a vast iron bridge straddled the broad street with its viaducts spanning about fifteen city blocks.

As she approached the entrance Lola passed by a group of young men camped beside one of the park benches outside the superblock high-rise. As she took the ramp that lead to the lobby door, Lola noticed three bullet holes in one of the metal uprights that supported the shelter at the front door. The jeers and catcalls didn't unnerve her because she was focusing on what she was going to say to Lemar but she could hear them shout after her, 'You must be lost' and 'I ain't seen anything that white in Harlem since the last snow storm'. Lola couldn't help but smile. It was probably true and it was also funny.

Lola's head tilted back once last time, following the stack of windows as they ascended in neat rows as far as her eyes could reach. She lost the top of the towers when she entered under the building's front porch.

Opening the heavy wooden door her nostrils were immediately assaulted by the sharp stench of urine. There was no evidence of actual bodily fluids on the brown tiles under her feet or on the grime-stained pale tiles that lined the walls. To her right, hung up on the frosted glass window, was a white bed sheet that had been covered with messages and condolences, each dedicated to a bright face that beamed out at Lola.

Lola realised that this was the young girl that the cab driver had been had been telling her about. She was dressed in gym clothes and had a basketball tucked under her arm as she smiled out confidently from the middle of the cotton bed sheet.

Lola looked about the hallway, wondering if this was where the girl had breathed her last breath. She stood in front of the memorial for a few minutes offering her respects.

An elderly lady emerged from the stairwell out of breath and Lola opened the door for her as she exited the building.

'You lost, honey?' she asked Lola; confusion clouded her creased eyes. 'No, I'm looking for the seventeenth floor.'

The elderly women started to laugh. 'Seventeenth.' She looked Lola up and down, concentrating on her legs. 'Well you sure look fit to me, honey, but I guess we'll soon find out. Those elevators haven't been working for over three months now. Damn Tenants' Association have been shouting about it to the city for god knows how long. Lights out, security doors don't lock.' She pointed towards the door that Lola now held open. Lola sucked in the balmy air as it seeped into the dank hallway, storing it for her journey. 'And they wonder why kids are getting shot in their own buildings.' The lady shook her head and walked on.

Lola let the door close behind her and decided to try the lifts just in case. After a while she gave up and took to the stairs. Her phone buzzed with an incoming message. It was Isaac. Where are you? Eugene is going mad. Is everything okay?

Lola stopped on the stairwell, glad of the break and texted him back. Out on assignment, be back soon as I can. Lola wasn't sure if it had sent, the reception wasn't great in the tower block.

Beads of sweat settled on her neck and back as she reached the tenth floor. A group of young women passed her on the stairs. They didn't say anything; they just stared at her disdainfully. 'She must be five O,' said one of the girls on the way past.

'No way,' said the other, 'she look more like some hack to me.' The girl sucked at her lip and gave Lola an incendiary look.

'Either that,' said her friend, 'or she be haunting the stairwell. She white enough to be a ghost.' Lola could hear the peal of their laughter rising as they descended the stairs and she was beginning to get irate now.

Her feet sloshed in her shoes as the sweat began to build, the smell of stale piss got stronger the further up the stairs she rose and on the sixteenth flight she had to step over a pool of vomit. Lola couldn't blame its owner, she felt like she was close to vomiting herself.

Finally, she reached the corridor for the seventeenth floor. She looked at each door for number seven hundred and seven. Of course, steamed Lola as she came to the end of the corridor, it had to be the end one. Lola gingerly knocked on the brown door, part of her hoping that no one would answered. The corridor light kept flickering on and off. It buzzed and hummed threatening to extinguish at any minute. The corridor was narrow and the discoloured wall tiles had the remnants of graffiti smeared across them.

She knocked the door again and this time there was some movement from within. Lola still hadn't gotten her breath back when the door opened a fraction and a woman peered through a chain on the door.

'Yes?'

'Hi. My name is Lola Paige, I'm looking for Mr Lemar Jenkins.'

'What you want my Lemar for?' said the woman suspiciously eyeing Lola.

Lola hadn't had time to think about this clearly. Between the taxi driver and being busy concentrating on breathing coming up the stairs, she hadn't finished working out what she would say when she got there.

'I just need to talk to him about something,' said Lola lamely.

The woman closed the door and for a second Lola was about to turn and go. Then she heard the numerous locks being unbolted and a woman around forty or so stood in the doorway. She was small and a pair of blue nurse's scrubs hung loosely on her narrow frame. She had a cup of coffee in her hands. Taking a slow sip from the steaming mug she stepped aside and invited Lola in.

'You'd better come in Ms... what did you say your name was again?'

'Lola Paige,' said Lola politely.

Lola guessed the lady she was talking to was Lemar's mother. There was a lot of grey in her aura but underneath it there lay aquas and leafy greens, with some lavenders and yellows. The grey subdued the more vibrant healing shades.

Her hair was plaited in thick braids and she wore a band to keep them off her fine face. She bore a close resemblance to Lemar and Lola might have been forgiven for mistaking her for his sister until she examined the woman's dark, smooth skin. She didn't have much in the way of wrinkles but her eyes gave away her age, they looked tired and worn despite the obvious beauty present.

'Thank you,' said Lola as she took a seat where directed. The apartment was a complete contrast to the corridor beyond and the entire building that it lay within. It was fresh with its walls painted a crisp white, which accentuated the light that crept in through the two small windows.

Coats and jackets hung on a hallstand and pictures were displayed on the walls, a gallery of the young Marine at different stages in his life.

The kitchen lay to the left with only one wall separating it from the living room, where a small couch and two chairs were arranged around a TV screen. The seats, like most of the furniture in the apartment, were old but such care had been taken with them that they didn't bare any of the grubbiness of old things.

'He's in the shower, I can't hold out to that boy since he's come home from Iraq, he's always in the shower. He's not the one having to wash and dry the towels but.'

'Maybe you should put him to work then, Ms Jenkins,' smiled Lola amicably. The woman smiled for the first time. 'Maybe I should, Ms Paige.'

'Lemar,' she knocked on the bathroom door with her knuckles. 'Lemar!' she shouted louder now. 'That boy gone deaf. Lemar, there's some white girl here to see you.'

Lola could hear the deep base of some rap music piping from the bathroom. It sounded like Tupac, but she couldn't be sure until the bathroom door swung open releasing the full sound and a plume of steam.

'What, Moms?' shouted Lemar Jenkins over the music as he stood soaking wet with only a towel covering his bottom half shocked to find a strange woman sitting in his living room. Lola's eyes betrayed her immediately, the screenshot she had did not do him justice. Lemar Jenkins looked much better in person as he stood looking from his mum to Lola and then back at his mum again.

'Turn that music down, boy,' commanded Ms Jenkins in her no-nonsense tone. 'This girl here, she says she's here to see you.'

Lemar Jenkins walked into the living room and stood directly in front of Lola who gaped almost open-mouthed as the water fell in pearls from his powerful frame.

'Sorry, Ma'am, do I know you?' His voice was deep and smoky and dazzled by the sound of it and the sight before her it took Lola a few seconds to muster an explanation.

'No,' choked Lola. 'I'm from the New York Torch,' she stammered, 'I've come to talk to you about...' She never got a chance to finish.

'Did Mr Kane send you?' Lemar interrupted, confusion narrowing his eyes. Finally Lola had been handed a lifeline, how he knew Isaac Kane didn't concern her now so she clasped on to this life raft with both hands.

'Yes, he did Mr Jenkins. 'Sorry I arrived unannounced but...'

'I need to go get dressed, I'll be right back,' Lemar retreated back into the bathroom, turning the music down as his mother had requested.

'Would you like a drink, Ms Paige? You seem pretty outta breath.'

'That would be great, thank you.'

'Soda or water?' shouted Lemar's mum from the kitchen.

'Water please, Ms Jenkins.'

'Less of the Ms Jenkins, it makes me feel old, please call me Adele.'

'Thank you,' said Lola. 'Those stairs are a killer. I never thought I was going to make it.'

'Well you know the vomit and pee kinda spur you on,' she smiled, handing Lola a bottle of water. Her colours bloomed opened and Lola understood that Adele was beginning to relax a little more. 'So you work for the New York Torch?'

'Well I'm an intern there for the summer and I'm working under Isaac Kane at the moment.'

'Isaac Kane, I wouldn't mind workin under him myself,' laughed Ms Jenkins.

'He seems to have that effect on women alright. I can put a word in for you if you like,' said Lola flashing her a cheeky grin.

'God knows having one man to look after is enough for me, Lola. I don't need any more worry. My Lemar is a good boy; getting him outta this neighbourhood was the best thing I did for him. Now he's going to college in the fall and going to make something of himself.'

'That's brilliant. Where is he going to?'

'He's going to Columbia; it's just a few blocks south of here. He's going to study law and say what you like about the military, but that's what's payin for him to go. On my salary at the hospital, I could never have afforded it.'

'You're a nurse,' said Lola motioning towards the scrubs.

'Yeah,' sighed Ms Jenkins as she leaned back into her seat. 'I've just got off night shift. I work in the emergency room so it can be pretty hectic.'

'I'm sure it can,' said Lola. 'It can't have been easy when Lemar was away.'

'Every night,' she said looking up from her coffee. 'Every night I prayed to the Lord to keep my baby safe from harm, Iraq, Harlem Miss Paige, it makes no difference. A bullet can end your life here just a quick as it can in some foreign country.'

Lemar emerged dressed in pair of loose khaki trousers and white trainers that looked as though they'd been taken straight out of the box. He wore a fitted white t-shirt that was tucked in just above the brown belt. His hair was cut neat to his head and his lips were full and pink and when he licked them it drew Lola's eyes to them.

'Ms Paige, you fancy getting some lunch?'

'Yes, sure,' said Lola as she rose from the seat. 'Thank you for the water, Ms Jenkins. I'll take it with me. I'll need it for the descent,' laughed Lola, as she followed Lemar out of the apartment door.

'You stay safe, Lemar, and be back here at a reasonable hour, you hear me?'

'Yes, Moms,' said Lemar planting a kiss on her cheek. 'Now get some sleep.'

~24~

Lola sucked in the humid air trying to dispel the sharpness of the building that had assailed her nose and throat. The group of young men that she'd passed on her way in were still sitting at the park benches in front of Grant House and she could hear them gearing up for more catcalls.

'Yo, snowflake,' one of them shouted. Lola thought it best to ignore them. Lemar followed out after her and the group were suddenly muted.

'Yo, Lemar, how's it going man?' The most vocal of the group stepped forward and greeted Lemar as they slammed hands and hugged.

'When'd you get back, brother?'

It was obvious that Lemar knew this guy well, there was an air of familiarity between them, but still Lola could detect that Lemar was uneasy and keen to get away. She wasn't sure if it was because she was with him or for some other reason.

'Been home a few weeks, been doing this and that.'

'Is this who's been keeping you away from our spot here,' he nodded towards Lola. 'Snowflake here.' The man smiled and laughed but Lola could tell there was menace in his gait. Lemar positioned himself between Lola and his friend. 'You got a bit of jungle fever out there in Iraq?'

Lemar looked at Lola and laughed. 'Hell no man, she's just someone I know, that's all.'

'Where you from, Snowflake? M'on on over here and talk to me. I wouldn't mind getting me a taste of that white skin and those green eyes.'

He started posturing holding on to his crotch.

'You wouldn't know what to do with it,' said Lola stepping out from behind Lemar.

'Snowflake's Irish!' He started pretending to Irish dance, jigging about to what he thought Irish music sounded like. Lola could see that Lemar was growing more and more uncomfortable. 'Me and you could dance a little jig, snowflake.'

'I'd say you're as good in bed as you are at dancing, mate,' said Lola, 'and from what I've seen you're pretty shit.' The group around him exploded into laughter.

'Leshawn just got burned by a snowflake,' said another of the young men between chuckles. Lemar said his goodbyes and beat a steady retreat from his apartment block.

'You on a death wish, Ms Paige. I mean it's bad enough that you come here on your own. I don't know what Isaac was thinking letting you come here. Then you have a mouth that's just asking for trouble.'

'What?' said Lola, genuinely confused. 'Can he not take a bit of stick? What did you expect me to do when he was standing taking the piss out of me? Let him? Should I have been intimidated by him?'

'What?' said Lemar, growing more agitated. 'Keep walkin.'

'Where are we going?' asked Lola as she struggled to keep in step with his long strides.

'Someplace we can talk. Someplace that's safe.' Lemar looked around behind him. Satisfied with whatever he saw, he continued around the block from his home and down towards the subway on West 125th Street.

As they walked Lola noticed a few flowers and wreaths laid at different points on the pavement. Lemar caught her looking.

'That's just some of the many sidewalk memorials at this end of town. You not used to that where you live.'

'I'm from the north of Ireland, believe you me we've had our fair share of sidewalk memorials.'

'I suppose you have,' said Lemar, rather preoccupied.

Lola offered no reply. When they got to the subway entrance Lemar paid the fare for both of them. Lola followed him up on to the platform, which was almost deserted. It was a stark contrast to her morning commutes in mid-town Manhattan; it wasn't as busy at this end of town.

'Where are we headed?' she asked again.

'Just a little further downtown into central Harlem, away from prying eyes.'

'Does it embarrass you to be seen with a white girl?' asked Lola apologetically.

Lemar smiled for the first time. 'Hell no, it's just we don't often see white folks that deep in Harlem so folks get suspicious.'

'Yeah, I kind of gathered that,' smiled Lola. 'I was accused of being five O and a hack earlier. Mind you,' said Lola with a light laugh, 'I was also accused of being a ghost.'

Lemar grinned again. His smile was contagious; he should smile more often thought Lola to herself. Lola thought about where he lived and where he had spent the last four years of his life. Perhaps he had little to smile about, she realised.

'Well you sure is white enough.'

'You think you'd never seen a white person before! I mean if someone white made those observations about someone black, they'd be called racists.'

'You sure have a lot to say for yourself, don't you, Ms Paige?'

'Well who else is going to say it for me?' shot back Lola. 'That sure as hell is true.'

The hairs on Lola's arms began to stir and bristle and suddenly she felt uncomfortable. As always, the ring dutifully respond to the deep force within her that registered the danger, long before her eyes were conscious of it. Lola looked around the platform now at the three men sat at different points on the narrow gangway.

One sat on the bench next to theirs and the other two stood at different points. What struck Lola was that they were all white and dressed in some sort of black non-descript clothes.

'Lemar,' she nudged him with her elbow. He lifted his head in acknowledgement. 'Yeah?'

'You said it was rare or odd to see someone white that wasn't police come to your neighbourhood?'

'Yeah, why?' Lemar read the urgency in Lola's eyes and took her lead.

'I think we may have company,' she said, urging him not to turn around. 'Just stay calm.' Lola thought back to the file she'd seen, she was sure that the men that surrounded them were not on official duty. They looked like they could be Carl Stein's men. One looked familiar.

Lola looked at him directly and when he averted her gaze, she had him placed. He was the guard on the stairs the night she was at the Pierre. She didn't know whether they were there for her or Lemar; it even occurred to

Lola that they could be there for them both.

Lola didn't panic, she was in complete control as she kindled the energy that built up like thunder inside her, ready and willing to be unleashed when she commanded it.

The grind and rattle of the incoming train sounded from the line and they were still the only five on the platform. Lemar was growing more and more uneasy as he shuffled and fidgeted beside her. Lola placed her hand on his. 'It's going to be okay. Just follow my lead.'

She could tell Lemar didn't trust her. He stepped away from her and his eyes darted from one point to another, seeking an exit and escape. Lola could see how bad it looked. She could very well have been part of the operation, but she wasn't.

Reading his thoughts, she decided to act.

'They are after me, Lemar, so just stay calm and play along.' Lola stepped into him, reaching up on her tip-toes to place her arms around his tall frame. She pulled Lemar down towards her planting a kiss on his unsuspecting mouth.

At first, he didn't respond as he stood rigid and frozen and then he finally took his part in this stage play. Lola's aura expanded and flexed like a ball of lycra around them both and even though Lemar's pursuers were unseen, she could feel their movements, no matter how subtle. Lemar began to move his hands down towards Lola's bum. She broke apart from him playfully, but there was no mistaking the venom in her voice as she smiled though gritted teeth.

'No need to take the piss, move your hands or I'll break them.'

Lemar smiled back and moved his hands upwards. 'You said play along, so I'm playing along.'

The train was almost at the platform now and the sudden movement alerted Lola that their would-be assailants were about to make their move. It was clear they intended to push both her and Lemar in front of the oncoming train but they hadn't banked on who and what they were dealing with. Lola let the power within her build and build until it gathered and scalded the palms of her hands and the tips of her fingers.

And suddenly time itself seemed to slow and she could see it all before her, every movement and every angle as all three men approached. Lemar broke off from her and turned to face them, their hands were outstretched in an attempt to push him over the edge. Just as they made contact with

Lemar, Lola let the sonic pulse pore from her, the entire platform shook underneath its force and even the electrics on the train were momentarily snuffed out.

Lola saw the flash and then as the three men were propelled onto their backs, she heard the nose as the train car's emergency alarms went off.

Lemar Jenkins stood in a state of stasis. His ears rang and hummed and although Lola was speaking to him and pulling on his t-shirt he couldn't focus on what she was saying.

The train's electrics whirred back to life and the doors slid open to let those inside out onto the platform. A few commuters looked on in bewilderment at the sight of three grown men staggering to their feet. Lola tugged at Lemar's arms, pulling him onto the train just as the doors were about to close.

Lemar didn't speak a word. Lola noticed he kept shaking his head. She knew his ears must still be ringing. They rode the train for about three stops before Lemar motioned they should get off.

As they moved through the crowds up onto Malcolm X Boulevard, they could very well have been on Princes Street for all Lola knew. This part of Harlem looked very different from Lemar's neighbourhood. There were various shopping chains and restaurants with patios out front filled with diners. Street vendors and market stalls offered and broadcasted their wares and there was music everywhere. The atmosphere was open and vibrant and despite being a lone white face Lola didn't feel intimidated or uncomfortable, in fact she felt better here than she had in parts of Manhattan. She wondered if Carl Stein's reach stretched this far north.

The lights turned green and Lemar guided Lola across the busy street. They walked a little further down the block and stopped at a stone-fronted building that said 'Sylvia's Soul Food'.

A line of diners curled out on to the pavement and she and Lemar joined the tail of the queue.

A gentleman in a waiting outfit came out to check on the line and spotted Lemar. 'Young Jenkins,' he waved giving Lemar a warm embrace. 'So good to see you, little brother. When did you get back?'

'I'm back a few weeks now. We have to go through the usual decompression activities before they release us.'

'Your momma told me your good news, said you was going to law school.'

'Well that's the plan,' said Lemar bashfully.

'Now who is this exotic little bird you've got with you?'

'This is Lola, Ken. She's Irish,' said Lemar as if being Irish was the reason Lola was with him.

'Come on you two, I've a great table inside that will you do you two lovebirds.'

Lemar was about to protest but the man he called Ken wasn't listening. Inside the restaurant was equally as busy. The tables were neat and only sat two people at a time; lucky for them theirs was against the wall, which afforded them a little more privacy than some of the other tables.

After they'd settled into their seats, Ken came back with a jug of water for the table and left two menus. Along the walls were pictures of the family that owned the place and all the acclaimed visitors that had eaten there. There were politicians, celebrities, and political activists. Every table was its own universe and soon Lola was content that no one was listening in on their conversation.

'Listen Lemar, you need to promise me that anything we discuss at this table will not be repeated. Do you hear me?'

'I was in the military, Lola, I know all about secrets,' said Lemar staring at Lola from over the menu he was pretending to look at. 'I've been in Iraq for over four years and I ain't never seen anything like that. What you did was like some supernatural Jedi bullshit. You better tell me what in the hell is goin on! Who are you?' Ken came back to the table to take their order.

'You ready to order?'

'You go first, Lemar, I'm having another look,' said Lola.

'Ken, I'll have some fried chicken and waffles please.'

'Course you will, my young brother. You know, Lola, this man of yours used to be our bus boy here, then he graduated to the tables, one of the best workers we had. My Moms broke her heart the day he left to go join the army.'

'Ken, I'm so sorry about Sylvia. I sent a card and a letter. I was in Iraq... I loved the old girl.'

'I know, Lemar, and she loved you.'

Lola picked the first thing that she saw and went for the red tortilla soup.

'This will be interesting,' smirked Lemar.

'What?' asked Lola.

'You get much spice in the Irish diet? Do you lot not eat potatoes or somethin?'

'Yes, that's all we eat in Ireland, Lemar. Potatoes. I see travelling with the army didn't illuminate your mind much then?'

'Oh it illuminated my mind alright. It made me realise that parts of Harlem, like the projects that I grew up in, look like parts of Iraq.'

'So you're going to study law at Columbia,' said Lola trying to lighten the mood. 'That's really brilliant.'

'Yeah that's if I live long enough. I mean, I followed my orders, I went where they sent me, I did as I was told and I did what it took to survive and now they want me dead, just like the rest.'

'Hold up here,' said Lola. 'Who are they and why do you think they want you dead?'

'How much has Isaac told you?'

'Enough,' said Lola, telling the lie seamlessly.

'The military, those guys looked like military to me.'

'They may very well have been military at one stage,' cautioned Lola, 'but I think they are now in someone else's employment.'

'What do you mean?'

'Do the words Operation Babylon or the Inanna project mean anything to you, Lemar? Were you involved in this?'

'Yes, like I told Isaac on the plane coming home, I had been stationed in Baghdad and suddenly I was reassigned to a town further south called Al Basrah. The town was where the Euphrates and Tigris meet. At first I thought that we had been called down to work at ABOT?'

'ABOT?' asked Lola.

'Sorry, I'm so used to speaking in military terms. It stands for Al Basrah Oil Terminal.'

'Why would you be stationed there?' said Lola curious. 'The US Army is fighting Al-Qaeda or ISIS, aren't they? That's why they invaded Iraq after all?'

'You're joking, right? USACE out of Fort Worth in Texas run that along with Stein Corp. They move over three million barrels of oil per day from that site. From time to time officers are called on detail; they say it's the safest place in Iraq.'

'Sorry! Can you take it back a bit there? What or who is USACE?'

'USACE stands for US Army Corps of Engineers.'

'So the US Government is in business with Carl Stein?'

'Yes, Lola. This isn't news; it's a matter of public record. Why do you seem so shocked?'

'It may be a matter of public record, Lemar, but how many broadcasters or newspapers actually talk about this, publicise it?'

'They don't, or they can't, because they are owned by the same people, for the most part. I mean when you think about it it's genius really.'

Ken came with their food. Lola picked at hers in between questions. 'So I take it you weren't sent on detail to ABOT then?'

'No, we were stationed in Al Basrah and debriefed there. There was a team of about ten Marines. We were told that this was strictly top secret and the information that we would be receiving was on a need to know basis. That's how OPSEC is. You follow orders because it saves lives.'

'Sorry,' interrupted Lola again holding up her hand for Lemar to stop. 'OPSEC?'

'It stands for Operations Security,' said Lemar before continuing his story.

'Every other day, we left in teams and flew to a site about two hundred miles northeast of Al Basrah. We landed in the middle of the desert, with nothing around us for miles, only some small farm holdings. As I told Isaac, we were at a place called Ur and what looked like an archaeological site. We were guarding some ancient site like a large pyramid only the top was missing. It wasn't smooth like the way you see the pictures of the Egyptian pyramids but tiered. They didn't call it a pyramid either, they called it...' Lemar searched the recesses of his memory to find the word. 'It sounded like a ziggurat or somethin like that. There were scientists and archaeologists all over the place. It was like something out of Raiders of the Lost Ark. I don't know who was involved, some areas were even off limits to us.'

'What where they looking for?' asked Lola fully engrossed in Lemar's story.

'Well the little that I heard, it was some sort of book, only they didn't call it that they called a...'

'A folio?' said Lola, leaning forward and whispering the words.

'Yeah that's right, a folio. From what I gather the site is related to some ancient civilization, the Babylonians or Sumerians or something like that and this ziggurat thing was dedicated to this Goddess Inanna.'

Lola slumped back in her chair, running her hands over her face. Now she understood why the Hell Fire Club wanted Lemar Jenkins dead, to them he was nothing more than a loose end.

'The others,' said Lola, 'where are they now?'

'Dead,' said Lemar pushing away his plate, his eyes focused on Lola. 'I'm the last one alive, Lola.'

Lola had presumed as much and her intuition had laid her to Lemar Jenkins today, not only to save his life but because he was connected with the bigger picture.

The Order now had evidence that the Hell Fire Club was searching for the lost Oracle of Danu, why their search had taken them to Iraq, Lola had no idea but based on what Lemar had said they stood to gain so much from the invasion of Iraq, not only financially but it gave them unfettered access to sacred locations like Ur.

How all this pieced together only time would reveal. Lola rubbed her head and sat back in her seat.

'You lost your appetite too?' asked Lemar.

'Yes,' said Lola getting ready to leave. 'You'd better come with me, Lemar. It's not safe for you to go back home just yet. One more thing,' said Lola as she reached over and showed him another picture. 'Do these numbers mean anything to you?'

'No not to me, but they look very like co-ordinates or something.'

Lola paid the bill. Lemar was about to protest but she waved it off. She dialled Isaac's number on her way out of the restaurant.

'Irish, where the hell have you been?' scolded Isaac down the line.

'I've been to Harlem, Grant Houses to be exact.'

'You've what? On your own? Girl, are you outta your mind?'

'Isaac I've no time for one of your lectures right now. We're coming into the office. Are you there?'

'Yeah I'm here and who's we?'

'Me and Lemar Jenkins,' said Lola and hung up the phone. Her mentor had some explaining to do.

~25~

A pair of boxing gloves lay on Lola's desk when she and Lemar arrived at the Torch. It had taken almost ten minutes to get him signed in and up into the newsroom. Isaac appeared at the door of his office when he saw them at the bullpen. His expression, which was dark and brooding, was becoming an all too familiar sight for Lola.

None of the other journalists around the booths that made up the bullpen acknowledged her arrival when she looked around them for an explanation but Bill was a notable absentee. Lemar looked at the gloves enquiringly as Lola placed them in her desk drawer and closed it.

'It's a long story,' she explained as they approached Isaac's office. She shut the door behind them and went around the room closing the blinds.

Isaac greeted Lemar congenially and while his tone was welcoming and warm Lola could tell he was irate.

'Is this room secure, Isaac?' Lola asked as she closed the last of the blinds, obscuring the three of them from view.

'What do you mean, Lola? What in the hell is goin on here?' He'd called her Lola, which meant she was in trouble.

'Take a seat, Lemar,' offered Lola as she got up and selected a record from Isaac's collection and set it on the record player. Soon the room was filled with the sound of a jazz trumpet singing its sorrowful tune. Happy that it was loud enough to absorb their conversation, Lola sat back down placing the record sleeve on the desk between her and Isaac. She glanced at the Vinyl cover, 'Dizzy Gillespie – Live at the Apollo'.

The table that separated Isaac and Lola expanded as if it were acres and not centimetres that lay between them. Isaac stared at her, his baleful eyes waiting for hers to meet his. Lola lifted her head to meet his accusing look. Isaac's jawbone pulsed in his cheek and she could see that he was trying to compose himself before he began to speak.

'Now,' said Isaac seething, 'you gonna tell me what you're playing at?' he demanded leaning over the table at Lola. 'Have you been going through my private notes, Irish?'

'What?' said Lola in disbelief. 'Going through your notes? What do you take me for, Isaac? I find my own stories, I don't need to steal anyone else's.' This wasn't exactly going as she had expected but Lola could see how it looked to Isaac so for that reason she remained passive.

'Hold up, hold up,' interrupted Lemar, standing up from his seat. 'You're saying you didn't send home girl here to my house?'

'No, I didn't, Lemar. You think I'd send Irish here into the middle of the Grant projects, a week after a major police operation? You think I'm outta my head?'

Lemar looked at Lola and back to Isaac. Lola could hear the questions jingle in his mind and she at the very least owed him an explanation.

'Sorry, Lemar, for misleading you,' she said apologetically. She turned to Isaac now. 'Isaac, I'm sorry but I tried to talk to you about this on Saturday night but you didn't want to know.'

'Was this before or after you got drunk and punched a senior member of staff in the face,' said Isaac, his tone as sharp as a razor.

'Listen, I'm not proud of that, even though he deserved it and the filthy word he was about to use to describe you. I thought I just got in before you did.'

Lemar smiled at Lola. 'You do that sonic boom shit on him too?' Lola give him a stern look urging him to be quite.

'What sonic boom shit?' asked Isaac, his dark eyes cutting through Lola again.

Lola stood up and paced around the office. The music coming from the record had softened and was more upbeat.

'You had better start talking, Irish? What had you rocking up to Harlem like... like...' Isaac stumbled over his words.

'Like what?' said Lola, 'Like Lois Lane – a real journalist?'

Isaac shook his head in annoyance. 'You know what I mean, Lola.'

'Well are you going to let me explain then?'

'Go ahead,' Isaac waved his arm in irritation, 'the floor is all yours.'

'I'm dying to hear what you have to say too,' said Lemar leaning back in his chair and resting his ankle on his knees. 'My day started well and then a white girl knocked on my door and shit just got strange.'

'I was at a party on Saturday at Carl Stein's penthouse, which as you know is on top of the Pierre Hotel. I can't go into the detail but I just happened to find myself unattended in his personal study. I was looking for something he has that belongs to me.'

'You what?' said Isaac rubbing his temples in consternation.

'Isaac, please don't start, I can't tell you, it doesn't concern you or the paper. Anyway, on the desk of his bureau there were a few folders. Being inquisitive I decided to have a look at what was in them.' Lola turned to Lemar now. 'That's when I saw your picture, Lemar. It was stamped Top Secret. It had your name, date of birth, address. I wasn't sure if you were a prospective employee because from the picture and your details I realised that you were military. As I investigated further,' Lola shot Isaac a cursory look as he gave a groan, 'that's when I found the info on this Project Inanna and the numbers that I showed you, Lemar. I'm truly sorry that I deceived you but I needed to know what part you played in all of this. Now, from what you've told me, I think I know what it was they were looking for at Ur and what Carl Stein's interest in the area was. When you mentioned Isaac, you handed me a lifeline but after what just happened we know why Carl Stein had your information and it wasn't because he wanted to give you a job.'

'Why?' asked Isaac. Lola looked at Lemar and back at Isaac.

'Well, when we were waiting on the train, three men approached us on the platform and...'

'Those sonsuvbitches tried to throw us out in front of an incoming train, Mr Kane,' finished Lemar.

'What did you just say? What happened?' Isaac leapt off his seat and paced around the room. 'This is just crazy, are you sure?'

'Yeah, Mr Kane, I'm pretty sure they were trying to kill us,' said Lemar. 'If it hadn't been for Lola and whatever the hell it was she did we'd be sprayed out on those tracks right now.'

'They were Carl Stein's men, one I could identify,' said Lola. 'It's not safe for Lemar to go back to Harlem just yet. He needs to stay somewhere they would never think of looking.' Lemar was about to protest but Lola's hand on his shoulder made him sit back down.

'Lemar, please listen to me,' said Lola taking a seat beside him again. 'You have information that they are willing to kill you over. You need to take this seriously. You have no idea what Carl Stein is capable of and you have no idea who and what he really is.'

'Carl Stein is a snake, a snake that has built his empire on the blood of the ordinary people, but what you are accusing him of, Lola, is crazy,' protested Isaac.

'You're wrong, Isaac, I know him better than any of you. We need to do something with this and we need to play a shrewd game.'

'Chris would never go for this, how could we sell this with no evidence, no facts, we'd be laughed out of the newsroom.'

'I have the screen shots,' said Lola.

'That could have been taken anywhere Lola, and even if we could use it they'd need to know how you came by it. How are we going to tell them you found your way into someone's private office? He'd have you for breaking and entering.'

'Then we get evidence, we get information,' said Lola growing more frustrated. 'We have a first-hand source here in this room.'

Lemar shifted uncomfortably in his seat. 'No way am getting involved in this. I survived four years in Iraq so I could go to college; I'm not getting killed in my hometown. I want no part in this bullshit.'

'You've no choice, Lemar. In case you haven't noticed you're in the middle of it. They just tried to kill you and they won't stop.'

'We'll go to the police, see if we can get those men arrested. There will be pictures on the station's CCTV,' said Isaac peaceably.

'Isaac, don't be so naive, the authorities are no good to us here and even if there are cameras I can guarantee that they didn't happen to work an hour ago. The Hell Fire Club's...' Lola broke off mid-sentence realising what she'd just said, she could have cut out her tongue.

'The who? Why do I feel that you are not being straight with me, Irish? Who in the hell are you?'

Lola sat dolefully with her head in her hands. This was such a mess. She had said too much, given too much away. There was no way she could reveal the Order's secrets, after all they weren't hers to reveal, only to protect.

'That's a complicated question, Isaac. Who and what I am,' answered Lola, lifting her head, 'is irrelevant. There are bigger forces at work here, larger than you and me and Lemar, larger than this city and this paper, larger than the authorities, than the government.'

Isaac sat down now and loosened the tie at his neck. 'What are you saying, Irish?'

'I'm saying this is dark; this is an organisation that controls everything. They create a cloak of chaos but those like me who understand are not distracted by the garment but we are more interested in what it veils.'

Isaac's body was rigid. Lola could see the same disbelief conflicting in him that she had once seen in herself. 'This is some conspiracy bullshit that those whack-jobs down at Liberty Plaza would conjure up.'

'Come on, Mr Kane,' this time Lemar was the voice of persuasion. 'You remember our conversation on the plane home, you been out in Iraq, you know they are not out there for anything other than oil and making money. We put our lives on the line, for our fellow soldiers, we live and we die for our brothers so that a men like Carl Stein can buy up our neighbourhood, can live in the a penthouse in the Pierre Hotel, can own papers, can do whateva the hell he likes.'

Then something struck Lola about her conversation with Jodi the afternoon before the Steins' party. She had felt that Jodi was keeping something from her about Carl Stein so Lola made a mental note to go and speak to the former news journalist, again trusting the current that flowed inside her.

'I know, Lemar,' Isaac was saying. 'I was there and I never want to go back. I will never get that place out of my mind. I got a visit from someone out there, before I left. He told me that it was time for America to know the real truth about why we went to war. I've been sitting on it since then. Not sure what to do with it. Then I just so happened to speak to you on the plane home but how do we tie any of this to Stein?' said Isaac deflated. 'It won't stick.'

'We do what real journalists used to do,' said Lola. 'We investigate. We find the links. We have Lemar, your source and me.'

Isaac rubbed his eyes. The music had stopped playing now, Lola hadn't noticed until they all fell silent. This was only another play in the great chess game for Lola so it wasn't a stretch of the imagination but she had once been where Isaac and Lemar where now so she understood what was going through their heads.

'You can't go home tonight, Lemar,' said Lola. 'You'd better call your mum and let her know. Just tell her you're staying with some friends.'

'If I can't go home, where the hell am I going to go?'

'They've seen you with me, so you can't come to mine, it would be too dangerous.'

'They know where you live too?'

'One of them does,' said Lola regretfully. Lemar looked at her for a further explanation. 'The son, he knows where I'm living.'

'He'll stay with me,' said Isaac.

'That's no good either, Isaac. I have an idea but first I need to speak to Jodi, I think she might be able to help us plus I have to return the dress and shoes. I'll be back in as soon as I can. We can't discuss this with anyone, you understand. I feel like this room has eyes and ears.' Lola's skin prickled as she looked around Isaac's office.

'Now you're really being paranoid, Lola,' chided Isaac.

'Am I?' she said as she walked out the door.

~26~

To the west the sky looked as though it had been smeared with damson jam as the sun set over the city. The low thrum of Manhattan's soundscape mingled and was muted by the sweet air as it ruffled around the boxed peonies. None of the grime and oppressive humidity from the streets below made it this far up. Out on the balcony Alex was waiting for his father to return. He could tell from their earlier exchange that whatever he had wanted to discuss it was urgent.

Alex closed his eyes and thought about Lola. His knuckles whitened from their grip on the balcony rail and his body tensed in response. He shook his head in resistance but it was no use as her name was borne from his tongue as he spoke it aloud. The familiar conflict of love and hate, want and duty tore and clawed at him. Like a chameleon, Alex was skilled at changing his camouflage, but here on the roof out in the open air he allowed himself a rare moment of authenticity.

He heard Maria's soft tread approaching from across the ballroom floor. 'Master Alex, your father has arrived, he will see you in his study.'

'Thanks, Maria.' Alex smiled tenderly. 'I'll be there in a few minutes.'

The maid left him alone with his thoughts once again. Alex watched the last glimmer of sunlight dance off the surrounding high rises as the city's lights began to twinkle and ignite below. All this would be his one day; he just needed to convince himself that he wanted it.

His father was sitting behind a stack of papers when Alex entered the office and he was surprised to find him in such a convivial mood.

'Alex, have a seat, son. I've something to show you.' Alex couldn't help but feel uncomfortable. He never quite knew how much his father could see. Since their last encounter with Lola he certainly had seen a change in his father – while his eyes were still lively and calculating, there was now a hint of uncertainty that had never dared dwell there before.

Carl Stein fought with his phone until he gave up. 'Here, son, do this for me, all this modern technology has me at a loss, I prefer the old ways,' he said surrendering his mobile to his son.

Alex tapped the phone screen and connected it wirelessly to the large screen on the wall. It looked like surveillance tapes from a subway station, the sepia image was distant but clear and Alex had no idea what they were going to reveal.

'It looks like our mutual friend has become quite the young woman and she appears to have become acquainted with Lemar Jenkins,' said Carl Stein ruefully. 'Now what are the chances of that?'

Alex's eye fell on the stack of files. He knew exactly where Lola had gotten the information but of course he couldn't reveal that to his father without compromising himself. He had to hand it to her she made one hell of an investigative journalist.

Alex watched as the two of them took a seat to wait for the next train followed by three men who, even to Alex, looked conspicuous and awkward as they spread out around the couple.

All the while, and under the scrutiny of his father's hard eyes which were polished and unrelenting, Alex remained impassive, but his stomach convulsed. He knew this was another of his father's tests as he poked and prodded him with the needle that was Lola Paige and he almost felt sorry for him as he waited in great anticipation for some reaction, but Alex didn't oblige.

The silence shot up around them as they continued to watch the CCTV footage of Lola and this Lemar Jenkins. He watched on edge as Lola subtly registered the presence of the three white men that had gathered in a wide noose around them. Inclining her head to one side, she considered each of the men before jumping playfully to her feet, taking her companion by the hand.

Carl looked around again excitedly to make sure that he was still watching and Alex understood that the real test was coming up. He could see his father's eyes as they shot sideways falling on him but still he remained emotionless.

Then came the money shot and Alex almost lost it as Lola reached up to kiss the Jenkins boy. He shifted in his seat but he never once took his eyes from the screen watching Lola kiss and fondle this strange man only to be restored to his placid self when he realised that she was only doing it to protect him.

Lola turned her back to lure the men in and just as they made their move she released an unseen force that exploded from the palms of her hands, a force so powerful that it caused the entire platform to shake and the train's electrics to short circuit.

Like water from a breaking damn, the relief poured out of Alex when the image returned and he saw Lola looking out of the moving train at three disorientated men scrambling to their feet.

'Absolute idiots,' said Carl Stein turning around in his chair to face Alex. 'They could have compromised our entire operation.'

Alex couldn't tell what had disappointed his father more, the fact that his men almost killed Lola, denying him the pleasure, or that he hadn't managed to extract a reaction from his son. Alex had passed this small test but he knew there would be others. He had a lot of work to do to convince his father that Lola Paige would not be his Achilles heel.

'They weren't to know that Lola was a valuable asset to us,' said Alex his voice pale and still.

'Indeed, I suppose you're right,' said Carl Stein in a conciliatory tone standing up to pour himself a glass of Cognac. 'Well,' he said swilling the amber liquid around the tulip glass and inhaling its aroma, 'it certainly looks like Ms Paige has risen to the challenge. This is the second time her pyrotechnics have been caught on camera, she is certainly growing stronger and more conspicuous by the minute.' Carl sat back down again, rocking back and forth in his seat. He always did this when he was in a dark mood.

'The old man would never have permitted such recklessness but I suppose he is dead,' he smiled, 'and that means Lola is all ours.'

'Why were they there?' asked Alex ignoring his father's reminder of his role in Arthur Delphian's murder.

'I know why my men were there,' answered Carl, evading the question, 'but I'm more interested in understanding why she was there. What are the chances of Lola Paige being acquainted with an ex-Marine from the Grant Housing slums? An ex-Marine that we need exterminated.'

Carl Stein looked down at the neatly stacked paper files on his bureau and while he said nothing his eyes asked the question.

'You tell me,' said Alex with a dismissive shrug, throwing the question back at his father.

'You don't need to worry about the detail, son,' said Carl with a short smile. 'The boy was assigned to our Iraqi project and he's nothing more than a loose link,' he said with a dismissive wave of his hand. 'But now things have become a little more complicated. My sources tell me that she took the boy to the newspaper and that they spent a significant amount of time with my friend Mr Kane, which further complicates things.' Carl swirled the glass again and inhaled.

'That son of a cotton picker has been hounding me for years but soon I'll be paying his wage so no matter what he has, it will never see the light of day.'

'There's no way that they could link us to this, Father. You've taken all the necessary precautions, I presume,' said Alex firmly.

'I certainly have, Alex. Have you?' said Carl annoyed by the challenge. 'You've made your choice, Son, and you understand what has to be done and you will do it. Do you understand, boy?'

'Yes, Father,' nodded Alex. There was no point in making any excuses. Although he was keeping a close eye on Lola, Alex would have been a fool to think that his father wasn't doing the same on him.

'I don't mind you having your fun, Son, but I just don't want you getting any more confused. I understand that Ms Paige is enticing but it will only make it harder for you to do what you have to do. I cannot have you disgracing me in front of the other members. You are heir apparent and these foolish games with this girl need to stop. She is the one thing that is standing in the way of what we want and once the time comes, she will have to be eliminated, like all the other pieces that no longer serve us.'

'Yes, Father. I won't let you down,' assured Alex.

'I know you won't, Alex,' said Carl, but there was more malice in his father's retort than there was comfort. 'So how are things progressing with Professor Moriarty? You have spent a lot of our money and taken a huge gamble in bringing him here.'

'Slow,' lamented Alex. 'Access is limited to the book. Lola and a Rocha Moone, apparently she is a relation of...' his father looked at him waiting to hear which name he spoke. Alex knew he feared his mother's name and he quite enjoyed the control it gave him over his father. 'A relation of Celeste, an auntie, I believe.'

'Do you think she thinks the book could be the Lost Oracle?'

'I wondered the same thing, Father, but Susie informs me that there was no indication that she had any connection with the book. However, Professor Moriarty has become increasingly inquisitive. There has been one development though and that is early tests have indicated that the skin is not calf velum but that of an elk. Apart from that,' said Alex rubbing his chin in consternation, 'the short time that I've had with it gives no indication that it is the Equinox Oracle that you're after.'

'That is a huge development,' said Carl as if he hadn't heard Alex's last few words, 'that would place the folio right at the heart of the Dé Danann's reign,' he said, his expression brightening again.

'Its magick might not be apparent to you or I,' Carl continued. 'The legends say that its magick is so advanced and complex that it will only reveal itself to she of the Dé Danann bloodline, therefore we seek it because we wish to destroy it.'

'You make it sound like it's a living thing,' said Alex, searching his father's face for the information that he wasn't revealing. 'Why is this book so important to you, Father? What does it contain that you need to destroy?'

'It contains many things and each of those things in some form or another threaten what the Club has built and worked hard to suppress over millennia. We are at the tip of the pyramid for no other reason, Son.' Carl Stein's soft southern lilt gave him all the gravitas and conviction of a soothsayer as he leaned back in his chair imparting this wisdom.

'You see mankind needs to be enslaved to be kept down and dominated, that is how people like us thrive and survive, Alex. Of course we let them chose their jailers and we allow them to decorate their cells, convincing them that they are indeed free. But our current paradigm, despite the thousands of years in its building, is a fragile thing because you see, Son, the human spirit has an innate longing to express itself and to be free. So from time to time you will see it stir and awaken, like those fools down at Liberty Plaza. But our job – our job, Son – is to teach the others who remain asleep that what they seek is not something that exists within them but it's the latest car or house or a line of cocaine, that way we will always be in control.' His father was growing more demonstrative gesticulating as if to punctuate and emphasize his words.

Alex understood the Club's dictum and dogma well but what he couldn't imagine was how Lola Paige and what was left of the Order along with some old book could threaten the Hell Fire Club's vision for humanity, especially since it was almost complete.

'But, Father, why do you fear Lola and whatever is in this book so much?' asked Alex. Instinct almost made him retract his words but his uncertainty was fleeting and he sat upright as if supporting and giving his words buoyancy under the weight of Carl Stein's uncompromising white stare. But without acknowledging the slight his father took a slow sip from his glass and began to explain.

'The little information that I was able to acquire from the old man, Markus, and indeed my own father, says that the scribes of this long lost land, where the Dé Danann were said to have come from, constructed this book. The story goes that each of the four folios were created in the four ancient citadels of the once mighty continent of the Túatha Dé Danann. These were Falias in the north, Finias in the south, Gorias in the east and Murias in the west. Each of the four cities represented one of the four alchemical elements of earth, fire, air and water and as a result once united they housed all the wisdom and knowledge that ever was or ever will be. The Ancient Oder of the Golden Dawn believe that the sacred mother herself breathed on its very pages bringing their words to life. In the beginning there was the word.' Carl Stein stared into his glass as if his words swirled on its golden liquid. 'In the beginning there was the breath,' he continued in pious reflection.

'Some believe that this book, along with other items, was brought to Ireland when the Túatha Dé Danann had to flee their homeland after some cataclysmic world event and while the people of this once great civilization looked for shelter in the corners of the globe the knowledge needed to make humanity great again was contained in this sacred Arcanum.'

'What other things?' asked Alex. Since initiation into the Club, Alex had never heard his father speak so openly, it was as if he had been cautious about revealing these things to him or perhaps it was because until now Alex had never had the courage to ask him.

'Well one such item, the Lía Faíl, you've already seen,' said Carl, 'when we took our mutual friend to Tara. Others include the Spear of Victory, which has been in our custody for the last two millennia, even Hitler wanted to get his hands on that,' he chuckled.

'Then there is the Sword of Light which was said to have been forged in the city of Finias by the smith and alchemist Goibniu, the last on the list is the Cauldron of Plenty, and while many believe that this is a metaphorical term rather than a real physical object, its contents were said to offer everlasting life. These items have been written about since the time of the Sumerians, Egyptians, Greeks and Romans but some believe, and I tend to agree, that the root of all these stories and myths lie in the story of the coming of the Túatha Dé Danann to Ireland.'

'So we know that Lola is one of the Dé Danann?'

'Not only is she one of them, she is the last of them,' a spark ignited in Carl Stein's flinty eyes and Alex knew that Lola wouldn't leave this city alive.

'When Ms Paige's life as Brigid ended,' continued his father, 'the trail ran cold on the Arcanum and the other magickal objects. Well, apart from the Spear, luckily we have it and it is the only thing that can kill her.' This was a revelation to Alex and he desperately wanted to find out more but he knew that if he were to seem too eager his father would pull back.

'It's a pity we didn't have it when we needed it.'

'We did,' said Carl sternly. 'You just got in the way. Remember?' His mouth curled up into a terse smile pleased that he still had the ability to render his son acquiescent. The shame made Alex wilt back into the seat.

'Your dagger?' Alex asked, trying to remain stoic.

'Yes, Son, my dagger. Its blade is forged from the strongest gold and magick and it is the only item that can take the life of Miss Paige.'

Carl swallowed the contents of his glass, their conversation was now at an end.

'Keep an eye on things,' he said rising from his seat, 'and keep me informed. As you know, the Club will be expecting a full debriefing on our findings at the equinox ritual, but I plan to have everything in place by then and what a show we will give them.'

'What brought you to Iraq?' asked Alex, standing on the threshold of the door.

'As I said, Son, this object has appeared in many different pantheons, those of the Babylonians and Summerians included. One theory talked about Ur so we went to have a closer look. Had those towers not come down we wouldn't have been able to get near the country let alone the site.'

Alex could see that his father had not intended to be so candid.

'Besides,' said Carl ironing over his last statement, 'we have archaeologists all over the world working to find this missing Arcanum. If our visiting professor doesn't trust us, it could be he is withholding information and there may come a time when we will need to remove him and his book from the equation.'

'Would you like me to take care of that, Father?'

'Not just yet, that can wait for another time. I have more pressing matters, like Lemar Jenkins and this lot in Liberty Plaza. It has been brought to my attention that they have a private benefactor. Every time I get that old man arrested, he keeps making bail and whoever owns that park refuses to remove them but it's only a matter of time before I find out who is bankrolling them.'

'Anything I can help with?'

'No,' said Carl. 'Your part will come soon so you best prepare for it.'

Alex excused himself and left the room. There was so much he had not known about the Club and the Order, all in equal measure. He had never really asked his father; instead he had been happy to do as he was bidden. Alex paused as he passed the house's large library. Opening the door he stole in and climbed the stairs to the top landing and walked along it until he found what he was looking for – The lost City of Atlantis. Lifting the worn book he sat down and opened the heavy cover. Alex's source had instructed him to read it.

~27~

Lemar sat motionless in the back of the cab disguised in a stranger's coat, hoody and a baseball cap that Isaac had managed to get him from the paper's lost and found storage.

Lola watched as the buildings floated past feeling guilty that he'd been dragged into a dispute that was not his to fight, but then this was nothing new to the former soldier. Lola was lost in thought, her conversation with Jodi before she'd left the Torch building had confirmed her suspicions that she knew more about Carl Stein than she had disclosed. Lola suspected that she had been hiding something but she'd no idea that it would be so close to home and her mind toiled now as it tried to knot together all the little threads that led back to Carl Stein.

Each piece of information was like one tiny fibre and Lola believed that if she could weave them together they would reveal a sordid tapestry that she could use to expose the Hell Fire Club and its leader.

Her gaze remained fixed on the skyscrapers that reflected, with absolute perfection, the deep crimson and red slashes that lay across the evening sky but Lola's eyes found no beauty there because they craved the comforting hues of home. The myriad shades of green in the trees and grass, and the blues and greys of the sea and clouds. She was so tired of mirror and steel and the rigid concrete and iron.

Nem nglas, muir mas, talam cé. The voice that whispered these words of comfort were not her own but a direct response to her soul's longing to be back in Ireland. Nem nglas, the blue sky, muir mas, the beautiful sea, and talam cé, the present earth. Her bones and flesh and pumping heart missed it all.

'I'm sorry, Lemar,' said Lola, pulling her eyes away from the darkening city and back into the cab.

'Sorry!' said Lemar turning to meet her gaze. 'If you hadn't been there today, I sure as hell wouldn't be sitting here going to wherever it is you're taking me. I don't know what you did back there; I don't think I want to know. God knows I seen some crazy shit out in Iraq, but I ain't never seen anything like what you did. All the same, I owe you my life so the way I see it is you have nothing to apologise for.'

Lola's tired eyes searched his, she knew he was right, she had saved his life on this occasion but what if she wasn't there the next time that Carl Stein's men tried? She forced the thought to the back of her mind, bidding her doubt to rest, even if uneasily. She would just have to work harder to ensure that Lemar remained safe.

'Where we're going now,' she smiled at Lemar, 'it's rough but the weather has been good and you'll have somewhere to sleep and something to eat tonight.'

'Rough,' said Lemar, a wry grin curling his full lips. 'You've seen where I'm from and you know where I've been. I think I can handle rough.'

'There's a man called Prospero and he's going to help you,' said Lola. Of course she'd no idea if Prospero had returned to the camp; the few times that she'd been able to make it down he still hadn't turned up.

The taxi pulled up to the side of Liberty Plaza and Lola paid the fare, her eyes scanning the sky above until she found what she was looking for. In the falling dusk it took a while for them to locate it but there was a little patch of sky to the left of the park where the air and light wavered around an unseen edge of the veil giving off an iridescent glaze that allowed her to trace the rest of its border.

As she made her way through the encampment to Prospero's cardboard shack, Lola immediately knew that he was back. The mood in the camp had been restored to its vibrant self and her pulse quickened when she saw Hermes lying guard at the front of the gaping brown mouth of the cardboard box.

He barked his greeting and sauntered over to meet her and Lola bent down to pet him.

'Ms Paige,' said a disembodied voice from within. 'I thought I told you to stay clear of here for a while.' There was no animosity in his tone as Prospero emerged from his shelter with the New York Torch folded under his arm.

Deep welts the colour of ripened plums spread across his left cheekbone and travelled up to his eye which was bloodshot and swollen. He leaned on his staff and Lola noticed the yellow bruises on his wrists and forearms where he'd tried to protect himself.

'What happened?' cried Lola. Although she'd only met Prospero she couldn't shake off the familial feeling she had towards him. She reached out and touched the aubergine skin of the old man's creviced face. 'Who did this to you?' she demanded covering her face with her hands as if to wipe the distressing image from her mind. 'Did they do this while you were in custody?'

'Oh it's only a bit of bruising,' said Prospero retreating from Lola's outstretched hand. 'Edel and Mary have swathed me in every unction under the sun and nursed me well, no need to fuss, Ms Paige, I'm tougher than I look.'

'What precinct did they have you in?' Prospero looked now towards Lemar and back to Lola waiting to be introduced.

'The 7th precinct, Mr...'

'Sorry, Prospero,' said Lola, regaining her composure. 'This is a friend of mine, Lemar Jenkins. Lemar this is Prospero.' The two men shook hands while Lola gave Prospero the abridged version of events.

'Let's just say that Lemar has come under the attention of Carl Stein and he needs some place to stay, just for tonight, just until I figure out my next move.' Prospero considered Lola for a moment.

'So you decided to bring him here, right in front of Stein Corp and you thought he would be safe?' Lemar turned to where Prospero's staff pointed at the colossal black and golden building whose shadows in the falling sun invaded the camp. 'You could be smarter than you look, Miss Paige,' said Prospero shaking his head. 'Please come and join us, Lemar. Have you eaten, son? You're very welcome here at Liberty Plaza and you're more than welcome to share my deluxe penthouse with me and Hermes here, it's dry and it's warm.'

'Thank you, sir, I've slept in worse.' Prospero guided them towards the camp's kitchen and Lola let Lemar go on ahead hanging back so she could speak to Prospero privately.

'Are you mad with me for bringing Lemar here?' started Lola. 'I'm really sorry about what happened before, I phoned almost every precinct to try and find you and I called here to see if anyone knew where you might be but it's like finding a needle in a haystack in this city. I just couldn't control it,' continued Lola in earnest. 'That policeman was about to crack your skull open, I couldn't let that happen but now it looks as though I've made things even worse, for you and for me.'

'Don't be ridiculous, Ms Paige. I like my head the way it is so I'm very grateful that you were able to protect it,' said Prospero, skilfully omitting the particulars of how Lola had helped him that night. 'If the young man is a friend of yours and he needs help he'll get it here, but may I ask why has he come to the attention of Carl Stein?'

'Well...' Lola thought about this for a moment and her eyes found the veil again as if that was the only confirmation she needed that Prospero could be trusted. 'He's a former Marine,' said Lola looking awkwardly at the ground, 'and he was based in Iraq for the last four years. He's left the military and he's due to start college in the autumn,' said Lola skilfully dodging the question.

'That's all very interesting,' said Prospero winching as his mouth widened into a grin, 'but it doesn't explain why he is in danger. So why is he in danger, Miss Paige?' Lola was about to make an impulse judgement and prayed that she wouldn't regret the loosening of her tongue.

'Prospero,' she said stepping closer to the old man her expression serious. 'What I'm about to tell you has to remain between us.' Prospero gave her a sharp look, as though he was offended by the suggestion that he couldn't be trusted.

'Let's just say I'm good with secrets, Ms Paige,' he said curtly. Lola looked at the patchwork of bruises on the old man's face and had no doubt that he was. She hoped that he could keep hers as safely as the others he held.

'Well, I'm just piecing things together myself, there are so many threads and strands to this, so many little connections and I'm trying to tie them all together so that I'll see the bigger picture. I know it's all connected but it's so frustrating...'

'That's usually how it works, Ms Paige. As Sherlock Holmes said, it's all about the trifles, the small things. A chance meeting, a fleeting connection, a small piece of information that leads you to where you're meant to be. That is life and there is no such thing as coincidence, Ms Paige, we are all on our path and we learn something from every experience and every encounter. Each of us are connected in the most beautiful of ways, some connections can be seen and others are yet to be revealed.'

Lola couldn't doubt Prospero's logic after all she'd found Lemar because she'd gone searching for the Cube. Lemar knew Isaac Kane. Isaac Kane had arranged an interview with Carl Stein and that's how she had met Prospero. She could go on and on.

'So, Miss Paige, let's get to the point,' said Prospero gently. 'Why have you brought this young man here?'

'Well firstly,' said Lola, 'I know he'll be safe here because of the veil,' her eyes reached up to the sky, which glowed a deep purple and pink, almost like Prospero's battered face. 'I know it helped me the day I was in the Stein building, the day I took the nose bleed. I know what you really are, Prospero.' Lola said the name in a way that insinuated that she knew it wasn't the man's real name.

'I don't know what you're taking about, Ms Paige.' Although his expression and tone never altered, Lola sensed a slight tightening in the old man's bones as if he feared what she was about to say.

'Listen, I know why you are named Prospero,' said Lola undeterred. 'I know the effect you have on this camp and what you bring to it. It's magick,' she said giving him a knowing nod but still his face remained impassive.

Lola was beginning to panic a little, fearing that she was way off the mark but she couldn't turn back now, she had gone too far to backtrack so with all that was in her she continued.

'I know,' she said her voice pleading now, 'because it's in me too, as you've seen for yourself. Listen, I don't expect you to talk about it; I understand some secrets are not ours to tell. What matters is that we are on the same side.' Lola stopped to look at him, trying to see him, but it was almost impossible.

'We are on the same side, Prospero?' said Lola her voice searching for some reassurance. 'All I want is a yes or a no.' Lola tried to sound assertive, but there was an unease in his eyes that made her fear she'd said too much.

'Yes,' he smiled finally, 'it would seem we are, Ms Paige.'

'Carl Stein has made an attempt on Lemar's life already, I know that he won't stop at that, he's used to getting his own way.'

'Lemar will be safe here for a while, but the young man, I'm sure will not want to stay here indefinitely. You said he lives with his mother, no doubt she will be worried about him.'

'I've already told him to contact her and let her know that he is safe and staying with friends for a few days.'

'Will she buy it?' asked Prospero with a sharp intake of breath as if he'd been struck in the ribs.

'She works nights at the hospital so that may gave him some grace until I figure out what to do and how to help him.'

'Well this is a start, Ms Paige. Men like Carl Stein think that Lemar is expendable and that if he were to shuffle off this mortal coil that the world wouldn't notice. The sad thing is, he's right, so perhaps what we need to do is make sure people know all about Lemar Jenkins, who he is and where he's been. It would certainly make killing him in broad daylight a bit more difficult.'

'That could be an idea,' said Lola, the solution already beginning to form in her mind. 'Perhaps I could write a piece on him for the paper, or get Isaac to do it. They'd need an angle though,' said Lola, her mind pacing from one idea to the next.

'Well I'll leave that for you to figure out, after all you're the journalist, Ms Paige.'

'I'll think of something,' said Lola as they re-joined Lemar.

'So, Lemar,' said Prospero placing his hand on the young man's broad shoulders, 'Lola tells me you're ex-military. Well, we'll have plenty of work for you here at Liberty Plaza, you can earn your cardboard box and food for the next few days,' he smiled.

The three of them sat down with the rest of the large group and tucked in to their evening meal. Campfires, which were forbidden by the city authorities, began to crackle and ignite in little pockets around the small park warming the faces of the protesters who were happy to enjoy the heat.

As they settled down to their fish and vegetables, Lola could hear the strings of a guitar begin to sing and whirr as its owner tuned it. After plucking and refining the musician seemed satisfied and finally broke into song.

The chattering stopped immediately as the people listened to the melody of the guitar's strings and the singer's raspy voice. When the first line of the song issued from his mouth Lola's awareness moved across the busy street to where Stein Corp sat in darkness.

'Come you Masters of War, you that build the big guns, you that build the death planes, you that build all the bombs. You that hide behind walls, you that hide behind desks, I just want you to know I can see through your masks.'

As the singer continued the gooseflesh on Lola's arms migrated to the back of her neck. Not one sound could be heard only the man's voice and the determined thrum of the guitar cords.

'You've thrown the worst fear that can ever be hurled,' he continued, 'fear to bring children into the world.'

Lola looked at Lemar Jenkins and she could tell from the sorrow in his eyes that he too felt the writer's pain. She wondered what horrors this young man had to see and endure all because he wanted to go to college. He'd survived four years at war and now his life was once again on the line because of some other faceless rich man. The thought brought tears of anger to Lola's eyes and as the song drifted on she let them come.

'Let me ask you one question, Is your money that good? Will it buy you forgiveness? Do you think that it could? I think you will find when your death takes its toll, all the money you made will never buy back your soul.'

As the song finished, the city's acoustics drifted back into the camp again and Lola wiped her tears away with the back of her sleeve while Lemar ate on in silence, his mind far from Liberty Plaza and New York City.

Lola wasn't so hungry anymore. After giving Hermes what was left on her plate, she gathered her things to go.

'It's time I was getting home, I've so much to do tomorrow,' said Lola hugging Lemar goodbye. 'I'm so sorry about all this but I'll fix it, I promise.'

'None of this is your fault, Lola; there ain't nothing to fix. You don't owe me anything, girl. Besides I don't mind chillin here with Pops for a while. He seems cool, I'll be alright.'

'You will,' said Lola, 'you'll be safe here. I'll see you both tomorrow.' Hermes let out a bark. 'And you too Hermes, how could I forget you,' said Lola bending down to ruffle his coat.

Prospero walked Lola to a waiting cab. 'Please be careful, Ms Paige. I know you can look after yourself but this city has eyes everywhere.'

'I know,' said Lola. 'I carry their lead stares every day.'

'Indeed, Miss Paige,' said Prospero. A deep sadness had settled in his eyes as if some conflict was playing out behind them. 'The true method of knowledge is experiment and that is often the hardest road.' Prospero smiled mournfully and, denying Lola the opportunity to reply, he closed the taxi door.

Lola sat bemused, what are the chances she thought. Prospero is a Blake fan. The revelation served to fortify her certainty about the old man. She knew it was foolish to see this as a reason to trust Prospero; after all even Carl Stein could quote the finest poets and playwrights. She knew what was happening, the story that she was creating in her mind. He was old, he was knowledgeable, he had a beard, and he possibly was familiar with magick.

Lola chastised herself. He wasn't Arthur, nor could he ever replace him. She needed to be guided by her discernment and not her heart. When the taxi finally arrived at Princes Street Lola's feet barely touched the pavement as she ran in through the door and up to the apartment keen to see Rocha.

'Here she is now, Aíbgréne, I'll have to go.'

'Rocha, no! Don't hang up. Please, let me have a word with her.'

Lola didn't notice the angst in Rocha's face when she took the phone from her. 'Aíbgréne,' said Lola slightly out of breath from the short run from the taxi to the elevator.

'Lola, where the hell have you been?' rounded Aíbgréne, shocking Lola. 'Rocha is out of her mind with worry.' Lola looked around for Rocha who was filling the kettle in the kitchen and while she couldn't see her face she could see her aura and the grey mist was only now beginning to return to its usual colours.

'Aíbgréne, will you just shut up a minute,' said Lola, 'and listen to me. This is urgent.' For once her friend did as she was told. 'First of all,' said Lola, 'how is Celeste?'

'She's good,' said Aíbgréne, her tone a touch cold. 'She's doing much, much better. Being here has really helped her and your parents have been fantastic.'

Lola spoke to her parents almost every day so she knew that Celeste was making a speedy recovery but her encounter with Carl Stein, by all accounts had taken its toll on her.

'Good, good,' said Lola. 'Is Daithí with you?'

'Yes,' said Aíbgréne. 'Why?' 'Could you put him on?'

'Yeah, but what's going on?'

'I take it Rocha has filled you in on the book; well there have been a few more recent developments. I don't have time to go through everything now, Aíbgréne, but I need Daithí to help me out with something.'

'What do you mean more recent developments, Lola? I want to know what's going on.'

'Please,' pleaded Lola. 'It's been a long day and I've had to take in a lot of information, not to mention foil an attempt on my life.' This was the wrong thing to say as Aíbgréne became apoplectic.

'What?' she wailed down the phone. 'Lola, you need to come home. Do you hear me? You need to come home. I've seen it all. I've dreamt it. I didn't want to tell you that but I've seen it.'

'Seen what, Aíbgréne?'

'Your death.'

Lola hadn't expected to hear that, she stood stunned on the phone. 'My death.'

She could tell Aíbgréne was crying now. 'I'm sorry, Lola, I shouldn't have blurted it out like that, but they wouldn't let me tell you the real reason why I was so against you going to New York. I had a dream that you were laying on a stone table with your arms all cut open and it was him that killed you.'

'Who?' said Lola, her mind a shroud of mist. 'Who?' she asked again. 'Carl Stein?'

'No' said Aíbgréne. 'Him.'

Lola knew whom she meant and while she was disturbed by her friend's revelation she had no time to get side-tracked by whatever Aíbgréne believed she had seen.

'Lola?'

'I'm still here, Aíbgréne. Not every dream is a prophesy,' said Lola trying to reassure herself as much as Aíbgréne. 'Now I really need to speak to your husband. I don't plan on dying out here, besides my powers are getting stronger by the day.'

But Aíbgréne couldn't be reasoned with. 'Lola, please just listen to me.'

'Perhaps it's time you listened to me,' said Lola sharply. 'Perhaps it's time you trusted and believed in me.' Daithí came on the phone his soft voice disarming Lola.

'Is everything okay?' Lola choked up. She could hear Aíbgréne sobbing inconsolably in the background.

'Yes, Daithí, it's good to speak to you. Listen I need your help with something.'

'Yeah, Lo, anything.'

'I need you to get a pen or pencil and a piece of paper and write these numbers down. We think that they may be coordinates but something tells me that there's more to it, something that I'm not seeing. I know with your expertise in the deep web that if there is something to be found that you'll uncover it.'

'Okay, Lo, go ahead.'

Lola read out the series of numbers and letters. She could very well have looked up the sites on her own but she understood that Daithí was capable of finding out more than she was. It was clear that it was all connected in some way. There was a series of numbers and letters on the screenshot. Lola just needed a few to get the ball rolling. 'The first one,' said Lola, 'is 29.9792 degrees North by 31.1342 degrees East. The next one,' her eyes scanned the page and picked another series of numbers at random, '53.4441 degrees North by 7.0645 West.'

'I've got it,' said Daithí, 'what's the next one?'

'30.96250 degrees North by 30.5745 East,' said Lola, her eyes already moving on to the next one. '38.483182 degrees North by 22.4993 East, 30.96250 degrees North by 30.5745 East and I'll give you one more for luck.'

'Okay,' laughed Daithí, 'go ahead.'

'It's 54.1959 North by 6.1952 West.'

'I'll have a look at these, Lola, and see what I can dig up. If you want a more thorough check it might take a couple of days.'

'That's no problem. Don't contact me via my email or my new work number, if you call this landline, it should be safe enough.'

'Of course, Lola. I see I've taught you well.'

'Yes,' laughed Lola. 'Thanks, Daithí, and give your wife a hug from me please. I'll speak to you soon.'

'Daithí,' said Lola just as she was about to hang up, 'I almost forgot, could you check out Project Inanna and Operation Babylon. In the files I saw they were marked Top Secret. See if you can find anything on this as well.'

'I'll see what I can do.'

'Thanks,' said Lola. She hung up the phone and went to find Rocha. She thought about Aíbgréne and felt guilty for being so abrupt. Lola thought about what her friend had said but it was only a silly dream she told herself.

'Well by all accounts you've had a very busy day, Lola. Come and sit with me,' Rocha patted the seat beside her for Lola to sit down.

'I don't know where to start, Rocha.'

'Where all adventures start, at the beginning would be a good place,' she smiled.

Lola didn't hold back, she explained it all to Rocha who didn't once interrupt. She told her about Chateau Le Ciel, she told her about Alex's visit and Aíbgréne's vision, although Lola figured that Rocha knew about it already.

She told her about Lemar and Harlem and what happened at the subway station and why she dropped him off at Liberty Plaza. When she was done talking the weight of all that she'd been carrying had lifted from her body, the freedom of that honesty and sharing left her feeling light and hollow.

'Well,' said Rocha when Lola had disseminated all the information. 'That's quite a busy weekend and few days you've had, Lola. Now normally I would scold you for being so silly and reckless by going to Carl Stein's house but your investigations have saved the life of a young man, so on this occasion, I won't. As for the coordinates, Daithí will be able to help you and I've no doubt that the information, once we establish what it is will be useful to us. However, there is still the small matter of your dalliances with Alex Stein and your partial disclosure to this Prospero character. You say you think he could be a member of the Order? Well if he was I'm sure I would know about it, Lola. This concerns me a little.'

'He knows magick, Rocha, I could see the veil over the camp, it's the same as the one over Brook Mill Manor and I know it certainly helped me when I emerged from Stein Corp almost unconscious. Prospero said himself that Carl Stein had been trying to evict them.'

'Hmmm,' said Rocha remaining unconvinced. 'If this Prospero knows magick, Lola, I think I need to pay a visit to Liberty Plaza and meet him for myself. What were the words he spoke to you that made you think he was a member of the Order?' Lola thought back to the first day that she met him and while her memory was still a bit foggy from the attack she remembered his words to her very clearly.

'He basically spoke the Order's maxim: what lies within, reflects without. Those are Her words and the words that activated the portal at Tara and opened up the Cube. I spoke them in Gaelige but I've never heard anyone else using them. I can't describe it, Rocha, but I trust this old man. There is something about him.'

'And did he admit that your suspicions were correct, did he confirm any of this to you?' asked Rocha gravely.

'Not exactly,' admitted Lola.

'Not exactly,' pursued Rocha. 'What did he say?'

'Well,' admitted Lola gingerly. 'He denied any knowledge of magick but he didn't get the name Prospero for nothing.'

'Only time will tell, Lola. Let's hope he is a bit more honourable than his namesake. But I think you might be right. The information that you've acquired from Jodi and Lemar as well as what we know about the book, it could all very well be linked.'

Rocha draped her green cotton shawl over her shoulders and settled back into her seat as if she was about to begin a lecture.

'The stories,' began Rocha, 'which have been handed down through the oral tradition for millennia have foretold of one book that was penned in the four cities of the Túatha Dé Danann. In the city of Falias in the north and in communion with the element of earth, the scribes of that great city imparted their knowledge about our sacred land, the energy ley lines and meridians. While in the southern city of Finias and through the element of fire, they filled the book with the knowledge of creation, alchemy and magick. In the east lay shining Gorias and guided by the element of air the scribes filled this great book with philosophy, writing and perfect wisdom. The port city of Murias lay in the west, and here, commanding the element of water, they filled the book with their acute knowledge of healing and rebirth.'

Rocha pulled her shawl around her closer as if she could feel the wind that moved across the waves of Finias.

'This one book,' she continued, 'along with the Cosmic Cube is said to have been the cradle for the first and last golden civilization this planet has ever seen. It is said that the book was passed down to the head of the house of Danu and that the very breath of the divine mother gave it her life eternal. Some believe, and Arthur was one of those people, that the last custodian of the great Arcanum was Brigid. It is thought that before she passed out of this world that the book was separated into four folios and distributed to her Guardians who each went their own way.'

'What did you call this homeland of the Dé Danann?' asked Lola. 'It says they came to Ireland in the high air, but where did they come from and where did they return to?'

'That is the million dollar question, Lola. Some believe they came from Atlantis but there are so many theories and so many stories that it's hard to know. The Lost Oracle is said to detail all of this and more that's why it is so coveted.'

'Atlantis,' snorted Lola, 'isn't that just some myth?'

Rocha laughed and shook her head. Her tone wasn't sharp but one of tender bemusement. 'Myths and legends are the perfect way to preserve a truth, Lola. Just because it's a myth doesn't make it untrue.'

'Like the Book of Kells?' said Lola.

'Exactly. It certainly fits the description and the fact that you could communicate with the book leads me to believe that it is what we have been searching for. Ogham has long been associated with the Ancient Order of the Golden Dawn,' said Rocha, but before she could finish Lola interjected.

'That reminds me,' said Lola cutting Rocha off, 'your email.'

'Yes, indeed, Lola. Well it's actually very interesting based on what my colleague found. As I just said Ogham has been used since the infancy of the Order. It is a very interesting form of writing with an alphabet based on different trees, each with a special meaning and attribute that only the initiated can decipher. The language is written in linear forms.' Rocha found a notepad and pencil on the nearby coffee table and began to draw lines and slashes on the pink paper.

'Using a series of lines, dots and slashes,' explained Rocha continuing to demonstrate, 'each of the outlines denotes a certain word or group of words. This was the language of the Dé Danann and certainly a means of communication amongst the early Guardians of the Ancient Order of the Golden Dawn and that is exactly why I think that she has chosen to communicate with you in this way.'

'So what about what it said?'

'Well,' said Rocha, 'as I explained in the email Professor Cartwright was able to translate the small bit of what you picked out and as you know from my email it read My daughter, my light. The great even time will soon be upon us.'

'Now it doesn't take a genius to figure out who the daughter of light is,' Rocha nodded affectionately at Lola, 'but Charles said that there was another word in the text that he hadn't noticed until he looked again which for me shed some light on the second part of the translation. I had thought about what "the great even time" was and when Charles gave me the rest of the translation it suddenly became clear to me. It was a term that I had never heard before: Cleamhnas Naofa,' said Rocha with perfect pronunciation.

'Scared Marriage,' said Lola unmoved by her knowledge on the matter.

'Yes,' enthused Rocha clapping her hands. 'Yes. You know about this?'

'I'm sure I do, well I'm sure she does but sometimes I remember what she remembers, but I don't know what that means for us or for me.'

'Well, it's only a theory mind, but it's one that brings me back to Alex Stein and you.' Lola's face flushed again, thinking about their union, she wasn't exactly sure it was sacred.

'Well I had never heard of the term in Irish before, Lola but I am very familiar with the principle in Greek, the Hieros Gamos. Basically this is sacred marriage played out through the sexual unification of the Female/ Goddess energy and the Male/God energy and when the two are unified we will have balance and order in the world, so the theory goes.'

'And you think Alex and I are this Cleamhnas Naofa or Hieros Gamos?'

'Well, yes. I mean you're both two sides of the same coin, you're the light and he is the dark, for want of a better word. Like the equinox we have perfect balance and perfect union,' said Rocha.

'I don't think it goes that deep with us, Rocha, it's more of a physical thing.'

'Nonsense, Lola, that may be what you tell yourself, but I don't think either of you believe that for a second, your bond, your hunger for each other is as old as these words. What do you remember of Alex in your previous life?'

'Alex?' asked Lola. 'Nothing. I remember nothing of him.'

'What do you remember of your death?'

'She's never shown me that. I get fragments in my dreams every now and then but nothing substantial, like smoke, by the time I'm awake, it's gone.' Lola searched for the memory. 'I remember the forest. I remember the Cube, the Sword, and the four Guardians. I remember standing in the Brú in the ever-growing darkness waiting for someone but I never get to see their face, I always wake up.'

'Interesting,' said Rocha as she mulled over Lola's words. 'You need to work harder in your dreamtime to access these memories and her knowledge, your knowledge. I know that it might be easier for you to think of Brigid as someone separate from yourself, Lola, but she's not, she's you and you are she. Look what happens when you don't resist it. You remember, you save lives.

'Arthur searched for you for a long a time, Lola, initially he thought that Aurora might be Brigid reborn, she had many of your traits and qualities but he soon realised that she was not the one. When she died at the hands of Carl Stein, Arthur blamed himself, because he believed that Carl Stein thought that he and Aurora where the prophesised Sacred Marriage, and when it transpired that she was not the Goddess returned, he decided to cut her loose. She had Alex and moments later he took what was left from her when she was dying. Arthur never quite forgave himself for planting the seed.

'Then he met you and he knew then who and what you were. He watched from a distance until it was time for your schooling to begin, until it was time for the two of you to be reunited. He has been with you many lifetimes, Lola, that is why your bond is so strong and I believe the same for both Alex and Carl Stein.'

'Alex said it himself, he will never leave his father, even after he found out he killed his own mother, he's in too deep. He won't ever choose me. He's already made that decision, just like we all have, Rocha, we've chosen which side of the chalk we stand on.'

Lola continued. 'Carl Stein has been hunting books and ancient sites for the lost folios, we need to secure the Book of Kells. We need to secure Lemar Jenkins and expose whatever it is that's been going on. I need to write something in the paper about all this. Prospero made an interesting suggestion on how we can perhaps help Lemar.'

'Well,' asked Rocha, 'what did this great Prospero have to say?'

'He made a very interesting point. He said that no one would miss a young man from the Grant Projects if he was thrown in front of a train or "accidently" got himself shot. At first I was mad with him for being so rude,' said Lola, 'but then I realised what he was really saying. The media or anyone outside of Lemar's neighbourhood wouldn't care; they would just put it down to gang related violence or an accident. What we need to do is give Lemar Jenkins a voice, a face that would make it harder for Carl Stein or anyone to harm him. I'm working in features for the next few weeks and I think I'm going to write a feature on this amazing young man who was raised by his mother in Harlem, graduated top of his class at High School but couldn't get a scholarship or afford to go to university so he joined the army because they said they'd pay for it. He survived four years in Iraq and now has been accepted into Columbia Law. He's down helping protesters in Liberty Plaza in his spare time.'

'Sounds like you have it all worked out.'

If only she had, thought Lola. Since she arrived in New York she felt like she'd been walking on quicksand, just when she thought that she was on solid ground the earth moved and sank beneath her.

'Earlier when I was with Lemar and Prospero, we were having something to eat and this fella was singing and playing a guitar. I'd never heard the song before but it was about war and those that wage it to line their pockets. Masters of War or something.'

'Aah, the great Bob Dylan.'

237

'Is that who sang it?'

'Yes, many a time we sang it with him,' smiled Rocha. 'It's sad, Lola, that those words are even more prevalent today than when he wrote them in nineteen sixty-three. The military industrial complex has wreaked havoc on our planet, on our lives and we have been complacent in our slumber. But things are changing, people are wakening. Of course they will be ridiculed and slandered and belittled and marginalised but it is happening. The change is here. You can feel it, I can feel it and you can be damn sure Carl Stein and his cronies can feel it. Great Gaia is stirring and we all have our part to play.'

The two women sat in silence because words seemed trivial and awkward things. After what seemed like hours Lola finally got up of the seat.

'I need you to do me a favour, Rocha. Is there any way you could get Professor Moriarty to meet me at Liberty Plaza? We need to secure that book and I can't risk going back. Alex will know for sure that I've been there and he's already suspicious about my interest in it.'

'Of course, honey, I'll get it sorted. I'll text you tomorrow.'

'No texts, call the desk from a landline, not your mobile.'

Rocha nodded her head in agreement. 'You're getting a bit paranoid, Lola,' said Rocha. 'Good,' she smiled, 'it shows your learning.'

That night Lola dreamed she was speaking to Aíbgréne, they hugged and talked and cried. She could still smell her apply scent and when she woke early the next morning, she missed home.

~28~

Isaac Kane was already in work when Lola arrived at her desk. The morning news meeting was just about to start, but she would be working on features for the next few weeks so she lifted her pencil and notebook and made her way to the feature editor's office, which lay at the opposite side of the newsroom.

After an hour Lola emerged beaming from ear to ear, she'd gotten the go-ahead for the feature on Lemar Jenkins and she planned to get to work on it straight away.

She called Erin to see if she was able to come take his picture later that evening and made a mental note to go and speak to Jodi again. She sent the fashion editor an email but first she needed to speak to Isaac.

He could see her coming through the glass front of his office but he made no attempt to acknowledge her presence. Lola shuffled awkwardly outside the door, waiting to be called in. He was writing something in a black notebook, once he'd finished he locked it in his top drawer and beckoned her to come in.

'Irish. How'd your meeting go over in features?'

'It went well, I've got my first feature to write up and John said that if it was strong enough, he'd give me a double page spread in this weekend's paper.' Lola beamed. She loved being a journalist, the buzz she got from words, from connecting with people, from researching and learning never seemed to get old.

'That's impressive, Irish, so what's the big story?'

'Lemar Jenkins.' Lola smiled a smug grin, Isaac had been leaning back in his chair and he almost fell over in alarm.

'What? Are you out of your mind?'

'Will you just listen to me for once before you fly off the handle?' Isaac was about to interject again so Lola lifted her things and went to leave.

'Irish. Lola, come here a minute. Sit down.'

'Are you going to listen to me, Isaac? Or are you gonna shout me down, like you usually do?'

Isaac looked at her and a smile crept across his face. 'I don't remember being as annoying as you when I interned here. You and that mouth.' Lola reached for the door handle. 'I'm listening, I'm listening.'

'Good!' said Lola taking her seat again. 'Something occurred to me yesterday,' she started. Lola had decided to take the credit for the idea, it was only a small dilution of the truth but a necessary one all the same, and she knew Isaac didn't have much faith in Prospero or anyone at Liberty Plaza.

'When Lemar and I were walking to the train station to come downtown, there were wreaths and flowers along the pavement, just a spot here and there.'

'The sidewalk memorials,' said Isaac.

'Yes, said Lola. 'This got me thinking. This was someone's life, someone's child and they had been struck down in cold blood and inside the block where Lemar lived there was a memorial to young girl on a bed sheet. It was so sad. Then I thought why do I not know about this? Why does the world not know about this? If it happened in Manhattan they would but not in Harlem and it's the same in Iraq and Afghanistan and Africa and Palestine. Children, mothers, fathers, families killed and we never hear about it because our media have an unwritten code that some lives are more noteworthy than others. So when I looked at Lemar Jenkins, when I heard his story I realised he deserves a name, a face, a narrative.'

'And you and your Malcolm X complex are gonna give it to him I suppose. Good little white girl helping the poor black boy.' The acid in Isaac's tone momentarily stunned Lola. It took her a few seconds, as he stared her down, to untangle her thoughts.

'What? Are you actually serious, Isaac?' she said in disbelief. 'You're playing the race card? I'm not white Isaac, I'm Irish. Those signs, if you remember said "No Irish, No Blacks and No Dogs" and where I'm from we're no strangers to discrimination, in case you need a history lesson. Add to that the fact that I was born female makes the struggle as real for me as it does for you. So don't you dare lecture me on struggle, when I've known it since birth. I'm doing this because I can and because it's the right thing to do, which is more than you have done for the community that you profess to come from,' Lola knew she had overstepped the mark again.

'And does Lemar think it's the right thing to do? Oh let me guess,' mocked Isaac, 'you haven't even bothered asking him what he thinks.' Lola couldn't argue with him. It had never once occurred to her that Lemar would be adverse to the idea.

'How did you win four Pulitzer prizes?' spat back Lola. 'What a fraud you are,' she said, slamming the door behind her in a rage. Lola could feel the tears welling up and while she forbade them to come, come they did. Instead of returning to her desk she walked straight through the newsroom and out towards the garden.

The tiny square of grass and trees may as well have been the Hill of Tara itself, as she threw off her shoes and stood on the small tuft of grass. She took a deep breath and allowed the earth beneath her feet to centre her.

Her feet and skin and cells registered its sweet song, as the tension fell away from her body, section by section. Calm now, Lola's mind struggled to understand why Isaac was so sore with her. The grass moved between her toes and she could smell the soil beneath. The sun filtered dim and light behind her pale eyelids. She couldn't stay long, she'd have to get back to her desk and start the story.

Lola decided that perhaps Isaac had been right. She really should have asked Lemar first before she proceeded. She'd bring the article with her tonight and show it to him. If he wasn't happy, she'd can it.

On her way back into the newsroom, by the coffee station, she almost collided with Jodi. 'There you are, Miss Paige. I came down looking for you, Isaac said you'd just gone out.'

'Did he now,' smouldered Lola. 'Did he tell you he was the reason I went out?'

'No, but don't let that old fool get to you. Now what can I do for you, little sista?'

'Jodi, when we spoke before you said that you moved from news before you were pushed because of a story you were covering on Carl Stein.'

Jodi pulled Lola to the side. 'Keep it down, this newsroom has ears and eyes everywhere. What about it?'

'Well your source, could you perhaps put me in contact with her?'

Jodi's eyes welled up and dark pools of water gathered in her ducts. 'I would if I could but the story died when she did.'

'What? She's dead?'

'Yes, Lola, that's what I said, isn't it? Her body was hauled out of the East River two years ago. The paper wouldn't print it. Chris said that there wasn't enough evidence, even though I had a direct first-hand source not to mention a few other girls who were willing to talk off the record. The police said it was suicide, but Lucy was my best friend, my roommate. There is no way that girl took her own life.'

'Did you get an autopsy report? Were there any marks on her body?' Jodi eyed Lola suspiciously. 'I'm looking into something similar,' lied Lola with a faint smile.

'Her arms were cut on the inside down the main artery, which the coroner deemed compatible with suicide.'

'Was she black or white?'

'What's with all the questions, Lola?'

'It's a long story but let's just say I covered a similar case at home, last summer, when the Steins were in Ireland.' Jodi's eyes widened but she didn't offer up her thoughts to Lola.

'White, long blonde hair, about 5'9. She was a model, but smart and kind and funny. She had been with Carl Stein a while and said he belonged to some club and that he was into some freaky shit. She said there were others and even gave me names but when I went to follow this up there was no trace of them. It was as if they'd vanished into thin air.'

Lola felt frantic now, this was one way to get to him, if she could link Carl Stein with these women, dead or alive, she could at least publically discredit him. She didn't have much in her arsenal, but she could certainly try and tarnish his much-polished public persona.

'Did you look into any other deaths that fit this profile, Jodi?'

'No. I was pulled of the story, it was cut and then when Lucy turned up dead, I'd just had enough. Chris said that there was a job going upstairs so I took it.'

'Did you discuss this with Isaac? What did he say?'

'Isaac was in Iraq, Lola, earning his fourth Pulitzer. I was a black woman in a predominately male white newsroom, what chance did I have?'

'What precinct did you deal with?'

'The seventh. Everything is there, Lola, all the case files. You think there were others?'

'I don't know for certain but I think there are and if I can find them, we may have something.'

'You know he paid for everything for her. Her apartment, clothes, jewellery, he treated her like a queen. He even had the audacity to turn up at her funeral. There's a darkness in that man, the coldness just radiates off him,' said Jodi shivering. 'Some girls tell me his boy is just the same.'

Jodi continued. 'Lucy told me once that he was very well connected and very powerful. She was afraid to leave him, she said that she had overheard conversations she shouldn't have.'

'Like what?'

'She didn't give me much detail, but it had something to do with September 11th.'

'And you didn't pursue this?' Lola hadn't intended to sound so scathing, she was genuinely surprised by Jodi's revelations.

'Like I said, who was going to listen, I had no one, Lola.'

Lola's head was buzzing as one idea sparked and gave birth to another. The silver threads that connected each point of reference were there, she could feel it but she just couldn't see the big picture for the tangle.

'Do you mind if I try to resurrect this story, Jodi?' asked Lola. She thought it was only right that she ask her permission.

'Go right ahead, Lola, but be warned, they won't let it go to print. I almost lost my job over it. No disrespect but you're only an intern, which may give you a bit more freedom.'

'Thanks, Jodi, and I'm truly sorry to hear about your friend Lucy. I know what it's like to lose someone close.'

'Good luck, Lola. I'll see you around.'

When Lola came back to her desk there was a yellow Post-it stuck to her computer screen with the message Call Prof Moone scrawled on it and a number. Lola called the number and waited for Rocha to answer.

'Rocha Moone speaking.'

'It's me, Rocha, sorry I missed you.'

'Lola, I managed to get speaking to our mutual friend this morning, in the cafeteria of all places and he is eager to meet you tonight. We'll both see you at Liberty Plaza, say around five-thirty?'

'That'll do fine.'

Lola hung up the phone just as her mobile buzzed with a message. It was Erin; she couldn't be at the park until six-thirty. Lola texted back to confirm. After opening up a page on Quark she began her feature on Lemar Jenkins. It had been a while since she'd done any feature writing and she found herself immersed in the freedom it offered. She was able to flex and bend her mind and her words; here on the features page they were allowed to move and breath, free from the rigidness of the news column.

Lola diligently read and re-read the article, making a few amendments here and there. She scanned for spelling and grammar, knowing that she wouldn't catch it all, but that's what copy editors were there for she thought. Satisfied at last, she hit the print button and went to the print-er to retrieve the hard copy. After glancing through she folded it and tucked it into her bag for later.

It was almost three in the afternoon. Outside above the city the grey clouds began to gather in knots ready to burst. Lola thought of all the protesters at Liberty Plaza crouching under thin covers from the rain. On the up side, she thought, at least they'll be able to harvest the rainwater for cooking and washing.

Lola remembered being told during their first week that if they were looking for anything from the paper's back catalogue they could search the archive icon. Gene Rush had said there were over thirteen million articles in total in the digital archives. Lola was unsure what to do, she had thought about asking one of the other journalists, but decided against it. She'd have to learn for herself.

Raindrops streaked down the long windows of the Torch as the heavens opened on the pedestrians and traffic below.

Clicking the browser Lola chose the bottom option, which gave her all articles from 2001 until the present. She typed in the basic search words, suicide, East River, blonde, slashed arms, red dress as she didn't have a headline. The search button rotated for a few seconds and then the page was flooded with article after article.

Lola sifted through them until she found ten different articles spanning over a sixteen-year period that had all the buzzwords. She quickly separated them into individual folders and sent them all to the printer closest to her.

Lifting the pages as they came out she read down the first article. The words she had searched for were highlighted in yellow. Once she had collated everything, Lola took a note of the twelve names.

Already she could see that each of the young women who smiled out at her with varying poses fitted the same bill. Each had worked as a model at some point and each, according to the reports, had the same markings and each wore a red dress.

Lola couldn't believe that the authorities or some journalist hadn't been able to put them together. She looked for a by-line on the articles. Lola looked again, believing her eyes to have deceived her, but there it was in black and white: Bill Ogle, Senior Reporter. Each of the press statements from the police came from a spokesperson at the 7th precinct, just like Jodi had told her.

While Lola's computer was shutting down, she went to the stationery cupboard and picked up a folder for the printouts. Isaac's office door was open; she could see him glancing over at her desk now and then. Lola checked the time again it was nearly four now. Her stomach rumbled begging for something to eat. Grabbing her coat from the back of her chair, she left the office.

Gene Rush gave her a furtive look on the way past checking his watch but he didn't say anything. Lola knew this was because she had been sitting at her desk, working all day. It was still raining when she stepped out of the building and out into the street.

The air was thick and warm and it felt like she was in a green house. The rain hung and hissed in the temperate air.

Lola held her face up to the deluge and it felt wonderful as each droplet bathed and touched her skin. She just stood there in the rain, asking it to wash away all the grey and give her some clarity.

She wished Arthur was still here, she wished Aíbgréne was by her side and for a while Lola felt her loneliness gather around her. She wanted to hug her mum and her dad and fight with Liam. Such a big part of her still lamented for her old life but here she was, an adult now out in the big bad world standing in the pouring rain like someone who had lost their mind.

Lola was soaked through by the time she managed to hail down a cab.

'Liberty Plaza,' she told the driver.

Another message had come through on her phone; it was from an unknown number.

Thanks for the chat last night. It was so good to spend some time with you. Daithí says he has news. Call when you can. A. XO

Lola could only laugh because her meeting with Aíbgréne hadn't been a dream after all.

The taxi pulled up outside Stein Corp. Lola crossed the road quickly to find that most of the protesters had taken cover in whatever ramshackle shelters they had managed to pull together. Some had found heavy-duty plastic to cover their cardboard boxes, but others weren't as fortunate.

The rain was unrelenting and as Lola looked around the drenched holdings she wondered what fire made them sleep night after night in all conditions. Then she realised it was the same fire that had her in this city that made her throw her own life in the mix. It was the fire of truth, the fire of passion, the fire of love.

Lola was surprised to find Prospero on his own. His box had recently been covered with a blue tarpaulin to keep the wind and rain out.

'I see you've had an upgrade,' said Lola slipping out of the rain and talking a seat on a pile of newspapers.

'Yes.' Prospero smiled from behind his book. 'Your friend has proven to be quite an asset. He's only been here for a couple of days and already he's helped us set up a shower cubicle using our rainwater harvester, he's helped us keep what meagre dwelling we have watertight and he's helped the volunteers fix the kitchen stove.'

Lola took a seat. She felt quite shy now that she was on her own with the old man, she was unsure what to talk about and Prospero didn't seem compelled to fill the silence with conversation.

'You like Blake?' said Lola looking out at the slackening rain.

'Yes. He's a fine poet, not to mention illustrator. What makes you ask?'

'You quoted him the other night, before I left.'

'Oh yes, "the true method of knowledge is experience". You know Blake?'

'A bit. A friend of mine was particularly fond of him,' said Lola. Her eyes travelled around the small space. She couldn't believe how much you could fit into a box. She hadn't noticed the stack of books that were neatly piled in the corner of the makeshift room before now.

'Well your friend is a very learned man or woman then,' joked Prospero.

'He was,' said Lola. Even after all this time she still couldn't mask the pain that seeped from within her every time she thought of Arthur and she often wondered had she really grieved for him at all. But there was no manual on how to grieve and no magickal solution that could cure you of its wounds, save time.

'You lost him?' said Prospero looking up from his book.

'I did and I carry the void every day. I seem to feel it more here in this city; the chasm that he left in my life is a void that can never be filled. He left me with so many questions and little or no answers.'

'I can tell that you cared for this man deeply,' said Prospero, 'but more often than not the answers we seek lie within ourselves. We are too quick to look toward an external source, something separate from ourselves for direction and guidance which means that we no longer trust or listen to our own instinct. Your friend may no longer be here but that doesn't mean that he isn't right by your side.'

Lola thought about what he had said for a moment before answering.

'What lies within, reflects without.'

'Exactly,' said Prospero. 'It certainly does, for those with eyes to see and ears to hear.'

'I think I feel him sometimes,' she said. 'I mean Arthur. Sometimes I think he's right beside me and I go to ask him a question or tell him something and then it's like finding out he's dead all over again. You know, I mostly try to block it all out, the pain I mean. I try to block out the hopelessness and the sadness that assails me each time I speak or even think his name.'

'It's called grief, Lola, and it's very natural to feel that way, honouring how you feel is a good thing.'

'It's all for him,' said Lola unsure where all this was coming from and why she felt the need to share it with Prospero. 'Everything I do, it's for him,' she said dolefully, 'and the love I had for him. He give his life for what he believed in but sometimes I wish he hadn't, sometimes I wish that I was at home in Ireland living my life like every other nineteen year old instead of trying to...' Lola broke off.

'Instead of what?' asked Prospero.

'Instead of trying to save the world?' He laughed. 'At the risk of sounding like Yoda the force is strong in you, Ms Paige, your eyes blaze with it. I've known it from the first day we met. Only someone very special and very worthy would react to the Stein Corp building in the manner in which you did.'

'Who are you?' asked Lola.

'I'm Prospero,' he smiled from behind his peppered beard. His face looked like time itself, creviced and weather-beaten. His cheeks were sullen but the excess hair gave it a fuller look. Prospero ran his nimble fingers down the length of his beard, shaping it into a point at the end where it fell on his chest. Lola examined him, but he was giving nothing away. Why can't I see you, she asked herself.

When Lola couldn't see someone's aura she felt a natural sense of unease. In all the times that she had been with Carl Stein, she had never once been able to see his, that was until Erin took the pictures. The photographer was due down later that evening, perhaps that might work again.

Prospero's grey eyes seemed a shroud of mist and cloud as Lola watched them observe her and each time the old man looked at her she didn't quite understand if what she found there was tenderness, sadness or pity for her.

'What is it those eyes of jade search for, Ms Paige?'

'You,' answered Lola truthfully.

'"If the doors of perception were cleansed everything would appear to man as it is, Infinite. For man has closed himself up, till he sees all things thro' narrow chinks of his cavern."'

'Blake again,' said Lola.

'Let's see how faithful a student you were to this Arthur,' smiled Prospero. 'Can you name the poem?'

Lola raised her eyes to the sky, feigning boredom, as though the question itself was an affront to her knowledge. '"The Marriage of Heaven and Hell",' she answered smugly.

'You've read it then?' He had Lola now, she could have lied and said yes, but her face immediately gave her away.

'Perhaps you should, Ms Paige. It makes an interesting read. You can be sure that your friend Mr Stein knows every word of it.' There was a warning in the way Prospero spoke, a point half made or nudged at and it stirred something in Lola that made her agitated.

'I have tried, but it's way too cryptic for me. You know I wish people would just say what they mean and mean what they say. It's exhausting having to dig and plough on your hands and knees through subterfuge and deceit,' she declared.

'Lola,' the name seemed familiar yet strange on his tongue and it caught her attention. 'We don't receive wisdom, we must discover it for ourselves but only after a journey that no one can take for us or spare us.'

Prospero turned to face her again, his gaze made her feel loved and chided all at the same time. His smile was gentle, like his deep chalky voice. He placed both his hands on her shoulders.

'Opposites attract, you understand that?' Lola give him a dark look, but her face flushed a light pink.

'Child, how do we know how good the summer sun feels on our skin if not for the cold of winter? How do we know how beautiful and tranquil the night is, if not for the heat and bustle of the day? Opposites are what bring order and balance, Ms Paige. Opposite does not always mean opposing, sometimes it can mean completion. Like night and day, dry and wet, cold and warm. The tree needs both sun and rain to flourish and after all what is light without the darkness and what is darkness without the light? Together they can weave a graceful waltz but I hear what you're saying, Ms Paige, the waltz has become a Paso Doble.'

'Yes,' said Lola as she thought of Alex and her – or was it Carl Stein she was dancing with? 'But who is the matador and who is the bull?' Before Prospero could answer Lemar popped his head around the corner of the hut.

'I thought I heard you, Lola,' he smiled. His coat was dark with rain and he shook the water off as he stepped into the makeshift cabin.

'Lemar, good to see you. I hear you're fitting in very well.'

The young man smiled at her, his teeth were white and perfect. 'There's someone looking for you, Lola. She's been wondering around the camp taking pictures.'

Lola stepped out of the hut to find Erin pointing her camera at different areas of interest. It was the rainwater harvester that was holding her attention now.

'Lola, this place is amazing,' she said as walked into the hut. Prospero sat with his nose in a book. Lola hadn't realised but he wore reading glasses. They were round and only had one leg, but his long thin nose seemed to keep them on his head.

'Wow!' said Erin when she saw him. 'Sir, you look amazing. Would it be okay if I took your picture? That face.' Lola was quite enjoying herself because Prospero clearly wasn't. He shuffled uncomfortably in the chair.

'Please, sir, it'll take two minutes.' Erin didn't wait for an answer she just started to snap away. 'This is the last,' she said. 'If you just could look at me.' Prospero looked up from his book and the camera flashed. 'Thank you so much. Now, Lola, where is this Lemar Jenkins.'

Lola was caught unawares, she hadn't even had a chance to speak to Lemar yet about the picture never mind the story.

'What about Lemar Jenkins?' he asked.

'Lemar, I had an idea,' said Lola giving him an apologetic smile.

'Did you now? What idea is that?' Now it was Lola's turn to squirm. She searched her bag for the article and handed it to him, hoping he wouldn't flip. 'Now don't go mad at me, Lemar,' she urged. 'Just read it first and if you really don't want to go ahead with it, that's fine. I'll explain later.' Lola nodded her head, hoping he would get her meaning. Lemar didn't speak, he took the page from Lola and sat down and began reading it. Lola ushered Erin out of the hut. The rain had stopped and the camp was starting to come alive again, as more people emerged from their makeshift shelters.

'Holy shit, Lola. You didn't tell me he was so handsome? Is he single?' Erin laughed.

'I don't know, I think so,' said Lola. 'Never mind that. Let me have a look at the picture you took of Prospero.'

'Prospero?'

'Yeah, the old man.'

'What a name, what a face. I could win awards with that face,' she laughed.

Lola lent over her friend as she clicked through the images until she came to Prospero. 'Ah dammit,' said Erin. 'I mustna put on the right filter. Dammit!'

Lola took the camera from her and looked at the picture in question. It was the one where Prospero was looking straight into the lens of the camera. His face looked even more weathered than in real life, Erin had captured every deep crack and drill that time and experience had ploughed into his terracotta skin.

Then she caught a sight of it. 'How do you zoom in on this picture, Erin? Have a look and tell me if you can see anything.'

Erin looked at the picture and then at Lola. 'You don't think that is what I think it is?' Lola nodded her head.

'I think it is. It's beautiful, isn't it?'

Lola looked at the picture again and just above Prospero's head and all around what you could see of his shoulders hung a translucent mist. Its colours were like the feathers of a peacock, shimmering and iridescent blue, turquoise and greens. Every now and then a fleck of deep gold could be seen. It was magnificent. It was the most complex aura that Lola had ever observed and she trusted those colours.

The sound of Prospero's stick hitting the ground made them turn around.

'I'm on dinner duty tonight, Ms Paige, so I'll see you a little later. You and your friend here are more than welcome to join us for some food.' Prospero headed toward the wafting smell of smoked peppers and soup drifting from under the kitchen tarpaulin.

Lemar emerged from his temporary home, his face was like stone, and it gave nothing away. Lola's heart sank, he didn't like it, or even worse, he was angry with her for being so presumptuous. She could hear Isaac's voice in her head, you and your Malcolm X complex are gonna give it to him I suppose. Good little white girl helping the poor black boy.

'Listen, Lemar,' started Lola. 'I hope I haven't offended you, I just thought about what you said, about another faceless victims and your story is a positive one plus if you had a face in the media then you wouldn't be an easy target. I won't run it,' Lola trailed off.

'The New York Torch has actually agreed to print this?' Again Lola couldn't gauge what Lemar was actually was thinking.

'Yes. They have agreed to publish it. My editor in features thought it was a great story.'

Lemar stood and looked at Lola for a while. 'It's really beautiful, Lola, nobody has ever said anything like that about me before, well except for my moms,' he smirked. 'Hell I'm not sure anyone has ever seen me like that before. You think this will help me?'

'I think it will, but I can't be sure,' said Lola uncertain now. 'This will give you a platform, Lemar. You're intelligent, you speak well, you've seen things I never want to see, you're going back to school and even Prospero said you've been an amazing asset down here.'

'It's been great down here. It's another world. To think all this going on in my hometown. These people are talking about the same issues brothers be talking about in Harlem, hell, the same shit we be talkin' about in Iraq and all over the world. I wanna continue to help them in whatever way I can.'

'Then stay alive and finish that law degree.' Lola smiled.

'I'm happy to go with the story, Lola.'

'Are you sure?'

Lemar nodded his head. 'Can I hold on to this, I wanna show my moms.'

'I'll get you a copy of the real thing when it's out.' Lola called Erin over to take the picture.

251

She positioned Lemar beside the rainwater harvester that he had mended and took a few snaps.

'Mr Jenkins, I'll need your cell number, just in case I need to contact you,' asked Erin, winking at Lola when he went off to get his mobile.

Lola shook her head laughing. 'You are shameless, Erin O'Connell.' After they exchanged numbers, Erin give Lola a goodbye kiss on the cheek and headed off to her next job.

Lola suddenly felt hungry and she followed Lemar to where Prospero was serving the evening meal. As she sat down beside Lemar and Hermes to eat, she could see Rocha Moone and Professor Moriarty in deep conversation as they tracked across the camp.

~29~

The orange and blue flames of the fire hissed and crackled when Lemar threw another few sticks into the bespoke brazier. Lola, Rocha and Manus huddled around the small point of heat as the night settled on the city. Dotted throughout the encampment, the various flames of little suns ignited as the protesters gathered in loose groups to talk and read.

Rocha pulled her woollen scarf around her shoulders against the light wind that spread between them. The soft mauve material accentuated her silver hair giving her profile a regal air and as the umber glow wavered and stirred it highlighted how gaunt Moriarty's face had grown. His skin looked looser around his cheekbones and his eyes bore the dark circles of insomnia and restlessness. Seeing him, Lola realised that she wasn't the only person that New York wasn't agreeing with.

Prospero was not at camp; he and Hermes had taken off for a walk after dinner so Lola didn't get the chance to introduce him to her guests. Rocha had been particularly keen to meet the old man but that could wait for another time.

The positive energy fell like silver from the veil above and Lola was relieved to the see that Moriarty was finally beginning to relax. Rocha must have sensed it too because every now and then her keen eyes rose to the darkening sky in search for the silken thread of the veil as it hung and flexed like a fine gauze far above them. She and Moriarty listened intently to Lemar's story about the mission he'd been assigned to in Ur and how

253

he'd ended up at the camp, being kind enough to leave out the part about how he'd actually managed to live long enough to see Liberty Plaza.

'And you think all this is linked to my book?' asked Moriarty, looking at Lola for some explanation.

'Yes,' said Lola simply. 'Professor, I can tell how much you love the book and how committed you are to keeping it safe. What we are about to discuss and the reason I had to meet you here is of the utmost importance, not only for your safety but also for the book's safety. You need to promise me that our conversation tonight will go no further and I mean you tell no one, do you understand?'

'What's this all about, Lola, and why all the secrecy?' asked Moriarty in weary despair.

'Professor,' said Lola, carefully picking her words. 'I know how uneasy you felt about bringing the book here to New York. I know because I saw it with my own two eyes.' Lola paused again to allow her words to settle on Moriarty, hoping he would understand. 'I saw it the very first time we met, back in the airport in Dublin. Your suspicion and concern emanated from you. Let's just say that you have a truly unique connection with this book and that it is deeper than I think you understand. Do you know what I'm saying to you, professor?' asked Lola prudently.

Moriarty didn't answer her but from his pensive expression she could see he was considering her words and what his face withheld his colours expressed.

'Professor, it's my belief that on some level you've always known this connection existed,' said Lola growing more self-assured, 'but I can't quite pinpoint if you've had some experience of this or you genuinely don't understand what it is that draws you to this book.'

Moriarty's face grew paler in the dancing light but his colours ignited in a plume of lapis and cobalt blue and Lola trusted it, she was sure that this was the key to unlock him and to convince him to help.

'It can't be true; it was only a dream, a childish fantasy. No it can't be true,' whispered Moriarty his eyes staring at some unseen memory as if it danced and swayed in the fire's flames.

'What can't be true?' coaxed Rocha gently. 'What is it that troubles you, Manus?'

'When I was about seven or eight,' said Moriarty, his voice brittle and unsure, 'my father brought me to the Long Room at Trinity for the day to see the Book of Kells. My dad, he knew someone that worked in the preservation lab and they were doing restorative work on the document. I remember being so excited when we were lead away from all the tourists to a room downstairs to where the book was being held before it underwent its checks. I can't describe the feeling I had the first time that I laid my eyes on it. It was housed behind a glass casing and I wanted to protect it, to shelter it. After the visit I kept having this dream about a young woman,' said Moriarty searching Lola's pale face for some remembrance.

'She was beautiful with hair the colour of autumn and eyes of green that held such strength and tenderness. I remember she wore a long hooded mantel that had a golden broach on it in the shape of a triple spiral and at her side hung a sword that glowed as blue as a new-born star. For years the dream came to me but then as I got older and became more sceptical of these things, the dreams and the lady faded from my memory until now,' said Moriarty tenderly as a smile curled on the edge of his dry lip.

'Nothing happened again until I was well into my studies, it was my thesis,' he said diving into the dark pool of his memory.

'I'd been working so hard that I couldn't tell day from night. I don't recall how long I'd spent with the book but it felt like I hadn't left it in days,' Moriarty paused for a moment because his thoughts seemed absurd now that he was about to give birth to them by speaking them aloud.

'Manus, you're safe to speak freely here,' soothed Rocha again placing a comforting hand on his shoulder.

Nodding, Moriarty continued. 'For years I convinced myself that it had been a dream but deep down I knew what I experienced that night was not some fantastical imagining.'

'What did you see? What did she show you?' asked Lola gently, trying not to push him too far.

'The truth of the matter, Lola, is that I still don't know, all I remember of that night was these golden forms as they permeated and lifted off the pages. I now understand that those unfamiliar shapes and markings were Ogham and that one glimpse is what has driven my research all these years. It never happened again, well that was until you showed up.'

The uncertainty in Moriarty's voice betrayed him and even if he could have disguised it from them the milky grey that pervaded his aura gave him away. By now Lola had decided that he deserved the truth, however irrational and delusional it might sound to his virgin ears, she believed

255

she owed it to Moriarty. She would offer him the truth and hoped that in exchange he would make the right choice.

'Professor,' said Lola, certain that she was doing the right thing. 'What I'm about to tell you will no doubt make you think I'm a raving lunatic but for the sake of your book and in honour of your own true experiences, I beg you to listen with an open mind.' She paused and took a deep breath.

'Do you believe in past lives, Professor Moriarty?' said Lola, conscious of how bizarre those words sounded. She remembered her own scepticism when she was confronted with the very same words.

The professor snorted nervously. 'I don't know that I do, Lola,' he said with a half-smile. Unabashed by his candidness, Lola continued undeterred, spurred on by his colours.

'When I first met you,' said Lola, 'do you remember? You dropped some papers and I handed them back to you.'

'Yes,' said Moriarty shifting closer to the fire. 'That was my manuscript for my new book, I was reading over it and making some changes.

'Yes, the Equinox Theory,' said Lola. 'We'll get back to that in a minute but first I want to explain what happened to me when I touched you.' Lola explained where she had gone and the fragments that she herself could recall.

'I know that was me in that chamber over five and a half thousand years ago,' said Lola confidently as if she had always known and believed the things of which she was now trying to convince Moriarty. 'How I know, I don't have time to go into that now, professor, but I also believe that you were the young boy in front of me that fateful night and that I was the young woman in your dreams. I believe this is why you have such a connection with the book and I also believe that you were called Manus then too and you were its Guardian and that you still are its Guardian.'

Moriarty sat in stunned silence and for a moment Lola feared that she'd pushed him too far but he didn't lurch for the nearest exit instead he sat in perfect stillness weighed down by his own thoughts.

'It wasn't a dream, Manus, my child,' said Rocha as if she could hear the clangour of his internal conflict, 'it was a memory. Please,' she said reaching out a hand to both him and Lola, 'let me show you. Lemar, perhaps you would be so kind as to keep watch while we're away,' said Rocha her warm grip finding Manus's hand and then Lola's.

'Take a deep breath and close your eyes,' she said. 'What I am about to show you, I hope, will clear away the mist of doubt.'

Lola gripped her soft hands and the city with its tightly stacked buildings and the endless sound of all its traffic disappeared in a spark and she was back in her Temple where she was surrounded by the familiar columns of decorated granite. This time the scene was so sharp that she could even smell the cold and dirt beneath her feet. It made her feel like she was safe, like she was home.

As before, a young man stood in front of Brigid. Lola's eyes were transfixed on the ancient manifestation of herself and she recognised nothing of herself in Brigid, who stood majestic and assured. The spectator Lola's eyes traced around the womb of the Temple to where Rocha stood in a conclave with the others, her long hair was bright and silver and she was dressed in a cloak of deep purple.

'Manus,' Brigid was addressing the young man now. 'Take this octahedron, you understand that you must protect it with your life?' She spoke in her own primal tongue and the lyricism and beauty of how she spoke struck Lola deeply. Lola watched the scene play out before her as the young man called Manus nodded gravely and stepped back into line. Then another stepped forward, an old man this time, and Lola's heart was once again Brigid's and she felt the pain and angst in it as it fluttered and faltered with the deepest sorrowing and Lola knew who the old man was because she loved him too.

Brigid's eyes looked beyond the wisest of her Guardians for a moment, searching the back of the room where Lola stood breathlessly watching and for a second the matching eyes of both women found each other but in that instant the Temple, the Guardians and Brigid were gone. Each of them inhaled deeply as if resurfacing from water and opened their eyes to find themselves once again around the dying embers of the fire.

'Did you see that, Rocha?' burst Lola. 'She saw me! And the old man she gave part of the Oracle to...'

'Who?' urged Rocha. 'Who was there?'

'Prospero,' whispered Lola in disbelief.

'Are you sure?' said Rocha, her brow furrowed in doubt.

But Lola wasn't sure now, the man was old with grey hair swept back from his face and a long grey beard. Perhaps it was the beard. 'I don't know, I can't be sure,' said Lola shaking her head in confusion. The name Brigid had used hung on the edge of her tongue but the more she tried to remember the more the name eluded her.

'Didn't you see anyone else, Rocha? What about you, Manus?'

'It wasn't a dream,' answered Moriarty, confounded by the experience. 'It wasn't a dream,' he repeated over and over to himself.

'I saw no one else, only Manus and you, Lola,' said Rocha her eyes examining Lola's face. Lola sucked in the cool air hoping it would stave off the dizziness. Her head ached and swirled just like when she'd touched Moriarty at Dublin airport.

'How was ya'll's trip?' Lemar looked at each of them with a bemused grin. 'Lola, you're green! Here drink this,' he said, shoving a bottle of water under her nose. Lola took a long drink from the plastic bottle but she wasn't thinking about herself, she was more concerned about Moriarty.

'Are you okay, professor?' Lola asked, handing the water bottle back to Lemar. Moriarty still hadn't spoken other than to say 'It wasn't a dream'. But when he turned to her smiling, relief flooded Lola's body.

'I'm fine, Lola,' said Moriarty. 'For so long I'd doubted myself but you've shown me that I was right all along. This book is special and now I understand why. Before, all I could do was speculate but now I know I wasn't crazy.' Moriarty's face welled up with emotion as he tried to hold back the tears that wanted to escape from his eyes.

'Which leads me on to my next question,' said Lola rubbing her temples. Her head felt like someone was beating a bass drum inside it. 'What is the equinox theory?'

The professor laughed. 'I don't think I really know anymore, Lola.'

'Well, what did you think it was?' she asked winching as another sharp pain drilled at the inside of her skull.

'As I said before, talking about what I'd experienced that night was more than my career was worth, besides I was so tired that I wasn't one hundred per cent sure whether it was real or a dream.'

'What makes you think it couldn't have been both?' asked Rocha.

'Go on, professor,' said Lola. She shot Rocha a terse look. She didn't want a full philosophical discussion on the reality of dreams. Rocha shrugged her shoulders and nodded for Moriarty to continue.

'It was one of the many late nights I spent with her and like I said I'd been working on my thesis back then.' Suddenly Lemar's ears picked up at the mention of 'Her'.

'The book, Lemar,' said Moriarty laughing.

'It may seem a bit strange but I've always seen her as a beautiful woman.'

Lola could fully understand this analogy because that was exactly how she had experienced the book as well. The voice that had called and beckoned her was one of love and compassion. As strange as it sounded Lola believed that the book had empathy, that it had a consciousness all of its own.

'You found yourself drawn to her too, Lola, and now I know why,' said Moriarty, his voice thick with emotion. 'I know that she is part of you and you are part of her. Thanks to you I now understand why I felt so compelled to dedicate my life to her. It was many years ago that she spoke to me and gave me that fleeting glimpse into her beautiful depths. When the letters rose from the page I remember thinking 'what does this mean?' and as if reading my mind she translated them. Like a golden mist the letters spiralled and took form in front of me and what they read was "Equinox". You must understand, Lola,' said Moriarty almost apologetically, 'to a rational scientific mind it seemed ridiculous. I blamed the lack of food and too many late nights spent burning the candle at both ends but still the experience lingered with me. It clung to my mind and wouldn't let go. Eventually I gave into to it and indulged it. I thought that what I had seen was a trick of the light and perhaps lay underneath the existing script. To me that could be the only rational explanation for what I'd seen but the technology that we had at our disposal at the university didn't reveal anything.

'Of course there were other signs in the text and in the legends that I began to research and when our Gaelige professor at the college brought the story of the Túatha Dé Danann to my attention, stories I had heard told around the fireside as a child, some half-remembered truth burned and simmered in me.' Moriarty's dark eyes reflected the teal and saffron flames as they licked the side of the brazier.

'I knew there was something more, something I wasn't seeing. Then the funding dried up and I started to write my third book to try and create some revenue so that I could continue my research. About six months ago, a patron of the Butler Library at Columbia, approached the university provost expressing an interest in the Book of Kells and funding my research. That patron was Alex Stein.'

The name made Lola's very soul twist and writhe but her face remained unmoved as she encouraged Moriarty to continue.

'I've met Alex on a number of occasions,' he said, 'and I must say I always found him very courteous and quite knowledgeable about my work, but after your first visit, Lola, something changed in him. I couldn't quite put my finger on it but I was very unsettled by the way he looked at the book. That sounds silly, doesn't it?' laughed Moriarty shaking his head.

'At first I thought he was getting frustrated with me because all our research, which didn't come cheap, was yielding nothing but as I observed him a bit closer my intuition told me something else was at play.'

'The Steins,' seethed Lola, her voice clear and ringing with authority, 'as you now know from what Lemar has been able to tell us, have been searching for this book for a long time and I fear that Alex suspects that this is the Lost Oracle of my people, the Túatha Dé Danann. But can I ask you again, professor, why the equinox theory?' The title plucked on the strings of Lola's mind because of a half-remembered conversation she'd had with Aíbgréne.

'Initially it was because "equinox" was the solitary word that she offered up to me,' shrugged Moriarty. 'But when I revisited our ancient heritage and culture, looking into our rich mythology and oral tradition, I learned that the equinox was a very important time for our ancestors.'

'It's said that the great Oracle of Danu was born on the equinox when the world was in a state of great balance,' offered Rocha. 'The Order had in their possession a later fragment that tells of the return of the Dé Danann's light.'

'Yes!' said Lola remembering the document that she'd been given by Arthur's solicitor Felix Tenneyson. 'A time will come as blackness falls on the inside of our sacred walls, but lying there as before, will be our Goddess with her blazon core, Only she and she alone through her sacred spiral will lead us home. The Oracle will free us all, as she awakens to the divine cosmic call.'

Lola scrambled to explain her random outburst to the group. 'Those are the lines from an old Irish fragment that I had translated last year. Arthur left it to me in his will. Do you think that this could be what you're talking about, Rocha?' said Lola hopefully.

'It could certainly be, Lola, and that along with the stories that have been handed down through the generations of the Order also mention the Oracle but they tell the tale of the four folios each one from the four great cities of Eirlandis that make up the "Equinox Oracle",' explained Rocha, slipping into her scholarly voice now.

'There could be something in this equinox then,' said Moriarty nodding his head thoughtfully. 'After my experience – well after being in denial for some time,' said Moriarty, 'I was intrigued about the equinox and I soon found that for our ancestors in Ireland and indeed all around the world, this was an essential passage in the process to enlightenment. They believed that all things must die before they can be reborn and that all spiritual ascent requires descent first. The equinox, I soon understood, was therefore a time to discover your own inner light by firstly facing your internal darkness and overcoming it. This is just a very simplistic view but it runs deep,' said Moriarty looking intently at Lola now, whose mind was miles away trying to catch another string that dangled in front of her.

'You know,' said Moriarty with an air of discovery and pride, 'Ireland is like one huge open air temple. I would eventually go on to visit sites with equinox alignments all over the world but my journey started in my hometown in Oldcastle, County Meath,' he laughed, 'who would have thought it?'

'Loughcrew?' asked Lola eagerly.

'Yes,' said Moriarty tilting his head towards Lola. 'I'm impressed.'

'Well I can't take the credit for that...' But Lola stopped herself from finishing.

'As I'm sure you know cairn T at Loughcrew is aligned to the spring and autumn equinoxes, each year the rising sun illuminates the beautiful symbols on the back stone of the cairn. I don't know if you've ever been to Newgrange but there is a similar phenomenon there at the winter solstice each year.'

'Yes,' Lola smiled. 'I know a little bit about that.'

'Another interesting thing I found,' said Moriarty, his voice full of passion and wonderment, 'was that the entrance, which faces south east looks directly at Sirius, the brightest star in the night sky and the milky way flows directly above the complex and it made me think what did the people that built Loughcrew know? What were they observing or what were they trying to tell us? That was only the beginning of my research. After that I travelled to Chichen Itza in Mexico, to the Giza Plateau and Abu Simbel in Egypt, Angkor Wat in Cambodia, each with sacred temples aligned to the equinox and yet ours was the oldest. I kept coming back to my book wondering if what it held explained all these things or connected all these sacred sights but all I seemed to be getting was more and more questions and very few answers.'

'The Order that we belong to,' said Rocha, 'and that you once belonged to, Manus, believes that this book guards an eternal truth that will bring the current hegemony to its knees and this,' Rocha motioned with her open hand towards Lola, 'is the young woman who is going to give it to the world. So I have no doubt that this is all interconnected, your research, your sites, us, this city, the book – there is a common thread to all of this,' said Rocha, 'but it's just a matter of untangling it.'

Not knowing how she should respond Lola, uncharacteristically, remained passive and stared at the ground both embarrassed and unsettled by the truth. Moriarty and Lemar looked at her and she could read their doubt. After all she shared it, how could one young woman deliver all of humanity from this invisible war that the Hell Fire Club was waging against them?

But Lola didn't take Rocha's prophesies so literally. She didn't have some convoluted Messiah complex and she didn't see herself as the saviour of the world. The world would continue to spin when she was long gone, just like it did when Arthur had died and the other countless members of the Order that came before them. But she was here for now and while this might not have been the path she'd chosen she had accepted to walk it so she would do what little she could while she could.

Then Lola remembered the conversation she'd had with Aíbgréne.

'Back at Brook Mill Manor,' she explained to Moriarty, 'Aíbgréne had been exploring Arthur's log books and she came across some data that she said related to the vernal equinox.' Lola rummaged about on the shelf of her memory for what she needed. It felt like her thoughts had a sell-by date and if the information wasn't offered up in a timely fashion her brain just canned them. It was something specific, some phenomenon, and then she had it.

'Precession of the equinox,' she declared delighted with herself for remembering. 'It has something to do with the rising and falling of different ages. Every 2,160 years the sun will rise on the spring equinox in a different sign and every age is equated to that sign.'

'Anyway,' continued Lola, 'Aíbgréne believed that Arthur was looking into this for the coming of the new age but like most of his knowledge it died with him. Did you ever find anything like this in your research?'

'Yes, Lola,' enthused Moriarty waving his index finger excitedly. 'Would you believe I have heard of this. When I was carrying out my research in Egypt I meet some really interesting people. There was an archaeologist

I met who had been looking at the Giza Plateau and he believed that the Sphinx was actually older than mainstream antiquities have argued. His team's research was really very accurate and interesting and their evidence suggests that the Sphinx may actually have been constructed as far back as 10,800 years ago and that it would have been looking directly at the constellation of Leo, which is its celestial counterpart in the night sky. They believe that this deviation was in direct relation to the procession of the equinoxes. But still,' smiled Moriarty, 'this is all conjecture and how this relates to our book, or even if it does relate to our book, that still remains a mystery.'

'I only think it's a mystery because you're using the wrong technology, professor,' said Lola, hit with a sudden burst of insight. To me, and you even said it yourself, it's like the book is alive and conscious of all that is going on around it. Imagine if it could speak,' said Lola growing more animated by her own insightfulness. 'Perhaps it can speak only we just don't know how to communicate with it yet? I've no doubt that there is magick protecting the book. I don't know why but I think that if we could get some equipment that would allow you to check for electrical energy or something you might get more results.'

They all looked at Lola in bewilderment but it was Lemar who actually gave what she said any credence.

'Lola's right,' said Lemar clearing his throat. 'That's what they had back in Iraq, when we were at Ur. They weren't Geiger counters and they weren't using an AD651, they did look a little similar, but when I had the chance to actually hold one I could tell their device was like nothing I'd seen before, nothing the military used anyways.' Lemar quite often remained silent but when he did speak, Lola thought every word was like a prophesy.

'Were there any markings on this machine, any symbols or logos?' Lola wasn't sure why she'd asked the question but she felt any information might have given her some sort of clue.

'Aztec it said and it had a little symbol like a mask on it. Those white guys were crazy about that mask it was on their tech, their SUVs, their jackets it was a freaky looking thing too. It gave me the chills.' Lemar drew closer to the fire's dimming light and the cool night air slid around them.

Lola's mind was like a mangle, wrenching and ringing the juice from all the theories and possibilities that they'd discussed, laying them to waste like pulp.

Suddenly the weight of the city bore down on her again and she wondered how Rocha had managed all these years in this city with its hard buildings and sharp edges.

But there was no turning back; she'd given up that option the moment that she'd stepped off the plane.

'So where do we go from here?' asked Moriarty, as if reading her mind. Lola could see the grey swirl around his indigo outline. He was a crucial part of the plan and she needed to be able to trust him.

'Professor, what I am about to ask you will be a hard decision,' said Lola, swallowing the fizz of nerves as they bubbled in her stomach and throat. 'This is my path and my journey and I won't encourage anyone to walk it with me but that book belongs to me...' Lola stopped and corrected herself when she saw the suspicion rise in Moriarty's eyes.

'What I mean,' corrected Lola, 'is that it belongs to my people and I must have it. I have to keep it safe from the Hell Fire Club, namely Alex Stein and his friends at the Butler Library. And you, professor, are the only one that can help me do that. It might mean compromising your position and I don't need reminding of how much that book means to you and what you have sacrificed for it. But some very dangerous people want it and their reach goes very far and you can be assured that you're on their radar and if they get a hint that you've been speaking privately with Rocha, or with me, I'm afraid you too will become a target by proxy, just like Lemar has. These men will stop at nothing to get what they want.'

'Can't we go to the authorities?' asked Moriarty half-heartedly but he'd already made his decision.

'I wish we could, professor,' said Lola with a pang of guilt. 'I wish it were that simple. You, you both,' she said looking at Lemar, 'have been caught in the spider's web. This is a war. It's not like the war they sent you to, Lemar, it's not a war for oil or land or coin; it's a war for our very consciousness. It's a war waged for the control of our hearts and our souls. Believe me, I understand how ridiculous this must sound to you both...'

'Evening comrades.' Startled by the deep baritone voice they all turned to find Prospero silhouetted against the dying light of the fire. The strands of his beard shone like silver spider threads in the growing breeze and the bruises on the side of his face had begun to pale and yellow.

'Hermes and I are back from our evening stroll to the 7th precinct, it's part of my bail conditions that I check in there each night,' smiled Prospero looking at Lola.

'Prospero, this is Manus Moriarty and this is Rocha Moone,' said Lola eager to change the subject, she wondered how much the old man had heard of their conversation.

Prospero stooped to shake Rocha's hand and Lola caught a spark in Rocha's eyes when she saw the old man, but as quick as it came, it disappeared. Manus looked at him for a moment.

'You look so familiar,' he said to Prospero. 'Have we met somewhere before? I definitely recognise your face from somewhere.'

'I'm sure we haven't, Mr Moriarty, but after tonight,' laughed Prospero in his usual genial manner, 'that's the last time I'll be able say that.' Despite his casual demeanour, Lola thought she noticed a grain of discomfort flicker through him as he gripped his staff a little tighter, but reading Prospero was like trying to grasp mist.

'So, Miss Paige, you're down here plotting revolution?' Lola's insides jolted, he'd heard so she decided not to divulge any more information.

'Not exactly, it's the only place in this city that I feel comfortable enough and safe enough to talk.'

'And did it not occur to you,' said Prospero pointing his staff at Stein Corp, 'that this may be the very reason that certain people may be watching us at this very minute?' There was nothing in his tone to suggest that Prospero was angry or annoyed but his words upset Lola all the same, she was annoyed by her lack of foresight. Lola was grateful for the cover the darkness offered as she stared at the ground like a scolded child.

'Lola is doing the best she can,' said Rocha defensively. 'So why don't you cut her a little slack? Since her mentor died,' her eyes bored into Prospero's locking them to hers, 'she's had little guidance. I think it's time we left, Lola,' said Rocha curtly. 'If holding theses meeting,' she said turning back to face Prospero, 'are going to cause trouble for you and the others at the camp, we'll gladly met at another location.' With a nod to Lemar, Rocha turned on her heels. 'Come on, Lola, honey, let's get you home. I've a phone call to make to my niece.' Without a word Lola rose bewildered and followed Rocha and Manus.

'What do you need me to do, Lola?' asked Moriarty as they left Liberty Plaza.

'I need you to get that book out of there so we can get it somewhere safe.'

Lola thought he would argue or protest considering the things that would have to be taken into consideration. This was a priceless artefact that belonged to the university and it wouldn't go unnoticed if it mysteriously disappeared but Moriarty offered no such protest.

'I know a way but you need to give me time.'

'Okay,' said Lola trying to hide her delight. 'We can stay in touch through Rocha, it will raise less suspicion that way. Prospero was right back there; it was silly of me to bring us all together here. Let me know when things are in place, but please keep in mind, professor, time is not on our side.'

~30~

'There you are, young lady, that's all the files we have. Sign here.'
Lola wrote her signature where the duty officer had directed and followed him into the viewing room. He was a tall, slim man in his late fifties with greying hair and despite the air of diminished interest with which he conducted himself, his well shaven face and keen brown eyes told Lola another story, so she scrutinised him further.

The badge read Officer Mendez, but even though they were diluted, there was pride and authority in his colours, which intrigued Lola.

Startled from her reverie, she jumped back when the logbook smacked down on to the Formica table top. Mendez flashed her a grin as if this was the only pleasure he could command in a day.

'Written on the front of each file, as you can see,' he said tracing underneath the words with his index finger, 'it says that these documents are the property of the New York Police Department and the Records Administration Branch. No material is permitted to be removed nor added to this file without the approval of the Records Administration Branch by Order of the Attorney General,' said Mendez with little or no expression as he rhymed the words off by heart. 'Is that clear, young lady?' He gave her cursory look to which Lola nodded in agreement.

'On the front you'll also see a sign-in log, if you choose to take notes or look at a particular file, you must also fill out your details on the front, I will date and sign it off when you return it to me at my desk.'

She eyed the boxes that were stacked in front of her disheartened by the sheer volume of material that she'd have to sift through. Lola contemplated calling Erin for some help but that would require too much explaining and she needed to keep things quiet. It was best she worked alone.

Lola couldn't help feeling a little vulnerable when Mendez closed and locked the gate behind him leaving her in the musty room alone but she shook off the feeling, turned on the desk light and went to work on the boxes. Her mind enjoyed the linear task of organising; the job allowed her brain respite from trying to work out her next move while simultaneously anticipating what the Steins had planned.

Beyond her, in the room across the hall where Mendez had now settled back behind his desk, rows and rows of boxes sat neatly stacked and filed and Lola thought about the lives and stories that each box housed. Focusing back on the task at hand, she consulted her list and began her search for Jodi's friend and the other names that she'd unearthed.

For over an hour Lola trawled through the boxes, removing the case file of each girl. Marking them off against her printout, she rested them on the table in front of her.

Lola organised each file into their respective years, cross-referencing them with the information that she'd taken from the Torch's online archives.

She noted the cause of death. Suicide each file said. She noted the place they were found and what markings appeared on their bodies, refining the search by adding the background and social circle of each girl, trying to see if there were any links. After two hours Lola took a step back from the table covering her mouth in disbelief.

Before her lay three piles with four girls in each pile. Scrambling for her notebook and pen she frantically began to write down a tally of similarities between these young women and their deaths.

All twelve women had similar, if not the same, markings on their bodies. Each fell into a group of four, with just three months between their deaths. Over an eleven year period, so far as Lola could tell, from 2001 until 2012 four women were murdered every five years. Another correlation, realised Lola, her hand struggling to keep up with her brain's commands, was that all the bodies were found along the East River. Lola tried to orientate herself. Tommy had shown her some of the sights and they had passed the East River. She lifted her phone and did a quick search and just as suspected Chateau dans le Ciel, Nassau Street and Stein's old headquarters at the Rockefeller Centre were all close by the East River.

In just a few hours she had found a pattern that she was certain would connected these deaths, so how on earth had the authorities not?

Exhausted, Lola fell into the stiff plastic chair and stared at the uniform piles. Her eyes travelled out of the room and across the hall again to the endless stacks of files and she understood exactly why these cases had not been connected. Mixed in with the other so- called suicides and homicides and unexplained deaths, these women's murders – and Lola was convinced it had been murder – would have easily gone unnoticed.

According to an article she'd read in the paper, crime in New York had dropped significantly in the past number of years so suicide was better than homicide for the statisticians and bureaucrats. Still, she wondered looking at Mendez, this was surely more than coincidence.

Neatly folding back the covers of the files so that she could see the names and face of each of the victims, Lola read each aloud.

Speaking gave life to language she thought and as her tongue birthed their names to the walls of the empty room, those twelve girls were once again alive. Each of them had once walked the streets of this city carrying their hopes and aspirations, their fears and dreams and a deep sadness settled on Lola when she thought about how their lives were now reduced to a picture and a few lines on yellowed paper.

'Lucy Davis,' she said reverently, 'Susan Harris, Kimberly Adams, Kristi Cooper.

'Ashley Cox, Carmen Barnes, April Myers, Beth Powell, Elsie Price,' she continued. 'Joy Butler, Jo Morris, Nora Evans.'

Twelve individual faces smiled back from their respective pile. If the pictures had not been there and with only the personal information of each girl to go on, based on their age, height, weight, eye colour, hair, complexion, give or take a few variations, she'd have thought they were duplicates. While their pictures made them individuals their vital information made them almost like clones.

It was immediately clear that this was a particular type, and the descriptions looked sickeningly familiar as she was reminded of Victoria Jones, who had been murdered at the hands of the Hell Fire Club last summer back home in Ireland. Still, she realised, this wasn't enough.

She felt herself getting excited, if excited was the appropriate word to use in these circumstances. Lola grabbed a pen from her bag and an A4 writing pad. Using the edge of one of the case files she drew five lines down the length of the page sectioning it into a table, where she added the names of the twelve young women. She charted what she'd read so far, their names, age, particulars, and place of the death. She would add as she went along. Her eyes floated along the crammed page of Lucy Davis's report for something significant. The language was cold and bureaucratic and there were codes but no key was available so she couldn't decipher them.

Then she found what she was looking for under 'Identifying Marks or Scars' – this was the one that she had been pinning her hopes on. She already knew from what Jodi had told her that Lucy's body had been found with two deep incisions on the inside of her left and right arms. Lola's stomach leapt when Lucy's report confirmed this. Quickly, Lola moved to Susan Harris's file hoping to see the same thing but there was a note to check the diagram on page twenty-three. Lola flicked through the file until she came to the coroner's report at the back of the document, where a diagram of the body displayed similar marks but this time they were on the quads of the young girl's legs. This seemed strange at first but then Lola remembered that the main arteries travelled down the legs too. As she moved on through the files, some had the same markings as Lucy and Susan while other scars appeared under the collarbones and around the pelvic area on others. Lola could feel her stomach knot, it would have been too neat to expect synchronicity in each case file.

Lola continued to scan the files noting down anything that she felt was similar or that could tie into the Hell Fire Club's rituals. The women were all wearing red dresses the night they were found. The colours and styles varied, which was only to be expected given the six-year time period between the groups, but Lola noted it down. Time of death in all of the cases was an approximate, but Lola was startled when she examined the dates a little closer. At first all she could gather was that two girls had died per year in the last six years. As she continued to take notes, it transpired that all twelve girls were registered to three companies. Some were aspiring models, some were TV presenters and some were actors. Lola jotted down the names of the agencies Ephémère, Reign Management and Metro Model Agency. She'd never heard of them but a quick search online would no doubt identify them and their owners. If that would be of any use, she wasn't sure yet.

Lola's head began to throb. Her eyes stung as she tried to rub the tiredness and rigidity away. Her head was crammed full, with each idea trying to fight its way out of the melee to the fore of her mind. Already it was clear that these young women were connected and Lola's gut told her that it wasn't just their untimely deaths that they shared. She could feel something stronger under the surface but she would have to mine deeper to unearth it. There were obvious similarities but whether there was enough to connect Carl Stein or the Hell Fire Club that was another matter entirely.

Lola slid back her chair and stood to stretch. Beyond the iron grill in the room's gate she could see Mendez busy at his desk, he looked up and tapped his watch.

'It's almost time to go home, young lady, you've been here over four hours.'

Lola checked her watch and was shocked to see it was well after eight pm. She looked down at the sheet of paper again and jotted down all the case file numbers. She'd have to come back after work again tomorrow, but it was time to call it a night for now.

Gently she closed over the documents and signed the front as she'd been instructed. As she was doing so, something caught her eye on each cover, Lola checked and rechecked them all twice, just to make sure she was right and then she wrote down the name A. Jessop.

The name appeared on every file apart from Lucy Davis's but it was the most recent. Nora Evans's file was the last one she closed and she took one quick glance at it before she delivered it to the rest of the case files. Her eyes were drawn to the words 'Known to Police' and underneath the answer 'YES' in bold type with six different number codes. Lola kept it to the top of the pile, gathering her things she brought the boxes out first and then returned the twelve files to Duty Officer Mendez.

'Officer, these codes,' Lola pointed down at the report, 'what do they mean?'

The officer eyed her for a moment before looking down to where her finger instructed. 'Let me see,' said Mendez, taking off his glasses to read.

'These are incident report codes,' he said, 'but if you're looking for them you have no chance tonight, young lady. You gotta come back tomorrow.'

'Do you mean that this lady Nora Evans was known by the police?'

'According to these codes and the fact that the answer to that question on the page is yes, I'd hazard a guess that she was.'

Lola shot him a cold stare. 'Yes,' she smiled, 'but what I'm saying is, are those incidents related to this case?'

'I don't know. Take a note of the numbers, come back tomorrow and then you might find out.' It had been a long day and Lola just wanted to get out into the fresh air.

'Oh, sorry, officer?'

The old man sighed and sat down in his seat again but there was no venom in his demeanour. 'What now, kid, won't it wait till the mornin?'

'It's just a quick question, there was a name on the front of all the files...' Lola dipped her hand into her bag searching for her note pad, when she pulled it out, half the contents came with it, which only compounded Officer Mendez's irritation.

'An A. Jessop. That name appears on all the files apart from one. I was just wondering if you might know who that was.'

There was a sudden flourish of blood red around Mendez which caught Lola's attention immediately. She realised that the name had struck a chord and an emotional one at that.

'Your name's on it, kid,' said Mendez giving nothing away in his languid tone, 'but I ain't never heard of you.' Despite the rebuttal he humoured her and looked down at the files on his desk. He flipped through another couple before lifting his head to answer.

'That seems to be the signature of Detective Andy Jessop and before you ask,' he said, pre-empting Lola's next question before it had fallen from her tongue, 'he left the Department about six months ago, he went into private work. On this salary, I can't say I blame the guy. Now good night,' he looked down at Lola's name on the front of the file again, 'Ms Paige. You did remember to take the case file numbers down? It'll make your search a lot easier next time.'

For a moment Lola began to panic but then she remembered that she'd just done that before she left the room.

'I have them here. Night, officer, and thank you for all your help,' she said with a hint of sarcasm.

'Night, kid, and safe home.'

The brightness of the 7th precinct's command area attacked Lola's eyes when she emerged up the stairs from the basement into the busy room where the smell of polished floor tiles and disinfectant reminded her of her old primary school. Three men and one woman sat along a bench, accompanied by their arresting officers waiting to be booked in by the desk sergeant. The lady, dressed in a white shirt, called them over one at a time and one of the men called out to Lola, she couldn't make out what he said and when the man smiled back all his teeth had disappeared apart from two lonely incisors at each side of his mouth.

'It's your lucky day, kid,' said the cop who was bringing the toothless Lothario to the desk, 'Donny here says he'd like to marry you.' The man smiled hopefully at Lola again and she politely smiled back.

'Tell Donny, I'm bad news,' said Lola humorously, leaving the cop and Donny laughing.

Heading for the front desk, Lola caught sight of a familiar outline as it disappeared through the precinct's security doors. Quickly confirming her slot for the following day with the TSO she ran outside to try and catch up with Prospero. As she emerged on to the busy street she searched up and down Delancey but there was no sign of the old man amidst the strings of patrol cars that lined the pavements and fire engines from the neighbouring station. One of the engines roared to life momentarily blocking Lola's view but when it passed she caught Prospero's silhouette as it disappeared down the road with Hermes proudly trotting alongside him. Lola shouted out to him but her call was drowned out by the scream of the siren.

Deciding to follow after him as he headed towards a nearby underpass Lola finally caught up with Prospero but he wasn't alone. Unsure, she hung back listening. The obvious anger in his voice sounded unnatural to her forcing her back against the wall and out of sight.

'You've got to go through with it!' Prospero was saying to the shadows. 'You're the only person who can. This is what we have been working towards, you are not the only person to have made sacrifices and taken risks, Mr Stein.'

Lola felt her breathing halt and her knees slacken, the shock that Prospero was speaking to any of the Steins made her belly twist and contort. She toyed with the idea of stepping out into the middle of their clandestine meeting but her anxiety wouldn't allow her to move.

He was a fraud. Prospero was a fraud! The revelation hit her with such propulsion it felt as though a breezeblock had been placed on top of her heart. Why had she trusted him? Lola berated and mocked herself. He had a white beard like Arthur's, answered the voice in her head meekly. That was the sum of it, she wanted him to be like Arthur. How utterly needy she was. Still, she was looking for someone to rely on to tell her what to do and how to do it.

'Things are moving much quicker than I anticipated, her strength is growing daily, I can feel it and so can my father. We need to move soon if we are to stand a chance.'

Alex's voice punctured Lola's chest once again, she wasn't sure if it was better or worse that Prospero had been conspiring with him instead of his father, but what did it matter? Yet again here she was standing on the other side of the line, alone and exposed, having shown her cards on the open palm of her hand.

'The book must be secured immediately, you must see out your end of the bargain, Alex.'

'Moriarty rarely leaves the book, he doesn't trust me, or anyone else for that matter,' said Alex, his tone terse and defiant against Prospero's commands.

'Well our mutual friend has told him what it is so I would imagine that he'll trust you even less now.'

'Leave it with me,' said Alex irritably. 'Is that it?'

'For now,' answered Prospero, leaning against his staff.

'I can give you a lift back to the camp; my driver can drop you off,' mocked Alex.

'No thanks, my driver will be here soon,' said Prospero. He didn't catch the absurdity of Alex's offer in time. 'Yes, Mr Stein,' he said finally realising, 'that would help both our causes exceedingly well. I'm sure my comrades are wondering why I'm down here every night as it is.'

'They know you're signing in as part of your bail conditions, at least that much is true. They just don't know it was the son of their tormentor who has enabled you to pay your bail and legal fees.'

'How do you keep up this veil, old man?' continued Alex with genuine interest. 'I mean don't you ever get tired or worry about it slipping.' Lola wasn't sure if Alex was talking about his co-conspirator or himself. The same thing could be said for them all she supposed.

'Lola is smart,' said Prospero, his tone soft and understanding now. 'She can cut through all the deceit and lies and I think it's only a matter of time before she figures it all out.'

'So how come she hasn't sniffed you out then?' said Alex. Prospero must have been thinking because it took him a short while before he answered.

'I suppose the pretence is secure so long as people continue to see with their eyes and not their hearts, Mr Stein. Lola will discover the real me at a time of my choosing. It appears she has already seen through your veil, Mr Stein.'

There was no reply as Lola could hear the purr of a car engine and it was clear that Prospero was alone again. Unsure in what direction to go she concealed herself among the group of nearby pedestrians as they waited on the sidewalk for the green light.

Her head was in a fog but her feet seemed to lead her to the subway station on Delancey Street. She travelled across town and walked the short distance to Princes Street. Closing the apartment door behind her she watched passively as Rocha rushed to her. Rocha's questions felt distant as they echoed and bounced off Lola's ears.

'It's over,' was all she could say. 'It's over, Rocha.'

~31~

'You don't know for certain what you overheard, Lola,' said Rocha in a conciliatory tone. 'Perhaps Alex Stein is helping Prospero, and perhaps they are on the same side.' Rocha who was normally relaxed and methodical paced up and down the open living room, her actions in direct conflict with her words.

'They're on the same side alright, but just not on ours. This is all my fault, Rocha,' said Lola with despair. 'Prospero knows almost everything now. He knows about the book, he could have heard us talking that night with Moriarty and I'm sure Alex knows about the new dates, Susie is bound to have told him.'

'But he couldn't have heard everything,' reasoned Rocha, still pacing back and forth. 'He didn't return until we had almost finished. Which means someone else has informed him,' she said. 'Unless Lemar has told him?' Rocha dismissed the thought with a wave of her hand. 'No,' she declared and continued to pace.

Lola couldn't understand why Rocha had been so quick to defend the old man. There had been an uncomfortable exchange between the two when she'd first introduced them. It was very subtle but she'd picked up on it. At the time it felt like Rocha was unsure about Prospero and it seemed as though he sensed it himself. Lola's mind raced, what if Rocha was part of the plot too, what if she had been feeding him and Alex Stein information the whole time and that's how Alex had known where she was staying? Lola's mind toiled and raced, she wished she could get out and run. She wished Aíbgréne was there. Talking a deep breath she centred herself stifling her rising paranoia.

'I heard it as plain as day, Rocha,' said Lola testily, '"You've got to go through with it. You are the only person who can. This is what we have been working towards, you are not the only person to have made sacrifices and taken risks, Mr Stein."'

'I came a bit late to the conversation, I know but it doesn't take much deduction. Alex Stein is the enemy, Prospero, who I thought was on our side, is meeting with him in secret. If it was all above board and we were all one big, happy Hell-Fire-Club-fighting family why would they be meeting at night under a bridge at the 7th Precinct?'

Finally Rocha sat down. She was clam now, restored to her normal self. Her eyes locked on Lola's and when they did Lola felt so guilty for having doubted her because all she found there was honesty and love.

'The truth is I don't know, Lola, but this is a dirty war and the Hell Fire Club do not play fair. Perhaps we use this to our advantage. You're always saying that you feel ten steps behind, well now you're a step ahead of the game and I say let's make the most of it.'

But as reasonable and logical as Rocha's words were, Lola was exhausted. It was too much to always try and keep ahead of the game, always trying to outthink and out whit your opponent, but she understood this was a fight worth fighting. She'd been up against worse odds before. Perhaps Rocha was right, maybe it was time to change her perspective and view this as serendipitous discovery.

'I'm afraid that Moriarty is not wholly convinced about the book,' said Lola, rubbing the worry and stress away from her temples with the tips of her fingers.

'I can hear her,' she said finally admitting it to Rocha. 'The communication is getting stronger but he can't. Maybe if I find some way to prove what I'm saying to him, with him fully on board the Hell Fire Club doesn't stand a chance of getting their hands on her.'

'It's almost midnight,' said Rocha sitting down and pulling Lola close to her. She smelled of lavender and musk and it mollified Lola's anxiety. 'Perhaps we should both sleep on it,' smiled Rocha. 'A new day can quite often bring a new perspective.'

Lola didn't resist, instead she took Rocha's advice and went straight to bed. She didn't realise just how fatigued her mind and body was. No sooner had she rested her head on the pillow than the darkness of sleep crept over her.

A slight depression on the bed stirred Lola from her slumber. Opening her eyes a crack, she found the room was still in darkness, she could feel the presence on the bed beside her but she wasn't fearful; she knew it wasn't there to harm her. Turning, she smiled when she heard the familiar voice.

'Finally, you're bloody awake. I've only been sitting here staring you awake for the last half hour.'

Lola sat up and greeted her friend with a warm smile. She wasn't sure how this worked, as she had never really engaged with Aíbgréne on the astral plane before.

'Move over there and give us a bit of room,' said Aíbgréne shoving Lola over and sliding under the quilt cover beside her.

'I'm so glad to see you, Aíbgréne; I've missed you so much.' Lola's voice was thick with sleep. It was easier to be honest in the darkness. She was unsure whether she could hug Aíbgréne until her friend put her arm around her and it felt solid and real, Lola could even smell her friend's perfume. It was an apply scent that she made herself and matched Aíbgréne's aura perfectly, if Lola had been able to smell Aíbgréne's colours, this is how she imagined they would smell, fresh and fruity.

The hug spoke their apologies and addressed each transgression so there was no need for words to explain why Aíbgréne hadn't turned up at the airport to see Lola off or why Lola had taken so long to contact her or why they had argued over Alex. None of it mattered and gradually Lola began to reassemble the hope that had been so fractured earlier. The two women chatted for hours as Lola filled her in on all that had occurred both inside and outside of the paper, while Aíbgréne informed her of all that had taken place across the Atlantic. She never mentioned her earlier prophesy about Lola's death and Lola didn't quite have the energy to ask.

'So you're definitely sure that this is the Lost Oracle we've been looking for?'

'Yes,' said Lola stretching and yawning. 'I wasn't sure at the start, I mean the first time that I saw it, it definitely had an effect on me. I could hear her sing but I couldn't understand what it was she was saying. But lately, after seeing it a second time the connection seems to have gotten stronger. It freaked me out a little at first, the voice,' Lola paused to explain. 'I can hear her, Aíbgréne, she speaks to me.'

'You're hearing voices in your head now, Lola,' said Aíbgréne playfully nudging her with her elbow.

'I know,' laughed Lola. 'I sound like a right rocket, don't I?

'What does she say? What does it sound like?' asked Aíbgréne her tone serious again.

'She speaks in old Irish, Sengódelc, she calls it. Her voice is like the whisper of a wave, hushed and soft yet there's no mistaking the power in it. "Come" she sings, "come to me In Rúad Rofessa. It is time to heal the Brón Trogain and the time has come for the Túatha to hear of the Imbas forosnai."'

'Yes,' said Aíbgréne waiting for Lola to elaborate, 'and what exactly does all that mean?'

'Oh,' Lola smiled into the opaque room; she'd missed Aíbgréne's sharp tongue. Everyone in America was so polite but Lola doubted most of them really meant what they said, well apart from old Bill the bigot he never held his punches, but then neither had Lola.

'Come to me the Red one of Great Knowledge. It is time to heal the earth's sorrowing. The time has come for the nations to feed off the great knowledge that illuminates. Then she spoke the words Dírgas,' Lola decided to translate this time, 'righteousness, Eólas, Knowledge, Fír, truth.'

'Righteousness, Knowledge and truth,' repeated Aíbgréne. 'You use a pronoun to describe this book, it's like you think it's a living thing.'

Lola threw a scolding look at Aíbgréne, even though she wouldn't see it in the blackness around them but she felt the change in her body language.

'What!' said Aíbgréne. 'I mean it's a book and a powerful magickal one at that but alive...'

'You amaze me, Aíbgréne, and you have the cheek to chastise me sometimes. Listen to what I'm tellin you. This book contains the spirit of a living conscious entity. She calls herself the first Bile Máthir of the Cethardúil, the Túatha, Mother of the nem nglas, muir mas, talam cé.'

Without being prompted this time, Lola translated. She is the first Sacred Mother of the Cosmos and the nations. She is the mother of the blue sky, the beautiful sea and the present earth sent forth, she says, from the Crann na beatha, the Tree of Life.

'There is so much more I can learn from her but I haven't been able to get any time alone with the book or my thoughts for that matter. I can feel her pull and her draw, it's like I was called here by her, that's what your auntie Rocha thinks and I'm inclined to think the same now.'

Aíbgréne thought for a moment. 'You may be right, Lola,' she agreed. 'It would explain why my mother supported the trip from the beginning but it doesn't explain why Markus was intent on you coming here.

The Order has been infiltrated at every corner, I mean look at Markus, now even I didn't see that coming.'

So much had happened that Lola hadn't really had time to digest it all. Markus's role in Arthur's death was heaped into the ever expanding 'must process' pile along with the rest of the issues she would need to face.

'Markus,' said Lola regretfully, 'I haven't been able to get my head around that one yet, I mean, why?'

'Who knows, Lola? Who knows what motivates some people to make the decisions they do? People do shitty things for all sorts of reasons – fear, greed, power, control, jealousy. In the end I think Markus was confused himself about whose side he was on, that's why he was so convincing. Celeste has no idea I suspect anything,' continued Aíbgréne, 'but I know she's hiding something from me. I think Carl Stein was tying up a loose end, Markus had become a liability and that's why he killed him. I mean,' Aíbgréne moved and sat at the edge of the bed as if she was readying to leave, 'if he was still of any use to him he would have kept him alive.'

'Carl Stein plans to finish us all in the same way,' said Lola darkly, 'yet he continually underestimates the forces that we have at our disposal. He wants the book, but the stronger my connection with it gets and the more I learn about it, the more I'm convinced that he'll never be able to unlock its secrets. She would never permit him to. My worry is that he knows this too. I think he covets the book not to unlock it but to destroy it.'

'Well it's up to you to make sure that doesn't happen and we're all here to help you, Lola. You must always remember that you'll never walk alone,' said Aíbgréne laughing bashfully as she stood up. 'How cringe worthy was that reference? But I knew you'd appreciate it,' she grinned, reminding Lola just how much she missed Aíbgréne's counsel.

The dull dawn had begun to creep around the inside of the blind reminding Lola that she'd soon have to go to work. She could see Aíbgréne's silhouette against the milky light, the outline of her buoyant hair and as her eyes adjusted she could see her pale face and for the first time she realised that the person before her was not the real thing but a facsimile.

'Before I go, Lola, the reason I actually paid this visit was because Daithí asked me to,' said Aíbgréne moving back into the shadows in the corner of the room.

'Thanks a million!' replied Lola feigning offence.

'You know what I mean,' said Aíbgréne apologetically. 'He didn't want to risk using the phone or the Internet so he decided this was the best way to communicate plus it's good practice for me. I think he was just looking for an excuse to get me to speak to you face to face, he's had to deal with my behaviour this past few weeks and in truth I'm surprised that he's still even with me. Anyway. He wanted me to tell you that... get a piece of paper and pen, you're going to need to write this down.'

Lola always kept a notepad at the side of her bed, she'd done this since she could remember, so she could jot her thoughts down if she got a sudden burst of inspiration. Her fingers found it in the growing light of the room. 'Right hit me,' said Lola, poised, ready to record the intel from Daithí.

'Don't tempt me,' Aíbgréne smiled. 'Well, he said to tell you that the numbers you gave him were co-ordinates to various sites of interests but he said you already knew that. They included Newgrange, Loughcrew, Dowth, the Giza Pyramids, Abu Simbel, Glastonbury Tor, a place called Ur in Iraq – I've no idea what that is all about – Tara, Lisnagade Fort and the Temple of Apollo at Delphi,' finished Aíbgréne.

'Now that's quite a list, Lola, and as of yet we're not sure what exactly connects them, apart from the fact that they're all ancient sacred sites.'

'Well that amongst other things,' said Lola thinking about her recent conversation with Moriarty. 'Most of them have some astro-archeological connection, well Newgrange, Giza, Abu Simbel, Loughcrew and Dowth do,' she added.

'He also found something even more interesting,' said Aíbgréne. 'Daithí said that the numbers corresponded to patent numbers of some sort of quantum technology, which is placed in or around these locations. He hasn't quite figured out what they are doing there but he discovered that the items or patents are registered to a tech company called Aztec Systems and they're owned by...'

'None other than Stein Corp,' finished Lola.

'You've really got him excited now, Lola, he is obsessed with this but this is deep web stuff so he has to tread very carefully. So you've heard of this Aztec?' asked Aíbgréne.

'Only just,' replied Lola, deep in thought. 'It turns out that Aztec Systems have been searching for something. The last night you were creeping about my bedroom,' said Lola with a cautionary glance, there was no animosity in her tone so her declaration went unchallenged. 'Well before... You know,'

Lola could feel herself blush as she stumbled over her words.

'Before you had a sex marathon with your arch-nemesis,' shot back Aíbgréne all piety.

'Yes,' conceded Lola, 'I had managed to wangle my way into the Stein party.' Lola could see that Aíbgréne was about to reproach her so she dismissed the incoming lecture with a wave of her hand. 'Anyway, I could sense that the Cube had been there, then I thought that it still was but when I went to the place that my vision showed me, it was gone but on the table was a stack of files and papers that's how I got the co-ordinates, you see. I also saw a file for an ex-Marine, we don't have time to go into all the particulars,' said Lola trying to condense the story as best she could. 'But that Marine was a young man named Lemar Jenkins and he was on Stein's hit list.'

'Why?' asked Aíbgréne.

'Well that brings me back to what Daithí has uncovered. The place in Iraq you mentioned – Ur – it turns out Lemar was part of some protection detail at this archaeological site and he said that they were searching for something, a book. He was able to tell us that the company Aztec was using some sort of new tech and now Daithí has confirmed what this could be. I've no doubt that they were looking for the Oracle in Iraq.'

'But why Iraq?' said Aíbgréne. 'What's the connection there?'

'That I don't know. I mean it could just be the Hell Fire Club hedging their bets but you're right, something must have prompted it. Aíbgréne, every day there is another thread to this, another loose end that I have to connect. I mean I think I've just uncovered twelve ritual murders at the hands of the Hell Fire Club, why this information has presented itself I don't now but I feel it's all connected in some way. It's crazy.'

'That's how it all works, Lola, six degrees of separation,' said Aíbgréne as if she was some seasoned sage. 'Look at how you and I met. I needed you and you needed me.' She was absolutely correct.

'Well these girls need me at the moment and perhaps if I can help them, they just might be able to help me.'

'They will,' said Aíbgréne, 'trust your gut, Lola, it's rarely wrong and besides, it's a much better judge than your heart.' Lola threw a pillow at the corner of the room where her friend stood, but it hit the back of the wall, passing through her as if she were made from mist.

'Thank Daithí for me,' said Lola peaceably, 'I knew he'd come across. But before you go, can I ask you a favour?' Lola stretched her body awake and wondered what hour of the morning it was.

'The procession of the equinoxes thing, would you be able to send me something on what you found in Arthur's log books about this or anything that your mum might know that could be of help to us? Moriarty believes that there could be some connection with the equinox and this Oracle. I don't know what it is but I think it's worth looking at.'

'Yeah. No bother, Lola, anything I can help you with please just ask.'

'So how's married life been?'

'Active,' smiled Aíbgréne. 'Stay safe, Lo,' she said and then just like dew on a warm day, she was gone.

Minutes later Lola's alarm sounded announcing it was time to get out of bed. Groaning, she reached over and turned it off. Tempted to press the snooze button she shuffled clumsily from bed, she washed. Picking a light grey pencil dress and a pair of kitten heels, she quickly dressed.

Lola looked longingly at the empty bed tempted to jump back in, it wasn't as though they would miss her in the newsroom, she told herself. Most days it was like she was invisible to her colleagues. Interns didn't really count; they were treated as more of a nuisance than a help, but resisting the temptation of her still-warm bed, she straightened the duvet and headed down to the kitchen where Rocha was clearing away her breakfast dishes. The smell of toasted bagels and coffee made Lola's stomach growl.

'Did you sleep well, Lola?' Rocha's keen eyes scrutinized the contours of her face and the dark circles underneath her eyes.

'Not a wink,' yawned Lola. 'I had a late night visitor.'

'I didn't hear a thing, I went out like a light when my head hit the pillow.'

'Well you wouldn't have,' said Lola stuffing some granola and yoghurt into her mouth, 'they didn't visit the traditional way.'

Lola could see that Rocha was becoming confused. 'It was your great niece, I believe she calls it traveling on the astral plane.'

'All night?' asked Rocha in astonishment.

'Well for the most of it anyway.'

'Goodness me, you're not the only person who's seen a substantial rise in their powers. Aíbgréne must have become very proficient to be able to stay so long on the plane. She will be exhausted today no doubt,' said Rocha matter-of-factly.

'She'll be okay, Rocha?'

'Oh yeah, she'll be just fine. Very tired, but she'll be fine. Are you good to go, Lola?' Lola nodded her head and followed quickly behind Rocha, waiting while she locked the various bolts on the apartment door.

'Daithí was able to find the co-ordinates that I gave him, it seemed straight forward enough, but what his expertise did unearth was that there is some sort of device at these sites. He said that it was some sort of quantum technology and you'll never guess who owns the patents for them.'

'Let me guess,' said Rocha. 'Stein Corp?'

'Almost, Professor Moone, Aztec,' said Lola raising her eyebrows with a conspiratorial nod. 'And we know from talking to Lemar that our friends at Aztec were searching for something of interest in Ur and the co-ordinates for Ur that I found on the list in Carl Stein's office also corresponds to one of these devices. So my feeling is that they are at all the other sites as well, including Ireland and Egypt.'

'That's fantastic work, Lola, I'm not sure if you're in the right profession,' laughed Rocha picking up her stride. Lola noticed an air of determination as she walked, it was as if her mind was preoccupied with some other issue other than the one at hand.

'He said he'd get in touch. Daithí,' repeated Lola quickening her stride to stay in line with Rocha's. 'He's going to keep digging and I'm going to look into this company to see what I can find too. I've a crazy day ahead of me with so many irons in the fire I don't know which way to turn, add to that Moriarty. I don't know how I'm going to encourage him over the line.'

'Sometimes, Lola,' said Rocha now fully invested in the conversation again, 'the light of inspiration guides us when we least expect it. Things will be revealed when the time is right and not a moment before.'

Rocha stopped before they approached the entrance to the subway.

'Aren't you coming?' asked Lola expecting Rocha to follow alongside her.

'I'm afraid I have to leave you here, honey; I've a meeting this morning,' explained Rocha evasively as her eyes fell on some imaginary stain on her dress that she rubbed and fussed at. Her suspicions stirred, Lola watched as Rocha's colours plumed a muddy orange and grey and she knew then that Rocha was concealing something.

'Who are you meeting?' probed Lola, perhaps a little too hard because she could see a flicker of impatience in Rocha Moone's hazel eyes.

'I'll see you this evening when you get home and we can discuss this all then.'

She bent over and gave Lola a hug, planting a kiss on her forehead. 'Have a good day, Lola, and please stay safe.' Lola watched as Rocha crossed the road and hopped onto the downtown bus. As it took off from the kerb Lola read the street names as they moved across the digital bus screen. Fulton Street/Trinity Place, they said. That was the route she'd taken to Liberty Plaza and she wondered if Rocha was heading for the same destination.

Resigned to find out later, Lola headed down to tackle the subway alone. She had tried to avoid it as much as she could. The New York Subway was like the crucible for humanity, you learned so much about people and about yourself. As the doors snapped shut behind her and Lola tucked herself into the bulging carriage thinking of the layers of earth above her, she hoped that Rocha's promised light of inspiration would come sooner rather than later.

~32~

The pace of the features desk was a welcome contrast to the immediacy and competition in news. It was twice the work at times but Lola had really found her niche. She enjoyed the research and time afforded to explore options and stories and the bonus of being able to work at her desk unhindered, save for the interruption of the odd phone call that was rarely for her.

Lola stared at the busy page of her note pad as though she was expecting it to organise itself and tell her how to start piecing this puzzle together. The name Nora Evans, written in pencil, caught her eye; she was one of the deceased who'd been previously known to the police. It might be a long shot but Lola typed her name into the large achieve search engine. Who knew there could be so many Nora Evanses in the city.

Going by the proposed time of death, according to the case file, she typed in the year 2001. The computer churned and calculated before displaying the picture of a young woman, not much older than Lola was now, with long blonde hair that fell in a middle parting across her narrow face, the proportions of which were perfect, as though they had been chiselled from marble.

Nora Evans wasn't pretty in the common way, Nora was supermodel pretty. She had that look that made her appear other-worldly. Her milky skin had a few light freckles across her nose and although her mouth opened into a wide smile there was a deep sadness in her grey eyes.

Lola couldn't quite quantify it, perhaps it was Lola that was sad, here was this young woman full of life and blind to what lay ahead of her. But then, thought Lola, it was the same for her, for everyone. One minute your life was 'normal' and the next it was pulled inside out and sent reeling upside down. One thing the past two years had taught her was that life wasn't like a book, it wasn't linear it didn't happened in straight lines, life was like a river, it turned and twisted, it was sometimes calm and sometimes turbulent. The truth was that not one person could see the path ahead of them and Lola wondered if it was better that way.

Lola looked at the picture of the smiling Nora again, taking in her company this time, two other young women who were variations of her – model types. Lola consulted the caption underneath: From L-R, Ms Kimberly Adams, Ms Nora Evans and Ms April Myers enjoy a night out at the Stein Corp Charity Mixer. All three ladies are represented by Reign Management.

Lola couldn't believe what she was reading, she ran her eyes down the list of names on her note pad. Nora Evans, found in the East River on 22nd December, 2001; April Myers, found in the East River on 21st March, 2001; Kimberley Adams found in the East River on 23rd June, 2001. All three women were known to each other and represented by the same company. It wasn't exactly watertight, but it was, at the very least, more than circumstantial. Lola looked at the dates their bodies had been found.

March, June, December repeated Lola to herself.

She looked down at the rest of the deaths on the page and the table that she had drawn up back at the 7th precinct. The ring around her neck began to pulse and throb confirming that her gut instincts were right, she was on to something and every part of her body acknowledged it.

There it was in front of her a pattern of ritualistic murders, just like Victoria Jones's, each woman fitted the same profile, same line of work and had been murdered within three months of one another. Although there were years between each block, each fitted the same pattern. Her eyes fell on the list again, this time she made another note beside the names and dates.

April Myers – Spring Equinox, 2001

Kimberley Adams – Summer Solstice, 2001

Carmen Barnes – Autumn Equinox, 2001

Nora Evans – Winter Solstice, 2001

Based on the dates that she had in front of her there was a five-year gap until 2006 when the pattern continued with four more girls' bodies being pulled from the East River.

Elsie Price – Spring Equinox, 2006 Joy Butler – Summer Solstice, 2006 Jo Morris – Autumn Equinox, 2006 Ashley Cox – Winter Solstice, 2006

The final block of four were found back in 2012, this time there was six-year gap between them. That year Beth Powell was the first to be found in March of 2012 she was followed by Kristi Cooper in June, Susan Harris in September and, finally, Jodi's friend Lucy Davis in December.

Lola sat back and looked at the list again. Sure there were gaps but there was definitely enough here to merit further investigation. That the evidence led to Carl Stein and the Hell Fire Club was clear, but it was only clear when you understood what was really at play, only then could you see the pattern. If Lola was to convince Isaac that this could be a way to get to Carl Stein she would need more than a few dates and she would need help with this. There was no point going to Isaac until she had built a case.

Lola lifted the phone and called Erin. The phone rang off but just as she was about to replace the receiver, someone pounced on her from behind.

'BOO!'

Lola almost jumped out of her seat. 'Flippin hell, Erin,' she said placing her hand on her heart as if to keep it from exploding out of her chest, 'you near scared me half to death!'

'It's coffee time, let's go,' Erin smiled unapologetically. Without reply, Lola lifted her bag and followed her out of the newsroom.

'I was just calling you there,' she said as they boarded the elevator. There were a few others from the newsroom going down to the café so Lola didn't say anything else until she and Erin were out of earshot.

'So what's the big secret?' asked Erin intrigued.

'Listen, Erin,' said Lola with a slight hesitation, 'I need you to promise me that you won't discuss this with anyone and I mean no one,' she added sternly.

'Cross my heart and hope to die,' said Erin as she ran her fingers across her chest.

Lola pulled her closer and whispered, 'I'm looking into a series of deaths and I happen to believe that they are all connected.' Lola didn't want to divulge too much information but she needed Erin's help so she decided to tell her just enough. 'Let's just say that I think that the same organisation is responsible for these deaths.'

If Erin hadn't been fully serious before, she was now and Lola had her undivided attention. 'Do you have access to the photo archives up there?' asked Lola.

'Yeah,' said Erin her face open and sincere. 'I can even access the archive on my laptop too.'

'Brilliant,' smiled Lola. 'Would you be able to come down to my desk later maybe?'

'Sure. I'm free now if you wanna do it when we get back?'

'Yeah, that would be a great help. I have to go back down to the 7th precinct tonight again, so I don't know when I'll get home. It was late enough for me last night and then I hardly slept a wink.'

'You look tired alright, Lola. I can come down the station with you if it would be any help?'

'No, I'll be grand,' said Lola placing her hand on Erin's arm in acknowledgment of the offer. 'Thanks anyway but I've got things under control. If you could help with the pictures that would be great.'

Lola's back and shoulders felt tense and stiff as she settled into their usual spot and allowed her eyes to slip shut for a moment. The mid-morning sun had climbed high enough so that it streamed down onto the small square garden at the centre of the building. The light coaxed her muscles to relax as it beamed on her skin and her tired eyes. Erin was preoccupied with her phone and the tip tapping and the growing heat, like a warm blanket lulled Lola to rest. All she needed was five minutes shut eye and she would be ready to go.

'Right, sleepy head you've got work to do. Time to get up.' Erin shook her lightly as Lola sheltered her eyes from the growing sun. She felt as though she'd been asleep for hours.

'What time is it?' said Lola disorientated. 'How long have I been asleep?'

'Don't panic, Lola, it's only gone 11am, you were only out for a half hour.'

'Shit,' Lola sat upright and fumbled to get her shoes on. 'Can you come and help me out now?'

'Yeah. Sure. I just need to nip up and get my things first.'

As Lola settled at her desk, foggy from the abrupt interruption to her sleep, it took her eyes and head time to adjust to the artificial lights. Lola thought about her bed back at the loft. She would have to get an early night tonight, that's if she didn't fall fast asleep on her desk before then.

The newsroom was busy this morning and there seemed to be more activity than usual. Isaac had been in meetings upstairs for most of the morning and he and Jodi had been in deep conversation when she'd arrived earlier this morning. She wondered what they were working on. Now that she actually looked around Isaac, Chris and other section editors were nowhere to be seen.

The bullpen stalwarts gathered in flocks talking in hushed tones, flitting like little sparrows from one hub to the next. Whatever was going on, Lola was the last to hear and at the minute it was the least of her concerns.

She was wondering where Erin was when she saw her proudly walking across the newsroom with so much confidence, like she'd always been part of the Torch, and Lola loved her for it.

'Sorry I'd have been down sooner only all hell has broken loose upstairs. Apparently there have been meetings all morning and they're talking lay-offs of some of the top staffers.'

'What? Why would you let your best people go?' said Lola thinking immediately of Isaac. 'It doesn't make any sense.'

'I know, right? But it all comes down to dollar bills, Lola. That's all these people care about. They're only in it to make money, these guys in suits, like they could give a shit. They don't care about news, as long as it keeps their bank balance rising and when it doesn't? Well...' Erin rubbed her hands together as if she was wiping dust from them, 'they discard them as if they were nothing. There is some good news though,' she beamed, 'your sparring partner Bill, well apparently he's accepted his redundancy package.' This made Lola laugh but she still felt ashamed for striking him, even if he did deserve it. She could have really hurt the old hack.

Lola thought about Isaac and wondered if he could be on the brink of losing his job too. She glanced at the darkened office.

'The word is that the redundancies are a last ditch attempt at dealing with dwindling sales in print, they are in trouble. Word is,' said Erin fully animated and with her South Boston charm, 'Carl Stein has been looking to increase his shares and bail out the paper to become a majority shareholder but there are some on the Board that are reluctant to let him. I heard two suits arguing about it on the way to the elevator,' said Erin enjoying the intrigue.

Here was yet another source of concern for Lola – Carl Stein taking over the paper. But in the great scheme of things it would have to go to the bottom of her slush pile.

'That's quite a bit of information you've gathered there,' teased Lola. 'I think you might have chosen the wrong specialty.'

Erin laughed as she opened up her laptop and wheeled her chair closer to Lola's. The newsroom was so preoccupied with the emerging news that no one paid them any heed.

'Okay, Erin, I'm going to give you a list of names first and I want to see if anything comes up.' Lola took a glance round to see where the nearest printer was. It was halfway across the newsroom and this made her feel a bit edgy.

She lifted her phone and texted Isaac. She didn't have the nerve to call him, not this morning, so she took the coward's way out and texted him. Ten seconds later her phone pinged with a reply.

'Sure' was all it said. Lola lifted her notes and bag and beckoned Erin to follow her. When she got into Isaac's empty office she closed the door and the blinds on the windows.

'Jesus, Lola, what's all this about? It must be some story you're working on. Is the newsroom that bad that you have to go to these measures to protect it?'

'I'm not worried about anyone stealing my story, Erin,' said Lola as she settled at Isaac's desk. Lola wasn't exactly sure if this was true but she liked to believe that it was. 'It's the actual story itself I'm trying to protect, that's until I can decide if my hunch is right. There are higher powers at play than nosy journalists.'

'Can you connect to that printer there, Erin, just in case we need to print stuff out?' Erin played with her laptop for a moment. 'Done,' she said. 'Now can we get started?'

Lola began to call the names out one by one, starting with the most recent block of four. She had already gotten some information from the news archive but she was hoping that the photo archive would prove more incriminating.

Sure enough pictures existed of the all four girls but what she needed was something more specific. 'Could you add Carl Stein, Stein Corp, Reign Management, Metro Agency and Ephémère to the search?'

Erin typed in the extra words and waited for the computer to respond. Lola felt nervous. It wasn't the end if nothing came up it just meant that she would have to work a little harder and dig a little deeper.

Erin sat back gazing at her screen. 'One hundred and twenty-three matches. Look, Lola,' she said sliding away from the screen.

Lola took over the reins and flicked through the pictures. It was soon clear that the blocks of women that died in the same year all knew or had meet each other at some point.

Various pictures confirmed that and although the captions detailed that they may have been signed to different agencies she was definitely on the right track. Lola hit print as she went through the pictures, as of yet Carl Stein wasn't present in any of them. Hoping she would find something she continued to flick through picture after picture of some social event or promotional mixer. Then there it was – a group picture, the caption read January 2001 Aztec Gala Ball. Lola's eyes widened as she leaned in to get a closer look at Carl Stein. He was a good fifteen years younger in the picture, his hair was dark black, a stark contrast to the ice of his blue eyes. Dressed in a dinner suit and his legendary politician's smile, he was flanked on either side by two young women. Lola recognised their faces but she read the caption anyway.

Stein Corp owner and Chief Executive Carl Stein enjoying champagne and canapés with young models (right) April Myers, Kimberley Adams, (left) Carmen Barnes and Nora Evans at Aztec Solutions First Anniversary bash.

There it was, proof that Carl Stein knew these women and that they all knew each other. 'How could the authorities conclude that these women took their own lives?' said Lola in disbelief. 'I mean I've been researching this for two whole days and I'm able to make these links.'

'You think Carl Stein killed these women?' said Erin, her brow furrowed with scepticism. 'Yes,' said Lola solemnly. 'I have reason to believe that he was involved in these murders.'

'How?'

'I can't say too much at the moment Erin, but I've seen this kind of thing before, back home in Ireland. I've gone through every case file and each death has at least five similarities. How on earth the NYPD did not see that this was not suicide is beyond comprehension.'

'Look at your dates, Lola,' said Erin pointing at the screen. 'Anything after September 2001, you may as well forget about it. Once those towers came down, this city changed, the world changed. The NYPD wouldn't have been spending too much time looking into the deaths of some random girls, if what you're saying is right and it was made to look like suicide that meant more time for trying to catch terrorists.'

Lola had been very young the day the twin towers came down but her father had always maintained that something wasn't right about the official story. In many ways she had inherited that distrust from him. She'd always been quite cautious of the establishment and now as a grown woman having had the experiences that she had, she understood that it wasn't without good reason.

'Anyway, what led the police to call it suicide, did they leave notes or somethin?' asked Erin.

'I just saw it on the file but I never thought to look for the actual reason. Good woman, Erin,' said Lola writing a note to check this out.

'Glad to be of assistance, Ms Paige. You're a regular Lois Lane,' laughed Erin. 'Does that mean I'm your Jimmy?' she added, tipping her head humbly.

'You're hilarious,' said Lola. 'On that note,' she said searching her pages again. 'What I did find out was this same detective has viewed all these case files. I don't know if he was involved in the investigations but his name was on the front of each file. I asked the desk sergeant about him but apparently he left the force and went off to work in the private sector. I've no idea where, but I wouldn't be surprised if Stein Corp has set him up in a nice job somewhere.'

'Jesus, Lola, I know you hate the guy and all but this is hardly proof that Carl Stein is involved. I'm at these gigs all the time and it's what you do, I mean these girls might not even know each other at all, never mind Carl Stein. Just cause they're in a picture together don't mean shit.'

Lola knew she was right but then Erin didn't know who and what Carl Stein was.

'I know, Erin, I know,' said Lola in a conciliatory tone, accepting her point. She wondered if she was trying too hard to make all this fit and she was thankful for Erin's scepticism because this would be nothing compared to what Isaac would give her.

'All I can say is that it's a start.'

'You've done some great research here, Lola,' said Erin as she printed off the rest of the pictures that they'd earmarked, 'not to piss on your parade, but even if you do have a watertight story here, good luck getting it printed. If things are going down so that Carl Stein is going to be a majority holder at the Torch, try getting that into his paper.'

At every turn there was another obstacle, he'd all angles covered, business, law, banks, the media. Those were all the tools that he needed and the people like him to literally get away with murder, amongst other things.

'I hadn't thought of that, Erin.' Lola rubbed her eyes and wondered why she was doing this, what she hoped to find when there were far more important matters that she could be dealing with, like securing the book. Although she was becoming increasingly disillusioned with the world of journalism, there was still something noble in holding power to account, something noble in the pursuit of the truth. The pillars of the fourth estate were being eroded at an alarming rate and only a noble few fought against the decay. Lola thought of Jodi and how her story had been canned. It showed where the power really lay.

'Well if not the Torch, then perhaps the National Outrage will take it,' said Lola with a weary smile. 'Thanks for your help, Erin, anyway.'

'All you gotta do is ask, my little Irish fairy! Right I better get going and don't worry my lips are sealed.'

'Thanks, Erin.' Lola smiled at her friend as she slipped the pictures back into her file. She tidied around Isaac's desk before she returned to her own seat. It was lunchtime and while some of the reporters typed at their desks, quite a few had left the newsroom, but Lola was too distracted to have an appetite so she decided to do a bit more research.

She typed in Aztec Solutions to the computer's search engine and in seconds page after page of information sprang up on the screen. The company's website was top of the pile and it was the usual slick corporate jargon. As Lola scrolled on down through the page she finally saw something promising, clicking on the headline, which was from an old Torch article, she read 'Aztec Solutions wins Patent "theft" Case'. Lola clicked on the article to see who had the by line. It was by someone called Len Carnegie. Closing the window she made a note of the name and then checked the paper's email database to see if he was still there. She had no idea where the business section of the paper lived but it was worth a try.

For ten whole minutes she had been wondering aimlessly around the third floor trying to track down the business editor's desk when finally someone took pity on her.

'You okay there?'

'Oh hi,' blushed Lola, she didn't know whether it was from embarrassment or because her rescuer was very handsome. He didn't look much older than her. His dark eyes softly considered her as he waited patiently for her to answer.

'Yes, I'm looking for a Len Carnegie. I'm a bit lost,' apologised Lola with a sheepish grin. 'I don't get out of the newsroom too often,' she laughed.

'You're Isaac's girl,' said the young man. Lola liked how that sounded a little too much, so she forced the warm feeling it elicited to the back of her mind.

'I hear you've got quite a left hook on you,' he started to laugh. If Lola's face was flushed before, she was sure it was like a beacon now. It wasn't often that she found herself bereft of a retort but it felt like her brain was struggling for oxygen.

'I'm only messin with ye. I saw you at the bar that night. I was about to offer to buy you a drink and then I saw you whack Bill and I decided to leave it.'

Lola laughed. She liked this guy.

'I'm Ritchie Young by the way.' Lola leaned over the booth to shake his outstretched hand. 'I'm Lola Paige, nice to meet you.'

'So what you looking Len for? He's gone to lunch. Anything I can help you with?'

'I don't think so; it's actually a story he covered a few years ago about Aztec Solutions.'

'Oh, the court case. Is that what you're talking about?'

'Yeah. You know anything about it?'

'I actually worked on the story with him. I was just an intern then, so you know how it goes.' He didn't elaborate but Lola understood the implication. He did a lot of work and got little or no recognition. 'What is it you want to know?'

'We'll I'd like to know who they are. Who owns the company? What do they do? Who brought the case against them and why?'

'I was just going to grab a bite to eat, if you wanna come along I can try and answer some of those questions.'

'Yeah, that's grand,' said Lola. 'Thank you. But I'll need to go get my bag and some money.'

'I can buy you lunch; I mean if that's okay with you. You're not going to assault me for suggesting it.'

'Shut up,' smiled Lola. 'I'll throw the money up to you later and thank you.'

'You're welcome. After you, Ms Paige,' said Ritchie as he watched intently as Lola led the way to the elevator.

'You know Bill didn't get a slap for offering to buy me a drink,' said Lola pressing the button for the bottom floor.

'I know, I know. I'm just messin with ya!' smiled Ritchie. 'So why are you interested in Aztec Solutions?' Lola hadn't anticipated this question so she had to think quickly.

'Oh I'm in features for the next few weeks so I'm just sounding things out. I heard about some of the technology they are pioneering and I wanted a bit of background on the case when I saw it.'

'There's a place just around the corner, called Ameren's, you ever been in there?'

'No. Erin and I usually just go to the wee garden at the paper.'

'Yeah I see you there sometimes.' Lola didn't know if Ritchie Young had meant to say that out loud but judging by the flush on his checks, she'd guessed that he hadn't.

'So is it good?' she said changing the subject quickly. 'The food?'

'Oh it's real good. Busy but it's worth the wait.'

They only had to wait five minutes before they were seated. The only available seat was right by the window. Lola didn't mind as she enjoyed looking out onto the street and feeling the heat from the sun as it came through the window on her skin. The back rooms were teeming with men in suits, some from the paper, some from the various businesses and banks that were close by and she didn't have to guess too hard to know what the topic of conversation was. Carl Stein's heist. The waitress brought their drinks and took their order, leaving them free to talk uninterrupted.

'So Aztec Solutions was set up back in late 2000. It's a subsidiary, one of the many subsidiaries of Stein Corp. Have you ever heard of Stein Corp?'

'Yeah. I've heard of them,' said Lola forcing a light smile onto her face.

'I suppose everybody has,' conceded Ritchie. 'Carl Stein is a very shrewd businessman not to mention a multi-billionaire. He has his hands in lots of different pies from private banks, real estate, media and now pioneering technology,' said Ritchie in full appraisal. 'Of course the big news today is that he is on the brink of buying the Torch but there's talk that he has privately funded all sorts of research in the new frontiers of quantum technology and research. That's why he set up Aztec. So fast-forward a few years and a man called Ezra Cohen files a case for patent breach. It turns out that this Cohen guy was a professor at Stanford University out in California and that he belonged to some Club out there, what was it you called it?' Ritchie thought for a moment.

'Oh you see all these nut jobs online protesting outside it... The Bohemian

Club,' he spat, delighted with himself. 'That's it. Anyway, Cohen claimed that he had been working on these egg devices that housed Random Number Generators off the back of some Russian scientist's research that our thoughts can affect the physical universe, some whack stuff like that.' Lola could tell that Ritchie wasn't very taken by the idea of thoughts affecting the physical universe. She looked at his colours, there was a lot of bright orange and grey. He was proud, but nervous.

'So,' continued Ritchie, pausing to take a sip of his water, 'building on this, Professor Cohen set up a study at the university and it turns out that Stein Corp was one of its main sponsors. These RNGs are based in countries all over the world and they are connected to a central system that produces the data.'

Lola worked hard to keep her face passive, what a piece of luck she was having today, these were the devices that Daithí had discovered.

'Now his claim,' said Ritchie, enjoying Lola's undivided attention, 'is that these RNGs can measure global consciousness and that the numbers and research have shown a correlation in our global consciousness before, during and after major world events. There is science to back this up. It may sound crazy to you, Lola, but this is where the quantum field is at the moment. Anyway this Cohen guy was happy to continue working with Aztec as their chief scientist but he claimed that he discovered that Aztec, namely Carl Stein, was using these devices unethically by working with the military.'

'By doing what?'

'Well, this is the thing, there was so much that we never got to hear. Parts of the proceedings were heard behind closed doors. Anyway the old guy lost his case and that's the last we heard of him. Apparently he's living over in Brooklyn now. The case almost broke him when an anonymous donor suddenly weighed in to pay the legal fees. After that no university would touch him. I kinda feel sorry for him,' said Ritchie as an aside. 'I mean he's scraping along while Aztec's stocks and shares are off the charts, all because of his invention.'

There was a lot for Lola to digest. 'You got a pen?' Ritchie fished one from his trouser pocket and handed it to her. Lola wrote down the name Ezra Cohen and Brooklyn in the white napkin, folding it she placed in to the pocket of her dress.

She and Ritchie talked about the events of the paper that day and the trials and tribulations of the intern. It was a lovely reprieve for Lola. She liked Ritchie and he was by no means hard on the eye. She left to go to the bathroom while he kindly paid the bill. Emerging from the toilet Lola's heart leapt into her mouth when she saw that he was in deep conversation with a finely dressed gentleman. Lola didn't need him to turn around; she would know Alex Stein anywhere. As if he too sensed her, he turned around as she was approaching the table. Lola looked straight at her colleague, she feared that if she made eyes contact with Alex she would lose her nerve.

'Thanks, Ritchie. I'm good to go when you are.'

Alex shook his hand. 'Good to see you again, Ritchie, give my regards to your fiancée. When's the big day?'

This caught the young reporter off-guard as he stumbled over his reply. 'Oh err... December.'

'Only a few more months of freedom left,' smiled Alex.

'What about you, Alex, have you plans on settling down anytime soon?'

'It's all overrated,' said Alex his voice light and ringing with confidence, 'besides I haven't met anyone that can hold my attention long enough.' He never took his eyes from Lola.

'Ms Paige,' said Alex smoothly. 'It's always a pleasure to see you.'

'And likewise, Mr Stein, do be sure to tell your father I was asking after him. I must pay him a visit soon.'

'I look forward to it,' said Alex without a hint of unease. 'When should we be expecting you?' he mocked with a polite smile.

'Soon.' Lola smiled back with equal sweetness. Ritchie's eyes flitted from Lola to Alex uncomfortably.

'Good to see you again, Mr Stein.'

Lola chose not to ask him about his fiancée on the way back or why he had failed to mention her and nor did he.

'Are the Steins friends of yours? I mean you could have gone and got it straight from the horse's mouth.' Ritchie was smiling but Lola could see the uncertainty and panic in his eyes.

'Then I wouldn't have gotten the truth,' she smiled. 'And to answer your question,' said Lola, 'no. We aren't friends. Thanks for your help, Ritchie, I really appreciate it and I'll throw that money up to you before I leave today,' she added as they parted on the second floor.

The newsroom was like a morgue when Lola got back to her station. A light was on in Isaac's office but the door and privacy blinds were closed. She hadn't spoken to him for a few days now so Lola knocked on the door gingerly.

'Come in,' he beckoned from within. Lola opened the door a crack and stuck her ahead around the glass door to find him and Jodi deep in conversation again. Lola had the distinct feeling that she'd interrupted something and the awkwardness hung in the air despite their welcome.

'Irish,' said Isaac in great spirits, 'good to see you. Come in.'

'Hi, little sister.' Jodi beamed as she stood to leave. 'Isaac, that looks good to me, let's go with that,' she said nodding. Lola stood to one side to let her out the door. 'Good to see you, Lola, I hope you're enjoying features.' Jodi was a vision as always and her musky perfume lingered in Isaac's office long after she was gone.

'So how did it go this morning?' asked Lola, still loitering in the doorway.

Isaac held his hand up, 'I don't even want to talk about it,' he said but he didn't seem that concerned. 'What have you been up to? Besides going for lunch with Ritchie Young. Soon- to-be-married Ritchie Young.'

'Jesus,' said Lola rolling her eyes, 'we ate a sandwich together, it doesn't mean I'm trying to steal him.'

'It's not you I'm concerned about. That boy has been mad looking an introduction for weeks now.'

Secretly flattered, Lola didn't offer a reply. 'Listen, Isaac, I'm heading down to the 7th precinct here and I wanted to check in with you before I left.' This made him lift his head to look at her.

'7th precinct? What's taking you down there?'

Lola stepped into the office and closed the door behind her.

'I'm working on something; something that I think might interest us both. It's very early days yet so I can't say too much until I'm sure.'

'Okay,' said Isaac glaring at her over his reading glasses. 'I don't like the sound of this, you have quite an aptitude for finding trouble, Irish.'

'Don't start, Isaac. Please. This is very serious stuff and very important. I won't lie, it is huge and if I'm right, it's certainly going to be too much for me to handle on my own. I'm going to need you to have a very open mind, Isaac.'

'What? I'm the most open minded person in this newsroom.'

'Yeah you are,' mocked Lola, 'until it comes to moving into the twenty-first century.'

'Always an answer, Irish. Some day that mouth of yours is going to get you into trouble.'

'Bye,' smiled Lola, closing the door behind her. It had just gone two-thirty, which would mean that she had plenty of time to get to the precinct and home at a reasonable hour.

~33~

wo officers were escorting a drunk man into the police station when Lola signed in at the front desk. There was a different officer on duty than the day before. He searched for her name on the list, eventually finding it on the reverse page.

'Okay, Ms Paige, you can enter through the door to your left, just wait for the buzzer to sound.'

The main processing area was all but empty as Lola made her way across to the back of the room. Taking the stairs down to the basement floor she had to sign in again before she was allowed to proceed along the corridor to the file viewing room.

'You're back, Ms New York Torch. What have you got for me today?' Officer Mendez's sardonic smile spread across his face.

Lola handed Mendez the file numbers that she'd recorded on her previous trip, as well as the two additional files logged under Nora Evans's case.

'Take these,' he handed the twelve document folders she'd had the day before. 'It might take me a while to find the others. Go right on ahead into the room and I'll bring them when I've found them,' he instructed pointing at the grim room across the hall.

Lola lifted the files and crossed the hall, set them on the table. She didn't waste any time getting started. She was halfway through Nora Evans's file when the old police officer came in with another in his hand.

'This is all I can locate at the moment.' He set it down in front of Lola. 'You haven't found the other one yet?'

'I've located it but there ain't nothin in the folder.' Although his tone was even Lola could see the grey around his aura and she knew that there was something he wasn't telling her. He was very worried. His body might not have betrayed him but his energy field certainly did.

'You mean it's disappeared or someone has taken it?'

'Now, that's not what I said. I said it wasn't there. Typical journalist, making up stories.'

'Would anything as far back as 2001 be on a computer database?'

The officer scratched his head. 'I don't know. I'll have a look on the system here.'

There was a suicide note attached to the file and Lola's eyes poured over it again and again. The file said that it was left by Evans and written in her own hand.

The letter was generic enough, short and concise. In the note Nora Evans wrote that she couldn't take it anymore and that the world was moving into a very dark place and that while she had tried she couldn't fight them anymore. Lola read and reread it again. Reaching for the other file she opened it up to see an incident report. The format was slightly different on this document but it had all Nora's particulars.

Lola cast her eyes along the type. From what she could gauge Nora had contacted police to say that she thought her life was in danger. She said that she thought that she might have heard something that she wasn't supposed to. According to the report, the filing officer stated that when he asked Miss Evans who or what was posing a threat to her life, she became irate and uncooperative and left the building. Lola checked the date. It was two months before her death.

Lola couldn't believe what she was looking at. She flicked on through her case file. As she read the autopsy report it said that the cause of death was consistent with lacerations to the artery on her quads and drowning, as the lungs were filled with water. There was nothing out of the ordinary there.

Lola looked up to see how Mendez was fairing when he beckoned her towards the desk again.

'It says here the other report that you were after has been classified as confidential. Between you and me, kid, this is very strange.'

'Could you come with me a second?' said Lola. 'I'd like you have a look at something for me, just to see what you think.'

'Sure kid, what is it?'

'I'm no detective but something doesn't seem right to me about all this.

All these women, I believe, were killed in blocks of four.' Lola moved around the table separating the files according to the month and year they fitted into.

'Look these women all turned up dead in the same river, in the same city, within three months of each other. Look,' said Lola lifting out each file.

'April Myers, Kimberley Adams, Carmen Evans and Nora Evans, who we know, thanks to this report, was known to the police on one occasion where she told them that she feared for her life. Two months before she was dragged out of a half frozen East River. Now don't you think that's a little strange? I mean if you'd been a detective wouldn't you have followed this up?'

'I was a detective, kid,' said Mendez, his colours all a swirl. 'But 2001 was a crazy time. The force was stretched thin after the towers came down. Nothing else mattered. It sounds harsh, I know, but this wouldn't have been top priority.'

'Okay,' nodded Lola, 'that aside, and the fact that all these women were known to each other.'

'What? How d'you know that?'

Lola scrambled through her bag and pulled out the clippings she'd printed off earlier.

'This is how I know. Look at the caption, they all modelled or were represented by the same company. Look at the date, January 2001.'

'Yeah, yeah, I can read, kid.'

'Officer.'

'It's Sergeant, kid, Sergeant Mendez to you.' 'Sorry, Sergeant,' corrected Lola. 'That's not all.'

She picked up the next pile. 'Now fast forward to 2006 and on the exact same date in March of that year Elsie Price's body was found with cuts along her arterial artery, June, Joy Butler, September, Jo Morris, December, Ashley Cox. All girls found in the East River, all girls had lacerations to their arterials, all deaths were marked down as suicide with a letter.'

Lola reached for the last pile. 'Now we are in 2012, first up is Beth Powell, then Kristi Cooper, then Susan Harris, then Lucy Davis. The exact same as before. 9/11 cannot be blamed for overlooking the deaths in 2006 nor in 2012, Sergeant, surely even you would concede that?'

'None of these cases came across my desk,' he almost whispered to himself. A look of unease darkened his face but Lola was not deterred by this, instead she was emboldened by it.

'Sergeant' said Lola having decided that it was worth it to risk laying all her cards on the table. She had no reason to trust Mendez but something in his demeanour told her that these connections and revelations where as shocking to him as they were to her so she told him the truth.

'I have reason to believe that these deaths were not suicides, but murders and ritual murders carried out by something or someone with enough power to conceal it. They all occurred at the solstices and the equinoxes of that I'm sure.'

'Now hold on here, kid, with your conspiracy theories. You've put a few things together, I'll grant you that, but that don't build no case. You can't run around printing suspicions in that paper of yours.'

'Settle down, Sergeant,' said Lola as if she was in full control of this situation. 'I know that, plus Isaac, my boss, would kill me if I didn't come to him with something substantial. This detective whose name appears on the front of every file, I need to get in contact with him. Have you any idea where he went to when he left the force?'

'Hold on a minute.' The sergeant walked out and around behind his desk again and lifted the phone. Lola couldn't hear what he was saying from where she was. She studied the man, the grey was there again, it seemed to be everywhere in the precinct. Lola could never be a cop, in fact the very thought depressed her. Constantly having to deal with the worst of humanity, never trusting, always suspicious. Jolted by the familiarity with her own situation Lola laughed to herself – that pretty much summed up her life at the moment!

She could see that Mendez was a decent man. He looked close to retirement age and he was obviously seeing out the rest of his days down here but she could see that something was awakening in him. Her enquiries had sparked something deep inside the old cop. Lola wondered who he'd pissed off to be given this gig.

'I made a call there to someone who knows someone. It turns out Detective Jessop got himself a job with Aztec Solutions, he's head of security for the entire company.'

Lola fell to the chair, pulling her hands over her face. Of course, how had she not seen this, it had been staring her in the face this whole time. With everything that she knew about the Hell Fire Club and Carl Stein, they had to have someone on the inside and it looked like Detective Andy Jessop was their man.

'He's our link then,' she said looking up at Mendez.

'Now, kid, I don't like where this is going. You can't go around making accusations like that about police officers without good reason.'

'Good reason? His name is all over these bloody files and according to the reports he was not the detective assigned to any of them. For all we know there could be pages missing, statements missing. Look at this, Sergeant. Look at this picture.' Lola produced a picture of Carl Stein with Nora and company in 2001. 'You know he owns Aztec Solutions, he knew these girls as you can see from the picture, and now your man's hands who are all over these files has been handed a very well paid job with Aztec. This is not trajectory, these are the facts as we see them.'

'Hold on a minute, let me get this straight. You think these girls were killed in some pagan ritual by Carl Stein and the case files tampered with by Andy Jessop, who then was awarded for his fealty with a top job at Aztec?'

'Pretty much, but the killings have got nothing to do with Paganism,' declared Lola defensively.

'Have you gone and lost your mind, child?' the sergeant bellowed in laughter. 'You've been reading too much Sherlock Holmes or watching too much of that X Files.'

Lola began to gather her things. She could see how crazy it maybe sounded to a regular member of the public, but she knew better. She didn't respond as she gathered her things together, placing them neatly into her bag. It was almost seven o' clock. She had no idea that she'd been down there so long. So much for the early night.

'I'm sorry you feel that way, Sergeant Mendez, but now I know why you're no longer a detective.' This shot had the desired effect, as the smile slid from the old man's face.

'Perhaps you should take a look at the suicide notes in those files, you might find something interesting.'

Lola walked out of the room and back up into the custody area. Business had picked up since she'd arrived. Her stomach rumbled, angry that she'd deprived it of food for so long. As she was leaving the building she could smell the hotdogs and crepes that drifted from the food vendors on the street. She still hadn't braved it yet with the street food and despite being so hungry she decided not to.

The sun burned a deep red in the sky and Lola needed to walk. She was tired of air-conditioned buildings and rooms devoid of air and light. She was tired of being tens of feet underground or in the back of cab. She needed to think and tonight it was still light and pleasant so she trusted her feet to guide her in the right direction.

As she left the brown brick building of the 7th precinct behind her and turned onto Delancey, Lola seemed to follow the natural flow of the footfall as New Yorkers walked and talked. The longer she walked the more confident she got that her feet knew what they were doing. The ring around her neck purred and pulsed, reassuring her that all was well. As she walked up East 2nd, she passed the famous Red Webster Hall and Lola paused for a moment outside the historic building to pay homage to the place that had housed the Labour and Union rallies at the turn of the twentieth century, way before socialism became a filthy word in American discourse.

Continuing on she tracked up 4th Avenue and then on to Union Square. She was tempted to get the subway from Union Square but it seemed sinful to leave the heat and light of the street. Although the evening was growing later, Lola felt as though the sun was growing stronger. It gave her energy and seemed to make even a city as tough as New York a little softer around the edges. People were more relaxed in the evening, there wasn't the same jostling for a place on the footpaths and everyone seemed to be in less of a hurry. Lola hadn't really gotten to experience this side of the city until now and she quite liked it. Without realising why she followed the signs to Broadway.

Madison Square Park lay to her left and she felt the urge to go in and sit by a tree. Not like the small trees in Liberty Plaza or the tiny saplings at the Torch's garden but a real tree, with trunk and bark and leaves with their faces opened upward to the pink sky above but she didn't stop.

As the buildings grew larger and more concentrated she could tell that she was getting closer to the midtown area. Times Square was up ahead, where tourists took photos and soaked in the neon spectacle. Lola could feel the pull of the light and the sun; the feeling was totally over whelming as it urged her to carry on, to keep walking.

Checking the time displayed above Times Square, she realised her journey had taken over an hour. The clock, which stood astride the former New York Torch building, was a thing of great beauty. Surrounded by brightly lit billboards and advertisements, Lola wondered how many of the 330,000 people who passed through Times Square each day bothered to look up.

Still Lola's feet urged her onwards towards whatever beckoned her, and while her conscious mind remained in the dark, the skin on her arms prickled with gooseflesh as if it knew what it was that called even before she turned the corner onto West 42nd Street.

The light washed over her warm and vivid, stopping Lola in her tracks. She heard that soft voice again that sounded like the hush and whisper of the sea. Follow the light it seemed to say. Follow the light and your path will be illuminated.

Shielding her eyes from the burning light Lola looked up the broad avenue, where they found its source.

There, suspended on the horizon between two mammoth buildings that acted as markers, lay the sun wavering and glittering like an enormous garnet in the twilight sky causing a laser of light to beam from West to East 42nd street.

For a moment, as the voice continued to reassure her and urge her on, Lola thought that she was the only person in all of New York privy to this celestial display, but as she became more present in her surroundings she could see the road was littered with pedestrians with their phones out filming and snapping pictures. New Yorkers at a standstill, Lola didn't know what was more confounding, the alignment or the sight of the stationary city dwellers.

'Manhattanhendge, how cool is this?' one passer-by was saying to another.

'I missed it last year. God I'm so happy I got it this year. That'll be it until next Memorial Day Weekend.'

The sound of a car beeping brought Lola to her senses, where she found herself in the middle of the road.

'Yo, Dorothy, the sidewalk's that way.' Tommy Maloney was leaning out the side of his car, grinning at her, directing her towards the sidewalk where he pulled in.

'Tommy,' said Lola. 'Good to see you.'

'You hadda stayed on the middle of the road for much longer, that sun display is the last thing you'd a been seein'. You just outta work or what?'

'I was over on Delancey, at the police station there, I fancied a walk and I'm glad I did. Did ye see that?'

'You walked four miles across town? Whataya crazy?'

'At home I walk everywhere.'

'This is Manhattan, Dorothy, not Ireland.'

'I'm fine,' said Lola shaking her head dismissively.

'Get in and I'll give you a lift home.' Lola was reluctant to leave the street and the sun but she didn't have the heart to decline Tommy's offer.

'You live in Brooklyn, don't you, Tommy?' asked Lola hit with a sudden burst of inspiration. The voice was still in the fore of her mind and it seemed to accentuate her trail of thought.

'Yeah, why d'you ask?'

'I need to track down a man that lives in Brooklyn. How would I go about doing that?'

'You tried the phone directory?'

'No not yet.'

'Well, Sherlock, that might be a good place to start. You gotta name for this man?'

'Yes,' said Lola, 'Ezra Cohen.'

'Never heard of the guy. I mean Brooklyn's a helluva big place, Dorothy!'

Lola typed the name and Brooklyn into the search and she knew that she would find him. She just knew it and just as the search was processing, an address in Brooklyn came up.

'33 Slope Parks, Brooklyn,' said Lola reading the address out loud. 'You know it, Tommy?'

'Yeah. I know the street. I don't know anyone that lives there. This guy he must be rich if he lives in Slope Parks.'

'I need to speak to this man, Tommy, it's really important,' said Lola feeling the urge to go now to Brooklyn.

'Where to?' asked Tommy pulling out into the stream of traffic.

'What? Oh right. Slope Parks please.'

'Now?' asked Tommy unsure.

'Well why not?' said Lola full of energy. 'You're on your way home aren't you and I could just get a cab back into the city.'

'What's the hurry?'

'Tommy, please,' said Lola. 'It's important.'

'Alright, Dorothy, let's go.' Tommy jolted the car around mid-traffic and headed for the Brooklyn Bridge, earning irate insults as he went.

'So I was down with my friend Prospero the other day. He tells me he hasn't seen you down there in a few days and he was wondering what you'd been up to.' Lola noticed how Tommy's eyes darted sideways to catch her expression when he said this. She could see that he suddenly seemed a bit tense but she remained aloof.

'I've been really busy with work to be honest,' said Lola looking out the window at the buildings as they passed through the city. Well it wasn't exactly a lie, she had been. She had put Prospero to one side for the moment because she didn't have the strength to deal with it at the moment.

'Well you should go down and see the old man. The place is looking great and things seemed to have settled down a bit. I mean the cops are still busting their chops but that's nothing out of the ordinary. That dog of his doesn't half get around. How the pound haven't caught him I don't know. You never guess where I saw him the other day?'

'Where?' smiled Lola affectionately, thinking of the little terrier.

'Only up on Fifth Avenue outside the cathedral. I was parked across the road waiting on a client when I saw the little guy. He was just sitting there. That dog knows this city better than me.'

Lola made a mental note as another light bulb lit up in her mind, she was returning Tommy's smile while she was wondering if Hermes might be the link between Alex and Prospero. Lola still could not believe she had been so wrong about the old man. Every time she thought about it only compounded her lack of faith in her instincts. Then she remembered she couldn't read him, she only got a glimpse of his aura when Erin had taken the picture. It never boded well when she couldn't read someone, and now she knew what Prospero was hiding.

The betrayal chaffed Lola still leaving her feeling sore and angry. Lola slumped further into the car seat, weighed down by her leaden thoughts.

The car began to slow down and Tommy Malone directed her across the road. 'Welcome to Slope Parks, Brooklyn,' he said pointing across the street.

For the first time during their journey Lola was present enough to notice her surroundings and the sight was an impressive one. On either side of the street, flanked by Japanese Pagodas and Norway maple trees, stood rows of Brownstone town houses.

The dense legions of trees gave the street a light plum hue in the falling light like a life in pastels drawn by the Impressionists. There was a softness about the redbrick buildings and the steep step that rose from the street to the mouth of the various arched double doors.

'Number 33 is across there,' said Tommy pointing it out. 'The one with ivy growing on it.' Lola got out of the car and crossed the street ironing out the creases in her dress with the palm of her hand. She took a quick look back at Tommy who was on his cell phone. He smiled and waved as she approached the house.

The house was like something straight out of an Edith Wharton novel, elegant and classic with ivy that crawled up the front of the four-storey building, winding its way around the windows and boxed flowers that sat perched on the sills. Behind the cast iron railings stood an original Victorian street lamp that expelled a muted orange light making the scene below on the street look like a movie set. After the day that she'd had Lola wouldn't have been one bit surprised to find that it was.

The stoop was high and broad and Lola had to hoist her dress above her knee to reach the first step. She held on to the side for security but the railing was so thick she couldn't get any purchase on it. Finally reaching the top of the steps, the light of the front porch illuminated the door and the button for the bell. A light spilled out onto the street from the basement of the house and the hallway light was on so Lola guessed someone was at home. She tried the bell but there was no answer. She tried again and waited until she could hear the steady tread of footsteps as they approached the door from within.

The door swung open and a man in his late sixties dressed in a shirt, a jumper and suit trousers stood in the doorway. He wore house slippers and his fine glasses hung on a chain around his neck. He was clean-shaven and his honey-coloured hair was neatly swept off his face. The years had been good to Professor Ezra Cohen, as there were still traces of the handsome young man who used to inhabit his body. He was strong and upright, not entirely what Lola had been expecting. She didn't really know what she had expected.

Albert Einstein perhaps – grey hair and no socks. Lola stood floundering like a fish out of water for a moment.

'Can I help you, dear?' said the professor with a bemused look at finding some strange young women on his doorstep. His voice was very polite and he had the kind of American accent that wasn't really an accent at all.

'Yes, sorry. Professor Cohen?' asked Lola. The word professor triggered a tightening around his lips and he retreated back from the doorway.

'Who's asking?'

'Yes,' said Lola. 'My name is Lola Paige, sir, and I'm from the New York T...' The door slammed shut in her face. Stunned she stood blankly in the doorway. She looked around the empty street before deciding to try again. This time she knocked on the door but there was no reply. Again she knocked and finally the door swung open but by now the professor's face was impatient and closed.

'I am going to give you three seconds to get off my property or I'll be calling the police.' He was about to close the door again, when Lola jammed her foot in the way.

'Please, Professor Cohen, I just need a few minutes of your time. I've come all the way out here.'

'I've nothing to say to your paper. The Torch writes what it wants.'

'I'm not here about that, sir,' said Lola trying to adjust her position. 'I want to know what Carl Stein stole from you and why?'

His hold on the door slackened and Lola made the most of it. 'I need to know what Aztec Solutions have been up to.' The professor considered Lola for a moment before deciding to let her in. Widening the door open, he stepped aside for her to enter.

'You must forgive my behaviour. I don't exactly have the best relationship with the Torch. Every now and then some hack will show up on my doorstep looking for a story.'

'I'm sorry about that, professor. I won't take up much of your time; I understand it's late in the evening. Thank you for speaking with me.'

'You're not from around these parts, what is it you said your name was?'

'No,' smiled Lola politely. 'Lola's my name. I'm from Ireland and I'm interning with the paper for the summer.'

'From Ireland,' he laughed. 'I'd never have guessed. So what can I do for you, Ms Paige?'

Lola thought about her approach and how she should word it. 'Well like

I said at the door, sir, I'd like to hear from a primary source about the technology you were working on.'

'And why do you need this information? So you can open up old wounds for a few inches of column in that rag of a paper you call news.' Although his words were sharp and straight to the point, there was no aggression in his tone.

'I won't lie, Professor Cohen, that could be a possibility, but what I'm trying to ascertain at the moment is whether I have a story or not.'

'When did that ever stop any journalist before, Ms Paige?' said Ezra with a knowing smile.

'Well I'm not every journalist, professor. I'm here, aren't I? If I wanted I could have just regurgitated everything that has already been printed in the paper, why come the whole way out here?'

'Well I suppose you have a point. But it was all so long ago now. I've moved on to other ventures and so have Aztec Solutions.'

'Does that not concern you?' He looked at Lola, and she could tell that it did concern him. It did worry him.

'So what is it you want to know?'

Lola lifted out her pencil and note pad. 'Do you mind if I take few notes?'

'Go right ahead,' the professor shook his head.

'Firstly what is it you were researching?'

'Well my background is in quantum physics and in the late 90s my department at the university, I was working out west then, we began to look at consciousness and what that meant. The quantum field research had opened up so many new possibilities for us. I mean we had only just scratched the surface. Back in 1927 at the Solvay International Conference, Werner Heisenberg and Niels Bohr...'

'Heisenberg and Bohr were physicists?' asked Lola, she'd never heard of them or this Solvay Conference.

'Yes. Well at this conference Bohr and Werner approached Einstein, I take it you've heard of him?'

'Yes,' smiled Lola rolling her eyes.

'Okay good, so Heisenberg and Bohr approached Einstein about some experiments they had been conducting and how they believed that the researchers involved were actually affecting the results of the experiments. The math that they had at their disposal at the time was not repeatable enough to explain what was happening so Albert wasn't convinced, later on in his career he understood what they were saying. They came to understand that something else was at play. Still to this day quantum physics can't deal with an experiment where a human being is involved. You see what they discovered then and what we now understand in the field is that whenever a conscious observer is present it causes the collapse of the wave function. Therefore the data can't be empirical.'

There was way too much information in there but Lola tried to grasp on to the important bits or the bits that she thought where important.

'So what you're saying is that consciousness or thought has a vibration or energy that can affect or interact with the field around it?'

'Exactly, Ms Paige, Exactly.'

'But haven't mystics been telling us this for years?' This has been known. Lola's own experiences were living proof of this phenomenon, as was the equinox Oracle.

'I suspect you're right, Ms Paige, but science was not ready to come to that conclusion. Scientists were not prepared to jeopardise their entire career by suggesting any such thing. However, I was,' smiled Ezra crossing his legs and chewing pensively on the leg of his glasses. Lola could see that he was cautious but he wasn't nervous. Ezra Cohen exuded total confidence and sovereignty over the situation.

'So based on the findings of Bohr et al, I wondered what if we used this concept, if human thought could affect the field why not find a way to see that in action? Several systems of thought have told stories about an intrinsic connection between all living things, the Greeks called it the Anima Mundi – the World Soul and that's what I wanted to investigate. At the time it was my belief – and it still is, the frontier of science is building some major data – that we are energy and that we, like the entire cosmos, are all interconnected. Our thoughts have a vibration and what we think and how we think not only affects our bodies but the world around us.

'So my colleagues and I built random number generators. These sensors were placed at different locations all over the world. The idea behind them was to see if there was co-ordination of thought or direction of that universal consciousness.'

Lola was completely wrapped in thought. She and the Order had known this all along. If people understood how we are all connected to everything, each other, the trees, the animals, how different everything would be.

'So what did your study find?' she asked.

'Well for the first few years, not much but there appeared to be slight correlations before, during and after major world events like in March of 98 in Kosovo, April of that same year in your own country around the Good Friday Agreement, in August of 98 when the US Embassies were bombed in Kenya and Tanzania and before, during and after the Columbine High School shooting, we witnessed a correlation of sort and a pattern begin to appear. But it wasn't enough, we could not be sure that it wasn't just chance, the numbers were ambiguous.

'However, by January 2001, we could see that something was happening in the global subconscious mind or for some the conscious mind. Again we couldn't be sure but each month the numbers were becoming more and more synchronized, not just here in New York City or America but all over the world. Something was coming and based on the data, it looked like it was going to be big.'

'Let me get this straight,' said Lola, her head reeling from what she was hearing. 'Are you saying that these egg things have the potential to detect a major world event or attack?'

'Yes.' Ezra confirmed her question with such indifference that Lola had to check him again. 'I mean it's not as simple as that,' he said modestly, 'but there is strong data and indications that this is the case. The events of that September morning have haunted me. After that everything changed. I tried to warn them but they wouldn't listen. It was too late, I was in too deep.' For the first time, Ezra's voice dimmed and in his colours Lola could see the old hurts split and break open again.

'You're talking about Aztec?' she asked. 'How did they get involved?'

'Competition for funding at any university is tough, never mind when it's the field of quantum physics. Some institutions believe that it's like burning money, that it gets you nothing. We were struggling, if I'm being honest, until a colleague of mine who belonged to some exclusive club up in Sonoma County seemed to come up with an answer. He went up there to meet this club for a fortnight every July.'

'The Bohemian Club?' asked Lola.

'That's right, the Bohemian Club,' said Ezra, his bright eyes narrowing in suspicion. 'You certainly know a lot, Miss Paige, for an intern.'

'I'm thorough, Professor Cohen.'

'So, he told us he knew this guy who was very influential and he happened to have lots of money to throw around. He had just set up a new business and they wanted to explore the frontier of science. He heard about our project and asked for a meet up. So I went to Sonoma County, the place is in the middle of nowhere in the middle of nowhere, if you get me. It was a strange place, I felt very uncomfortable there. I had a chat with Mr Stein, he came to the facility, liked what he saw there. He set us up in a state of the art facility here in New York. I had been spending my time going back and forth, this has been my home all my life, so it suited me well to be full-time in the city. But cracks began to appear before September 2001 when I found out that Aztec had been in talks with the military. So much good science has been corrupted by the military and I didn't want my research to be the same. This caused problems and as a result I was being frozen out bit by bit.'

'Did you tell Aztec about your concerns that something was going to happen?'

'I did. Repeatedly. There was evidence to suggest where it was going to happen, but they didn't want to know.'

'Didn't they pass this information on to the intelligence community?'

'That's the worst thing of all this, I have evidence that proves they did.'

'What? So someone knew that this was going to happen but chose to do nothing?'

'That September morning, like thousands of others, my world changed forever.' Lola wanted to reach out and console the professor, she could feel his pain and anguish and it was excruciating. 'After my wife Anne died,' said Ezra, his eyes darkening with the sorrow, 'the girls moved in with me. My daughter Melissa and my granddaughter Susan. Melissa worked in the North Tower for one of the major companies there. She was one of the computer executives and they were working on some new technology. Melissa's marriage had broken up some years earlier and it made sense for us all to live here together. When Anne died, we all stuck together and got through it best we could but noting prepares you for the death of your child, nothing.' Ezra's voice began to crack and break and he took a few moments to compose himself before he continued.

'After the towers came down I was left to look after my granddaughter who was only ten then. As she got older Susan became obsessed with the events of that day and the events surrounding her mother's death. I blame myself in so many ways for that.'

'None of this was your fault, Professor Cohen, you didn't fly those planes into the World Trade Centre.'

Ezra shook his head as if to dismiss Lola's reasoning. 'You don't understand, Miss Paige, I may as well have.'

'Help me understand.'

'In the days and weeks before the Towers came down, Melissa had been acting very strangely. She wasn't sleeping, she was barely eating and was she really putting the hours in at work. They were rolling out some pioneering brokerage software and it had to be finalised by September 11th. Finally I confronted her about what was going on and she told me that one of the IT managers on her team had come to her about some concerns he had about a series of invoices. She had been investigating it. Then on the 10th of September, she received a call from her boss to say that she was wanted in work for a conference meeting the following morning about their findings on the matter. My Melissa was on the 98th floor that morning when the planes hit. She and 294 of her colleagues were killed that day.'

'Who owned the brokerage your daughter worked for?' Lola asked, half-knowing and half-fearing the answer.

'Stein Corp,' said Ezra, his face pallid and full of sorrow.

'But how did this affect your granddaughter?'

'Well, Melissa's boss, who called the meeting conducted it from his Upper East Side home that morning, he didn't come into work and I suppose this made me angry. I mean I hadn't long lost my wife and then my only child, you can imagine where my head was at and I fear some of that rubbed off on my Susan. Melissa had a laptop and it was my granddaughter who found a memo on it. A message was sent advising employees not to come to the office that day, as they would be carrying out work on security systems. But Melissa got the call after. That memo saved four thousand lives but Susan maintained that her mum was lured to her death.'

'Who sent the memo?'

'Well we tried to trace the sender, but it just kept bouncing back to us. Susan just wouldn't let it go, in the end it drove her to take her own life.'

'Susan,' and then like a bolt of lightning the realisation finally hit Lola making her leap of the seat and pace up and down.

'I don't believe this,' said Lola to the ceiling. 'Susan Harris? Your granddaughter, was she a model?'

'Susan? No not my Susan she was a journalism major at Columbia.'

Lola ruffled through her bag until she came upon the correct picture. 'Professor Cohen, is this your granddaughter?'

The old man seemed to age instantly; he lifted his glasses to his face to get a better look. 'It looks like my Susan, but it can't be her.' He looked at the caption. 'She was at school, she never worked for any agency that I know of.'

'Could she have signed up to one of these agencies for extra cash maybe?'

'No she wouldn't have needed the extra money. After her mother's death she inherited a substantial amount.'

'What did she know about Aztec?'

'Just what I'm telling you now. She got it into her head that Carl Stein was responsible for her mother's death, but he was no more responsible than I was.'

'Professor, you couldn't have foreseen this, none of this is your fault.'

'After Susie died I lost it. I tried to call Aztec Solutions out but it was too late and they had grown too powerful.'

'But why would they allow so many of their own people to be killed? It just doesn't make sense.'

'Come on, Miss Paige, surely you have more nuance than that? Look around you; you look at how the world has changed. Our civil liberties are being eroded bit by bit, we are pumped with fear every hour of every day, told we are not safe. We are under threat from global terrorism. Terrorism this country and others have fuelled and created. You keep people in fear, you control them. Fear is slavery, Miss Paige, and the war on consciousness has been raging for a long time. Follow the money and you see why it benefits men like Carl Stein to allow something like that to happen. Why it benefits those in the intelligence community to allow this to happen. Empire, Miss Paige. Empire.'

'But if the people knew. If the world knew what had happened and what's going on they wouldn't allow it.'

'Who's going to tell them? You know six companies own ninety per cent of the media in this country and of that ninety per cent Stein Corp owns over sixty-five per cent and it looks like he's going to be adding the Torch to his collection too. So you tell me who's going to tell them.'

'I am,' said Lola.

'Child, you are playing with forces you cannot possibly comprehend.'

'Professor, I know you are a man of science and this might not carry much weight with you, but I believe my path led me to you tonight. For the past number of days I have been investigating the deaths of twelve women, of which, it now transpires, your granddaughter is one.

'Based on what you have told me, it is now my belief that Susan got caught up in something she shouldn't have. Perhaps she was undercover looking into Stein Corp and Aztec Solutions. I need you to listen with an open mind, sir.'

'I'm a quantum physicist, child, you can't get more open minded than that.'

'We'll see,' shrugged Lola. 'With all due respect, Professor Cohen, what I've seen, what I've learned and what I myself am capable of confounds even the most leftfield scientists. This stuff is like something straight out of a fantasy novel. Carl Stein possesses powers that go well beyond the realm of money and politics. The man is darkness incarnate and his predilections are more varied than controlling the media and the banking system. I'm talking supernatural power. The battle on consciousness you referred to earlier is closer to the mark than you know, only this is a battle Carl Stein and my people have been fighting for millennia.

'I know that Carl Stein murdered your granddaughter in a ritual killing on the autumn equinox of 2012. As he did those eleven other women in 2001 and 2006.' Lola took the pages from her bag and began laying them out on the floor. Going through each girl, each year, she explained the dates and the significance of the dates. 'Nora Evans who was sacrificed at the winter solstice 2001 was known to the police, she bares the same marks as the other two December girls, Ashley Cox in 2006 and Lucy Davis in 2012. Two of whom I know were in a relationship with Carl Stein,' explained Lola. 'The marks on the spring equinox victims all match, the summer solstice victims, the autumn equinox victims all match. They all match. The suicide notes left look so familiar you'd think were penned by the same person and yet no one has picked up on this.'

The professor was shaking his head now, as if trying to repel Lola's words. 'You think Carl Stein killed my Susan?'

'I know he did. Let's just say I have first-hand knowledge of how they operate.'

'What he's into? Black magic?'

'There is no such thing as black magick. A wise woman once told me there is only magick, it is the exponent that is either good or bad. Carl Stein's organisation is privy to the same wisdom and understanding of this great cosmos as my people, only he has subverted it and corrupted it, he has taken something organic and sacred and desecrated it for his own self-fulfilment and greed. Now it looks as though he is manipulating these eggs that you created for his own means. Something that was to help raise global consciousness and illustrate how were are all one and the same and he has subverted and corrupted it into a way of furthering the Hell Fire Club's agenda.'

'The what? You're talking secret societies now!'

'Professor Cohen, have you not seen and heard enough to convince you? Open your heart to the truth. At the moment I have so many strings fluttering in the wind but having spoken to you this very night a number of things have become clearer. Do you believe in six degrees of separation, professor?'

'Well I understand the math and probability behind it.' This made Lola laugh.

'Well I know nothing of those things but let me give you an insight into why I believe in it and why I think it has lead me to you. I arrive here in New York to intern in the Torch, while at the Torch, I just so happen to get a mentor by the name of Isaac Kane, who has just returned from Iraq. Before returning home he is tipped off about a Project Inanna and an Operation Babylon, which it turns out is linked to Aztec and your work and Stein Corp. On that flight home he meets a Marine who was assigned to this operation while serving his country in Iraq. Fast forward a few weeks, I infiltrate a party at the Steins' and find codes, numbers and a picture of a young Marine. I take pictures and go to investigate this young man and end up saving his life, this it turns out is the same young man who was seated beside Isaac, my mentor. When I investigate these numbers I discover that they are patents and co-ordinates, which lead back to Aztec and your egg things. When I research Aztec, I am led to you. In the meantime I'm looking into the murders of twelve young women because I'm trying to find something on Carl Stein, now only to discover that you are the grandfather of one of the victims, Susan Harris, who appears to have been investigating Stein Corp's involvement in 9/11. What they were looking for in Ur, relates back to why I'm here in the first place and it also explains how and why 9/11 benefited Stein Corp. Not only financially but it gave them unfettered access to sites like Ur and the whole Middle East.'

'Who are you, Miss Paige?'

'Apparently I'm In Ruád Rofessa,' said Lola proudly. 'The Red one of

Great Knowledge.' Lola smiled unsure whether he believed her or thought she was just a lunatic.

'Who is she?'

'It's a very long story, professor, one we'll have to save for another time. Like you, the Steins have taken someone I loved dearly from me and they plan to harm something else that is close to me. I cannot and will not let that happen. I need a distraction and I believe that this story will give me one. It will give me enough time to figure out my next move. The information you have that Aztec and the intelligence community knew an attack was imminent, how did you come by it?'

'I'm afraid I'm not disposed to disclose that information. Emails were sent to me via a third party about two years ago. I figured I'd use it when the time was right and it looks like that time may have arrived. Hold on a moment, Miss Paige,' said the professor as he left the room. Lola could hear the shuffle of his slippers as he descended a flight of stairs. After a few minutes he re-emerged into the living room with a small memory pen in his hands.

'I have a few of these, Miss Paige, I hope I'm doing the right thing by giving it to you.'

'What does your gut say, professor?'

'Well I let you thought the door,' he smiled. Lola took the memory stick from him and hung it on the chain around her neck.

'I've taken enough of you time, Professor Cohen. Thank you for this and thank you for listening.'

Lola stood up to go but before she got to the door another thought struck her. She turned to face the old man. 'Professor, this Project Inanna, had you heard of it?' She could see from the change in his face that he had.

'Yes,' he said, his eyes lowering. 'I was going to mention it to you when you were talking but I was uncertain whether it would be beneficial at this point.'

He continued. 'Before I severed all ties with Aztec, I had been using the facility and the endless budget for my investigations into the heart. Anyway I'll not go into that now, but I built a prototype that allows you to detect the electromagnetic field and investigate the bio field.'

'This allows you to detect if something is living or putting out some sort of signal?' asked Lola the idea already firing in her brain.

'Well yes, but it's a bit more exciting than just that.'

'Do you still have this prototype device?'

'I do, Miss Paige,' he said hesitantly.

'Is it easy to transport?'

'Well it's a bit bulky but it would be easily transported in a car.'

'Could you meet me at the Butler Library tomorrow evening say around 6pm with it?' It was more of a command than a question from Lola as she walked back out onto the street.

'Why, Miss Paige?' asked the professor scratching his head.

'You won't regret it, professor, and it will do the world of good to get out of those slippers and get some fresh air,' said Lola with an impish smile.

Lola was surprised to see that Tommy was sitting in the car when she crossed the street. 'Jesus Dorothy, I thought you were going to stay the night!'

'Tommy, why are you still here?' The driver shuffled uncomfortably in his seat. 'You know, I just wanted to make sure you got home safe, you know.'

'Tommy, what are you like. You shouldn't have.'

'Shut up and get in will ya. I'm off tomorrow so it's no bother.'

There was very little traffic so they pulled up outside Rocha's apartment just fifteen minutes later.

'Tommy,' said Lola before she got out of the car. 'Could you do me a big favour?'

'Seriously, after tonight?'

'Would you make sure Professor Cohen gets to the Butler Library at Columbia for six tomorrow evening?' Lola threw fifty dollars into the passenger seat as she left. 'And thanks for tonight, you're a real knight in shining armour.'

'Yeah, whatever,' he said as he drove off.

It was just after 1am when Lola turned the key to her apartment. Isaac and Lemar looked up from their seats. Lola was about to ask what they were doing there when Rocha lurched at her.

'Lola, you're safe.' Rocha threw her arms around Lola who stood confused trying to understand what the hell was going on.

'Jesus, Irish, we've had a search party out for you all night. Goddamn rang the police and everything. Where in the hell have you been and why didn't you answer your goddam phone?' spat Isaac.

Lola looked at her phone. 'I'm sorry. I must have switched it off. I was in Brooklyn.'

'Brooklyn?' said Rocha who was now on the phone. 'Celeste, she has just arrived back home, safe and well. No she was out in Brooklyn. Okay darling, I'll call you tomorrow.'

'It's actually great that you're all here,' said Lola still high from all the revelations. 'What a day this has been. I've so much to tell you.'

'Damn right you do,' said Isaac still smouldering. Lola had been awake for over twenty-four hours now and it looked as though it was going to be another late night. She dropped her bag and fell down onto the sofa wondering where she was going to start with all this.

~35~

Everyone's eyes and ears belonged to Lola and they listened intently when she laid out her research over the past number of days. She felt exhausted and wanted so badly to wash the grime of city streets from her skin, but it had been quite fortuitous that Isaac and Lemar were there when she arrived home.

Although he sat and said nothing, Lola could see the questions burning on Isaac's tongue but he waited until she invited them.

'Isaac,' said Lola, 'you look like you may have a question or two.' The look in his black eyes seemed implacable, so she waited for the inquest. She expected it.

'Irish, you've done some amazing work here,' said Isaac, his voice ringing with praise. 'I'm truly impressed, but I just don't see where all this is leading. You understand I'm not undermining you. I'm just trying to get things clear in my own head. I mean why do you think that these deaths are all linked?'

'Isaac, I know for a fact that these women did not take their own lives, their deaths coincided if not to the day, in or around the spring and autumn equinoxes and the summer and winter solstices. The organisation that has been conducting these sacrificial killings offer these women at these very powerful times of the year, it's like their religion for want of a better word. I need you to trust me on this.'

'I trust you, Irish, but I just can't see your reasoning, and if I can't there is no way that we can sell this to Chris, no way.'

Rocha gave Lola a cursory look urging her to tread carefully. Lola thought for a moment before she answered.

'I know this to be true because I have seen it myself, back in Ireland. Let's just say that's how I know Carl Stein, he and I have history – a lot of it. I'm sorry I can't say more than that at the moment, Isaac, but even ritual killings aside, there is enough evidence here to a least link him with these women.'

'So,' said Lemar who had remained silent until now, 'Mr Kane don't know about that Jedi shit you got goin on Lola?' He and Rocha understood that there was more at play here. Lola shot him a cold look. 'He oughtta know, Lola, I mean you saved my life with your magic or whatever the hell it was.'

'I have seen it, Lemar,' said Isaac evenly. 'The whole Internet has seen it, just not in person. I don't know what sort of supernatural stuff you're into, Lola, but we can't sell that. The fact remains, a picture is not enough, or this former detective, Jessop, who's now working for Aztec. It's a start and a great one at that, but not enough to go to print. We're the New York Torch, not the National Outrage!'

Lola had wanted to hold something back just until she had time to figure things out but it was no use.

'There's more and I believe it's something that we can use. This has been a very peculiar day, where one thing has lead me further and further down the rabbit hole,' she said gravely. 'The old Sergeant down at the 7th precinct thought I was crazy just like you, Isaac, but there was something about those suicide notes, it was like they were written by the same hand.'

'I'm not saying you are crazy, Lola. I said no such thing but you gotta see where I'm coming from here.'

'Anyway,' said Lola shrugging him off, 'when I came out I just needed to walk. I had no idea where I was going or in what direction but I just trusted that my feet would bring me where I needed to be. I walked the whole way from Delancey to 42nd Avenue. It was like something was pulling me along on a massive string. I could feel it even before I turned the corner on to 42nd Street, the air around me was charged, and when I saw what had been calling to me in all its majesty, I understood she had been guiding me to that point. The sun hung between two buildings illuminating the entire avenue, the light felt as though it was from another place and another time.'

'Manhattanhendge,' laughed Rocha. 'Yes,' Lola nodded in agreement.

'I was standing there in the middle of the road, looking at this phenomena panicking wondering where I would go next and that's when Tommy Maloney showed up.'

'Tommy Maloney, the driver?' said Isaac unsure.

'Yeah. Earlier that day,' Lola looked at Isaac, 'when I was at lunch with Ritchie it had been to find out more about this Professor Cohen and his court case against Aztec. Ritchie told me that he was living out in Brooklyn and the first day I met Tommy he told me he was from Brooklyn.'

'Sorry,' said Isaac his face confused. 'But how do you know Tommy?'

'He picked me up at the airport and brought me to the Torch.'

'Tommy still works for the paper?' said Isaac with a shrug. 'I thought they had parted company some time ago.'

'Yes he still works for the paper, otherwise he wouldn't have picked me up,' said Lola continuing. 'So I found Cohen's address and Tommy dropped me off at Slope Parks. That's the kind of day I've been having.'

Lola looked at Rocha apologetically, 'I'm so sorry for causing you to worry, Rocha; I should have texted to let you know where I was. The battery in my phone died and I'd no way of charging it.'

'It's fine, honey,' said Rocha gently. 'I know how well you can look after yourself, Lola darling, but these are dark times.'

'So you went to see this man,' said Lemar, who seemed to be enjoying the story so far.

'I did, and here's where things get curiouser and curiouser,' said Lola. 'I made the mistake of telling the old man I was a reporter from the Torch and he slammed the door in my face. I thought I'd blown my chance and decided to try one last time before I retreated with my tail between my legs. He came back to the door and I explained what it was I wanted, it took him a few minutes but he let me in,' said Lola standing up and pacing back and forth. The motion helped her to think and organise her thoughts.

'So this guy is some sort of physics genius and his particular area of study is the quantum field and we got talking about Aztec Solutions before they dumped him and it turns out he'd invented a device that could measure global consciousness.'

Lola explained about the eggs and the Random Number Generators and how they worked, what the research had uncovered and the correlation in numbers whenever there was a major event.

'You see a friend of mine who was able to check into the co-ordinates that I uncovered at Stein's was able to tell me that the same numbers, which I now know thanks to Professor Cohen are these RNGs, also relate to different patent numbers,' explained Lola methodically.

She explained about 9/11 and how the Professor's data showed a correlation in the numbers before, during and after the events of that day. She told them about how Cohen had alerted Stein and Aztec that an attack was imminent but that they and the military ignored these warnings.

'You see the professor lost his daughter in the north tower that day and she had been called in to work by her boss after most employees at the brokerage had received a memo telling them not to report to the office on the 11th due to ongoing "security work". But the plot thickens,' exclaimed Lola grateful to have the time to think out loud and lay her findings bare. 'She and the others gathered that day had been investigating what they believed was inside trading on this newly installed software!'

Lola told them everything about Aztec Solutions and how they were now using the technology Cohen had pioneered and invented to control that consciousness.

'Now just when you think things can't get any stranger, this man was talking about his granddaughter Susan. At first the name didn't register with me. Professor Cohen said that Susan became obsessed with the events surrounding her mother's death so much so that she took her own life and that's when it hit me,' said Lola her eyes reaching out to the room, 'I knew the name Susan Harris, she was one of my victims. At first I thought this was insane. I asked Ezra if she was a model and when he said no, that she was a journalism major at Columbia, I thought it was just a co-incidence but to be sure I showed him the picture and it turns out it was his granddaughter. I mean,' said Lola growing more animated. 'You couldn't make this shit up.

'So from what I know this girl was posing as a model at one of these agencies and wound up dead. If she was looking into her mother's death, at this point we've no idea what she found if anything, but the fact that she ended up in the East River makes me believe she may have found something.' Lola was vivid and passionate as she spoke and her voice rang with certainty, so that even Isaac couldn't help but be convinced, however unwillingly, that what they had here was explosive. 'And look,' said Lola fishing the memory stick from around her neck and holding it up for them all to see. 'The proof we need is on this.'

A stunned silence swathed the room. Lemar sat with his head in his hands. He had put his life on the line and watched his comrades die only now to learn that people had known there was going to be an attack on New York, yet did nothing to prevent it. The wars in Afghanistan and Iraq and Libya and Syria, all that death, devastation and gratuitous destruction could all have been avoided. His stomach burned and lurched, he needed air. Lemar opened one of the large arched windows and sucked in the balmy night air.

'Don't you see, everything is connected,' urged Lola. 'It's just a matter of connecting the dots. These girls' deaths, which I only found because Jodi had been forced to drop her investigations into her friend's death...'

'Jodi?' Isaac stirred.

'Yes,' said Lola continuing at lightening pace. 'That, the rise of Aztec Solutions, 9/11, the site Lemar was securing in Ur, Project Inanna, Operation Babylon, the patent numbers I found at the Steins', the equinox Oracle it's all connected to the Hell Fire Club. They used the events of 9/11 knowing that it would open up the Middle East for them. They have been searching for the Lost Oracle for millennia and the war in Iraq has given them unfettered access to any sites of interest. I know that these eggs are placed at various sacred sites around the globe, at this point I just don't understand why. Not yet anyway.'

'Hold on a minute,' spat Isaac, he was up and out of his seat now moving about in agitation. So Lola took a seat to give him the space to think.

'How do you know you can trust this man Cohen? It sounds like he has a major axe to grind with Stein Corp. I mean according to you they owned the brokerage his daughter worked for and the agency his granddaughter worked for, they fired him. It seems a bit suspicious don't you think?'

When Lola thought about it like that, she could see that Isaac had a point and Cohen had been very forthcoming with his information.

'I accept that, Isaac, it does all look a little too neat, but my investigations led me to him, he didn't find me.' Lola threw the pen drive at Isaac. 'All the proof you need should be on that. I haven't looked at it myself but perhaps it's best you look first.'

'Do you understand what you are saying, Lola?' asked Isaac solemnly. 'You're saying that Americans, including sections of our military, were told an attack was going to take place and stood by and did nothing and not only did they do nothing, they benefited from it and that Carl Stein benefited financially and also used it as a way into Iraq to look for God knows what. I mean this is just absurd.' Isaac slumped back down onto his seat and hung his head in his hands.

Isaac's head was in turmoil, this was crazy but something in his gut told him that Lola was right. He cast his memory back to the night before he left the airfield in Kuwait and the conversation he had with the logistics manager. The world needs to know the truth about that September Morning, he'd said. Find the links, the man had told Isaac. He knew that since then he'd been avoiding the subject but as much as he closed his desk drawer on it, trying to lock it away, it had found him and now he and every other American would have to face it head on and stop avoiding the truth, no matter how devastating it was going to be.

'Lola,' said Isaac darkly. Her name sounded strange on his tongue and she could hear the fear that was present in his distressed voice. Lola could see it all around him and she knew that despite his protestations he was on board.

Isaac got off the seat and started to pace up and down the room again. Lola watched him do this in the office all the time, when he was thinking something over or trying to make sense of something.

'This is crazy; I mean it's like something out of an Oliver Stone movie. We are talking conspiracy at the highest level here. I am not a fan of the US military or war, I've seen enough death and destruction to last a lifetime but to think that young men and women like Lemar here were sent out there...' Isaac broke off and then something happened that completely threw Lola, something that she had not been prepared for or even thought was possible. Isaac Kane began to choke back tears. For a moment Lola thought that they would break through, that Isaac would losing the battle he seemed to be waging against himself but stoically he held fast swallowing his embarrassment by talking a sip of water from his glass.

'What is this Hell Fire Club?' asked Lemar, punctuating Isaac's outpouring. Lola was grateful when Rocha interjected, she felt totally spent. There was no way she would be in work tomorrow, she needed some rest.

'Lola pet, it's been a long day, you need to go and get some sleep. I'll fill the boys in on what they need to know about Carl Stein and the Hell Fire Club and you. I know they aren't part of the Order but they have a right to know what and who it is they are fighting against. After all,' said Rocha with an air of resignation, 'forewarned is forearmed.'

'Don't worry about work the next couple of days, Irish,' said Isaac now fully restored to his normal self. 'I'll clear it with Chris that you and I are working on something.'

'Isaac, you can't tell him anything yet. You can't tell anyone,' warned Lola.

Isaac gave her a bemused look, 'Now you're schooling me on the tenants of investigative journalism?' It was the first time he'd smiled all night and it gave Lola the reassurance that she needed.

'Oh one more thing,' said Lola before she disappeared up the stairs to her bedroom, 'it turns out Professor Cohen made some sort of prototype for project Inanna. He's meeting us at the Butler Library at 6pm tomorrow night. I think we all need to be there. Rocha, could you clear this with Manus? No one other than us can be present. It's imperative no one else knows about this.' Lola searched their faces. 'Professor Moriarty needs to arrange a time that he can be alone with the book. Lemar,' she said looking at the young Marine, 'same goes for you, tell no one.' Lola stifled a yawn as the others nodded in agreement giving her leave to get some much-needed rest.

Lola lay in the darkened room and allowed the last of the adrenaline that had been fuelling her body for the past twenty hours to finally dissipate. Her clothes lay in a warm heap at the foot of the bed and she thought of the Bile Máthir, thanking her for all her help that day. That was the last thing Lola recalled before the sweetness of sleep wrapped around her like a warm blanket.

Her dreams swirled and gathered around her in a fog. Tense and crowded, Lola struggled to grasp hold of any one image. On she slept and on her subconscious mind rolled out vision after vision none of which she could fully capture.

Then she heard that soft elemental whisper as the sea called to her, 'In Rúad Rofessa,' it beckoned her to follow. The scene rolled out before Lola of a city alien to her eyes but as familiar to her soul as Brook Mill Manor.

Its buildings and narrow streets were fashioned from industrial slabs of clear quartz and granite. Huge crystal domes, some the colour of rose quartz and amethyst, others garnets and jade dominated the skyline of the city below and although she could not see her, Lola could feel the calming wisdom and serenity of the Bile Máthir. Lola had never felt the presence of so much unconditional love and tenderness as it poured from her like fine pink mist.

As before, with a quiet understanding, she let the Sacred Mother guide her steps. She spoke in a language Lola had come to realise was the native tongue of her Túath. Lola Paige would not have heard or known these strange words but Brigid did and so she understood them. Down a narrow cobbled street they walked towards this shimmering city that beckoned her.

Lola's bare feet fell on the warm crystal bricks underfoot and underneath the pads of her feet she could feel the small incisions that had been scratched on the top of each tile and somehow understood they were for grip should it rain.

Lola continued to walk through this familiar place and from time to time a little jolt of electricity ran up her arms circuiting around her body when she allowed her finger tips to run along the smooth crystal surfaces of the houses and buildings she passed. The sun shimmered and danced off the pearlescent structures and although she could not see it she could hear the gentle song of the trampling waves as the sea exhaled on a nearby shore.

The question had only partially formed in her mind when the reply came, 'Murias,' it answered, 'The Autumn City, Home of the Sacred Cauldron, a shining jewel on the West of Eirlandis. Each of our cities taught perfect knowledge and perfect wisdom,' explained the Sacred Mother. 'Rocha, daughter of the great healer Arimid, is the guardian of Murias. In the North lies the land of the Winter sun, the City of Falias. There the greatest of all the Eirlandian druids lives. He is Delphius of the white raven, who guards and commands the Lía Fáil.' As the words were spoken one scene dissolved as another materialised and now Lola was looking out over the darkened city of Falias.

Falias's shingled rooftops and streets were illuminated by a vast canopy of stars and the aurora that flickered like a warm fire above, washed over the vast spires that almost touched it in the sky, bathing them in ice greens and pinks. Lola turned to face the east as if following an invisible finger that pointed in that direction and again the current scene melted away like a snow drop while another took its place. A gust of cool wind brushed her face.

'You feel the winds of change on your face that herald from the city of Gorias in the East,' she told Lola. 'The land of the Spring Star and of youth, it is home to Manus óg the Ollam, highest of all our Filí. He is the guardian of the East and was protector of the Spear.'

When the city of Gorias came into focus Lola could see a central golden domed building surrounded by smaller holdings. Some of the domes were garnished with gems and precious stones of pale gold like the dawn sky and opals of blue and white. The central dome was a library with acres of books and parchments, maps and spells and Lola knew that they held all the wisdom and understanding of the world. She could see and smell and sense this all at once and with slightest of effort.

'To the South,' directed the Bile Máthir, 'lies the City of Finias, the land of the Summer Star and your place of birth. It was here, in the blessed fires of Finias that An Claidheamh Soluis was forged by the great alchemist Goibniu, made only for your hand. Here in the land of the stag resides Luna, descendant of the great Lugh, she is the guardian of the south. These are the four great cities of Eirlandis that serve the great Óenach in Uisneach. Where the Queens of Eirlandis have ruled since the beginning of time.'

The Queens, thought Lola, and as before her query was answered as quickly as the question took form. 'Yes, only Queens led this land before the great cataclysm struck this sacred isle. We have never ruled over but ruled with our people. I am Danu, the first of my people and the first of the Bile Máthirs to sit at Uisneach, where Éiru, who was the Goddess of my people in a time long forgotten, once sat. Uisneach, Brú, and Temple situated at the very heart of our land and centre of the eternal Cethardúil.' Lola understood the word Cethardúil to mean cosmos. 'At the foot of our sacred valley lies the mystical river which mirrors the milky river in the sky above. What lies within reflects without. As above, so below,' she said. 'This is who you are, Lola, those eyes of jade may be a stranger to this land, but your soul was birthed here. You are the last in the line of the great Queens and Goddesses and much rests on those narrow shoulders of yours. More than my spirit resides within the pages of the Lebor Solus. It tells the tale of our Túatha, our culture and our knowledge. After an aeon of sleep, the earth is once again stirring and awakening and now the earth's great sorrowing can come to an end but we find ourselves walking a fine line. The forces of ignorance and deceit are stronger than ever and like a wounded animal they will fight to survive. Trust this kinship you have around you and believe that you have friends that are yet to be revealed. All is not what it seems.'

The scene began to fade and Lola could feel the bed beneath her and the weight of the blanket around her. Where is this place, she thought. 'We call it Eirlandis but today you call it Erin.'

~36~

A dust-filled light flooded through the un-curtained windows rousing Lola her from sleep. She stretched and yawned to greet the day; her body was warm and heavy and Lola felt rested and calm. For an instant she thought about work but then settled again when she remembered that she'd been instructed to take the next few days off.

Her dream was still vivid and very much to the fore of her mind as she grabbed the pencil and notepad that sat on her bedside table and jotted down the particulars, fearful that as the day progressed they would somehow be expunged from her memory.

Lola listened for some activity down below but the house felt quiet. She wanted to speak to Rocha and tell her about the dream. Lola thought about it again, running through it all. It was probably easier for her to be contacted in the dreamscape because her conscious mind was at rest, giving her subconscious mind time to understand, see and explore without the constant nagging and over thinking.

She put on some clothes, opened the windows and headed downstairs, disappointed to find that she was alone.

Rocha must have gone to work; she wasn't sure where Lemar had gone. Lola felt guilty for not having gone back to Liberty Plaza to check on him. She was the reason that he was there in the first place.

As she busied about in the kitchen making some breakfast, she flicked on the radio to kill the silence. Movement from above stopped her in her tracks and she turned down the radio, straining to hear. Lola walked halfway up the stairs hoping to see Rocha come out of her room, listening again. The door to Rocha's room swung open, but instead of her host it was Lemar who came walking out, wearing nothing more than a pair of crisp white boxing shorts. Lola stood open-mouthed glaring at him.

'Has Rocha gone to work?' fumbled Lola after he'd caught her gawping at him. 'Yeah,' yawned Lemar, 'she left early this morning. She gave me her bed last night.'

'Did she indeed,' smiled Lola, wide-eyed, looking into the room, just to make sure that Rocha wasn't there.

'She slept on the coach,' said Lemar, rolling his eyes. 'Come on, Lola, the woman's old enough to be my grandma. Don't get me wrong, she's one fine looking woman, but a little too old for me. Damn it felt good sleeping in a bed,' said Lemar stretching his contoured arms up towards the ceiling. 'Where's the bathroom at?'

Lola dumbly pointed down the hall and watched intently as Lemar Jenkins headed for the shower. Lola's face flushed when he caught her watching him again.

Lemar Jenkins was one fine human being, thought Lola, as breakfast for one became breakfast for two.

'Damn that was good,' said Lemar, pulling the stool out and taking a seat at the breakfast table. 'It feels great to finally get a proper shower. Rainwater is hard and coarse and it doesn't seem to clean you.'

They sat eating for a while and talking things over until Lemar's phone began to ring. Lola gave him some space to chat and started to clear away the dirty dishes.

'Maw. Maw. Calm down,' said Lemar, the fear caught in his throat. 'Maw, I need you to calm down.' Lola stood barley breathing. Her mind toiling about what she was going to hear now.

'I'll be right over, Maw. Stay where you are. Do not let anyone into the house, you hear me? No one.'

Lemar ran upstairs to get dressed, pulling on a t-shirt and jeans. 'What's going on?'

'Those guys came to my ma's house and started tearin' the place up, roughing her up, looking to know where I was.' Lemar's jaw flexed as he gritted his teeth, trying to keep a lid on his temper.

'Wait and I'll go with you,' said Lola. 'You can't go there alone! Please, Lemar.' Without waiting for a reply, Lola raced to her room grabbing her guddies and a hair band. Pulling her hair into a ponytail she collected her bag as they rushed out of the door.

It must have been later in the afternoon than Lola had realised, they only had to wait a few minutes before they managed to hail down a taxi. Lola gave the address, she could see the caution in the taxi driver's eyes but he kept his concerns to himself just nodding and talking off into the river of traffic.

Lemar sat in silence ringing his hands but Lola could see how anxious he was as he clenched and unclenched his fists into balls, his eyes urging the cab on. The traffic was gridlocked, but as they left midtown and headed towards Harlem it eased and they were at the Grant House projects in a few minutes.

The car just about stopped at the pavement when Lemar sprang out of the back seat like a horse in the stalls. The taxi driver was about to protest when he saw Lola's outstretched hand with the fare over his shoulder. Lola raced after Lemar but he was way ahead of her.

The same young men who'd gathered around the entrance to Grant House were still there and the one Lemar had called Leshawn, who'd taken a particular interest in Lola before, made towards her when he saw her approaching the doors to the high rise.

'Snowflake, you back! I knew you couldn't stay away.' He grabbed at his crotch. 'You after some of this, my boy Lemar ain't satisfying you? You know where I be at.'

Lola really didn't have time for this right now. Normally she'd have some witty retort, but she needed to catch up with Lemar, she hoped the lift would be working now. As the door closed behind her, Lola saw Leshawn making a call on his cell. The hairs on her arms prickled but Lola's attention was firmly fixed on the seventeen flights of stairs she had to tackle to reach Lemar and his mother. Two at a time she raced up them and by the time she reached Lemar's floor her lungs were screaming for air. She clamoured to the end of the hall where the door to his mother's apartment lay open and broken, clasping at the doorframe she called inside between breaths.

'In here, Lola,' called Lemar.

The once neatly furnished and arranged apartment had been ransacked, with tables laying on their heads and the entrails of the sofa, disembowelled on the floor. Glasses and the little ornaments and pictures that had been scattered around the space now lay broken. Miss Jenkins sat shaking, clutching a picture of Lemar in his military uniform. Tear stains streaked down her fine cheekbones like road tracks and a deep purple bruise had begun to rise on her wrist and the side of her face. Lemar hugged and soothed his mother, who was still dressed in her nurse's scrubs.

Lola fetched a glass of water from the fridge and handed it to her. 'Take a drink of this, Miss Jenkins, it might help you.'

'Maw,' said Lemar, he touched her face with such tenderness. 'Can you remember what these men looked like, what they said?'

She nodded her head. She was calm now, settled that he was with her and he was safe. She took a long drink from the glass Lola had given her, smoothed her hand over her hair to compose herself and then began to tell them what had happened.

'They came about,' she looked at the clock that lay broken on the carpet, 'well it's almost five now, so it must have been around four or so,' she said. 'I had just gotten in from work and I was just about to sit down when I heard the door, it damn near sounded like the door was coming in around me. At first I thought it was just some kids acting up, you know how it can be round here, but they persisted. When I opened the door, I had it on the chain and this guy he looked to be in early forties, tall with mousy hair, was rough looking, you know, hadn't shaved in a while. Well he was with another man, big big guy. Ugly as ugly can be, shaved head with a scar down his face. The mousy haired one seemed to be in charge and he asked where you at home. I asked who he was and what he wanted with you, that's when he flashed his badge.'

'What kind of badge?' interrupted Lola.

'Police badge, NYPD,' said Miss Jenkins. 'He said that he needed to speak to you,' she looked at Lemar, 'but when I told him that you weren't in and that I didn't know where you were, his body language changed like that,' she clicked her fingers. 'Anyway, I was about to close the door, when he lifted his foot and bust it open hitting me on the side of the face. They both came in and started smashing everything up. I asked them what this was all about and what they wanted with you. They said that they had information that you were involved in gang activity. I told them they was outta their mind, that you were a good boy. I asked to see their warrant and when I went to lift the phone, that's when the big one grabbed my wrist and damn near broke it. He sounded like you, Miss Paige,' she rubbed her wrist, as if the memory had reminded her of the pain. 'The big ugly one, he had an accent like yours.'

'Derek,' said Lola more to herself, sliding down onto the chair.

'What is it, Lola? You know this guy?' quizzed Lemar irritated. Lola needed to think so she stood up again as if that would help her.

'This was no police raid, Lemar. The man your mum described works for Carl Stein, I know because he nearly broke my jaw last year.'

'The other guy definitely had a police badge,' interjected Lemar's mum again. 'When you live in Harlem, you know what a real police badge looks like, Miss Paige. I mean us black folks get stopped whenever the boys in blue feel they want to. It was a police badge all right and I got the sonuvabitches badge number and name,' she said. 'Andy Jessop 710.'

When Lola caught Lemar's eyes they were clear and full of understanding. He knew just what was happening and he knew his mother wasn't safe in her home anymore.

'Miss Jenkins,' said Lola mastering the growing sensation of foreboding that prickled all over her now, 'you need to take everything of value to you and we have to get out of here.' Lemar's mother had begun to come around and was about to protest. She looked at her son waiting for him to interject and to tell this silly white girl to get out but his expression silenced her objections and she went about the house lifting pictures and the few valuables that didn't lie in smithereens on the floor.

In just twenty minutes Lemar and his mother had their entire possessions packed into three suitcases.

She took one last look back at the ransacked house. It was no longer her home, what feeling of place she had lay broken on the floor with her little worldly possessions. Besides, home was were her son was.

Lola sensed the danger as soon as they reached the top of the stairwell; there was only one way up and one way down. Lola allowed the ring to do its job and she worked in unison with it. She could feel the fluid membrane as it eased out inch by inch. She brought all her concentration to centre on the warm honey coloured buffer that expanded in front of her.

'Is there any other way out of this building, Lemar?' she asked hopefully. He shook his head wearily. 'No,' he said.

'We need to move now. I don't know how far up they are. I can't hear them on the stairs, but I know they are back. We need to move as quickly as we can. Lift those cases, try not to make any noise and stay behind me,' Lola instructed.

Lemar knew she had a specific set of talents and he trusted her to protect them. Lola didn't feel half as confident as they began their descent. As her defence stretched out ahead, they climbed down ten floors without encountering anyone, but Lola could feel that it was only a matter of time.

Lemar had taken two cases while his mother, who was so slight of frame, hauled the other with otherworldly strength. She didn't question the scenario or protest and when she looked at her son Lola understood why because when Lemar turned, as he did every now and then to look at her, he gave her a smile with such love and reassurance and her silent reply was a look of such unequivocal trust. It moved Lola, making her more determined to protect them both.

They were twelve floors down when she heard the first clumsy footsteps below. Lola hugged the inside wall of the stairwell, she understood how important the element of surprise was; after all, it had worked for her before. Her powers seemed to work better when she allowed instinct to lead. Lola moved her finger to her lips, motioning for them to be quiet.

Holding her hand up she halted the party so she could get a sense of how far away the footsteps were. Lemar tilted his head this way and that trying to listen.

'About four flights below,' he whispered. 'Two men,' he motioned with his fingers.

Lola knew that if it was the same two men who had visited before then they had come back on a mission and that mission was to kill. She had never used her powers against bullets before and she wasn't prepared to give them that chance.

The more nervous she became the stronger her force field grew as it spread its pearly tentacles protectively in front, feeling out the potential danger, like tiny nerve ends that seemed to communicate back to her heart centre.

Down she guided them, counting all the while. Their movement was freer and quicker than the encroaching footfall. Unlike those hiking up the stairs they had gravity on their side and Lola planned to use it.

The air around Lola began to tingle and vibrate and she understood that it would soon be time to act. She had only used this ability intentionally twice when she'd rescued Celeste and Lemar Lola took a deep breath and hoped that she could make it work again. She could hear the laboured breathing now, both parties would soon be on a collision course and for once she was going to be ready.

She was momentarily side-tracked as she stepped over some bodily fluid that she couldn't quite identify and when she looked up again she was staring into the pale grey eyes of the man Lemar's mother had described.

Soon Derek, who was panting and bending over trying to get some air in the hot narrow passage, joined him. He grinned when he lifted his head and saw Lola.

Both parties stood off. Lemar's mother let out a little gasp when she saw the men in front. Lola didn't take her eyes off the pair but she could feel Lemar's restlessness behind her. She could understand why he wanted to rip these men from limb to limb after what they had done to his mother. Without looking Lola reached back and placed her hand on him; he took a step back.

'Hello, bitch,' said Derek opening his gaping mouth into a grin.

'Derek,' smiled Lola as if greeting an old friend. 'Long time no see, I see you haven't gotten any better lookin' since I saw ye last.'

His expression darkened. 'I should have smashed your skull in when I had the chance.'

'Ach Dee, you don't really mean that, look at all the fun we would have missed out on,' said Lola titling her head flirtatiously. She was ready now, she could feel the power surge in her blood and in her veins but she held it back just a little longer. It fought with her, like a wild horse, as she soothed and reined it in building up momentum before she would unleash it.

'Our business is with Lemar here,' said Jessop, 'we have no business with you or his mother.' 'It didn't seem that way when you was breaking into our house, you piece of shit.'

Lola motioned for Lemar to stay cool and to let her handle this.

'I don't think that's going to happen, Mr Jessop,' said Lola, her eyes catching the confusion on his face. 'Yes,' she smiled. 'I know all about you and your dirty little tricks when you were hiding behind that big blue wall at the NYPD, but you're not a cop anymore, only a hired goon. So here's how it's going to go down,' Lola almost cringed when she heard the words that were coming from her mouth, it was like some cheesy movie, but she was blazing and she didn't care how clichéd she sounded.

'Myself, Lemar and the lovely Miss Jenkins here are going to walk the rest of the way down this filthy, urine littered stairwell and you're going to let us past without so much a whimper!'

'Would you listen to this kid?' said Andy Jessop playfully, as he reached for his holster and pulled his gun.

Lola had no idea what kind of a gun it was, but it looked like one that could take your life. As he took aim at Lemar, it happened. She let go of the reins and the energy poured from her in an almighty blast lifting both men of their feet and pinning them against the landing wall. Blood poured from Derek's head as both men lay unconscious and bits of plaster began to break away from the wall where they had impacted it.

Lola kicked the gun out of reach. When she looked behind her Lemar and his mother were standing like statues, for a moment she feared that she'd hurt them too but then they blinked and began to follow her down the stairs. Both men began to stir. Lemar set down the cases, towering over them now.

'Lemar, we've no time for spectating, hurry the hell up,' urged Lola.

After landing a punch flush on Jessop's nose, Lemar moved on to Derek and offered the same parting gift before following his mother and Lola down the remaining floors and out into the bright forecourt. Each of them sucked at the fresh moist air as if they had just resurfaced from the bowels of the earth.

The group that had been milling about the front of the high rise looked on with a passive interest. Lola, able to offer help now, took the case from Lemar's mother and wheeled it. They needed to get out of there and quickly.

'Why every time you come up her snowflake, you in a hurry to get away?' Lola tried to walk on but Leshawn blocked her way. She really didn't want to go there with this guy, not here, not in broad daylight.

'Lay off, Leshawn,' said Lemar, guiding Lola out of the way. The tension between them that Lola had felt when she first met Lemar, fizzed and bristled to the surface.

'Who you talking to, bitch? You think just cause you was in Iraq, you some kinda hero.' This had the desired effect, stopping Lemar in his tracks.

'And what would you know, Leshawn? Hell, you ain't never left Harlem. Shit, you ain't never left this spot. You don't know jack shit.' There it was again, that tingle in the air, that volt of electricity cautioning Lola and again she was ready for it.

'I know you is worth a few Benjamins dead,' said Leshawn pulling out a small silver handgun from the back of his jeans.

The other kids began to move away, some protesting, telling Leshawn to quit fooling around. But not Lemar, he stood calm and tall, looking straight down the barrel of the gun that was pointed directly at him by a kid he'd known all his life.

'You're going to play me like that, Leshawn?' spat Lemar from between gritted teeth, stepping in closer to him and the gun. Lola realised who Leshawn had been calling on the phone when she had run into the building after Lemar earlier, that's how Derek and Jessop knew he was there. Lola dropped the case and moved to position herself between Lemar and his old friend.

'You best move outta the way, snowflake, I only get paid for one body.'

'Lemar,' said Lola gently placing her hand on his arm. 'Please, go to your mother, she's scared. Let me handle this.' Lemar took a step back.

'You gonna let your bitch take bullet for you,' he laughed. Without understanding why Lola pushed both her hands into the air in front of her as the sound of the gun cracked. The force threw Leshawn into mid-air and over the railings into the brush as the gun fell at Lola's feet. The smell of the hot gun registered before the pain in her shoulder but as the tension, which she had been carrying since they arrived, slowly disintegrated, Lola felt the pain of her wound more severely. It burned like nothing she'd ever experienced before. Her baby blue t-shirt was soaked crimson as Lemar took off his belt and garrotted her arm, strangling the blood flow.

'You one hell of a soldier, Lola, I mean I believe everything that Rocha told us last night, but this is some crazy shit,' said Lemar as he adjusted the belt and placed his finger on the wound. Lola let out a piercing scream, she thought she was going to faint.

'We need to get you to a hospital,' insisted Lemar. 'The wound is clean; the bullet must have gone straight out the other end. It could be worse,' he smiled at Lola.

'I can't go to a hospital, Lemar, and tell them what. I was shot in Harlem? Get me to Rocha, she'll be able to do something.' Then she remembered that they were supposed to be at the university. 'What time is it, Lemar?'

'It's almost six. No way, Lola, you need help,' objected Lemar realising what Lola was about to suggest.

'We need to be at the library,' commanded Lola. All this time Miss Jenkins stood stock still staring at Lola. She may well have gone into shock.

'Get me a t-shirt from one of the cases, Lemar. We don't have time for this. Those two,' Lola gestured toward the Grant building, 'will resurface soon and I'm not taking another bullet for anyone,' she sucked in the air through her teeth as another flame of pain seared through her shoulder.

By now Miss Jenkins had come around and was trying to flag down a cab. Lola had just managed to change into a clean shirt when the cab pulled up at the curb. As Lemar packed the bags into the boot, she sat cramped in in the back seat her shoulder ablaze. Her head began to feel light and pearls of sweat gathered on her upper lip.

'Where to?' asked the cabbie.

'The Butler Library,' said Lemar, much to Lola's relief. Just as they pulled away from the curb, Derek and Jessop came staggering out of the darkened entrance into the late evening sun, which dazzled their eyes, concealing Lola's get away.

'Lemar,' asked Lola meekly, 'call ahead to Rocha and tell her to bring something. Don't alarm her.'

Lola closed her eyes and let her throbbing head rest on the cold window. The silence stretched out between them as the pain from her wound rang in Lola's head.

‘Holy mother of God, would you look at the state of you!’ Rocha met them at the entrance to the Butler Library, it had just gone after six and the building was closed for the day. She guided them through the door and bolted it behind her. The reception area was deserted.

‘The guard is doing his rounds,’ she said gesturing towards the empty desk. ‘And just as well or he’d have the bloody police here, seeing the state of you.’ Rocha’s Northern Irish accent was more pronounced when she was exasperated about something.

Lola felt weak and light headed, it would waste too much valuable energy talking right now. The pain was getting worse and she couldn’t hide the immense discomfort she was in.

Lemar’s quick thinking had certainly helped as the blood flow was stemmed but still it oozed out onto the clean t-shirt he’d given her out of one of the suitcases.

Rocha looked towards Miss Jenkins expecting an explanation. ‘We had to bring my mum, she wasn’t safe at Grant House,’ explained Lemar. ‘Lola insisted we come here and that you would be able to help her. She has lost a lot of blood, but the wound is clean. The bullet went straight through her shoulder.’

‘Jesus Mary and St Joseph,’ said Rocha, her eyes reaching to some unseen vision on the magnolia ceiling. ‘You’ve been shot? What in the name of all that’s sacred happened?’ Lola had never seen Rocha this angry before, she was always in control, calm and reassuring but now the fury in her voice rang like a bell, yet despite losing her temper, she still carried herself with a visible strength never failing to be elegant.

'It wasn't Lemar's fault, Rocha,' managed Lola as the lift doors opened and she was guided out into the hall. 'Anyway,' she said, growing irritated, 'we don't have time to explain now; I'm in too much pain, besides we have more important things to worry about. Is everyone here?'

'Yes,' answered Rocha. 'More important things to worry about she says,' she muttered under her breath. This time Lola let her comments go unrebuked, she was cold now and her body began to respond as she convulsed and trembled. Tiny prickles of ice began to rise on her clammy skin; she needed a blanket or something warm.

Isaac and the two professors rose to their feet when they saw Lola stumble into the preservation lab aided by Lemar and his mother. Questions flew at them as Rocha ordered Lemar here and there.

Lola closed her eyes and slumped on the floor against one of the work stations, it was like she was in a dream, she could no longer feel the weight of her limbs or get a sense of them as they touched the concrete floor or the wooden partition, but she could hear the buzz of activity around her. Someone gently placed a blanket over her legs and another around her shoulders.

Rocha gasped when she cut the sleeve off to address the wound. A scream was torn from Lola's throat and she heard it rise violently in the air around them when Rocha poured some unseen liquid into the opening. It was like hot lava and Lola was sure she heard the skin sizzle and hiss; she struggled to remain conscious as Rocha cleaned and applied some salve to the wound.

'Nettle and St John's Wart with a hint of mint,' hushed Rocha as she dabbed the thick ointment onto the tiny hole in Lola's porcelain shoulder. Lola whimpered asking for help, for strength and then she heard the voice of the Bile Máthir, the soft melodic hum washed over her like a cool wave. 'Come to me, child,' it said over and over. 'Let my light heal you.' The voice was like a soft lullaby distracting Lola from the explosion in her shoulder. 'The book,' she whispered pulling Rocha closer to her. 'I think the book can help me.'

'Lola, darling,' there was a stiffness in Rocha's voice. 'You've lost so much blood...'

'The book,' insisted Lola, shuddering violently now. 'Please get the book, she's calling me.' Lola opened her eyes to find a semi-circle of bewildered faces staring back.

'I'm not delirious,' she smiled. 'Professor Moriarty, please can you take me to her?' The young professor looked anxiously from Rocha to Lola. Rocha nodded her head giving him the permission he required.

'Isaac, Lemar, you'll need to help her up,' she instructed. Lola hadn't realised how flimsy her legs were until she almost fell over trying to stand up. Lemar caught her just in time and carried her into the viewing room where there was a significant drop in temperature, as the conditions for the vellum required it.

'Professor Cohen, I'm sorry about all of this drama,' apologised Lola as Lemar placed her down on the seat. 'Do you have your equipment with you?'

'Yes, Miss Paige, but if you don't mind me saying, you look like you need to get to a hospital. Can't this wait until another time?' Lola could see that he was growing more concerned about her health, they all were, but they had only half of the picture. She was sure that the book would do as promised and she was determined to capture this using the professor's prototype.

'We don't have another time, it is now or never,' said Lola looking around them all. 'Two attempts were made on our lives today in the space of ten minutes. I was lucky that my talents were able to stave off the first wave but not the second.'

'You're wrong, young woman.'

Everyone turned to look at the small figure at the back of the room in the blue nurse scrubs. They seemed to have forgotten she was there. Miss Jenkins walked towards Lola, with an air of strength and pride in her demeanour, and placed her hand tenderly on her head.

'Girl, you saved my life today, I don't know what the hell you are or what it is you can do, but not only did you safe my life, you saved my boy's life and that child is my world.' Tears scalded Miss Jenkins's face as she dismissed them with the back of her hand. 'That bullet was aimed straight at your head, I seen it with my own eyes but when you waved your hand in the air, I don't know how! But it changed the direction of the damn thing and that's why it's in your shoulder and not your skull, child.'

Lemar placed his steely arms around his mother's narrow frame, a mixture of comfort and pride. She almost seemed childlike compared to the bulk of his broad physique.

Lola appealed to Professor Cohen once again. 'Please, we need to do this now, for you and for me,' she urged. The professor offered no reply but moved to unpack the small grey case that housed his equipment. Lola was surprised when he unlocked the carbon-fibre casing to find a grey box no more than twelve inches long by six inches wide. He lifted it out and placed it on the table and proceeded to attach five wires with very long cables to the back of the device.

One line was linked up to a small screen and the other four were fitted with gel pads like you would see on a regular electrocardiogram machine.

Another spasm of pain attacked Lola's shoulder making her wince. Isaac, who had remained passive, now protested, pleading with her to get help.

'Irish,' he said kneeling in front of her. 'This is just plain crazy, you need a hospital.' Lola's face remained closed. 'Once the book comes, I'll be okay.'

Lola looked around the room for Professor Moriarty, what was keeping him? She gritted her teeth as another lash ripped through her shoulder. Finally the door to the storage room slid open and Professor Moriarty carried in the Leabhar Cheanannais with such reverence and majesty, then softly lay it on the table beside Lola.

Immediately, the pounding in her shoulder eased off and she understood that she had done the right thing. She wanted to touch the book, to cradle it in her arms like a new-born child; she wanted to protect it and as she made the connection, Lola seemed to understand the book felt the same way about her.

'Professor Cohen, we're ready for you now,' said Lola waiting for him to attach the leads to her chest and to the book, but he hesitated for a moment. Lola could see he understood what she wanted him to do but a conflict played out in his warm face.

'I know it sounds like madness to you, Professor,' said Lola, 'and you too, Professor Moriarty, but you have to believe me when I tell you that this book is a living thing. Not only does she hold profound knowledge and wisdom, she is a conscious entity. The spirit that lies interred in these pages is what has kept the book safe and disguised for millennia, ever since its creators and scribes imbued it with life.'

Lola was unsure where this knowledge came from, but she trusted it. 'Please, Professor,' she said shifting her body weight in the seat. 'I believe your technology will prove what I'm saying. Tell them what you've created,' she urged, 'tell them what your research has found.'

'I have made great advances in studying the human bio-field and consciousness even that of a tree, but never a book.'

'All I'm asking is for you to give it a go. Please, Professor. You've come all this way. Be like Bohr and Heisenburg.'

This made the professor laugh. 'Okay, Miss Paige, in the spirit of science, let's give this a go.'

Lola wasn't the only one to sense Professor Moriarty's anxiety; he was very protective of the book and guarded it fiercely.

Ezra Cohen introduced his equipment. 'This, ladies and gentlemen,' he said fixing the lines to the front of the book, 'is a SQUID or if you prefer, Superconducting Quantum Interference Device. This is the most sensitive detector known to science, normally they don't have to even come into contact with whatever they are testing but I don't want to leave anything to chance.'

'What is it exactly they are testing?' asked Isaac moving in to get a better look.

'I'm glad you asked that, Mr Kane,' said the professor, now in full academic mode. 'I have built this prototype to examine the impact that the sun's, along with the earth's, geomagnetic activity has on us humans. The early results were staggering.'

'I don't understand,' quizzed Isaac, ever the journalist. 'You're saying that earth's magnetic field has some sort of effect on the planet other than to protect us from harmful rays and such?'

'That's exactly what I'm saying, sir. Now let it be known, I don't for one second believe that it will work on this old book but I am humouring my young friend here, her passion and conviction are almost impossible to resist,' he shot Lola a scolding look.

Isaac gave a weary smile, 'I can attest that everyone in this room agrees with you there, professor.'

'Normally,' continued the professor who examined the book searching for the best place to rest the pads, 'my research is only conducted on humans, animals, trees, things that are actually alive. The heart is an amazing piece of machinery,' he continued finally settling on a spot. 'Not only does it provide our bodies and cells with life-giving oxygenated blood; my studies have shown that it has an intelligence. It gives new meaning to thinking with your heart and not your head. Well it transpired that there is some truth in that saying. So like the earth and sun we too have an electromagnetic field around us, and our heart powers that field and it is all part of the Anima Mundi.'

'The World Soul,' said Rocha in admiration, running her fingers along the device.

'Yes,' smiled Ezra. 'This field is so powerful that some people can even claim to see it in colour and surprisingly it has a greater amplitude than brain waves, sixty times greater to be exact. My early research was very interesting. After my granddaughter Susan was born, her mother would lay her on her lap and talk and coo to her. I found it very moving so naturally I wanted to test it and see if I could understand that bond between mother and child. This equipment was in its infancy then and the device was extremely crude but it allowed me to test my daughter's brain waves and detect my granddaughter's heart rhythm. Of course there was no correlation when each where doing their own thing, Susan laying googling to herself and my daughter busy about the house, but the moment she held the child and her concentration was focused on her something amazing happened. Melissa's brainwaves began to sync with Susan's heartbeat and thus that one observation has lead my research to look at the wider picture.'

The professor had moved to the small screen and began typing in a number of commands. Lola could feel her connection grow with the book and as she closed her eyes she felt as though warm water flowed through her veins, the sensation travelled up her legs and into her torso, up across her chest and to the top of her head, which tingled with heat. As she allowed her eyes to open she actually could see the warm amber and pale gold tones as they pulsed and danced around the wound in her shoulder. The light flowed with a rhythmic evanescence and Lola knew she was being healed. The Bile Máthir poured the light of love and healing and wisdom on Lola's frail body and it drank the earthy shades of pale ochre like a thirsty desert flower.

Neither Professor Cohen, nor anyone else in the room, could see the light that flowed like the aurora from the book to Lola but his screen detected it nonetheless. He stood back scratching his head, laughing to himself. He walked over to the book, examined the leads, and then over to Lola to make sure that nothing was attached to her. The equipment had never failed him before, but everything that science had taught him was imploding around him. The data was there on the screen that this book was indeed sending out an electromagnetic signal, the strongest he had ever seen. Stronger than any human, stronger than any living thing he had examined.

He rubbed his eyes again and stepped back from the screen as if that might correct his vision. By now the colour had started to flow back into Lola's cheeks, the burning and throbbing in her shoulder was gone. She lifted it gingerly expecting it to refuse, but the joint obeyed without the slightest protest.

'This can't be right,' mulled the professor. Everyone began to gather around the screen, trying to make sense of the lines and data that was presented.

'What does it mean, professor?' asked Isaac leaning forward. He couldn't follow this Ezra Cohen to the apex of his knowledge but even he could tell that the book was showing something. Lola stood up to a chorus of protests which were immediately hushed when she took off the gauze from around her shoulder, revealing fully intact flesh and bone. Lola craned her neck to try and see, running her fingers across the place on the skin that was punctured; there was nothing there.

Each of them gazed at her frog-eyed as if she was an apparition and their eyes had deceived them. Professor Moriarty fetched himself a glass of water and sat down beside the book with a look of such beatification on his face as he stared at its pages.

Even Rocha was in a static state because what they had just witnessed tested even the most open-minded person. The only person who seemed to be excited by the prospect was Ezra Cohen.

He was rummaging around in his case when he pulled out a helmet, made of what looked like plasma. The incisions and tiny microchips reminded Lola of a pineapple, but instead of lozenges the helmet was made from a mosaic of squares.

'This is just amazing, Miss Paige, what a wonderfully intelligent young woman you are,' he declared as he fitted the headpiece onto Lola's head, adjusting it here and there. 'This is a helmet I designed using the same technology. It's apparently clear that the book is communicating but let's see if it has intelligence.'

'Look at my shoulder, professor, look at me,' said Lola earnestly. 'Surely that's proof enough, even for the most rigorous scientific mind.'

'Now it's your turn to humour me, Miss Paige.' Despite his protestations, something had happened and like everyone else in the room, Lola could tell that Ezra Cohen was galvanized.

'Now, Lola,' said the professor, his eyes glistening and urgent. 'I need you to centre yourself and I need you to engage in a dialogue with the book.'

Lola turned to look at him. 'She won't speak back, professor, we communicate on a...' Lola considered this for a moment, how exactly did she communicate with the book? 'We communicate on – the only way to describe it – is on a telepathic level.'

'Well I gathered that, Miss Paige, but I need you to form a question. For the purposes of this experiment I'd like you speak your question aloud and then tell us what the book says.'

'Okay,' said Lola suddenly feeling self-conscious. She shifted awkwardly in the chair and tried to ignore the silent eyes that she could feel fixed on her back. Now that she was attuned to the book's rhythms and energy, she made the connection with ease. As her aura began to swell around her she could feel the book reaching out to it, both fields mingling and folding into one another thick and slow like nectar. Lola's mind had decided to be silent and suddenly it was a blank white sheet, bright and clear and clean, with not so much a shadow of a question on it, but as one thought sparked another, she thought of Moriarty and the book provided the response. In the background she could hear the undulating oohs and ahhs from Ezra but she tried to focus on one thing at a time.

'She wants to say something to Moriarty,' said Lola.

Professor Moriarty tore his eyes away from the book long enough to listen to Lola.

'Thank you she says,' all the while the book spoke in a language long forgotten. The lyrical beauty of the syllables as she heard them in her head made her translations sound dry and graceless in comparison.

'Thank you for loving her, for protecting her for dedicating your many lifetimes to her. She says that the day you found each other again, when you as a young child rested your eyes upon her, was a day of great joy. For millennia she had waited for one of the Guardians to find her and you were the first.'

'How was she made?' The question came from Rocha this time and Lola didn't even have to think it, because it seemed the book could hear it.

'I was penned in the four cities of Eirlandis by the great Ollam of the Fili. In the city of Falias in the North, I was given the knowledge of all the world, the earth and all its living creatures and organisms; my Guardian there was the great Delphius. In sweet Gorias in the East, the land of the rising sun, I was gifted the wisdom of the great cosmos and all its mechanics, after all we descended from the very stars that burned at night and it was there where your soul's journey began, young Manus. In the south, the city of Finias where the magickal sword of the Dé Danann was forged and the light of the world that promised to the Dé Danann came forth. She of the flaming hair now sits among you. The Guardian of the southern folio was Luna descendent of Lugh. Finally, it was in the west my life began, underneath the great Crann na beatha, underneath the Tree of Life, where the Leabhar Solus was completed with the knowledge of magick, healing and alchemy. The Guardian of the west was Rocha, Bandraoi and descendent of Árimid of the herbs. On the autumn equinox North, East, South and West became united bound by all in magick and truth. It was then, I the Sacred Mother was invoked to process and protect this knowledge until the time came for the light of the Dé Danann to return. Eirelandis has been long forgotten and its four shinning cities relegated to the realms of myth and time. People have searched and theorised about a great civilization lost beneath the waves, but yet it has stood in plain sight for those who have eyes to see and ears to hear. Great philosophers have known our humble land. Much blood has soaked her soil since my people had to retreat. Born on the autumn equinox when our world was in a time of great balance we knew the time would come when the shadow would swallow our land and our light. We are still in a time of great shadow and the future hangs on a silver thread. Those same forces that have pursued me through many lifetimes are closer now than they ever were...'

Lola stopped talking she could feel the book shut down completely sensing the incoming threat. Lola lifted of the headpiece and the wires from the book, just as the door to the viewing room slid aside.

Susie Delaney observed the scene with incredulity, her dark eyes narrowed as they fell on the motley crew assembled in her lab. A flush rose on her neck as if she had been caught doing something she shouldn't have been.

'What's all this, Manus?' she asked, failing to hide the irritation in her voice. 'I wasn't made aware that you'd planned a visit tonight.'

The professor rose to his feet deliberately obscuring her view of the scene, giving Ezra and Lola enough time to pack away the equipment. Susie's flint eyes darted from Moriarty to the activity behind him. The professor was faltering now, stumbling over his words trying to offer an explanation.

'Professor Moriarty was kind enough to let us see the Book of Kells,' smiled Isaac, reaching his hands out. 'I'm Isaac Kane.' Susie Delaney nodded her head in acknowledgement, indicating she knew who he was. 'I'm Lola's mentor at the New York Torch and when I found out she was doing a story on the Book of Kells I just had to get a look at it and the professor here was very good to give us a private viewing. I hope we haven't gotten him into trouble,' laughed Isaac casually. This accounted for his presence but what about the rest? He could see Delaney's eyes move to Lemar and his mother. 'Please excuse me. This is my nephew Lemar and my sister Kathy, they are in town visiting for a few days, they have just arrived and I thought it would be cool to show them a piece of real antiquity.'

'Hi, Susie,' waved Rocha. 'Ezra and I have a dinner reservation with Lola later so we came along too.'

'What has you here this late in the night, Susie?' asked Moriarty innocently. Now it was her turn to answer some questions and Lola noticed that she wasn't anywhere near as proficient a liar as Isaac.

'I...' she tripped over her reply. 'I forgot something and I just came back to get it.'

Moriarty, looked around the room in exaggerated earnest. 'What was it you left behind, Susie?' he smiled.

'Oh just a file, I must have left it in the other room.'

'Well we're just about the finish up here,' said Moriarty. 'We'll be out of your way in just a moment. The professor delicately closed the book and brought it back to the holding container, planting a reverent kiss on her cover.

The company were about to move on when Delaney saw Lola's t-shirt.

'Miss Paige,' she said pointing dramatically at Lola's shoulder. 'You're bleeding.'

For a moment Lola's heart stopped stock still. The staining was dark brown now.

'It's not blood,' laughed Lola airily. 'I lost a fight with a cola bottle. Serves me right for drinking the stuff,' she said as she slipped out behind the rest of the group.

They all crammed into the small elevator, united in their conspiracy a mild giddiness erupted as the intensity of the situation lifted off each of them.

'Kathy?' shot Miss Jenkins at Isaac. 'You damn near blew our cover, Mr Kane, giving me a white name like Kathy.'

~ 38 ~

Summer had all but disappeared from the city and it had rained solid for three whole days making the streets of New York dull and foreboding.

After the attack on Lemar's home it was arranged that he and his mother would stay with Isaac, that way Miss Jenkins wouldn't be far from the hospital and Lemar would have a proper bed to sleep in at night.

Despite the inclement weather, Lemar visited the protesters and the camp every day helping to fix their meagre holdings and inventing more ingenious ways to capitalise on the rotten weather by harvesting the rainfall.

Of course Lola had him sworn to secrecy and she trusted that Lemar would keep his own counsel but she had agonised over letting him return to the camp. In the end her instinct told her that, for now, it would raise less suspicion if he continued to visit Liberty Plaza and Prospero. Besides, she thought, it might not do any harm to have a pair of eyes on the ground.

They were in contact each day and every day he passed on Prospero's regards and every day Lola had to invent another excuse as to why she couldn't visit.

Since their first introduction at the preservation lab, Rocha had been spending a lot of time with Ezra Cohen and although she said it was merely in the interest of the book, Lola wasn't so sure that's all it was that brought them together.

She could see the connection between them grow with each encounter. Lola could tell by the way Rocha subtly touched her neck or played with her collaret when she spoke to Ezra that there was energy between them and one night over dinner she decided they'd make a great couple as she watched their unspoken exchanges.

The sadness that was never too far from Ezra Cohen's eyes subsided when he was with Rocha. Her aura, Lola observed, danced and folded in shades of violet, carmine and lichen green when they spoke or shared a joke and his changed from bronzes and coppers to cornflower blue and saffron. It was so interesting to see the beauty of the interaction.

This, Lola understood, was what sexual energy looked like, manifest in Technicolor and yet the two had not touched each other physically. Here it was, the passion, the dance sent forth from one heart to another in all its splendour, raw and exhilarating and yet not so much as a kiss had been exchanged. Lola understood how this felt, the intoxicating fizzle in the solar plexus the rising pull of one heart on another. Even the thought of Alex Stein's name evoked this spirit in her but to see it at play in another was something truly sacrosanct.

Granted a rare break from Isaac's office, Lola clasped on to the warm cup of tea while her eyes stared blindly out through the colossal sheets of glass. The lights of the surrounding buildings and shops below were blurred and distorted by the beads of rain that raced down the huge panes of Torch Tower making the entire scene below look like a water colour painting.

For the past two weeks they'd been holed away in the office compiling research and pouring over the information on the pen drive that Ezra had given them frantically following and chasing up leads. Lola thought about the morning they'd first accessed the documents. It felt like hours had passed before either of them was able to speak. They had sat dumbfounded as they read and re-read the emails, between Aztec, Stein Corp and a mysterious contact that went by the name of Mockingbird.

The emails proved what Ezra had told them, that Aztec and Stein Corp were aware of his concerns about an imminent attack on American soil but as of yet they had been unable to link it to the military. Both she and Isaac suspected that Mockingbird was very likely a military source but proving that was another thing entirely.

The revelations had taken their toll on Isaac and she could see the anguish and conflict that played out in him. Each day his face became a bit more drawn and his shoulders a little more slumped. Jodi was the only other person permitted to enter the office and when they both did emerge from their work, the eyes of the entire newsroom questioned them.

What they were working on was not a run of the mill exposé, this was major and not only would it shake the very foundations of American society, it would have repercussions all over the world. So when Lola found Isaac quiet or despondent, which she often had over the past number of days, she worried that he might be losing his nerve. She'd laid a huge responsibility on his shoulders but this was the most important thing either of them would ever do as journalists. They had a moral duty to stand up and tell the truth no matter how revolutionary or ugly it was.

By now they certainly had enough to link Aztec and Stein Corp with the data from the Random Number Generators and warnings that Ezra Cohen had expressed. They soon realised that linking the murders to Carl Stein was going to be a hugely difficult task but Lola was certain that there was enough negligence in the case to at least have it re-examined and Susan Harris was the sole link between the two. Perhaps, she'd argued, that by highlighting her case, they would be able to create an opening for the other so-called suicides to be re- examined.

But Lola knew that she would need something more substantial. She had a hunch that Susan Harris had found something but hunches could not be translated into print. Ezra had already told Lola that Susan had become obsessed with the events surrounding her mother's death and that she had no financial worries, so why would she have been working part-time for an agency? Lola decided to find out and for the past week she'd been trying to find any old friends or fellow students who might have known Susan. One name kept showing up, Eli Shultz, no matter who she spoke to or tracked down every person named Eli as being a close friend of Susan's.

Lola had tried for days to get in touch. She found four Eli Shultzes in New York. Luckily for her it wasn't a very common name and after she tried the phone directory as well as the obligatory social media route she'd narrowed her search down to one. Leaving a generic message online for him to contact her at the Torch, Lola hoped that something would come up.

Each day brought them another lead and with it they found themselves falling deeper into the rabbit hole.

Lola had contacted Daithí with the name and what details she could muster abut Susan in the hope that his talents would unearth something that she couldn't. She'd also given him the codename Mockingbird.

There were so strands and lose ends that Lola was becoming increasingly fearful that she was losing control. Daily reports came from Moriarty at the library and he was able to inform her that Alex was there almost every day and while he never asked to see the book, Moriarty was suspicious that something was afoot, because he and Susie always seemed to be deep in conclave.

Moriarty was fast realising that he would soon have to wrap up his research at the Butler Library but he needed a safe exit strategy and that would take time.

'Miss Paige. Miss Paige!'

'Yes,' smiled Lola turning around in her seat to greet the voice. 'Sorry I was lost in thought there.' She vaguely recognised the young man that stood in front of her. His hair was neatly styled and he wore a crisp white shirt and dark trousers. She thought he might work on the online desk but she couldn't be sure.

'A message has come up from reception, there's a police officer here to see you.' He smiled politely back at her. Lola's heart leapt, there was no way Andy Jessop would be so bold as to walk into the Torch!

'Did he give his name?' Lola asked, swallowing her anxiety. 'Yes,' said the young man as he was about to leave. 'Mendez.'

Lola breathed a sigh of relief and deposited her empty cup into the bin before heading to reception to meet her visitor.

It was a pleasant surprise to meet the old detective outside of the precinct. He looked completely different dressed in civilian clothes. Mendez looked smart dressed in slate blue suit trousers with a v-neck jumper and shirt under a matching suit jacket. From a distance he looked more like a librarian than a cop, but when Lola greeted him there was no mistaking the steel in his chestnut eyes.

'Sergeant Mendez,' greeted Lola extending her hand out to meet his firm grip. 'I'm surprised to see you here. To what do I owe the pleasure?'

Mendez's demeanour was pleasant but Lola could feel the stiffness under the casual greeting because kept looking about the open reception area as though he thought he was being watched.

'Can we go somewhere a little more private, Miss Paige?' he said, with another furtive look over his shoulder.

'Of course,' said Lola guiding him towards the elevator. 'Please, come with me.'

Lola made straight for Isaac's office, closing the door behind her. She was about to introduce the two men when Isaac rose from his seat ceremoniously, pulling Mendez into a warm embrace.

'Detective Mendez, good to see you, man! It's been too long,' smiled Isaac.

'Irish,' said Isaac smiling and animated for the first time in days. 'This guy here used to walk the beat in Mornington Heights. He taught us all how to play baseball and wasn't afraid to catch a whooping to our asses if we acted out.'

'Great to see you, Isaac,' beamed Mendez, so transformed by the encounter Lola barely recognised him.

'I'd no idea this little chica here was working with you.' Lola waited patiently as both exchanged stories of Harlem and what each had been doing in the intervening years since they'd last seen each other.

'You're a big shot reporter now, Isaac. I've followed all your stories. You always had brains and heart, son,' said Mendez as he settled into the seat. Despite the joviality, Lola could see that he was still uncomfortable so she offered him a glass of water, setting it down beside him on the table. He drank it and asked for a refill. Lola obliged.

'So, Sergeant, can I ask why you've come?' said Lola hopeful that he had some good news for her.

'Well, Miss Paige, it was something you said when we last met, before you left.'

'Was that before or after you laughed me out of the room?' asked Lola. There was no bite in her tone but Isaac shot her a reprimanding look.

Mendez's smile showed he wasn't offended.

'I'm sorry about that, Miss Paige,' he said shuffling in his seat as though he was sitting on something sharp.

'In truth, your words lingered with me, so much so I looked at the so-called suicide notes that you referred to and when I looked at them they seemed to be written in the same hand, not all of them but it is my belief that each block of four were penned by the same person. Well, this got me to thinking and the writing on the most recent case of four back in 2012, the writing looked familiar to me. Sorry,' said Mendez again, taking another gulp from the glass. 'I'm not making much sense. Isaac here will tell you, Miss Paige, I've been a police officer since 1970. I've had a great career and in that time I moved my way up through the ranks, being from Spanish Harlem that wasn't always easy, especially in the seventies and eighties, but I forged on and became a Detective Inspector. Now I'm about to retire and I've worked damned hard over the years to throw that away but the changes I've seen in the force are terrifying. Two years ago, I was given an ultimatum to basically shut up, get my pension see the rest of my time out quietly or face consequences. To my shame, Miss Paige, I chose the latter.'

'Why were you given that offer?' asked Lola. 'Whose feathers did you ruffle?'

'You're a shrewd young woman, Miss Paige, no doubt Isaac here has taught you well.'

Isaac held his hands up in surrender. 'In fairness to Irish here, I can take no credit for this, this is all her work. I'm afraid like you, Carlos, I laughed at her. But I ain't laughing any more,' said Isaac in earnest. 'So, tell us what happened. Why was a man of your calibre relegated to the evidence room?'

'The force I dedicated my life to and the communities that I worked hard to keep safe and protect are in the middle of a civil war and the good guys are losing. It breaks my heart to say it, but the NYPD is fast becoming the biggest gang in New York. It's war out there on the streets and they're targeting the poor, the minorities, from your community and mine. This new enforcement strategy is targeting those that can't afford to fight back. Making crazy arrests, and everyone is making money out of it. I was investigating a certain police officer, whose rapid rise in the force was, let's say interesting.' Mendez turned to face Lola. 'Miss Paige, I believe you're familiar with the name Andy Jessop?' Lola nodded and looked at Isaac, who knew all about him now.

'Well, in 2012 there was a significant rise of internal investigations into police harassment even murder charges and Jessop's name kept cropping up time and time again. Myself and my team were convinced that he was dirty; I mean the guy seemed untouchable. The whole investigation, which we had to hand over to the top brass, was a whitewash and I soon realised that nobody asked the right questions because nobody wanted the right answers. I couldn't take it anymore and when I went to the Captain to explain this, a man I've known my whole career, he basically told me to leave it, do my time and get the hell outta there with a nice pension.

'Soon after that meeting, Andy Jessop upped and moved on. He left the force and as I later found out got a top job with Aztec Solutions. Now the reason I came here today, is to tell you that when I looked at that writing on the suicide notes, I knew I'd seen it somewhere before and when his name was all over those files, I knew it was Andy Jessop's.'

Mendez reached his hand to the inside of his suit jacket and pulled out some papers that were folded up. 'I could lose my job for what I'm about to tell you. The boys in blue don't like whistle blowers but I couldn't live with myself if I didn't. I mean it's not definitive but it might be enough to at least elicit a conversation.'

Mendez unfolded the thick pile of papers and spread them out on Isaac's desk. 'You know, Carlos, we will protect your identity,' reassured Isaac.

'I know you will, Isaac. I'm an old man now and not many will take notice of me anyways. It's sad that it's come to this,' smiled Mendez.

His words struck Lola deep and she felt Mendez's despair. The man was completely torn between the force he'd dedicated his life to and doing what was right.

'Silence has its rewards, Isaac, but the price on my soul and conscience is too high to pay. I've made copies of the front of each of your files, with Jessop's name on them. I've also made copies of various statements, hand written by Jessop. I'm no expert in graphology but I've been in the force long enough to know the same handwriting when I see it. If the paper gets an expert in, you may be able to at least link him to the cases.'

'This is amazing, Sergeant,' added Lola. 'I'm sure the decision to come here today isn't one you made lightly. I wish there were more people in our profession with your courage and integrity.' Mendez just nodded his grey head in thanks.

'Can I ask you one thing before you go, sir?' The question had been plucking at Lola since Mendez had started talking. It was a long shot but she felt it was worth a try.

'Of course go right ahead.'

'In your time working in the precinct, did you ever see Carl Stein there?'

The former detective thought for a while before answering. 'No,' he said shaking his head. 'That man always had somebody to do his bidding but his boy.... He's different. He's a regular Bruce Wayne,' laughed Mendez. If he noticed Lola's expression change he didn't draw attention to it. 'He's down at the precinct from time to time, usually whenever that old hippy from Liberty Plaza gets himself arrested, he's the one that cuts bail for him. Now who'd have thought that,' he coughed as he laughed.

Isaac got up from his seat and led Mendez from the office towards the elevators.

Lola buried her head in her hands and rubbed her face.

Her body felt cramped and sore. Mendez's bombshell revelation should not have been the hit it was; after all she had seen Prospero and Alex's exchange outside the precinct only weeks ago. So it shouldn't have come as such a shock that Alex Stein bailed him out. Prospero had told her himself, remembered Lola now, that the protesters had a very wealthy benefactor and now she knew who it was. What she didn't know was why? What was it the two were scheming?

Lola was gathering her research up placing them neatly into her brief. She needed some fresh air and to clear her head and organise her thoughts. She was about to leave Isaac a note when he came back into the office.

'You going somewhere?' Lola could tell he didn't approve but Lola was resolved, she needed out.

'Isaac, I've been holed up in this office morning, noon and night for two past two weeks now. I need to get my head straight and I can't do it here,' said Lola.

'You're right, Irish,' said Isaac. 'I'll come with you.'

'Please I just need a bit of time on my own, but you should go home and get some rest.

'I guess you're right,' sighed Isaac. 'We both need a little time away from the office. You go on and I'll get cleared up here. Mendez has given us a great breakthrough on you murder cases.'

'Yes,' smiled Lola, 'some good news at last. I'll call by later this evening,' she said as she pulled her raincoat around her.

'Isaac,' he looked up from his papers. 'Don't leave anything in this office. Not a scrap of what we've been working on, make sure you bring your laptop home. Leave nothing.' Isaac looked at Lola and the sadness and understanding in his face almost broke her resolve as they both understood that this office would soon have someone else's name on the door.

'Isaac,' said Lola softly, 'now is not the time for sentimentality.'

'I know. I know,' said Isaac taking of his glasses and rubbing his tired eyes. 'Hell, kid, you'd think I was the rookie here.'

As Lola moved through the newsroom the other journalists pretended not to notice her but she could feel the heat of their enquiring eyes as their minds burned with the desire to know what she and Isaac were working on and Lola smiled, suddenly she wasn't so invisible anymore. At the far end of the floor, Gene Rush was making towards her and she could tell from his knitted brows and flexing jaw that he wasn't looking to engage in pleasantries.

Lola looked beyond him, out towards the sky where a mountain of blackness loomed over the city waiting for her. The rain continued to fall in a great deluge to the streets below but before she could let it wash her clean, Lola turned to face the torrent right in front of her.

'Miss Paige,' the words crept from the side of Gene Rush's mouth in a sneer as his jaw continued to pulse when he clenched it. 'Are you leaving?' He looked at his watch dramatically and then back at her. Lola glared at the large clock that hung at the top of the newsroom. It was almost four in the afternoon and she'd been there from six-thirty that morning.

'Isaac said it was okay to go considering we've been practically living here for the past two weeks,' said Lola evenly. 'I didn't think that would be a problem.' Normally Gene Rush's face was enough to incite her but she remained composed.

'In case I needed to remind you, I'm the person who determines when you come and when you go.' The other journalists weren't even pretending not to notice now, as Lola looked around the newsroom. Still she was unmoved by the standoff. She was suddenly filled with compassion for Gene Rush as she looked at him, urging her to speak out of turn and she wondered what had made him so insecure and mean.

'I think Isaac is still there, Mr Rush,' said Lola magnanimously. 'If you want to discuss it with him, I'm happy to wait until you both come to an agreement as to when I can leave.' Gene Rush's eyes narrowed as he stepped towards Lola but she didn't recoil or retreat.

'By tomorrow Isaac Kane probably won't have a job,' he grunted as he brushed past her towards Isaac's office. Lola continued on through the newsroom and out into the pouring rain. Without knowing where she was going or why, she trusted her legs to take her where she needed to be.

The rain slid off her raincoat and down onto her tights, soaking right through to her legs. The city streets were unusually clear as most people stood in out of the downpour or found refuge in the cafés and shops or in the back of cabs. The wind and rain that swept at her face and bathed the sidewalks and skyscrapers helped Lola to wash away all the debris of her mind, leaving only what was important. By the time she looked up again she was standing outside a large cathedral, trusting that this is where she was supposed to be, she entered the church.

Business was slow today as she shared the cavernous building with only two other people. It was beautifully lit and the amber light that poured from a large central chandelier high up on the columns gave it a sense of warmth, which was a stark contrast to the darkness of the day outside. Lola let the heavy door creep closed with a sudden burst of wind that sent the spearheaded flames of the votive candles that lay around the edge of the pews waltzing and wavering.

Lola thought of all the petitions that each point of light held and offered up. So many prayers she thought. How long had it been since she was last in a church, Lola wondered, as she settled into one of the narrow pews halfway up the central aisle. There was something calming and tranquil about an empty church and the smell of wood and incense permeated everywhere. It always reminded her of her da's worn work jeans, and the tiny shavings of wood that used to fall out of the turn ups. She still loved the smell of wood because it reminded her of him.

Lola took off her coat, interring it between the gap in the seat and the cushioned kneeler. Her wet legs stuck to the polished seat and squeaked loudly as she made herself comfortable on the hard seat.

A deep red carpeted the marble steps that led to a sparse central altar and along the flanks of the church enormous stained windows displayed various scenes from the bible. In the alcove to the left there was a smaller chapel with kneelers and rows and rows of blue votive candles that flickered and swayed in front of a large golden picture of Our Lady.

Our Lady of Guadalupe it said. Lola examined the image for some time deciding that she was the Bile Màthir and the light around her reminded Lola of the shape of a vulva. This was quite similar to earlier depictions she had seen of the Goddess.

For a fleeting moment Lola felt guilty for having such a blasphemous thought in a chapel but the notion immediately made her smile to herself, after all there was nothing more sacred than the womb or vulva.

Lola didn't turn when she heard the door open momentarily permitting the sound of the rain and the traffic to seep into the quiet church again. It was the familiar military tread of the footsteps that pulled her attention away from the picture and without understanding why, Lola leant down pretending to retrieve something from her coat pocket so as to conceal her face. Flashing her eyes to the side, she saw the dark brown shoes disappear up the cream marble aisle, coming to a halt three pews back from the altar.

Lola wondered could this day get any stranger as she allowed her eyes to creep above the seat in front.

Alex Stein's suit was darkened from the deluge outside but his hair still sat immaculately on his head, nevertheless he ran his fingers over it, smoothing it down. He sat stationary for a moment before bending over in genuflection. The sight was farcical to Lola.

Alex sat back on the pew and paused for a moment before lithely bouncing to his feet and taking a quick look down the central aisle, forcing Lola to duck down behind her seat. Certain he'd seen her, she sat waiting with her eyes snapped shut, until she heard his footsteps retreating to a door at the right of the altar.

Quickly she lifted her coat. The water dripped onto the aisle as she hurried towards the seat that Alex Stein had just vacated. It was still warm and his cologne still lingered in the air, the scent made Lola's heart ache.

Lola looked around aimlessly trying to uncover what he was doing there; it wasn't like he'd found Jesus. She groped under the seats and crouched down into the narrow space to look underneath the long rows of seats but there was nothing to be found.

Sitting up again her eyes scanned around the pew looking for some clue and that's when she noticed the powder blue cover of the bible sitting perched on the lip of the pew in front. Lifting it, Lola flicked through its tissue thin pages. A small note fell out of the back pages and onto the floor. She unfolded the tiny piece of white paper and read the note.

A move will be made two days from now.

Lola struggled to find the page that the note had fallen from; it was Revelations she was in as she flicked through the pages frantically. The main entrance of St Patrick's Cathedral opened and closed again as a few more tourists entered the building. Lola was just about to give up when she noticed markings on one of the pages. Brackets had been drawn around a passage and a little smiley face.

Lola read the highlighted passage which was from Revelations 21.9: 'Then came one of the seven angles who had seven bowls full of the seven plagues and spoke to me, saying "Come, I will show you the Bride, the wife of the Lamb".' She had no idea what this could mean or what it alluded to but she was sure that Rocha would. Gently folding the piece of paper so that it looked as though it hadn't been disturbed, she tucked it back in to the correct page and returned the book to its resting place on the shelf in front.

Lola pulled on her sodden coat and stepped out through the side door. The rain and wind whipped and lashed at her face and legs sending shivers over her body. For a moment she contemplated stepping inside the church again for shelter but she would have to face the elements sometime so Lola proceeded out into the cold in search for a cab.

How fortuitous, she thought, that she was brought to this place at just the right time. Something in her said it was all too easy, too neat, but her gut had served her well over the past few weeks so she tucked her doubts away, forcing them to sleep.

According to the note they had one day to secure the book. Moriarty wasn't going to like this mused Lola as she settled into the back of the cab. Finally she was one step ahead of the Carl Stein and the Hell Fire Club.

As her cab disappeared into the evening rush hour a dishevelled man long and lean, with a salt and pepper beard walked solemnly up the aisle of the church. A little dog, whose hair was wet and matted, trotted proudly beside him. They took their usual seat three rows from the altar and lifted the book of Christian Scripture.

He always had enjoyed reading the Bible, picking out the little nuggets of wisdom and truth that had managed to survive from a time long since forgotten.

His worn hands nimbly traced down the pages until he located Revelation 21.9. He let out a chuckle when he saw the passage highlighted in brackets. The boy had his father's dry wit. Taking the small note, he placed it gently into a concealed pocket on the inside of his coat.

Tension lifted from his shoulders, so many strings and so many faces he thought, how exhausting it all was becoming. Finally, things were set in motion. What they had been searching for was almost within reach, now there was just the girl to deal with and she would know the truth soon enough.

Lola would no doubt feel betrayed, he thought to himself, but it could not have been any other way. Running his hands across the sky-blue canvas cover of the book, Prospero laid it carefully back in its place.

So many battles had been fought over or in the name of sacred books and now another was about to begin. It saddened him as he urged his stiff bones up off the seat. He lifted his staff and stepping out into the aisle he bent his knee and bowed his head before the vaulted altar.

'Let's go, Hermes,' he said to the dog with a sombre smile. 'All the pieces are in place, let's hope this game will be ours.' He turned and walked down the central aisle and stepped back out into the noise and bustle of the city.

~39~

The news that Carl Stein had won his fight to take over the Torch spread like wild fire. Lola had been in the office since early morning drawing up the first draft of their story with Isaac. She had briefly mentioned that she would be visiting the library that night but she didn't go into detail with Isaac because something didn't feel quite right in the newsroom. Lola felt uneasy like there were eyes everywhere. Perhaps it was the nature of the story they were working on and the secrecy that it involved.

Isaac was unusually calm this morning and was nonplussed by the story at the heart of the Torch. She'd gotten a call from her mentor not long after she'd left the church the previous evening. Gene Rush had taken great pleasure in breaking the news of the takeover to him. Lola remembered what he'd muttered to her as he made for Isaac – 'by tomorrow Isaac Kane probably won't have a job.' Yet Isaac was calm, so calm that Lola was beginning to worry about him, but when she voiced her concerns all he told her was that he had everything under control.

When Isaac approached Chris to verify the news his old friend didn't deny it. It had only just been fed down to the section editors from above he'd told him. While Isaac had been expecting it he was still sore that his friend hadn't given him a heads up. He didn't buy that they were under strict instructions not to tell, Isaac felt that didn't count when it came to him and Chris.

This was very troubling news, not just for their story but for the paper as a whole, the Hell Fire Club had now gotten their hands on one of the only remaining independent papers in the city. Carl Stein had won a major victory in convincing the board to take his funding. No doubt he'd made them all kinds of promises but even Lola knew, as inexperienced as she was, that it would only be a matter of time until he was dictating and interfering with the editorial content.

There was a gentle tap on the door, startling them both, as they looked to one another as if they were fugitives on the run. Isaac got up from his desk and opened the door.

'Mister Kane,' it was Erin. Lola hadn't gotten a chance to speak to her face to face in days. Lola shouted for her to come in.

'Erin,' greeted Lola as she gave her a hug.

'Lola, I know you guys are busy, but I think you maybe wanna see what I have. It might help you with your story.'

Isaac looked at Lola, his eyes accusing her of treachery. 'It's okay, Isaac,' said Lola. 'Erin was helping me with some research, when no one else would listen,' cautioned Lola. This nullified any anticipated rebuke from Isaac.

'What have you got, Erin?' asked Lola as she cleared a space for her in the office. Isaac had his record player on, he said he thought more clearly when his music was on, but there was only so much saxophone Lola could abide, so she welcomed the excuse to turn it off.

Erin produced a large A4 envelope from her bag. Lola was relieved that she'd had the insight to conceal the information, it felt that there were eyes on them from every corner.

'Before the news broke about the takeover,' said Erin, 'you two were all anyone was talkin' about. Everywhere I went, "I hear Kane and that intern have something big cookin'". Erin mocked the way some of the suits in the office spoke.

'Anyways, I think you might like this, Lola. I had a little time on my hands and began to go through the photo archives, also those three agencies that you gave me that those girls worked for. All of them are owned by Stein Corp or a subsidiary of the company and it looks like Daddy Stein has been helping himself to the goods.'

Erin laid the pictures out one by one. 'I've the names below. I said it myself, Lola, just 'cause you're in a picture with someone it don't mean you know them, however, when you're in a picture with them at different functions, I'm pretty sure you know them.'

'Look,' she said as she began to shuffle and organise the pictures. 'December 2001, Nora Evans and Carl Stein at the Aztec annual ball, October of that same year, here they are again at a Children's Charity Fund and again in July of the same year at an art exhibition.'

Erin pulled out picture after picture of girl after girl proof that these girls were personally known to Carl Stein.

'That takes us up to 2012. I could only find pictures of him with Susan Harris and...' Erin checked her notes again, 'and a Lucy Davis. If you look, there are quite a lot with these two women and I believe that they were also friends. They worked for the same agency.' Lola and Isaac flicked through the pictures again and again. This was certainly a major breakthrough.

'This is great work, Erin,' commended Isaac. 'I really think that we'll be able to use this.' Isaac leaned back in his seat and rubbed his face. As he stretched, his toned torso was visible through the crisp white shirt he wore unbuttoned at the neck with the sleeves partially rolled up. Erin made gestures to Lola, indicting how hot he was. Lola laughed, she had missed seeing Erin; she always managed to lighten things up.

'What?' quizzed Isaac. Erin flushed and giggled at Lola.

'None of your business.' Lola smiled back at him. The door was rapped again and this time Chris Auld walked in without waiting to be invited. Erin and Lola began to gather all the pictures off the desk but it was too late, he'd seen them.

'So Isaac, you gonna tell me what all this is about?' asked Chris looking down at the table. While his body language and tone were informal the news editor's eyes told the real story. They told of his panic, his worry, and his resentment. Lola could see that Isaac understood this too but he was a much cooler customer than Chris. He was adept at working under pressure and thinking on the spot. Isaac Kane gave nothing away.

'Chris,' said Isaac, 'the very man. Would you believe, we are just working on our final draft to give to you.' Only Lola could see that Isaac was lying. He had no intentions of giving anything to Chris, not now that Stein had his hands on the paper and not now that he knew whose side his old friend was on. Isaac, like a skilled fisherman, was baiting his line.

'Final draft,' smiled Chris tightly. 'I thought,' he said picking one of the pictures up from the desk and considering it for a moment before continuing. 'I thought the news editor had to be consulted at every point. Erin, Lola, perhaps you ladies would give me and my buddy here a minute to talk.'

Erin was already up and out of the room before Lola even had a chance to pick up her things.

'What's this all about, Chris?' said Isaac firmly. 'Irish stays. This is her story, her research, her damn hard work. Irish,' commanded Isaac, 'you stay where you are.' Lola froze stranded halfway in and halfway out of the door.

'In,' demanded Isaac, getting up from his seat and slamming the door behind her making her jump.

'What the hell is this all about, Chris? Are you seriously tellin' me this is because you weren't consulted? You know how I work. I want to have the full picture before I go anywhere with it. It's the way I've always worked, you never seemed to have a problem with it before.'

What little gusto the news editor had carried in with him had now evaporated. 'Dammit, Isaac,' he said flailing his hands in the air. 'I'm trying to help you out here, can't you see that? The storm is here and I can't protect your ass anymore. I can't keep smoothing over your eccentricities just because you happen to be a good journalist. I've got upstairs on my ass and Gene Rush and now Carl Stein. I'm just trying to throw you a lifeline, Isaac. I mean we've been friends since forever.'

Lola sat silently in the corner waiting for Isaac to reply but it didn't come immediately. Isaac went to his laptop and hit print. The silence seemed to expand between them as the printer spat out four A3 sheets of paper, with their article on it. Isaac handed it to Chris. 'Read this.'

'Irish, why don't you go and get us a couple of coffees.' Lola, delighted to break free, ran from the office to the small café.

Outside, the rain continued its lament and not once had there been a cessation as it continued to baptise the city. She took the time to sit and drink a cup of green tea and get something to eat before heading back to Isaac's office.

Chris was sitting with his head in his hands, while Isaac lay back in his chair composed and collected. She sat the coffees down on the desk and took a seat.

'Hell, Isaac,' he finally said. 'Could your timing be any bloody worse? How am I going to sell this to upstairs now, when the man you are accusing of,' he flicked the sheets out of his way, 'god know what, has just taken over our paper? I mean legal would need to look at this and all these so-called sources and check the evidence before we could even think about considering it let alone printing it.'

Lola's stomach twisted and knotted, churning. She could see where this was going and why Isaac had been so keen to spend so much time fact checking and making the story as watertight as possible. They had certainly done that but Chris was faltering. Isaac knew he was lost but he enjoyed seeing him squirm. This was Isaac's revenge for the betrayal.

'"So-called", "timing", "sell it to upstairs", said Isaac evenly. 'Please tell me what's happening here, Chris, because in all the years I've known you and we've worked together, I've never once heard you use those words. Legal, yes, by all means that's procedure and I understand that, but as for the rest of the bullshit you're spouting, I can't get my head around that, not for one second. When have I ever,' Isaac leant across the desk, staring right into Chris's eyes, his face like stone, 'brought you anything that cannot be substantiated and backed up with evidence? We have a meeting in this very newsroom in,' Isaac checked his watch,' about fifteen minutes, when I'll know for sure what they've promised you, so I'm giving you the chance to tell me now, as your friend, what's in this for you, Chris?'

'I was just trying to help you, Isaac, that's all,' said Chris as he got up to leave. 'You've been lead down the garden path by a rookie who, from what I hear, has a bigger grudge against the Steins than you do. I'm not sure what hold this kid has on you, but all I can say is that I hope for your sake it's purely professional, she sure as hell isn't worth destroying your career over.'

Isaac snapped, leaping from his seat he lunged at his old friend and grabbed him by the throat, shoving him against the glass windows of his office. Lola tried to pull him back but he was too strong.

'You seriously coming to me with this bullshit,' spat Isaac and he squeezed Chris's throat. Chris's eyes bulged and his face turned puce until finally he broke free.

'Get your damn hands off me,' he said fixing his tie and shirt.

Isaac threw open the office door, 'Get the hell outta my office. This paper will never have the heart to print this story, lucky for me I know one that will.'

'Good luck with that, Isaac, even the National Outrage wouldn't take that.'

Isaac slammed the door shut, his body heaving as he let his temper vent. Suddenly he started going around the room pulling his vinyl off the shelves and stacking them in piles. He made a call to the mailroom asking for some boxes and wooden crates.

'What are you doing, Isaac?' said Lola. 'You can't quit, we need to get this story out there.'

Isaac stopped and turned to face her, his expression was drawn and his eyes glistened with such sadness that Lola wanted to embrace him. He had the disposition of a man not defeated but resigned. 'We will, Irish, but my time at the New York Torch has come to an end. In truth the clock has been ticking for some time and Jodi and I have been making provisions. That's why I've been so pre-occupied lately. I made the decision when I last came back from Iraq that it was time to move on. For too many years I've felt like a cheap imitation, curtailing and being selective with the facts not because they weren't true but because the great American establishment found them too uncomfortable. Really when you look at it all, I'm no different to Chris or any of the rest of them. I put my career first for too many years and I'd forgotten why I wanted to be a journalist in the first place.'

Isaac slumped into his chair. 'You, Lola,' hearing her name in his mouth made Lola feel proud and sad. 'You, a young girl from Ireland, full of heart and intelligence and wisdom, you, Irish, have made me remember why I became an investigative journalist. Along the way, between Pulitzer prizes and awards, I think I'd lost sight of that. I feel ashamed,' he continued shaking his head, 'ashamed, nauseated and angry at how I won that Pulitzer. I was embedded to get the story, the scoop, but what I was sacrificing was my sovereignty as an investigative journalist. They had control over what I saw and what I heard and ultimately what I reported. The independent journalists who actually risked their lives in pursuit of the truth were marginalised and discredited for their efforts, just like the men and women who served and spoke out about the atrocities being carried out in the name of democracy. All the facts,' he threw the words with venom, 'that I expounded and held to be true were nothing but lies fed to me on a silver platter by a sophisticated disinformation machine. Deep down I knew it but I chose to have journalistic Alzheimer's. I chose to forget why I wanted to be a journalist in the first place, but you reminded me. You forced me to look the truth in the face and you held the mirror up that made me see what I'd become. You, Irish, with your passion and belief, you saved me.'

A lump, dry and piercing rose in Lola's throat as she tried to stifle the tears. Isaac was up again stacking his records and clearing his desk.

'I always wanted to set up my own paper and that's exactly what we've done. It's called Veritas,' he said laughing. 'That means truth in Latin.'

An announcement, that the morning meeting was to begin, seeped out over the newsroom. Lola and Isaac stopped what they were doing and went out to find the large news floor packed with journalists, administrators, mailroom workers and printers. Even the space above was jammed as people jostled for position along the railings overlooking the news floor below.

On the stairs there stood the outgoing Chief Executive and beside him were Carl Stein, Chris Auld and Gene Rush. A man from the mailroom that Isaac addressed as Earl wheeled some crates and boxes into and Isaac's office and came out to stand beside him and Lola. The room was humming with conversations and whispers each speculating about what was going to happen. Were there going to be job cuts? Who would go first?

The Chief Executive of the Torch, Charlie Bohme, called everyone to attention and a deathly silence fell on the building. Despite the scale, his voice rang clear and loud over everyone gathered.

'As most of you will know,' he began. 'I've been the CEO at this company for almost twenty years and worked at the Torch for neigh over forty years. In that time news has become a multi-platform service and we have tried to embrace the new as well as preserve the rich ethos of newsgathering and journalism that has made this paper great for over one hundred and sixty years.

'I can safely say that I am very privileged to have worked with some of the brightest minds in American journalism and business here at the Torch where we have a wonderful workforce from the printing factory, the mail room right up to the board level. I am saddened that today will be my last day with the Torch as I will be standing down. I have taken this paper as far as I can and I feel it's now time for new initiatives and new ideas to take root, to carry us into the next hundred odd years.' The old man's voice started to break as he struggled to compose himself.

Isaac shook his head. 'They're even getting rid of old Charlie, looks like I'm leaving at the right time,' he whispered to Lola. The old man resumed again as he read from the small piece of paper that vibrated in his trembling hand.

'One thing I will say to you all and to those whose task it is to preserve and expand the legacy of the Torch, please don't interfere with the editorial integrity upon which we have built our reputation. Please continue this beautiful editorial freedom upon which we have built this paper. I wish you all the best for your future, whether it is with the Torch or with another organisation. I think I'll leave it there,' said the old man folding the piece of paper and placing it in his breast pocket. A loud cheer erupted around the room, as people clapped and some cried. As the adulation subsided, he spoke again. 'And now I'd like to introduce you to your new CEO, Mr Carl Stein.'

A warm applause streamed around the room with the noticeable exceptions of Isaac and Lola. Lola noticed that Jodi, who was standing a few booths over from them, didn't join in either.

'Thank you all,' smiled Carl Stein. 'I won't keep you long, after all time is money,' a ripple of laughter rose to greet his smug face. 'I would like to thank Charlie for his many years of service to the Torch and of course his words of wisdom. I do intend to speak to all the heads of department so each of you in your various sections will be made aware of any changes. At this point in time everyone's job is safe.' There was a collective sigh of relief throughout the crowd.

'However, I will say that we will be looking closely at the print section. This is one area that has seen a steady decline and while some cuts may be necessary I will be seeking to invest some new impetus in that region. I am an old fashioned man if anything and loath all this technology and online news. I'm a paper man myself so I can tell you that I am determined to reinvigorate our news department in that area and helping me with that project will be Chris Auld and his colleague Gene Rush. Everyone's contracts will be evaluated but we can discuss that in due course. This is exciting and I am excited to be here.'

Carl Stein looked around the room at all the grinning, approving faces that gazed up at him as if he was the sun itself. Lola realised then that this would be her last day at the paper and possibly as a journalist.

Filled with a sudden wave of wild abandon she stood on a nearby table and raised her hand as if in school. Chris and Gene looked at her with derision and tried to usher Carl Stein away but when he realised who it was, Lola knew that he was never going to retreat.

'Miss Paige,' said Carl grinning his politician's smile at her and the whole room fell into silence once again. Isaac stood looking at Lola but he wasn't angry, he was proud, nodding his approval at her.

'Mr Stein,' replied Lola politely. 'Thank you so much for taking the time to speak with me.'

'Why how could I resist, Miss Paige? It's come to my attention that you've been busy working hard on something quite interesting.' To the others in the room it may have sounded like praise but Carl Stein couldn't hide the threat of his veiled tone from Lola. He could have been talking about so much that had passed between them, the Oracle or the investigations.

'I've been working on a number of projects that might be of interest to you, Mr Stein,' said Lola never once breaking eye contact. She'd noticed that he didn't like that. He could never look her in the eye as though whatever he saw there unnerved him. 'That's why I want to ask you a question,' said Lola her chin raised in defiance. 'Mr Bohme made a very interesting plea that the powers that now govern this paper should refrain from interfering in editorial content. With that in mind, Mr Stein, and in light of our current investigations, what is your stance on the matter?' Lola understood that this was a moot point because the article would never be submitted to the Torch but this was her opportunity to face down Carl Stein in public and she wasn't going to let such a rare opportunity pass her by. She, unlike the rest of the journalists actually employed by the Torch, had nothing to lose.

Every face in the room and above on the second floor cast their eyes to the ground submissively pretending they weren't titillated by the exchange between Lola and Carl Stein.

'Sorry, Mr Stein, but our interns are not usually this brash,' Gene Rush said in an attempt to intervene, 'she will be dealt with...'

'Miss Paige and I go way back, Mr Rush,' said Carl Stein brushing him aside with his customary laconic laugh. 'Perhaps if you'd like to continue this conversation in my office, Miss Paige, I'd be more than happy to oblige.'

Lola smiled back at him serenely. 'Thanks for the offer but with your track record, I'd say it's safer for me out here in the open.' She looked around the newsroom and watched as the seed of intrigue took root in every face that bobbed between her and Carl Stein. 'I'm sure there are many journalists standing down here who would like to know if you plan to have an input into editorial content or just the stuff that threatens you personally, Mr Stein?'

Lola could see the side of his mouth quiver slightly as he struggled to control his temper, and just for a second she felt his cold tentacles run across her throat, but her ring was alert and up went her amber shield. No one noticed but she knew him better than anyone in the room and

she understood the arrogance and elitism of the man. She understood how he viewed women, especially women like her, and that he was not accustomed to being challenged.

'Well, Miss Paige,' said Carl, his voice smooth and clear. 'I would expect any story to be able to stand up to the most rigorous scrutiny and I would expect each fact to be verifiable not just speculation and fancy.'

'It may read like a crime novel, Mr Stein, but I think we both know that sometimes facts can be stranger than fiction.' As he spoke, Isaac stepped up beside Lola on the table, his voice commanding and his eyes ablaze. A collective gasp rippled around the room; this was gold for all the spectators and all that was missing was the popcorn. The only sound that could be heard in the room now was the clicking and clacking of someone tapping at their computer keys, as though they were taking notes on the exchange as it played out. Isaac's show of defiance intensified the already highly charged atmosphere and the audience were lapping it up.

Carl Stein was never going to back down now, not in front of his entire workforce. Gene and Chris melted against the wall trying to find cover against the coming onslaught.

'Life in general can be stranger than fiction,' said Carl his eyes sparkling and full of venom, 'but I don't think you're going to find another Pulitzer at my expense, Mr Kane. You and I have had, and I don't think I'm being unfair when I say this, a strained relationship, but I would caution you, and any other reporter out there, to make sure your story can stand up and if it cannot, it will not be printed in my paper.'

'That's the most honest thing you've said this morning,' smiled Isaac. 'All my stories stand up to scrutiny and this one is no different than any other. Miss Paige here,' he said placing his arm on Lola's shoulder, 'will make a fine investigative journalist and what she has unearthed is momentous. It has been made clear that this story will not be printed by this paper but as we both know, Mr Stein, it is not because it lacks credibility or truth.'

Isaac's eyes moved around the newsroom at the faces he'd known for years, so many honest hard working journalists, assailed and diluted, beaten down by the system that was controlled by men like Carl Stein.

'I say this to each of you here today. If you really want to do your job, you must leave this paper because all you will get here is cartoon journalism, you mark my words, Mr Stein here and his stooges will make sure of it. Today after talking to a life-long colleague and friend I finally understood that. I'm no longer prepared to subvert and bury the truth and what Irish here has uncovered about this man would make the hairs on your neck stand. It will make this entire country stand still. Carl Stein is a wolf in sheep's clothing but the truth will rise to the surface just like those twelve dead bodies that were pulled from the East River, Mr Stein.'

The colour drained from Carl Stein's face and for a moment Isaac had him on the back foot. Security men started to move around the room forming a loose net around Isaac and Lola.

'You had better be able to substantiate those claims, Mr Kane, because you're walking on thin ice,' laughed Carl insincerely.

'I've always wanted to set up my own paper,' said Isaac, 'and I think now is as good a time as any. If there are any real journalists out there who'd like a job, you're more than welcome to come with me now.'

Isaac jumped from the desk and helped Lola down. They lifted their bags and files, clearing every bit of research they had from the office.

'What about your records?' asked Lola, as they walked through the throng of bodies that stepped aside in silence to let them past.

'Earl will have them delivered and sent to the house for me,' said Isaac as he smiled his goodbyes as they edged out of the newsroom.

'Looks like it's just us,' grinned Isaac.

Erin stood waiting near the elevators with her bag and camera. 'What the hell,' she laughed, 'I'm with you, Mr Kane! I feel like I'm in Gerry Maguire or something.'

Lola felt like a revolutionary as she strode to the lift with Isaac and Erin. Just as the door was about to shut, a slim hand prevented it from closing. It was Jodi. She carried a plant and a small box, panting and out of breath she staggered into the elevator. 'I thought we were in this together?' she breathed.

Isaac didn't say anything; he just smiled at her and they took the lift to the ground floor in silence.

~40~

The phone slid from Lola's hand hitting the floor with a dull thud as the room began to hum and sway. Her mind toiled over the multitude of possibilities and scenarios that could have led to this catastrophe. Isaac's voice, muffled and distant, pulled her back to the present, where she was already lifting her coat and opening the door to leave.

'Irish,' he called to her, his voice thin and panicked. 'Lola,' this got her attention as she came around with a start. 'What in the hell is goin' on?' said Isaac, his face heavy with worry.

'That was Moriarty,' said Lola drawing away from him, her eyes watery and vacant. 'They've taken the book. The book's gone. Moriarty is in complete shock. I need to go to the lab and find out how the hell this happened.'

'I'll come with you. You're not going on your own,' said Isaac, pulling his coat from the stand and following Lola out through the door of his apartment.

The journey from Morningside Heights to Columbia only took minutes but it wasn't swift enough for Lola as she fought against the cold terror that rose in heavy waves, crashing on her chest. They were almost over the line and now the book was gone, snatched from their fingertips. She thought about the note she'd found; she had been so sure that they were one step ahead, that they still had a little time.

Lola felt the loss so desperately it was as if a hole had been ripped in her very soul allowing all the darkness and despair of this malevolent city to pour into its void. Her chest heaved again as she sucked for air but it refused to come.

Isaac placed a reassuring arm around her and took her hand in his. 'Close your eyes, Irish,' he hushed. 'Now take a deep breath in and let it out slowly.' Lola did as she was told. She could feel the air on her eyelids as it fluttered in through the cab window.

'That's it now. Keep doing that and everything will be okay,' said Isaac. 'It's maybe just some misunderstanding, let's just wait and see.'

But it wasn't some misunderstanding. Lola had felt this dread before when Arthur died, before Celeste almost died, before she herself almost died. Things were not going to be okay and her mind was in darkness. She could see no illuminated path out of the blackness that closed in on her from all angles. Focusing on Isaac's alto reassurances, her breathing gradually became more regulated and she was calm when the cab came to a standstill.

When they made their way around to the central quad, a crowd of people who had been evacuated from Butler and the surrounding buildings had gathered in little pockets as the fire alarm continued to issue its shrill warning.

Black and yellow tape had been fixed across the gaping mouth of the library with a 'Do not enter' sign alerting any approaching traffic of the danger, but Lola had tunnel vision and nothing was going to get in the way of her entering that building.

To the left of the main entrance, students and staff continued to trickle through an emergency exit, ushered out into the grey afternoon by two security guards. Capitalising on the short distraction, Lola ducked under the tape with Isaac in hot pursuit making a dash across the cavernous foyer, heading straight for the elevator.

Frantically she tapped on the silver button urging the lift to open, all the while casting fearful glances over her shoulder. Finally, the lift doors opened and she and Isaac plunged in then entered Rocha's pass code that would take them to the levels below. When the lift door groaned open, they ran to the conservation lab. Moriarty's ashen face met them at the security door beckoning them in absently. His once clear blue eyes now looked worn and dead.

As expected the entire lab was empty, save for Moriarty, and Lola supposed the alarm must have driven them out into the quad along with all the others. Three floors down, they could still hear the faint sound of the main alarm ringing. The room was strange now that it was devoid of the normal hustle and bustle and there was a sharp acrid smell that peppered the air. It smelled like rotten eggs and it unsettled Lola, but any discomfort she felt was overshadowed by her concern for Moriarty and the stolen Oracle. She was so absorbed in the current tragedy that her usually sharp mind wasn't fully engaged.

'I've failed you and I've fail her,' said Moriarty, his teeth biting down on his fist in frustration. Pivoting he lashed out and slammed his fist down on to one of the nearby workstations so hard that it caused its pages and tools to fly to the floor.

'Please,' urged Lola trying to calm him. 'It's not your fault, Manus, we weren't to know they would strike so soon. I maybe got the days wrong,' said Lola trying to shoulder some of the blame. 'Tell us what happened,' she said, all the while her eyes looked about the empty lab not sure what it was they were searching for.

'I'd been so busy making plans to the get the book to safety. Everything was in place for tonight,' explained Moriarty momentarily restored. 'As arranged, Lola, I'd planned to come back late once everyone had gone home so I headed back to the dorms early to get some rest. That's when I got the call from Susie asking me to come down. She said she needed to speak to me urgently that it was about the book and that she didn't want to talk over the phone. Naturally, I jumped straight out of bed and rushed down, but when I got here the place was in pandemonium. Alarms were going off and people were rushing out of the building as if there was a bomb or something.'

Moriarty's words lingered with Lola and she knew that whoever had set off the alarms was more than likely to have taken the book. Her skin began to prickle with unease as she considered the scene. Isaac walked around lifting bits of paper, examining the vacated desks, and she could tell that he shared her unease.

'How did you get in then?' asked Isaac.

'Same as you two I take it. I waited until the security guards were looking the other way and made a run for it. They never noticed because there were so many people exiting the building.'

'So,' said Lola. 'How did you know the book was missing?'

'Come and I'll show you,' said Moriarty leading them to the viewing room. 'When I finally got into the lab, Susie was nowhere to be seen but I just supposed that she had left with the others. I thought that this the perfect chance to get the book out and to safety. A few days ago I'd identified another emergency exit at the end of the hall there. It leads to the back of the library.'

Moriarty pointed to a grey door at the end of the corridor opposite before leading them into a small inlet off the main viewing room. The walk in safe was glass-fronted and although it was locked Lola and Isaac could see that it now lay empty.

'Did you pass anyone in the building inside or out?' quizzed Isaac.

'As I said, the place was manic, people were flooding out of the building but no one stood out. I'm sorry,' apologized Moriarty. 'I'll fix this, Lola. I promise I will. I was meant to be her Guardian and I've failed.' Moriarty's face grew flushed and tense causing the veins in his temples to protrude.

'Stein had been here all day and he built this lab, so he would know how to get out of it undetected,' spat Moriarty. 'Why didn't I listen to your warnings, Lola, and act sooner?' Moriarty rubbed his neck with frustration.

'It's done,' said Lola firmly. 'Now we just need to figure out who has taken it and where.'

Lola was growing more and more apprehensive. 'We need to get out of here,' she said, looking around her again. There was something that she was missing. The ring had started to pulse and there was so much about this scenario that put Lola on edge, the convenient alarms, the missing book, the phone call to Moriarty and that smell. What was that smell that singed and clung to her nostrils?

'We need to get out of here and now,' she warned. They all nodded their assent and they followed Moriarty's lead as he ran his pass across the panel.

Before the door swung open, time seemed to slow for Lola who could feel every particle of air as it was sucked from their lungs and the space around them, muting the sounds of the door opening and their footfall on the soft carpet tiles below their feet. It was as though they were all in suspended animation.

In just nanoseconds her aura rapidly expanded around her and Isaac who stood behind her half in and half out of its protection. But her words of warning struggled to escape from her throat, there was no air for them to travel through, as she tried to alert Moriarty to the rising danger.

She forced her bio-field out a little farther, but it was too late, the door swung open and the violent blast ripped through the rooms tearing through glass, wood and plaster and Moriarty, who now lay broken and contorted on the floor.

A ball of fire roared above them as Lola pulled herself up from the ground. Dazed and confused, she was blind and deaf to the carnage that had exploded around her. She sucked in the blackness as shards of glass and paper rained down on them like confetti. It was like she was submerged in water with the air around her thick and heavy resisting her every movement. Her eyes blurred and the sound was muffled and insulated. Lola could taste the rust and metallic elements of her blood as it gushed from some unknown source. The carnage of the scene gradually came into focus though a filter of dust and ancient scripts that had bonded like papier-mâché to her blood-soaked skin.

She leaned forward towards Moriarty but she could see by the vacant look in his eyes and the way his body lay twisted that he was gone. His flesh was torn creating a charred patchwork of bone and tissue. It made Lola wretch and she expelled the contents of her stomach among the other debris.

An alarm was ringing and the sound grew more and more vivid as Lola began to orientate herself. There was nothing she could do for Moriarty now. Tears scalded her eyes breaking through layers of smoke and dust. Another fireball shot up illuminating the room, which was now unrecognisable. Lola tried to call for Isaac, but not one syllable was borne from her dry and cracked throat. Then as another plume of light ignited Lola saw Isaac's foot poking out from behind the large table that was now lying on its side with pockmarks and lacerations slashed across its belly.

Still too shaken by the blast to stand she crawled along the floor in the glass and ash until she reached her mentor. Summonsing the strength she pushed the table away dreading what she might find behind it. Something bright and white protruded from Isaac's leg. Lola was leaning over to check that he was still alive when a faint groan issued from his throat.

His face had been badly cut by the small shards of glass and wood that had been propelled by the blast. Isaac writhed in pain, choking and spiting on the dense smoke and air that surrounded them.

'Isaac. Isaac,' cried Lola in a panic shaking him until he responded. Isaac grabbed her hand and squeezed it to let her know he'd heard. Pulling him up to a sitting position Lola used the bottom of her dress to clean the blood from his eyes and mouth.

'My leg,' hissed Isaac between breaths. 'I think it's broken.' She looked down at the dark wound and the white bone that had sliced through his shin. She could feel the vomit rise in the pit of her stomach again but she forced it back. The blood from the cut in her head leaked into her eyes now and she tried in vain to clean them as the ringing in her ears grew louder and louder making it almost impossible for her to hear what Isaac was saying.

At the bottom of the room a phosphorous green light declaring the exit blinked but it may as well have been miles away. If she could just get to that door, she thought. Lola left Isaac slumped up against the wall teetering on the edge of consciousness and reeling in pain as she searched about the room looking for something that might aid their escape. Everything was bathed in a blood-red light from the alarm but she could see nothing that would help. She was on her own and she would have to pull him to safety.

'Isaac,' she said over the hammering of the alarm. 'Isaac!' Lola tapped at his face frantically. 'I need you to stay with me, Isaac, please.' He squeezed her hand again in reply.

'Okay, we need to get you to that exit sign and I'm going to take you there but first I need you to work with me, okay Isaac?' He squeezed her hand again. 'I need you to help me get you out of here. If you can use your other leg and any strength you have in you.' Lola tried to remove what glass she could from her pathway but as she hitched her arms underneath Isaac's shoulders and dragged him every jerk and pull sent him to the brink of unconsciousness again.

They were still in such danger and the chemicals that she was breathing in were beginning to make her drowsy and sick but Lola used every ounce of the adrenaline that coursed through her veins to heave Isaac's limp body across the floor and out of the room.

Isaac let out a gasp as the milky bone tore through what little muscle and tissue there was left on his shin. Lola lent forward and readjusted her grip, pushing and urging him onwards towards the faltering green light and to the safety that was promised behind it. Another piece of the ceiling collapsed just missing them by inches, burying what was left of Moriarty's shattered body. The pain and guilt of leaving him behind assaulted Lola with such vigour that it was more painful than a million such explosions. There was nothing more she could do for Moriarty now but she could at least still save Isaac.

Lola reached the door and slid Isaac out into the relative safety of the hall where the same acrid smell of death and decay followed them along the dark tunnel. She was able to pick up a little more speed on the smooth laminate surface. Unhindered now and clutching on to Isaac with all her might she reached the external door, bursting through it with such force she fell down onto the dewy grass still clinging tightly to Isaac. Lola lay on her back and sucked in the sweet summer air. Far off in the distance she could hear the whirr of the emergency services as they raced to the front of the Butler Library.

Clamouring warily to her feet she dug deep into her handbag until her hands felt the familiar smoothness of her phone. Surprisingly, it remained unscathed from the ordeal and without hesitation Lola dialled Tommy Maloney's number. She'd no idea where exactly they were other than it was at the back of the Butler Library. Lola described what she could see. Her eyes were still swathed in blood and dust but Tommy, who knew every nook and crag of New York, assured her he would be there in minutes.

True to his word, Tommy Maloney and his black Lincoln Continental screeched around the corner five minutes later, coming to halt on the path beside them.

'Jeesus, Dorothy!' said Tommy, holding his head in his hands as he scrambled from behind the driver's seat. 'What in the holy hell went down here? The cops are all over the place, I heard on the radio there was a gas explosion at the Butler and you call me in a state. Look at you both...'

'Tommy,' interrupted Lola, opening the car door. 'I've no time to explain. Isaac's in trouble and a lot of pain,' Lola gestured towards his leg and as Tommy's eyes followed, he began to wretch throwing up at the side of his car.

'Tommy,' shouted Lola, 'get your shit together and help me get him into the car!'

Tommy wiped his mouth and did as Lola bid. They maneuvered Isaac into the back seat of the car where he lay prostrate writhing in agony.

'Here, give him this.' Tommy produced a bottle of bourbon from the glove compartment as Lola glared at him.

'What?' he said defensively. 'It was a present from a client. Give it to your friend, it'll help.' Lola twisted the lid off and leaned in to give it to Isaac, who supped it like a hungry baby. 'Where to?' asked Tommy starting up the engine.

'I haven't got that far yet,' said Lola trying to organise her thoughts. She knew that she should take him to the hospital but something inside her said that it wasn't safe. She didn't have the book; if she had she would have been able to heal Isaac, just like it had healed Lola. But the book was gone and so too was poor Moriarty.

The despair and panic seized hold of Lola's chest again and she tried desperately to fight it. She lifted her phone and rang Rocha this time.

'Rocha,' croaked Lola, feeling completely numb. 'Moriarty is gone, they've killed him. The book's gone, Rocha, they've taken the book,' said Lola her head falling into her hands.

'Oh no,' said Rocha her voice brittle and distant. When I had heard the news report that there had been fatalities in the explosion I feared the worst but I never once believed that you would be there...' Rocha trailed off again. 'Poor Manus.' Was all she could say. Lola could hear Ezra comforting her on the on the end of the line until she found her voice once again. ...

'How bad is Isaac?' she asked.

'Bad,' said Lola looking at her mentor, who had all but finished the bottle of bourbon.

'Firstly you need to get to the nearest hospital, Lola,' instructed Rocha. 'Go to Harlem General and we'll meet you both there.'

'Harlem General, Tommy,' directed Lola as she hung up the phone.

The fire engine and police sirens wailed past them as Tommy avoided the crowded areas, taking the back streets to the hospital. The bourbon had served to settle Isaac and make him more comfortable giving Lola some time to collect her thoughts.

'So what in the hell is going on here?' said Tommy glancing back at Isaac. 'Is that Mr Kane?' Lola nodded her head, she didn't have the strength nor the inclination to talk right now and her mind was elsewhere.

'Tommy, you don't drive for the Torch anymore.' Isaac's speech was slurred as he let the empty bottle role out of his arms onto the floor of the car with a faint whimper. 'I told Irish here you don't work for the Torch no more but she said I was wrong. I ain't wrong, am I, Tommy?'

'You're a bit delirious there, Mr Kane,' squeaked Tommy as a tense laugh escaped from his lips. Isaac's ramblings had struck a nerve and for a while Lola didn't say anything, she just watched him fluster and stutter over his rebuttal and then she knew.

'You work for them,' said Lola slowly, her eyes narrowing with suspicion. 'You fucking work for them,' she said with a half-smile. Lola could see what had just passed in Tommy Maloney's soul and now it made perfect sense.

'It was you, outside the seventh precinct that night. He said he was waiting on his driver. That was you. Alex knew where I lived and that's how they knew I'd arrived in the city amongst other things.'

'I don't know what you're talking about, Dorothy, that blast has obviously affected your head.'

By now they were outside the emergency room of Harlem General. Two porters stood at the door smoking and Lola called out to them for help. One brought a chair and between the three of them they managed to get Isaac into it.

'You tell your boss, that I'm coming for him.' Lola hissed the words at Tommy Maloney kicking the door of his Lincoln shut.

The anger roared like a furnace inside Lola as an image of Moriarty's lifeless body, that lay twisted and broken in the bowels of the library, flashed before her eyes. He'd been set up, Lola was sure of it and it had almost worked out perfectly but they hadn't banked on her and Isaac being there. The only thing that didn't fit was why all of a sudden Carl Stein wanted the book when it would have been easier for him to let it perish with Moriarty.

Carl, Alex, Susie and Prospero, they were all complicit in the death of Manus Moriarty, a gentle and innocent soul who paid the ultimate price for their greed and depravity.

She marked each name on the tip of her tongue and let it settle there. The fire raged but she held it there, deep in her centre. The time would soon come for her to unleash it but until then, thought Lola, she would let it build some momentum.

~41~

Lola yawned and stretched ensconced in that beautiful purgatory between sleep and lucidness, where she wasn't awake enough yet to remember that the day would bring things she'd rather forget. And then like the breaking of a damn it all came flooding back through that hallow inlet in her chest, the death of Moriarty, Isaac lying in hospital, the stolen Oracle, Tommy, the entire basement floor of the Butler Library in smithereens. No, Lola admonished, refusing to allow the despair to take hold, Moriarty and Arthur cannot and will not have died in vain, she told herself.

Whatever draught Rocha had administered when they'd returned from the hospital had knocked Lola out cold. A dream seemed fresh in her mind like something she should remember but couldn't quite gain any purchase on. She tried to grasp hold of it but all she could see was the professor's body and the carnage of the preservation lab.

Lola trawled through the fog of the previous night. At the hospital they had stitched her head and checked for a concussion. Given the all clear, she had to give a statement to the police before she was permitted to leave so by the time she'd arrived back at Rocha's Lola was physically and emotionally exhausted, her nerves were so shot she had a complete breakdown when they reached the sanctuary of Rocha's loft apartment.

As she encouraged her brain into action, fragments formed in Lola's mind like a puzzle. She recalled falling onto Rocha's couch, her body aching and too tired to move an inch further. An insatiable longing for home gnawed at her because she was totally alone in a foreign and alien city with few friends. New York was so far removed from the warmth and familiarity of Ballyvalley where the buildings never obscured the sky or hovered over you in a menacing crouch, where she could see the Mourne Mountains from her old bedroom window in Cottage Park, pink and lilac as they folded into one another on the distant eastern horizon. For the first time Lola understood why she felt that way and it was because her soul belonged in Ireland. Blood and bone, skin and sinew, she was forged from its sacred earth and sky. The realisation that her life, like Moriarty's, could have been snuffed out like a candle induced such terror in her that she wanted nothing more than to get on the next plane home. She'd worked herself into such a fit of anxiety, and that's when Rocha had stuffed the small glass of lilac liquid under her nose and instructed her to drink it.

The taste of Parma violets still lingered in Lola's mouth as she remembered the peculiar sensation as the cold liquid slid down her dry throat. It did its job, knocking her out cold in minutes.

Lola raised her head over the back of the couch as the stairs creaked behind her to see Rocha lazily making her way down to the living room. She was rubbing at the dull circles of sleeplessness that had gathered under her creased eyes trying to yawn the tiredness away.

'Morning,' croaked Lola clearing the sleep from her throat. 'Any news from the hospital?'

'Lemar's mum called,' said Rocha, finally reaching the bottom of the stairs. 'Isaac is out of the woods and he's sleeping like a baby.' Rocha smiled as if to confirm her optimism but her colours, which were usually so rich and vivid, had grown pale and insipid.

The dim remembrance of a dream plucked at Lola's mind again. She tried to focus on it as Rocha checked the wound under the thick gauze on her head, but like a wisp each time she focused it was gone. Satisfied that everything was in order Rocha went off to make some tea leaving Lola like a cat stretching the last of her limbs awake.

Lola tried to organise her thoughts as she sipped at the fennel brew but thinking was taking a lot of effort this morning as her head and the rest of body were wakening to the aches and pains she'd sustained from the fallout of the explosion.

The question to the fore of her mind was why? Why had they decided to move earlier than planned? Or had she gotten it all wrong?

'Do you think they knew we'd found the note?' wondered Lola aloud. 'This is a mess Rocha,' she said, labouring against the dull pain that drummed in her head.

'So after I intercepted that message in the Cathedral, the only two people who knew about it were you and Moriarty. That's why he arranged to move the book last night, twenty-four hours before the Hell Fire Club, according to the note, were due to make their move. I mentioned that I would be attending the library that night in passing to Isaac when we were working in his office. I didn't go into any detail,' said Lola in response to Rocha's reprimanding look. 'I just mentioned it in passing. So how the hell has Alex Stein walked out of the Butler Library with the world's oldest piece of antiquity, unhindered and undetected and managed to manufacture a gas leak?'

'You think Alex set up the explosion and took the book?' asked Rocha.

'Moriarty said that he had been there all day, Rocha,' said Lola pointedly. There was an air of uncertainty in Rocha's words that antagonised Lola.

'So I've no doubt Moriarty was set up but there are so many other loose ends that I can't tie up. I mean Moriarty received a call to come back by Susie, when he got there the place was in chaos. They would have known he'd have gone straight to the lab but when he got there she was nowhere to be seen.'

'Well that's not the full picture, Lola,' said Rocha leaning off the seat to place her tea on her favourite little Kettle stand. 'I fear the plot thickens.'

'What do you mean it's not the full picture?'

'I mean,' said Rocha, her hands gesticulating as if they we conjuring the words from her mouth. 'Two bodies were found in the wreckage and they have been identified as Manus Moriarty and Susie Deleaney.'

'What?' said Lola the shock and confusion making her head throb again. 'How?'

'Well, that we don't know,' explained Rocha. 'The official story says that she was working in one of the chemical labs and was overcome by the gas leak. They haven't reported anything about the book but I spoke to Vivian and she is beside herself because they believe the book to have perished in the blast but naturally both Columbia and Trinity are keeping it hush hush. There is a replica at Trinity and the official story will say that the book had been returned to the College before the accident. This would suit our purpose perfectly, but only if we had the book in our possession and we don't.'

'How did we not see Susie when we were in the lab?' quizzed Lola. 'I mean it's not like you'd miss a dead body lying around! He must have killed her,' added Lola quietly assaulted by that same grotesque disappointment at Alex Stein's vile nature. Why did it still hurt? 'We walked right into it, Rocha, the Hell Fire Club came so close to hitting the jackpot.'

'You were never a target,' said Rocha with a shrug as if it were the absolute truth. 'You are too precious. Besides,' said Rocha, her face creased with consternation, 'Carl covets your bloodline and prefers more pageantry when slaying his enemies. No, you being there was just chance.'

For the first time since they'd met Rocha Moone looked her age as Lola watched her wrangle over the best way to articulate what was playing on her mind.

'So,' said Rocha, having come to some resolution. 'I think you're right about the set up. It would make perfect sense for Carl Stein to blow up the lab, destroying the book and any evidence of foul play but the problem is the book was already gone before the explosion. It doesn't make sense.'

'I know,' said Lola mournfully. 'We're missing something. The exact same thought occurred to me about why Carl Stein would suddenly want the book.'

'Maybe he wanted to see if he could control it,' mused Rocha. 'Think about it, Lola, a chance to see the legendary Lost Oracle, I don't think that even Carl Stein would pass up on that opportunity, after all the Hell Fire Club have been pursuing it for hundreds of years.'

'Perhaps,' said Lola in a placatory tone. 'But that still doesn't explain Susie's call to Moriarty, her winding up dead and the explosion. I mean they could have just taken the book, it was gone by the time Moriarty had arrived so why manufacture an explosion unless you wanted to destroy the book? Even if they wanted Moriarty and Susie dead, surely there could have been other ways to do it?'

'Two professors turning up dead would have caused a great deal of suspicion, Lola, but both perishing in a freak accident, now that is believable and very neat.'

Rocha thought for a while nodding and shaking her head against her internal dialogue. 'You intercepted this message?' said Rocha lifting her teacup and taking a sip before setting it down again. 'Which I have no doubt was nothing short of divine guidance from the Bile Màthir, of that I'm certain. However,' she said, 'events after this have me at a loss and I'm left with more questions than answers. I mean who was Alex leaving the message for? Why there?'

'Prospero,' said Lola in a matter-of-fact tone. 'He was leaving the message for Prospero. They've been working together, as you're already aware. Tommy Maloney, who it turns out also works for Prospero, let it slip that he'd seen Hermes, Prospero's dog, outside the Cathedral on a number of occasions. That's who he left the note for.'

Rocha offered no reply in accord or dissent but the sudden blast of grey in her aura told Lola that she was harbouring some disquiet.

'The verse, that you said the slip of paper was hidden in...' Rocha went to one of her bookshelves and sat back down with a Bible in her hands flicking through to the back pages. 'Revelations, you said it was?' she asked, glancing up and fixing her glasses on to the bridge of her nose.

'Yes,' said Lola her mind running over the small note. 'At first I couldn't find where it had fallen from but then Alex had drawn brackets around one of the passages. It was Revelations 21.9.'

Rocha found the corresponding passage and read it aloud.

'Then came one of the seven angels who had the seven bowls full of the seven last plagues and spoke to me, saying, "Come, I will show you the Bride, the wife of the Lamb".' Rocha pondered this for a moment, Lola watched as her eyes darted over the words again.

'There are a few things that stand out for me. Firstly,' she said removing her glasses and looking up at Lola gravely, 'the numbers twenty-one, nine, this just so happens to be the date of the autumn equinox.

'I understand that this is a Christian text and may have no actual relationship with the Celtic Calendar but if we look at the text that Alex chose in a Christian context then perhaps things may make a little sense. The Bride,' explained Rocha, 'represents the new world, a heavenly utopia if you like, where we have been cleansed and purged of our wicked ways, which would have been represented by the Harlot in earlier passages. The Lamb, as I'm sure you know, like most former Catholics, represents Christ or more specifically the creator of the universe. United with the Bride, the all-encompassing new vision or new way. As they would say in Greek it is a more equal and complete partnership, the Hieros Gamos, that we talked about before' said Rocha, in full flow now.

The knowledge that poured from her was a thing of great reverence for

Lola, as she sat like a sponge soaking every drop of it up forgetting the tangled web that was being weaved around them for just a little while.

'The Cleamhnas Naofa' said Lola, 'The Sacred Marriage?'

'Exactly, Lola. So in this passage, I believe, what is described is this sacred union and while it's not yet clear to me how this applies to you and Alex, I have every belief that it does.'

'After we first talked about this,' explained Lola, 'I tried to remember that fateful night when Brigid stood alone in the darkness waiting for her pursuer to reveal himself. But it's never come to me. Do you think it could have been Alex?'

'It is certainly a possibility, Lola. She is growing stronger within you, and I've no doubt that when the time is right all these things and more will be revealed to you' said Rocha in admiration. She consulted the passage again.

'Another thing that interests me and that I think is the main clue here,' she said, 'is the number seven. In just this short passage we have seven angles, seven bowls and seven plagues. The number seven appears three times in the course of the small passage, as you know, Lola,' schooled Rocha, excited by her own revelations, 'three times seven is twenty-one, again the date of the equinox.'

Lola nodded studiously as if she knew that three sevens where twenty-one, she didn't. She had never been able to learn her times tables very well and what she had learned, she'd forgotten. But Rocha didn't seem to notice as she continued in earnest.

'So here we're brought back to the autumn equinox. Now it doesn't stop there,' she said beaming. 'In the Celtic Calendar, or wheel of the year, we have eight seasons, they are the winter solstice, imbolc, the spring equinox, bealtaine, the summer solstice, lughnasadh and the seventh season being the autumn equinox and then samhain.'

'So you think they could be planning something around the equinox?' said Lola. 'It makes sense,' she said, 'after all why would Alex have highlighted that passage if not for some specific reason and it sounds like he was tipping Prospero off about something that had been planned for the equinox.'

'You're a step ahead of me, Lola,' said Rocha snapping the book shut. 'I'm convinced of it, the Hieros Gamos ties in very well with the equinox as does the passage, strictly based on the numbers of course.'

'How do you mean?'

'I keep forgetting that you've not had much tutelage in these things,' said Rocha dolefully, 'so let me explain, child. As I mentioned before, the

Hieros Gamos is about balance and so too is the equinox. As I'm sure you know from elementary science an equinox occurs when the sun crosses the equator making the seasons click into place. From a spiritual perspective the autumn equinox in particular is a time of harvesting and transformation, it is a time when nature and the world collectively inhales. The autumn equinox represents that beautiful pause before the darkness takes over and ushers in the coming winter.' Lola's body shivered in reaction to her distaste for the word darkness.

'You must not assume that the darkness is a bad thing, Lola,' chastised Rocha. 'There are dark forces in this world some so devoid of light that they cannot be reached nor trusted but equally in a balanced and well world the darkness too serves its purpose. After all, as an old friend once said, how would we appreciate the beauty of the stars if it were not for the dark blanket of night?'

These words had a ring of familiarity about them and Lola tried to remember where she'd heard them before.

'The darkness is essential to us, Lola, and we Bandraoithe embrace it and accept the lessons mother darkness wants to teach us. We are at a point in our great cosmic journey where the world finds itself begging for wisdom. Take for example your own personal journey, Lola, it is almost a microcosm of humanity. Your progress has waxed and waned yet gradually as you ebb and flow, you – like the wider world – will harness enough power so that you can hold the light of love and truth. You may fluctuate but in doing so you get stronger and stronger. As Manus explained to us about his own research, when we had gathered in communion some weeks ago around the fire in Liberty Plaza, all spiritual ascent first requires descent into the depths, those who fight for the light, must first face their own inner darkness and overcome it. The equinox invites us to do this. We now find ourselves in an age where we have become brainwashed and coerced into relinquishing our powers of discernment and powers of emotion. We have blindly handed these to men like Carl Stein and his Hell Fire Club. Their darkness gained a lot of momentum when we gave our sovereignty away and they learned how to manipulate through their war on consciousness. And in this present time when the masculine energy tries to move towards its feminine counterpart, they wish to prevent this shift because it threatens their current paradigm. Balance is the aim, it is what the Order and the Dé Danann represent and protect, true balance and partnership. After all we did not evolve by dominating but by adapting and working together. Yet despite all the danger and menace around us, the Goddess is rising Lola. She rises in you and she rises in humanity through the collective world soul. At the moment you have to carry this burden because not everyone is ready to bear witness to this change, so for now the sacrifice must be yours, but not yours alone,' said Rocha, her eyes creasing in a reassuring smile.

As poignant as Rocha's words were and while Lola harvested the lessons within, she didn't welcome them. The burden of her life path was becoming more and more like a prison cell that created the illusion of freedom. Lola's mind twisted, searching for meaning in the lines of scripture, she ran over the dates in her head again and suddenly her brain made the jump to the young women whose deaths she'd been investigating.

'Carmen Barnes, Jo Morris, Susan Harris,' said Lola, searching for her bag. She emptied the contents finally locating her notes under a mountain of paper and files. A rush of pain stabbed at her head again as she fell down beside Rocha on the couch.

Lola sifted through the pages until she found the information she was looking for. Her mind leaped ahead, it seemed to be full of connections and possible links now.

'I don't know if this means anything and I can't believe that I didn't notice it before but the girls that were murdered on the autumn equinox they all have the same birthday, do you think there could be something in that?' she asked Rocha eagerly.

'What are their dates?' said Rocha.

'Carmen Barnes, born on the 21st of March, Jo Morris, born on the 21st of March and Susan Harris, born on the 21st of March,' read Lola, hoping it might mean something to Rocha.

'Holy Mary...' breathed Rocha. Lola's eyes beseeched her for an explanation.

'They were born on the vernal equinox and sacrificed on the autumn equinox,' said Rocha, shaking some thought from her head to her tongue.

'You see, Lola, the spring equinox symbolises the Goddess and her divine feminine energy. It symbolises rebirth and creativity. By killing these women the Hell Fire Club are subverting the natural energies of this time. They are performing a powerful and destructive brand of magick, it's blood magick Lola and it's not to be trifled with.

'Our blood is sacred. It is the soil of our bodies carrying life itself. Without our mothers' life- giving blood we could not have been nourished and born. The Hell Fire Club's magick is nothing but profanity; they use it to defile our sacred ways and the Goddess from whence we all come. By killing these young women, they are effectively killing the Goddess herself. Something is being planned for the equinox but where and what, I don't know,' said Rocha. In the course of their conversation Rocha's face had grown more pale and gaunt and Lola could see that she was shaken by these disclosures.

Something Rocha had said about the Bride seemed to linger with Lola. At first she told herself it was nothing, a stretch too far, but in the end she decided to say it out loud anyway.

'A thought occurred to me earlier,' said Lola tentatively. 'When you talked about the Bride alluding to the new world. I don't know why but I thought of the west and in the wheel of the year the autumn equinox would be positioned in the west. I know the Club has some sort of gathering out west each year,' continued Lola. 'It's somewhere in California, it's called the Grove. Aíbgréne told me about it once and even Ezra knows about it. Do you think that might be something we could look into?'

'Your instincts are rarely wrong, Lola,' said Rocha with a pensive nod. 'I know the place you're talking about. It's in Sonoma County, outside a quaint little town called Monte Rio.

'I've been there once. It was way back in the sixties after another spate of disappearances. For about four years a number of young women who'd worked the summer season in the town had been going missing. Some of the local residents were growing more and more concerned about this as it always seemed to coincide with the Grove's two-week summer camp in July. I was part of a small community of women of magick who investigated cases of the supernatural nature, we were all Goddess Feminists,' remembered Rocha with a wistful smile. 'We had been contacted by a friend of a friend who understood these things so we arrived in the little hamlet to investigate. As soon as we entered Monte Rio we could feel the rise of something sinister and foreboding and like you, we knew then these disappearances were linked. The word was that they were sacrificed at the Grove and their bodies dumped in the lake that surrounds the high altar. Our contact had gotten this information from a young woman who was lucky enough to escape. Lola,' said Rocha, 'I would never want to return. Anything that you have faced back in Ireland, here in New York, it is nothing compared to the evil present there. Everywhere we went the cold shadow of fear stalked us, it was all around us and when we eventually made the hike over the Russian River and through the forest members of the party were collapsing under the pressure, they couldn't breath and we eventually had to abandon our expedition.'

The radio had been playing in the kitchen but the sudden change in pitch brought it to Lola's attention when she heard the news begin. Lola rushed to the kitchen to turn up the radio, wincing as an electric charge of pain ran across the back of her head.

'Two people have died and two others are injured in what experts have said was a freak explosion in a Preservation Laboratory at Colombia College's Butler Library. Police uncovered two bodies in the wreckage, which are believed to be that of a visiting professor from Ireland, Manus Moriarty, and Lab Manager Professor Susie Delaney. Most of the staff had been evacuated from the building after a call to the central campus operator reporting a gas leak in the lower levels of the Library.

'The Butler's Curator, Professor Vivian du Vaul was too distressed to be interviewed but she did tell our NYC105 reporter that most of the texts being worked on had been moved out of the lab earlier that morning. When asked if this included one of the most celebrated medieval texts, the Book of Kells, she said that the ancient book had been returned to Trinity Collage Dublin over a week ago.'

'Freak accident my ass,' said Lola snapping the dial on the radio to off.

'I need to get in touch with Daithí,' said Lola. 'There's bound to be CCTV footage of the labs or the main entrance. He might be able to access them and shed some light on the comings and goings. For now, it's time I took a trip to Liberty Plaza to meet my old friend Prospero. I have a few questions for him.'

Rocha didn't offer any words of encouragement but Lola didn't require them. She could see a clear path ahead of her now.

The 21st September was seven days away. That gave her one week to prepare and plan. She would need someone with her, just in case she wasn't lucky enough to get away.

This was her fight and it was time to see just how powerful she really was. Lola decided to keep her plans to herself but firstly she would have to focus on the here and now. Isaac lay broken in a hospital bed, Moriarty was dead and she needed to track down Prospero.

The game was in full swing and for the first time Lola realised just how much power the pawn could have. Carl Stein may well be the king but the king was only as strong as the pieces at play around him. The pawn could move the whole board and was even offered the chance of elevation if successful.

~42~

Alex rapped the side door of the church with his knuckle but there was no reply, only the echo of the knock in the empty passageway within. He twisted the copper handle hopefully and was relieved when the door jerked open with a groan. After a quick dart to his left and then his right to ensure no one on the street was watching, Alex stood aside to let the old man and his dog enter. Following swiftly behind he bolted the weathered oak door shut.

Both men shuffled into the gloom of the narrow hallway and standing apart, as if shy in each other's company, they waited for Monsignor Monaghan to appear as arranged.

St Patrick's Cathedral had closed for the evening with the last mass finishing over an hour ago but the small passage was still thick with the smell of incense. Alex's cool eyes watched with concealed scorn as the old man inhaled the aroma, it smelled of pine needles and lemon blended with the shavings of wood.

'Ah, frankincense,' said Prospero his eyes closing in appreciation. 'It's been a while since I've had the pleasure of that in my nostrils. You know, young man,' he said brightly pretending to be oblivious to Alex's discomfort, 'it contains elements that stimulate the part of the brain that controls our emotions – interesting, don't you think? Probably explains why the Church uses it.' He laughed at his own joke but Alex's face remained unimpressed. Alex too shared the old man's appreciation of frankincense, but he was loath to give him any more encouragement, their unholy alliance was enough at present.

His eyes stooped to consider his dishevelled companion. The unkempt beard, the wiry hair and his wrinkled clothes may have given Prospero the appearance of some homeless bum but Alex knew that underneath all that chaos was a shrewd mind, sharp as a brier.

His eyes, Alex noticed, were keen and bright and they absorbed everything. Sometimes he felt that they could see beyond his skin and bones right through to his very soul; his gaze made Alex feel uncomfortable, it made him feel exposed.

'Well, we both know, old man, that frankincense was in use long before the great cathedral of the Catholic Church was a force for good in the world,' said Alex, in his usual aloof manner.

'Right you are, my lad,' said Prospero heartened by Alex's response. 'They even found some in the tomb of King Tutankhamen himself.'

Alex was relieved when he heard Monsignor Monaghan's urgent footsteps approaching and finally the priest emerged from the darkness with his cassock flapping out behind him. 'Gentlemen, come with me,' he said gravely beckoning them with two fingers. Prospero commanded Hermes to stay, patting him gently on the head and turning he followed behind Alex.

Alex was glad that it was almost over. The months he and Prospero had been planning and scheming on ways to get hold of the Lost Oracle, the clandestine meetings and notes and yet, despite all their planning, it was blind chance that ensured success in the end.

Whoever had sounded that fire alarm not only had presented him with the perfect opportunity to get the book but had inadvertently saved his life.

With his father out west preparing for their equinox celebrations, Alex had lingered about the lab all that day, fine-tuning what had taken almost a year to organise. Well, that was if you counted his initial petitions to Trinity to get the book to New York in the first place. Prospero had warned him that it would take time to convince Moriarty to come to the city. He never did manage to completely win the professor over. Men like Moriarty were not driven by money or self-interest so they couldn't be bought. Men like Moriarty they were only driven by passion and a thirst for knowledge but thankfully for Alex the university's provost was a much more practical man and money won the day.

As he followed briskly behind Monsignor Monaghan, his steady footsteps echoing off the concrete, Alex thought about just how close he had come to losing his life. For all his rationale, even he was overwhelmed by the serendipitous evacuation alarms that had forced everyone to down their tools and leave.

It was perfect and he had immediately recognised the opportunity not hesitating to take full advantage. Calmly, he retrieved the mobile container that his team had been working on for weeks. The technology employed insured the perfect conditions for the precious cargo that it would soon house. Then Alex swiped the stolen security pass he'd taken from Susie's lab coat the day before and lifted the book from its resting place. Once it was secured in the casing he'd boldly strode out the emergency exit to the back of the library as if it was nothing.

In his mind Alex relived Susie Delaney's confused calls as she saw him head for the exit and for a moment a pin-prick of guilt needled at him. Alex shook off the feeling. She wasn't his responsibility he told himself again. He'd no idea that Susie was still in the lab when the explosion ripped through it. At the time he'd assumed she'd joined the rest of her team out in the central quad but when the news had come through that she and Moriarty had perished in a freak accident part of him wished she had pursued him out the door, then she would have been safe too.

Alex pieced the scenario together as he kept up pace with the Monsignor. He supposed that after he'd left Susie had discovered the book missing and as a result contacted Moriarty, unwittingly leading him to his death. They were collateral damage, Alex reminded himself sternly and in truth, he thought, it had all worked out perfectly. He couldn't have planned it better, because now everyone with close ties to the book assumed it had been destroyed in the fire, in spite of the university's false public claims that the Book of Kells was safely back in Trinity.

Alex should have been elated, but when he was informed that Lola had been in the lab too, he was almost broken. Much to his consternation, his apathy didn't spread as far as her. In matters concerning Lola Paige he was heavily invested and that's what had gotten him into his current predicament.

Alex's neck and shoulders tensed and knotted and the thought of Lola lying dead in the carnage stifled and stiffened his lungs again. That was the only time he'd felt happy in the old man's company, when he'd told him that Lola was still alive. Alex didn't believe him until he'd shown him the text from his aunt Celeste. All it said was She's safe! Those two solitary words had relegated Alex to his knees on the balcony of Chateau dans le Ciel as he fought against his delight and his shame. Lola was alive and every part of his being bathed in the joy of it. How she'd ruined him! She was the sole architect of his downfall and he despised her for it.

Alex tried to rub away the growing tension in his shoulders. He glanced back at the old man who smiled at him and not for the first time he regretted their unnatural union. Ever since they'd met, Alex found himself in a constant state of flux, he always threated to turn back, but if he did turn back where could he go? Alex continued to focus on the little bald patch on the back of Monsignor Monaghan's head as he led them to the foot of a fine spiral staircase. Despite his delicate look, the Monsignor was lithe and steady on his feet.

'Saint Bridget is looking after her,' said the priest as they were halfway up the cramped staircase. Alex seemed unsure of what he meant until Prospero let out a chuckle.

'Perfect,' he bellowed. 'Out of interest, Monsignor, what tone does Saint Bridget play?' asked Prospero, happy for the pause in proceedings to catch his breath.

'Cee,' the priest smiled down at him. It was then that Alex realised they were climbing to the bell tower. All the bells were housed in the north spire of the Cathedral and each of the nineteen bells were named after saints. He'd only managed to get a look in the tower once during the restoration project and it was very impressive.

Their climb led them to a small square opening before the next flight of steps began where the grey walls housed numerous inscriptions. Axel loves Anna, read Alex among the myriad of names and dates that went as far back as the 1920s but the one that caused them all to pause was the most noticeable etching: 2001 Bad Year! Never forget Sep 11 it warned. Below the message, two towers were carved deep into the plaster. The Monsignor pointed towards a small square lead trimmed window that lay to their right, where the falling light of the city struggled to break through the years of grime that had veiled the glass.

'The initials you see on that small window pane,' said the Monsignor, tracing them with his hands, careful not to actually touch the glass, 'those initials were written in the dust and they each belong to a fireman that carried out a safety check on the towers and attic here at Saint Patrick's. Each of those men,' he said solemnly, 'lost their lives when the towers came down.' Alex and Prospero read the initials in silence as the Monsignor made the sign of the cross with his crucifix slicing through the air in front of the pane. 'We managed to preserve them during the restoration project which Mr Stein's firm undertook.'

The marble steps of the bell tower had not been restored and they still wore their glassy sheen making them slippery. Unsure of his footing, Alex had to mount the stairs sideways as his feet struggled to fit on the narrow steps as they twisted skyward.

To Alex's surprise, Prospero was keeping up the pace as they came to a small landing area where enormous arched shutters on three sides of the tower let in the noise and smells of the city below. Alex sucked in the cool air and looked down at the street, the spires were over three hundred feet high, he remembered, and his head began to swim. He hated heights. He couldn't look down or look back so the only place for him to look was straight ahead.

'Not long to go now,' smiled the priest, as he tread a steady beat up the stone mountain. 'The bells lie above the next flight of steps.'

On they climbed until finally they came to the bell loft where the long ropes attached to each bell lay dormant on the dusty floor. Counting the ropes aloud the priest stopped at number twelve. Disturbing the dust, he dexterously fished out a key that was hidden inside the tassels of the long silken rope.

Alex raised his eyebrow in admiration. 'You've taken all the necessary precautions, Father,' smiled Alex, feeling a little more relaxed now that he was no longer having to concentrate on climbing.

'Well if this document is as precious as you claim, it's important to keep it safe. I'm not ignorant to the news, Mr Stein,' said the priest admonishing Alex with a flick of his wrist, 'nor am I ignorant of Latin, even Medieval Latin. I did spend twenty years in the Vatican. I will not pretend that I'm not deeply troubled by recent events and you turning up on my doorstep in the manner in which you did, but I have known you since you were a boy, Alex, and I have seen the love you have for this cathedral.'

Alex suddenly felt uncomfortable again. Feeling guilt and humility was a new experience for him and having discovered these sensations, he now seemed incapable of experiencing any other emotion. He thought of Lola again and once more he resolved to hate her. If only Monsignor Monaghan could see what a wretched case he was, the things he had done.

'Don't get me wrong,' said the Monsignor laughing, 'when I say love, I mean the love you have for the building, not what it represents, Mr Stein. You have love for its beauty and architecture, its aesthetics and as a result of that love you have invested a great deal of your own money into its restoration.' Alex was growing impatient now acutely aware of Prospero, who seemed impressed by the priest's revelations. Alex tried to change the subject, but the Monsignor persisted in his eulogy.

'I know, I know,' he continued raising his hands in the air. 'I know how you feel about anyone knowing this and I will keep your confidence, my son, the Good Lord knows I will. I am glad to see this object leave this church tonight, but you, my son, have been a great friend to this Church and tonight I repay that friendship.'

'Thank you, Monsignor, we are truly grateful,' offered Prospero. The key slotted into a small cabinet that housed sheets of music. The Monsignor handed the sturdy case over to Prospero.

Laying it gently on the floor, Prospero opened the container to check that the book was there. Alex watched as the old man closed his eyes and laid his hand on the hide covering. He wondered what it was he could see and feel. Leaning over until he was almost prostrate Prospero whispered words in some strange and ancient tongue as if he was speaking directly to the book.

Alex watched the tenderness with which Prospero touched and spoke to it. His eyes were not covetous but filled with love and reverence. Prospero knelt like that for a few more moments before gently closing the case and securing it closed again. Shuffling off his knees in sections he finally stood erect again.

Alex lifted the case, it felt lighter than the last time he had carried it and he hoped it would root him to the stairs as they began their descent. He wasn't relieved until his feet reached level ground again. The Monsignor led them back through the narrow passageway to the small door they'd come through just minutes earlier.

The fresh air was a welcome reprieve from the stifling passageway and the lights of Fifth Avenue were beginning to ignite as evening settled on the city. Prospero produced a canvas knapsack that was as creased and worn as his face. He stretched and opened the mouth of the bag allowing Alex to place the precious case inside.

'What now?' asked Alex.

'Now our plan really begins,' said Prospero placing the knapsack across his fine shoulders. Alex shuddered at the implication of the word 'our' as the shame began to rise in him again.

'I believe I have an appointment out west,' smiled Prospero, 'as do you. We both have a job to do and whatever sense of loyalty you think you have, Mr Stein, you have made your choice and if I might say, the right one. I see the doubt that hangs about you like a cloud, Alex, but the object of your consternation is nothing but an anchor. You have made the decision to cut that line and you must see it through, so much depends on it. There can be no turning back, you must be resolute.' Alex thought about Lola again and this time his heart wouldn't let him hate her.

Lifting his staff, Prospero called Hermes to heel and with a nod the two departed, leaving Alex to his turmoil. He contemplated calling his driver but instead he decided to walk the short distance home. He couldn't be alone tonight so he scrolled through his endless lists of women but nothing seemed to hold his interest. It had been months since he had been with another woman, the thought of what he had become depressed him. Forcing thoughts of Lola to the back of his mind, Alex checked his phone again and picked a number at random. A bright voice willing and eager answered. He would send his driver. She was thrilled. Alex hung up the phone revived by the act and feeling more like himself again.

He wrote out a text message, deleting it immediately, and then he wrote out another.

You are my sweetest downfall, I loved you first. He hit send as he entered the Pierre Hotel.

~43~

The atmosphere was altered around Liberty Plaza and Lola knew Prospero was gone again. There was a cloud of solemnity that gathered around the camp blocking and muting the usual light energy that had once been so tangible. The area remained a hub of activity as the protesters continued to go about their daily rituals and while they may have been oblivious to this subtle alteration in current, Lola wasn't.

Prospero's motives confused her. On one hand, thought Lola, he possessed such a strong and positive presence, she had experienced it each time she was in his midst, yet he was working with the Hell Fire Club. It just didn't add up.

Something had told her he would be gone and she had an idea where but her mind would not settle until she'd checked.

Lola read the text message again that had been sent the previous night and although it was from an unknown number she knew it was from Alex. *You are my sweetest downfall. I loved you first.* She read and re-read it again, her heart floating and sinking all at the same time. What did it matter who loved who first when nothing could be altered by that love? Alex remained chained to his darkness, a prison of his own construction, he had made his choice all those months ago in the temple when he left her for dead. He'd made his decision in the full knowledge that his father had murdered his mother like some ghoul and he'd made his decision despite professing his love for her. As if he could possibly be capable of love. How dare he, she thought, after everything that he had done. Killing Moriarty, killing Arthur, killing Victoria Jones. For the first time Lola was filled with revulsion for Alex Stein and she welcomed it. Too long had her love for him blinded and bound her and caused her to separate his deeds from his person as if they could be two separate entities. He and his father had tried to take everything she loved from her including her own life. The fire roared in her again but Lola bid it to simmer.

She hit the delete button, the only act of defiance and banishment immediately available to her and the text vanished. She was finally done with Alex Stein. Aíbgréne didn't realise it, but she had nothing to worry about now. He was the last chink in her armour but that narrow opening that she held for him had finally been welded shut.

Rainwater gathered in deep pools along the top of Prospero's hut making the roof sag under the weight. Lola poked her head inside but it was empty, just a shell. Without him, and his meagre worldly possessions, the little home had become nothing more than a barren box, reclaimed by time and the elements in its abandonment.

Lola realised when she stepped inside where the smell of old books and tobacco still lingered, that she'd been half hoping that it had all been a misunderstanding, that her initial instincts had not failed her. She realised that's really why she had come to Liberty Plaza today, not to confront Prospero but to vindicate him.

The remnants of some letters written in white chalk lay scrawled along the back of the cardboard wall. Lola leaned in more closely to read the words: No Harm. I have done nothing but in care of thee... Only the first two lines of print were legible, the rest of the letters having been claimed by the damp and wet of the encroaching autumn.

She had no idea what it meant. The word thee made her think it might be Shakespeare. Lola took a picture and was about to search her phone for the quote when a voice from behind gave her a start.

'He's gone, honey.' Lola swung around relieved to find the lady who'd helped to stem her aggressive nosebleed all those weeks ago, standing in the disintegrating doorway. Lola nodded and stepped out of the dark hut. Looking skyward, as if to confirm her statement, Lola's eyes felt for the edge of something that wasn't visible.

'He's gone,' said the woman again. Lola gave up her search and met the lady's gaze. 'When?' she asked, following her towards the camp kitchen.

'A couple of days ago,' she said re-adjusting one of Lemar's rainwater harvesters as they passed by. Lola looked at the black water and imagined Lemar washing himself making herself blush at the thought of it.

'When will he be back do you think?' said Lola, knowing the answer.

'I'm not sure he will be back, honey,' sighed the woman. 'We'll sure as hell miss him here at camp, I can tell you that. The place has been strange since he left...' The lady broke off trying to articulate what Lola could already feel. She shrugged her shoulders. 'It's heavier,' she finally said.

Lola looked again for the veil but again her eyes came away unsatisfied. It was gone and Prospero had taken it with him. She could feel the thickness that the woman referred to. Once shielded by the veil from the hostile city, its darkness now leaked in around them on all sides. She likened it to deep sadness. Lola wondered if she was projecting her own emotions onto the scene. She couldn't be sure.

'That's a pity,' said Lola, 'I never got to say goodbye.' Lola actually meant it this time.

'You or anyone else honey,' smiled the women warmly. 'When the old man arrived here out of the blue last summer, we'd been so worn down by the police and the Stein Corp bully boys that we were all about to pack up and go back to where we came from but Prospero's arrival seemed to reignite us all. He gave us hope. Suddenly we became organised and he rekindled something in us and taught us that what we were doing was making a difference.'

'Prospero,' asked Lola. 'Is that his real name?'

'He never told us his real name but we gave him the nickname Prospero because he brought so much calm to the tempest that was raging around us at that time and he kinda grew into the name, don't you think?'

'Yeah,' said Lola. 'Have you any idea where he's gone to?' she asked hoping to confirm her hunch.

'Actually, that I do. He said he was going out west, that one winter here was enough for any old man. That's all I know. I'm afraid.'

What had she really expected to find? He was gone and all his things, the book was gone and she knew that he had been working with Alex. The lady had confirmed her suspicions about him heading out west and she was certain now that the highlighted Revelations passage was a cryptic nod to the Hell Fire Club's equinox celebrations, but one thing gnawed at Lola.

Why? Why all the subterfuge and masked meetings? Lola's mind wanted a break from all her wild wonderings, it was exhausting.

A panicked voice called to the woman from behind one of the makeshift shower cubicles. Her name was Edel, Lola remembered that now.

'That damn shower again,' scowled Edel.

'Before you go,' said Lola. 'Can you remember when Prospero first turned up at the camp here?' A flicker of suspicion sparked across Edel's face but she answered the Lola's question.

'I'm not likely to forget it, honey. It was the summer solstice just over a year ago. I remember because we had a lovely ritual and meditation and I firmly believe that our camp was saved that day. He has been a God-send to us.'

The voice had grown more urgent calling her again. Edel shook Lola's hand goodbye before rushing off in the direction from which she'd been summonsed.

As Lola left Liberty Plaza for Princes Street, her mind set aside Prospero and began to focus on her impending trip. She'd a plan that, if successful, would put everything right and she was determined to see it through.

Lola had spent a great deal of time organising and preparing but even she realised that this was not an endeavour that could be taken alone. If she was to recover the Cube and the Oracle from Bohemian Grove she would need help. That's why she'd approached Lemar. He was discreet, he had military training and he owed her.

She felt a touch guilty when he said yes without even the slightest hesitation. Lola thought she had been so clever and had the best plan laid out for their mission but Lemar picked a million holes in it. He'd decided then that it was best to leave the organisation to him and Lola was relieved to have one less thing to worry about.

They had six days, he told her, to drive the three thousand, one hundred and forty-two miles across the vastness of America. They would pass through nine states and according to Lemar's military precision, they would have to drive seven point six hours each day, covering at least five hundred and twenty-three miles per day. That's why they had decided it best to leave the following morning.

She had completed her first draft of the exposé on Aztec Solutions and 9/11 and the so called suicide cases and tonight their very first Veritas meeting would take place at Rocha's. She would hand everything over to her mentor. Once this story went live things would change forever, even if she was not there to see it. It filled Lola with such pride to have played a part in that.

Rocha had suggested a short memorial for Manus, whose remains had been repatriated back to Ireland. It would be the last time that she would be with Rocha and Isaac and all her new friends in New York. They didn't know it but Lola did.

When she finally reached the apartment Rocha remained oblivious to her arrival because she was arguing with someone on the phone in one of the south facing recesses of the loft.

'I understand why you did what you did, Celeste, but he's gone too far. Yes,' said Rocha growing more frustrated, 'her powers may have grown but this was reckless. I don't care what you say, he's been working in the grey and it could have destroyed everything we've worked for.' Lola stood awkwardly conscious that she was eavesdropping. 'It doesn't matter how I figured it out. The thing is that if I can so can she.'

There was pause in Rocha's tirade as she was pacified by the voice on the other end of the line. 'Okay,' said Rocha peaceably, 'we'll speak in a few days.' With that she hung up the phone and stood staring out of the arched window, still oblivious to Lola's presence. Lola was presented with two choices, she could either confront Rocha about what she had overheard or she could keep it to herself and see how things played out. Tomorrow she would be off so what good was confrontation? She was on her own and now she supposed she may always have been. Lola opened the apartment door and let it close with a bang jolting Rocha out of her revere.

'Lola,' said Rocha, 'you made me jump. I was miles away.'

Rocha's colours gave nothing away but her smile was uneasy and her body, usually fluid and free, stood rigid and closed. Lola eyed her cautiously and wondered if she should ask her what it was she was hiding but Rocha moved to the kitchen and the moment was gone.

There was little conversation between both women for the best part of the evening as they readied the apartment for their guests who would be arriving any minute.

Ezra Cohen was the first to arrive. Dressed in a fine navy suit, he had placed at little snow- white daisy in his breast pocket. He greeted Lola with a hug and kiss before eloquently complimenting Rocha on her appearance. Rocha giggled, running her fingers through her silver hair, she waved off his compliments like a blushing schoolgirl.

Gradually the house began to fill as Jodi, Erin and Isaac arrived with Lemar and his mother running late.

'Sorry we're late,' apologised Ms Jenkins. 'The hospital was crazy today and I didn't get off my shift until late,' she smiled handing Rocha some flowers and another bottle of wine. Lola offered introductions to those that were new to each other and the conversation flowed seamlessly.

Isaac, his leg in plaster and his crutches resting on his chair, was in deep conversation with Jodi in the corner of the room. The intimacy of the scene stirred something unwarranted in Lola. Erin, her usual congenial self, was chatting with Ms Jenkins and Lola couldn't help but think her friend had an ulterior motive because Erin's eyes constantly flitted towards her son.

'We all set for tomorrow?' said Lemar discreetly as he followed Lola into the kitchen. Lola nodded her head in assent. 'I'll meet you at the corner at five am, we need to get out of the city before rush hour.'

Lola nodded, lifted a tray with nibbles and went back to the living room where she offered them to the guests.

Rising off her chair, Rocha called them all to attention and a quiet hush descended on the room. Lola's thoughts were with Moriarty and Susie Delaney. Here they all were, breathing and alive and getting on with their day. The sun still rose and set and the earth still turned for them, but not Arthur or those dead women, not for Moriarty and Susie Delaney.

Moriarty never ventured far from Lola's thoughts and she agonised over how she'd failed to save him. If only she'd been more tuned in and not so consumed by the Equinox Oracle, she would surely have seen the signs. Yet, here she was alive and no one would ever know the truth. Most of the waking world would know nothing of the battle being waged against them or the few who fought to protect them.

Everyday Lola thought of Arthur and the legacy he'd left her. She wondered if she should be angry with him but she could never bring herself to question her old friend. She could never allow herself to feel any animosity towards him. Disloyalty of that kind would only break her heart all over again.

Rocha smoothed down her skirt and fixed the mauve silk scarf that hung over her regal shoulders.

'I know you're gathered here tonight to celebrate the birth of Veritas,' she raised a glass towards Isaac and Jodi in the corner of the room.

'However, you will not need to be reminded that not everyone that should be here today is here. Of course I am referring to my friend in learning,' Rocha's voice began to crack and she took a quick sip of her chardonnay before she continued.

'Professor Moriarty died protecting something he'd dedicated his entire life to understanding. His death cannot and will not be in vain. At the moment the scales are teetering on the precipice, what way they will tilt, we can only guess. The forces that we work against are strong. I have been in this city for almost forty years and I have felt the monster rise and grow until it has almost blocked out the light. We are walking a tightrope and our balance is wavering.

'As we approach the equinox, we wait to see what and who will prevail. But our strength is in our numbers and even though we may feel we must walk this path alone,' Rocha looked at Lola now as though she was the only person in the room, 'there is much still to be revealed. Veritas will certainly be a step towards that,' said Rocha, her eyes glistened ruefully as they moved around the room. 'So let us work together for a better future for all. Each of us by rising from our sleep can make a difference, but now we raise our glasses to Moriarty, a true guardian of knowledge and to our friends in and outside of this room.'

Each lifted their glass and called to Moriarty and to friends. After a while Lola gravitated towards Isaac, Jodi and Erin to discuss business. In the days after the explosion she'd began to flesh out her research but with Isaac being in recovery, this was the first time that she would get the opportunity to debrief him. While the Eli Shultz lead had gone dead, Daithí had come up trumps! He had unearthed material and information that would no doubt help their cause. But first she listened as Isaac filled them in on how he and Jodi had been working as part of an underground group of activists and journalists who through social media were working to set an alternative news agenda.

Since coming back from Iraq Isaac had been resolved that it was time to take action and breakaway from the mainstream media, which he felt was becoming increasingly stifled and controlled. So along with Jodi and a man he named as Angelo Bailey they began to secure investment in an online news outlet. After months of planning Veritas was about to be launched.

It made sense to Lola now, his long absences from the newsroom and

Jodi's frequent visits to his office. This is what they had been working on.

'Jodi is a partner and senior editor, along with myself,' said Isaac. 'Angelo is more of a tech guy so at the minute content will really be down to Jodi and I. Erin, if you have no plans to go back to Boston anytime soon, I'd love if you would stay on with us. It would be a huge workload to begin with, just until we get our feet on the ground but it would be a great grounding for you and you'd have so much freedom to cover the real stories,' he offered. Erin didn't need time to consider an offer like that so she almost burst with excitement.

'So where are we at, Lola?' asked Jodi. 'What have you got for us?'

'Well I was really hoping to get in touch with this Eli Shultz, who was a very close friend of Susan Harris's but that has come up short. I was hoping that he could have given us some insight into what Susan had discovered about her mother's death but Daithí, a good friend of mine who is good with computers, was able to help. He hasn't managed to trace the source of Ezra's documents, yet,' added Lola. 'But, he found this.'

Lola lifted the report from her bag and gave it to Isaac. 'I think this is what Susan Harris may have found. It turns out the FBI had conducted an investigation into insider trading on the week before and the morning of 9/11. This is a matter of public record, you can look it up,' she said as Isaac's eyes narrowed in disbelief. 'This is a really interesting development,' said Lola earnestly. 'Daithí said that this report was buried so deep, it would never have seen the light of day.'

'So how the hell did he get it?' said Isaac warily.

'Like I said, Isaac, he's very good with computers.'

'You mean he's a hacker, Lola?'

'I mean he's a truth seeker,' said Lola. 'Like all of us.'

'So what did he find?' asked Jodi, shooting Isaac a scolding look.

'So as we know Melissa Harris was head of some IT programme for a brokerage in the North Tower,' continued Lola, pausing to call Ezra and the rest of the group over, so they all could hear what she was about to say. It didn't feel right that she should exclude them because what they were investigating had touched all their lives in some form or another.

'Ezra,' said Lola squeezing his hand. 'I hope you don't mind but we have made a few discoveries with regard to your daughter's death and I think you should hear it.'

Ezra nodded at Lola for her to continue and so she did, laying out what she'd found to date.

411

'Well when I first met you, Ezra, you told me that Melissa had been working day and night on a huge project at the time in her brokerage which was housed in the north tower,' said Lola. Ezra nodded his head to confirm this. 'You also said,' continued Lola gently, 'that you were worried about Melissa at the time.'

'Yes,' agreed Ezra. 'Like I told you, Lola, she had been working so hard, she wasn't sleeping, she wasn't eating. What they were working on was installing the very first wireless software which would allow banks and business to move money with the click of a button. I was growing more and more concerned for her health. I finally confronted her about it. That's when she told me that one of her team had come to her with some concerns about the costings of this software. Apparently this employee had gone to one of Melissa's colleagues but he was told to keep his nose out. That wouldn't sit with my Melissa,' smiled Ezra, 'so she began to look into things and that's when she went to her boss.'

'A meeting was arranged by Melissa's boss which was to take place three days later on the 11th September in their conference room,' explained Lola. 'But Susan, your granddaughter and Melissa's daughter, when researching her mother's death found a memo that had been sent out to all employees of the firm not to come to work on the morning of September 11th because of some system upgrade. But because of the scheduled meeting,' Lola looked at Ezra for confirmation, 'Melissa along with some others had to go into work that morning for the panel which was investigating claims of misconduct. We also know that the man who had called that meeting, Melissa's boss, didn't come into the office that morning but strangely conducted the meeting via conference call from his upper-east side apartment.' Ezra nodded in agreement. Lola could see that Isaac was growing more and more restless so she paused so he could unload whatever was on his mind.

'What,' said Lola with more irritation than she'd intended.

'Now settle down, Lola, all I want to say is that at this point what you are saying is conjecture, we don't know any of this for sure.'

'Ezra was told first-hand by his daughter that they were looking into misconduct,' said Lola defensively, 'and her old boss is still very much alive, so I think this confirms the fact that he was not in the North Tower that morning.'

'Yeah but we can't be sure what it exactly was that they were investigating,' said Isaac.

'Listen, Isaac,' said Lola. 'We have it on first-hand information. Melissa told her father and her father is telling us. Perhaps, if you don't mind, maybe you'll let me finish.' Lola glared at him.

'Anyway,' she said to the rest of the group, 'while Isaac has a point about what we can prove, Daithí also unearthed this document.' Lola held the printed report up like a piece of evidence as she continued to lay out her case. 'It turns out that the FBI recovered some of the data centre of the North Tower which was housed on the 98th floor and which was hit directly by the plane, the same data centre that housed this new software that Melissa was overseeing. This, amazingly, was salvaged from the wreckage of the World Trade Center and given to a German tech company that was able to recover information from it. Now this is where things get really freaky,' said Lola. 'According to this report,' she held it aloft again as though it was a prize trophy, 'evidence of huge surges in trades between this brokerage in the North Tower and a bank in the South Tower were shown to have taken place and according to this no other business in the entire planet was using this innovative software. Now if you know anything about banking you should know that insurance and investment banks are housed in different buildings for a reason.'

'Holy shit,' said Isaac covering his face. 'You think this was insider trading?

'Damn right I do,' said Lola. 'And here's the thing, there were huge movements in stocks and shares in the weeks and the morning leading up to the attacks, which was unusual enough to raise an eyebrow. But what caused major suspicion,' she explained leaning forward on her seat, 'was the amount of puts being placed on certain airlines and other stock.'

'Puts,' said Erin. 'You've lost me there, Lola.'

'From the little I know – it's a very complex area – puts are when you bet against shares,' explained Lola. 'So say I knew that someone was going to hijack a certain airline plane and because of this attack I knew that the stock of that particular company would be affected in a negative way, I would bet against those shares. I might get a crazy price and when it actually happened I would make a hell of a lot of money. But because of the amount of puts placed on the weeks and days before the attacks between these banks and companies it would be fair to suggest that someone had prior knowledge of an attack. So Daithí and I did a little further digging and it turns out that when Port Authority sold the world trade complex in 1998, guess who bought it?'

'Stein Corp,' said Isaac, shaking his head in disbelief.

'Top of the class, Mr Kane,' said Lola. 'Now here's the cherry on the top. When Stein Corp bought it over three years before the attacks, there was a multitude of intricate insurance packages put together. Some were so intricate that they had to break them into over twenty-five policies. Now not only did Stein Corp insure the buildings for ridiculous money, twice what Port Authority had insured it for, built into their packages they had insurance in the case of a terrorist attack, which,' admitted Lola before Isaac raised the point, 'considering the attacks in 1993 may be fair game, but they also secured the contract to rebuild the World Trade Center should it collapse. If it was just based on this evidence alone, there is certainly enough to build a healthy case for prior knowledge of an attack, but we have an even more complete picture because of Ezra's random number generators, they were confirming that something big was coming. What we have here is a very strong case that certain people not only knew about the attacks but capitalised on them, in more ways than one.'

'How have we not heard about this?' said Erin her forehead creasing in anger. 'I mean this is ridiculous.'

'You're right, Erin,' said Jodi. 'We have all been sleeping but any journalist or writer that has gone anywhere near challenging the official story of that day, is mocked and cheapened and run outta town and we valued our careers too much to challenge the status quo. What Lola has uncovered here is enough to ensure that we have a proper discourse on 9/11 in this country and Veritas will make sure of it!'

'I've emailed you both my notes and what I've written up so far,' said Lola. 'This is the rest of my research,' she handed Jodi her file. 'This is too big for me, guys.'

Everyone sat stunned by Lola's revelations, even her greatest critic, Isaac, was speechless, there seemed to be no end to this story as one thing bled into another.

'This event, which has transformed the shape of not just your country but the entire world, must be re-examined and at the heart of it all is the Hell Fire Club. They are the ones who have gained everything,' said Lola falling back into her seat.

She wished she could be part of their team but her fight was leading her down another path besides her place was in Ireland, that's if she survived her trip out west. This was a matter for the American people.

'Irish,' Isaac beckoned her to him with a nod of his head. 'I don't know what to say to you. What you've uncovered...' Isaac trailed off.

'I know it's a huge burden, Isaac,' said Lola. 'Believe me, I know the weight of what you carry but people deserve to at least hear the facts. It's important that the families of those murdered that morning and the countless millions slaughtered in the Middle East because of it, know the truth. This story must be told for them. Jodi is right, if not Veritas, who? No one is going to dismiss a four time Pulitzer winner, not without a fight.' Lola leaned over and hugged him. 'You'll be grand,' she smiled planning a kiss on his cheek.

'You'll be grand?' he warned with his eyes. 'You needn't think you're dropping this atomic pile of shit on my knees an' leaving, Irish.'

'I know,' lied Lola without so much as a flinch. 'Sure there's no way you'd be getting rid of me that easy now! Besides, it's my story,' she flashed Isaac and impish grin.

'It sure is, Irish, I'll never take that away from you,' Isaac shook his head, his eyes filled with admiration for his young charge.

'Jodi,' said Lola, 'I've also sent you all the material and what I've drafted on the murders. Isaac said before that you thought it would be best to run them as separate stories. There is enough to at least perhaps call for a closer inspection of the suicide line. I've included the reports from the graphologist as well.'

'We need to tread carefully with all of this,' warned Jodi. 'After our little newsroom drama, it looks like we have an axe to grind with Mr Stein and we don't want to make it easy for him to use this against us. I think the best way to approach it is to look at the investigations and the obvious gaps and links that were not picked up. I mean we can say that the girls were known to each other and that Stein Corp owned all the agencies they worked for. Then there's the information from Mendez. We can state the facts and let our readers fill the gaps,' added Jodi. 'Even if we could put these deaths in the spotlight and put enough pressure on the NYPD to look into the cases based on our research it would be a start.' They all nodded in agreement.

'Lola, I can't thank you enough for what you have done for those young women and for my Lucy.' Lola breathed in the sweet musk of Jodi's perfume as she pulled her into a warm embrace. It brought Lola back to her very first day at the Torch standing next to the goddess Jodi in the elevator. How far she had come. But her life was like that now, every day brought a cataclysm of some sort.

It was growing late and while Lola didn't want the evening to end, she was eager to get the final preparations for her journey in hand.

They had all decided to meet the next morning in Harlem, where Veritas's new headquarters would be. All the press would be there for the launch. Lola pretended to write down the address, as Isaac called it out again while Lemar and Miss Jenkins helped him out into the hall. Lola pulled him close to her, she held the embrace for a touch too long but she didn't care. This might be the last time she'd get to hug Isaac Kane.

'All right, Irish,' he joked pulling away. 'You're gonna break my ribs again.'

'Stay safe, Mr Kane,' said Lola, 'and thank you for everything.'

'I'll see you tomorrow, Irish. Nine sharp.' He grinned as he disappeared into the elevator.

Rocha watched Lola tentatively as she fussed around tidying the last of the glasses and cups placing them in the dishwasher.

'Everything okay, honey?' Rocha smiled.

'Yes. It was a lovely evening, Rocha.'

'You seem to be taking all this in your stride. You've been though a lot, Lola.' Rocha laid her hand on Lola's chin pulling her head up so that both women were looking at each other. Rocha looked into her eyes and for a second Lola feared that she would cave under the gentle stare but she didn't, she held herself together and lied.

'It is. I'm looking forward to getting home, Rocha. I need time to process all this and I need Ballyvalley and the Manor and my family. Every day I wish Arthur was still here,' said Lola softly. 'Some days I feel him so close to me and other days it's like he was never here at all. Those days when I struggle to remember his voice or his face or his laugh or his kindness, I feel guilty and when I force myself to remember the scar is torn apart again and I feel that deep sense of loss all over again. Sometimes, I'm angry at him for not preparing me for this but mostly I miss him.'

'You feeling abandoned is only natural, Lola. I can't begin to imagine how you have dealt with all that life has shown you in the past twelve months. Such a short time but the greatest upheavals in our life are quite often our greatest lessons. Arthur or no Arthur, you are the only person who can walk your path, no one can teach you what it is that you alone must learn.'

416

'You're right,' said Lola. 'I know you are. The truth is I haven't had time to process any of this yet, Rocha. I haven't had the time to really assess how my life has changed in the most profound ways imaginable, I've been too busy stumbling from one crisis point to another and it's exhausting. I'm tired now.'

Rocha let Lola's words settle between them. Her eyes searched Lola's face as if she was trying to read all the things that Lola wasn't saying.

'I'll finish up here,' said Rocha. 'Go and get some sleep. Tomorrow a new day will be born and the possibilities once again will be limitless. Lola returned Rocha's embrace and headed for bed.

'Lola,' called Rocha. Lola stopped on the stairs and turned around to see the indecision playing out on Rocha's face.

'Arthur...' Rocha hesitated again, reformulating what she wanted to say. 'Arthur, he loves you more than you know,' she said.

'Loved, you mean' said Lola. 'He loved me, not loves. He's dead, remember?' Lola turned and left Rocha standing at the foot of the stairs.

~44~

For five days solid they drove the vast expanse of America. They passed through nine states from the lush green fields and roads of Pennsylvania to the flatlands of Iowa and Nebraska. Each was a blur on the endless I-80 highway that cut across the country carrying them to California.

Lola and Lemar had made the humble campervan their home, sleeping and cooking in it as they travelled. They shared the driving each taking their slot dutifully but nothing prepared Lola for the vastness of the journey. When they had left New York, almost five days ago, the map seemed to tell a different story, the distances seemed manageable. On average they were covering 489 miles per day. Ireland was only 302 miles long and 174 miles wide so this was like nothing she'd ever experienced before.

Lola counted the tenth state as they crossed the state line from Nevada in to California. The terrain began to change as more vegetation and green could been seen until they continued toward Santa Rosa.

They had seen the sunrise in every state and stopped to sleep and eat when the sun began to set. Lola wondered where the cohesion came from in a country so large, when every state was like a different country. The people, the terrain, the laws. It was amazing how all this was going on every day, while she was tucked away in the book room of the manor or going about her business. The energy of the land hummed and shimmered, Lola could see it and the closer they got to the west of the country, the stronger it grew. Lola first registered it as they came close to Wyoming and then Nevada. It seemed strange to think of it but it was as if the ground was a little more ancient there and a little more alive. There was something special about the west, a calmness that Lola couldn't quite understand. She could feel it, but what it was, she was unsure.

As they drove the scene was in constant flux. The pallet slipped from greens to the blue grey of the mountains to the honey and yellow of the desert with the shimmering veil of heat that lay above every horizon. Each sunset was as beautiful as the next and the moon expanded with each mile they covered.

At first both Lola and Lemar had felt the need to fill the silences with conversation but after a few days they settled peacefully into one another's company and became friends through the comfortable silences. They had both decided that after five days of travelling they needed to stop for a night and treat themselves to a hotel, a bath and well-cooked meal and breakfast.

The evening sun was setting casting a soft shadow along the highway as towns passed them by. Lemar's plans insured that they became phantoms. They were completely cut off from the outside world. Lola wondered how Veritas had fared. They hadn't heard a news report or watched a television since leaving New York and because Lemar had strictly barred phones they had no access to the Internet. In a way Lola quite enjoyed the simplicity of it but from time to time her curiosity had gotten the better of her.

'Look out for a motel sign,' said Lemar turning up the radio. 'That's my jam,' he laughed signing along to the song. Lola looked out the window. A sign for a Motel 6 was up ahead. Taking her direction, Lemar pulled off the busy highway and in moments they were in the outskirts of another anonymous town. They pulled into the parking lot and gathered their overnight things. They would get a chance to wash their clothes. Lemar had instructed Lola to keep her phone back at home telling her it was like a beacon. She intended to leave it behind but there was no way that she could go into the Grove without calling her parents first, so she had switched it off and stuffed it in her backpack.

She'd left a note siting on Rocha's kettle stand saying that she'd returned home to Ireland. Lola knew that Rocha wouldn't buy it but it might be enough to gain them a little time. Once she discovered that Lemar was gone too, she would figure out that they had gone in search of the Book and the Cube. Lola had tried not to think about how selfish her actions had been. She tried not to think about Rocha and how responsible she would feel for her welfare but part of her didn't care because Lola couldn't be sure who to trust anymore. She tried not to think about her parents and Aíbgréne and Celeste. It would do her no good and serve no purpose. She needed to be focused on the task ahead and hope that she had gotten it right, that she had interpreted the signs correctly. Lemar would come to no harm and if things didn't go according to plan at least he could bear witness.

Lemar locked the van and handed Lola her backpack and they made their way to the reception of the motel. Lola had never been in a motel before, the only perception she had was formed by what she'd seen in films so she was pleasantly surprised to find the reception area bright and clean with a well-dressed lady behind the desk.

The lady wore the requisite painted smile and beckoned Lemar towards her.

'How may I help you this evening?' she beamed at him. Lemar was handsome; the more time Lola spent with him, the more she noticed it and she guessed the receptionist did too.

'Could we have two rooms please?' said Lemar returning the lady's smile.

'Two rooms,' her smile seemed to widen. Lola smiled back at the lady as she typed their details into the system. She was happy to take cash and handed them the keys to their separate rooms. They headed upstairs.

'I'll see you in the morning, Lola,' said Lemar as they parted in the hallway.

Lola's room was bright and spacious and with a huge bed. She ran her hands across the top of the bed before jumping on to it, sinking deep into the plush mattress. It felt like heaven after days in the back of the cramped van but she needed to wash her clothes, so reluctantly Lola hauled herself from the mass of feathers and down and gathering her smalls and other items she made her way to the laundry room which was in the basement floor of the motel. It took over an hour to wash and dry her things but finally Lola was able to settle into a much needed bath back in her room from which she emerged fully refreshed.

As she dried off her hair and crawled into the sprawling bed, the sleep that had pervaded her every move up until that point had left her. Beyond the black-out curtains Lola could hear the hum of the nearby highway, the rushing cars sounded like a gushing river, as their plan ran through her head again and again.

The Grove was situated in the middle of nowhere Lemar had said and from what little research and testimony they could find on the place, it was virtually impregnable from the main Bohemian Highway Road. For this reason Lemar suggested they waited in the forest until nightfall.

He didn't seem at all unnerved by their mission – having been in Iraq perhaps this seemed small in comparison. But Lola didn't share his nonchalance. Unlike her, Lemar didn't fully understand what they were facing and Lola hoped that he never would. She hadn't told him, but most of her intel was based on her intuition. She could feel the book call her or guide her and yet she had no idea what she would find once they closed in on the actual camp.

It had taken Lemar a full week to actually pinpoint a location as the site was over a mile from the staff car park, which was in turn a mile from the main road. Their map showed nothing but densely packed forest on all sides.

Restless, Lola's body burned as she tossed and turned and threw off the heavy blankets, which had once been so enticing. The hours ticked by and still she chased the hound of sleep. Admitting defeat, Lola picked up the remote from the bedside unit and flicked on the TV. Had she not already been sitting down, the sight would have knocked her over. There on the screen in front of her was a clean-shaven and well-dressed Isaac Kane with Jodi sparkling and resolute beside him, both glaring into a sea of camera lenses.

'Holy shit!' said Lola to the empty room. Scrambling out of bed she rushed to Lemar's door, and beat on it like a hammer.

He must have been awake too because he answered immediately. 'God damn it, Lola, what in the Hell is going on?' Lemar stood in the doorway in his boxers and Lola pretended not to notice as she walked past him into the room.

'Turn the TV on, it's Isaac and Jodi,' said Lola in a splurge.

'Calm down, Lola. What is it?' Lola could see Lemar begin to panic a bit. 'Has something happened to Mr Kane?'

'No. No.' Lola shook her head frantically. 'Just turn on the TV quick.

They're talking about my story, it's gone national, Lemar!'

'I couldn't sleep,' said Lola as she sat down on the bed, 'so I turned on the TV. CNN I think it is,' directed Lola as Lemar tried to find the right station.

It wasn't the same channel but there was Jodi and Isaac again, this time it was Jodi facing the onslaught but the journalist wasn't hallowed by the interrogation, the steel in her eyes showed that she was quite enjoying it. Lemar flicked through a number of news channels and every one was taken up by Veritas's explosive revelations. Lemar and Lola sat for over two hours moving from station to station. The media were in a total frenzy, some backing a new enquiry and others dismissing and attacking Isaac and Jodi. It was happening and Lola could not hide her sheer delight. This was major and there was no way that Carl Stein would have seen this coming. Finally Lemar switched off the TV and the darkness swathed the room again.

'Do you think they've figured out where we are yet?' said Lola as she settled into the bed beside Lemar.

'I'm sure it will only be a matter of time,' said Lemar, after a while. 'But we'll be on our way back to New York by that time. Besides, Mr Kane seems to have created quite a distraction for us.'

'He has,' Lola laughed.

'Lemar?'

'Yes?' Lola could feel the heat radiating from his body as she moved closer to him in the bed. The dark stretched out around them magnifying every movement and breath a hundred fold. They both turned onto their sides and although they couldn't see each other the vacuum that separated them felt charged. Lemar's breath was slow and steady as Lola placed her hand on his face. His skin was warm and smooth underneath her fingers.

'Lemar?'

'Lola?'

'I need you to promise me something,' said Lola feeling the emotion of what she was about to ask him. 'I need you to promise me that no matter what happens tomorrow night you'll get away safely. You get the Equinox Oracle and the Cube away to safety.' Lemar was about to protest but Lola gripped his face tighter and made him promise her.

'You get back to New York and you call the number that I have given you. The number will lead you to my friend Aíbgréne. She'll know what to do. What's at stake here is bigger than me and I need you to understand that, Lemar,' urged Lola.

'Thank you, by the way,' said Lola into the dark expanse. 'Thank you for doing this with me. Lola felt his hand move to her waist.

'You're welcome,' he said. 'You've saved my life twice now and the way I see it, I owe you. I've survived two tours of Iraq and I'll be damned if a forest in the middle of California is going to be the end of me... or you.'

Lola smiled but he wouldn't see it. For a moment she thought she wanted to kiss Lemar Jenkins, she had the urge to feel her lips on his and to feel his tongue on hers. They remained in the same position, each wondering if the other was going to make the next move, the move they both wanted. In the end they moved apart, turned over and finally went to sleep.

~45~

They were on the road early the following morning only stopping twice, once so Lola could pee and the second time to get some food on board and fill the gas tank. Anything they had shared the previous night in the dark had evaporated in the morning light. There wasn't any awkwardness between Lola and Lemar but something had altered. The game was already afoot thanks to Veritas and now their focus had to be on the second-prong attack and for Lola the most important. In another few hours they would be in Monte Rio and Lola would soon know if her trip had been in vain or not.

She and Lemar spent most of their journey discussing and reaffirming their plan. As they drove deeper into Sonoma County the landscape beyond the campervan transformed from sprawling fields to thick mountainous forest that seemed to mute and muffle everything, even the sound of the van's engine.

Their camper crossed the Russian River Bridge at exactly 4.44pm, pulling into the parking lot of Lucy's Lounge and Grill. Lola smiled when she read the sign and thought of Jodi's friend Lucy Davis, hoping it was a good omen.

A large arched white sign with green writing and piping that presumably illuminated the letters in the dark, straddled the road, suspended by fine lengths of wire. Welcome to Monte Rio Vacation Wonderland it boomed.

Lola's legs were stiff and her arms and neck felt cramped. She stretched and maneuvered her body, trying to restore life and blood to her sleeping limbs. They were deep in the heart of the woods now entirely surrounded by forest at every turn but instead of feeling closed in Lola quite liked the sensation. Her eyes welcomed the sight of the trees and the green as it climbed to meet the blue sky above. Today was the autumn equinox and Lola expected that the sun would set around seven o clock.

They would have just enough time to grab some food but she didn't feel much like eating anymore – her stomach felt twisted and contorted in knots – so she let Lemar go ahead into the café making some excuse about wanting some air. When he had gone, she fished her mobile out of the backpack. Switching it on, she crouched on the floor of the camper wondering who she should call first. She decided that Rocha was the best person to start with, speaking to her parents would by far be the hardest. She'd already sent the girls an email and a text message, nothing too detailed, she told them that she loved them. She could have called them and talked about this and that but really that was all she wanted to say, that she loved them and missed them.

She wanted to let Rocha and Aíbgréne know where she was just in case she and Lemar didn't get out alive. That way they could at least tell her parents.

Lola scrolled through her contact list and hit the call button when Rocha's number appeared. The phone went straight to voicemail and Lola felt disappointed and relieved all at once. She left a message thanking Rocha for all that she'd done for her and saying that she was sorry for not telling her where she was going and that she hoped she would understand. Next she dialled Isaac's number expecting him not to answer, she was caught short when he did.

'Irish, is that you?' his voice was strained and Lola could tell he was anxious. 'Irish,' said Isaac again.

'Yes,' answered Lola meekly completely caught off guard.

'Where in the hell are you?' Lola could almost feel the relief as it poured from Isaac. 'We thought that they'd gotten to you, we have been out of our minds with worry. What the hell were you thinking!' Now he was angry but Lola didn't blame him, she deserved his wrath. What she had done was selfish but she believed that there was no other way.

'I can't talk, Isaac, I just wanted you to know that I'm okay and if I don't see you again, please don't give up the fight.' There was so much more Lola wanted to tell him, like how much she cared about him and how sorry she was, but he wouldn't let her finish.

'You're talking crazy, Lola, now you need to forget whatever Lois Lane bullshit you're up to and get your ass back to New York. You hear me?'

'Bye, Isaac,' said Lola cutting off the call.

Taking a deep breath to compose herself, she dialled the number for Brook Mill Manor and Lola almost lost her resolve completely when her younger brother Liam answered the call.

'Lola, is that you?'

'Yes, squirt,' she choked, swallowing hard to stifle the dry lump gathering in her throat. She wanted nothing more than to reach out and hug him, to see his face and play football in the garden with him again.

'Well are you back to school yet?' she asked her voice still on the brink of breaking. 'Yeah, we've loads of homework this year and the teacher is really cross.'

'You probably make the teacher cross, ye wee shite.' Liam's laugh filled the line between them and Lola thought she was about to lose her composure. He seemed normal enough so perhaps Rocha hadn't contacted them. This seemed peculiar to Lola, but it would maybe make things a lot easier, for the moment anyway.

'Is Ma or Da there?'

'Maaaaaaaa. Our Lola's on the phone from America,' shouted Liam. Lola couldn't help but laugh. He sounded so grown up. She could hear him hand the phone over to someone. 'Tell her to bring me something back and not to forget.'

'Did you hear that, love?' It was her dad. Lola wasn't prepared to deal with her dad and the tears began to leak from her eyes as her throat grew more swollen and barbed.

'Well, my daffodil, how has your trip been? Rocha called to tell us you were away for a few days with a friend?' Lola couldn't speak immediately and the line crackled between them.

'Hello. Lola, are you there, love? Can you hear me?'

'Yes, Da, I can hear you,' she finally managed between the stone that was wedged in her throat. 'I'm good. I just wanted to check in with you and Ma and the boys. I'll see you soon. Okay?'

'Are you alright, love?'

'Yes,' Lola reassured him between the sobs that she prayed he didn't hear. 'The reception isn't great, Da. Give everyone my love and I'll see you soon.'

She didn't wait for the reply instead she hung up and slumped against the back of the camper, sucking in the evening air and trying to stave off her tears.

She thought about why Rocha hadn't told her parents anything and she wondered had it anything to do with conversation she had overheard. Lola contemplated calling Rocha again but decided against it.

Lemar emerged from the café with some food, giving Lola just enough time to stash the phone back in the bag. He handed Lola some tea and a sandwich and climbed into the camper. 'We'd better get a move on,' he said turning the ignition and doing up his seatbelt as they headed out onto Bohemian Highway.

Lemar had thought it best to stash the camper and make the trip through the forest to the compound. They were flanked by dense thickets on the either side and the towering trees bowed their heads, arching over to meet their cousins on the other side of the road. Houses half-hidden deep in the forest were still visible for a while as they travelled but as the road snaked ahead and the vegetation became thicker, the houses grew scarce. After travelling for another few miles, Lemar slowed the van to a crawl, finally pulling into an overgrown laneway.

'This should do the job,' he said packing some items into two small rucksacks before locking up the van. According to Lemar the forest was sure to be patrolled. He packed night goggles and a few other items that he felt that he would need. They were both dressed in black trainers and bottoms and black hooded tops. Lola had done as she was told and added layers as they would be sitting around for some time unable to light a fire and although it was a very balmy and pleasant evening, the sun was already dropping and the temperature would fall dramatically.

Slipping across the deserted road they dropped down a slight incline onto the forest floor. Lemar consulted a small ordinance map and his compass. Adjusting his position slightly he began to walk forward with Lola close behind.

Lola felt comforted surrounded by the huge Californian redwoods. Their bark was a warm russet and their limbs stretched like antennae as if they were communicating with the heavens above. It reminded Lola of the

Crann na beatha, the Tree of Life as it communicated with both the physical and spiritual realms. Lola guessed they must have been thousands of years old.

As she settled into Lemar's brisk pace, she tuned into the rhythms of the forest, the sounds of the birds bedding down for the night, the gurgle and hush of the nearby Russian river and the soft sound of their feet as their steady steps disturbed the undergrowth of the forest floor.

Every now and then Lola reached out to touch the trunk of a redwood. The smell of the bark and sap and leaves and moss ignited something in her and she knew that the forest was on her side. There was no sense of danger. The trees and soil and all the life that was cradled within it charged and energised her. The weight and grime of the city peeled away from her skin leaving her feeling light and grounded for the first time in months. Whatever happened deep in these woods, Lola understood that the life force of the forest did not conspire in it, instead it urged her on, whispering its approval by helping and reviving her spirits.

She wanted nothing more than to stop by one of those colossal trees for a while but the light was falling rapidly, casting long shadows on the floor of the forest so she continued apace with Lemar who was consulting his map and compass again.

He motioned with a finger to his lips for her to stop, raising his fist in the air commanding her to be still. They listened through the falling birdsong and silence of the trees. Far off in the distance, Lola could not be sure in which direction, but a faint buzzing sound could be heard approaching. Lemar looked around them and then finally skyward to the canopy of the trees. There was still enough light spilling through to make both Lemar and Lola visible. The buzzing grew louder and louder and whatever it was it seemed to be moving at an extraordinary pace.

'Drone,' mouthed Lemar, pointing up above them. He surveyed the terrain before grabbing Lola by the elbow and leading her to the trunk of a felled tree. Lying down, he tucked himself into the undergrowth and pulled Lola down beside him. Like spoons they sheltered under the trunk as the machine hovered overhead, the sound from its engine deafening as it lingered over their patch of forest.

'It's a remote control drone, we used them out in Iraq,' whispered Lemar into the back of Lola's head. She could feel his solid body tight against hers as he pulled her further into the protection of the tree. 'Let's hope it only has a camera on it and not heat sensors as well,' said Lemar, wrapping his arms tighter around her.

Lola's mind raced trying to employ the ring and what little domain she had over the forest but still she hadn't sensed the danger.

'We must still be a good bit out. As we get closer no doubt there will be guards on patrol. One guy I spoke to said that they would have dogs and arms,' whispered Lemar.

Suddenly the iron spider dropped and circled just meters above them. Lola feared they'd been discovered and for a second she thought about blasting it out of the sky with magick but that wouldn't aid their cause it would only serve to alert them to their presence. She closed her eyes and willed it away, but still it hovered. Up and down it moved searching and sniffing for intruders. The forest was almost bathed in night when it finally began to rise again, moving off into the air and away.

Lola exhaled all the breath that seemed to have stored up and loosened her grip on Lemar's arm where her nails had left little half-moon indentations in his dark skin.

'Damn, that was close,' sighed Lemar. 'I thought we were goners. Security is tight here. I mean we are still a good mile out and they're using drones and shit.'

Happy that it was safe to continue Lemar handed Lola a pair of night vision goggles.

'Very high-tech,' jibed Lola, as she placed them over her eyes. Suddenly the forest was bathed in a pale green light, as Lola's eyes adjusted to the glasses the forest sprang to life. The green light danced and enveloped everything. It ran up the trunks of the trees like rivers of silver right through the branches to the very tips of the leaves, where it flickered and pulsed. It was like the forest's life blood, flowing through everything, from the trees to the very moss and needles that carpeted the floor.

'These glasses are amazing,' said Lola turning a three-sixty. It was like she could see the very life-force of the entire forest and it was all connected, the same energy or light ran through every living thing, including her and Lemar.

'The forest, it's so alive. I can see everything,' she said in awe.

'They're just cheap night vision glasses, Lola,' said Lemar. 'You sound as if you're trippin'.'

'Can't you see it?'

'See what?' said Lemar keeping a steady pace up ahead of her.

'The light, the green light that's running through everything. It's like... It's like..' Lola couldn't describe it because it was like nothing she'd ever seen before.

'All I can see is you and the trees and the forest floor. I sure as hell can't see no flowing light or whatever you call it. Sounds pretty cool though,' laughed Lemar walking on again.

Lola watched as the light danced and flowed and gently pulsed. Then she realised what it was she was looking at it. It was the forest's biofield. The animi mundi that Ezra had been talking about, the world soul and there it was right in front of her own eyes, the thread that connected every living thing, the aura of the forest! Lola continued on enchanted by the majesty and magic of this hidden world that lay all around her.

But there was a sudden change in vibration and as always Lola's ring registered the danger moments before she did but with no time to react, it tore through her body propelling her to the ground writhing in pain. Crawling to her knees, her fingertips digging into the dirt, she wretched and vomited as the pit of her stomach burned and twisted in agony. Lemar fell to his knees beside her as Lola screamed in agony.

It was like a million little needles were piercing her skin. Anything that she'd experienced at Stein Corp was nothing compared to this. She bid the ring into action and could see its bright blue womb closing around her, giving her immediate relief.

Lemar pulled her to the nearest tree and laid her at the roots of the sprawling redwood. Immediately its bark was like a sedative helping Lola to regulate her breath and focus her vision. She still wore the glasses and when her focus returned she could see the wall of blackness that she'd just collided with.

Lola could see the outline of the ground and the trees beyond its thin veil and she was sure that in the daylight that the same section of forest behind the wall of blackness would look just like any other but to her eyes it looked dead and decayed. The light that flowed through every other tree, leaf and root had been extinguished and drained. The green light fizzed at the edge of the barrier and died, failing to penetrate the throbbing gauze of dark energy.

Lola, her vision clear now, could see it pulse and move and hum and she wondered how on earth she was ever going to be able to breach its walls and even if she did, at what cost. For all she knew if it didn't kill her it could alert the Hell Fire Club to the intrusion.

Exhausted and shaking, Lola's head fell against the huge redwood as she sat in the fork where the root met the trunk. She closed her eyes and removed the glasses from her sweating face, laying them on the earth beside her. Her lungs sucked in the mossy air forcing it down into the pit of her solar plexus. Again and again she drank deep mouthfuls of breath and with each one she became calmer and lighter until she could no longer feel the trunk of the trees supporting her or the damp ground beneath her.

Lola's eyes shot open but she wasn't on the forest floor anymore, instead she was suspended two feet off the ground. All around her was a halo of rich green light holding her up and restoring her. The energy flowed in a glowing circuit from the redwood and into her. Tiny roots of light attached themselves to Lola's aura imbuing it with vitality and reviving it until it merged with the electric blue of her own aura. All the while she watched this transfusion as if she was a spectator. The trees and forest although they could not speak told her that she was safe. We are with you, they said. We will protect you.

When Lola opened her eyes again she was seated at the great taproot of the ancient tree and she doubted if the experience had been real until she caught Lemar's face in his hands as he stooped over to get a breath, clearly unnerved by what he'd witnessed.

'Just when I think this shit can't get any more crazy, you go and pull that Yoda come Exorcist shit.'

Lola placed her hand on his face and immediately he fell silent, calmed, not by her but the eons of wisdom that flowed from the trees and into her body. Lola got to her feet and taking Lemar by the hand she turned to face the murky wall that spanned out in front of her.

'It's time now,' she said in a voice that didn't feel like her own.

Lola squeezed Lemar's hand tightly and glancing sideways to catch his face in her light she thought of Persephone and stepped across the barrier into the Underworld.

~46~

The air around Lola parted and stirred as an object whistled past her ear breaking the skin on the side of her face before flashing through the barrier that hung like a veil of obsidian, separating the vibrant forest from the wasteland that they now found themselves in. She had no time to orientate so it took seconds for her to register the incoming assault but Lemar, as always, was bright and alert.

Lola's outstretched hands groped around blinded by the darkness as she tried to gain a footing on the scorched earth below. The blackness closed around them like a sarcophagus but she was comforted by the grace of Lemar's unseen movements as he met the incoming footsteps. A muted groan escaped from someone's lungs as they slumped to the ground in a heap. Lola wheeled around towards the sound, which had risen up from behind her, calling for Lemar.

'It's okay. I'm here, I'm here,' said Lemar, gently touching Lola's hands.

'Thank god,' said Lola, her rigid body softening at his touch. 'I can't see a bloody thing from when we passed through that barrier. I left my glasses back there at the tree.'

Lola's eyes began to adjust until she could see the sepia hues of the nocturnal forest floor and the outline of the trees that loomed skyward, dead as stone.

Above, the canopy began to thin out permitting a few strands of light from the sickle moon to cut a path in front of her.

A radio sounded and Lola ducked to the floor, anticipating more company. Lemar stooped to meet the dark bundle that lay on the ground and flicked the radio off, helping himself to the guard's gun and night visions glasses.

'Wow, infrared stealth glasses! Now this is my kinda apparatus,' said Lemar handing Lola his old pair.

'I'm good, thanks. I think I prefer the moonlight,' said Lola reaching up to feel her left ear. The blood trickled down her neck and gathered in a pool at the root of her hair. She couldn't see the crimson stream but the night, like a whetstone, had sharpened her other senses so she could smell and taste the rusty blood.

Lemar pulled out the small map again and examined it underneath the light of his pocket torch. He crouched down onto his haunches and Lola followed, she felt stiff and tense and her head had a deep dry throbbing that made it hurt even when she breathed.

'Right, Lola, we're almost at ground zero,' said Lemar, consulting the map and looking towards the forest every now and then but she already knew that, she could feel it press down on her.

'We walk due north here and that should bring us to the lake and that's where we part. I'll be waiting for you on this side of the bank. You hear me?' Lemar squeezed Lola's shoulder and she felt reassured again.

'We've already downed one man.' Lemar gestured to the heap lying on the ground and Lola couldn't help but wonder who the man was and if he had a family or children.

'I'm sure he won't be the last,' continued Lemar 'but I'll do my best here to hold things off for you and you do your Jedi shit and then we can both the hell outta this place cause it's giving me the creeps.'

'Sounds like a plan,' said Lola, trying to muster a smile. She embraced Lemar planting a warm kiss on his cheek.

'Lemar,' said Lola resolutely. 'You've got to promise me that no matter what you see or what happens you will get yourself to safety. Promise me, Lemar,' urged Lola. 'Promise me,' she almost shouted.

'I promise. I promise.'

'Good,' smiled Lola. 'It's been a pleasure serving with you, Officer Jenkins.'

'Never mind that bullshit,' said Lemar, as his uncompromising brown eyes bore into hers. 'You just get your fine white ass back here so we can both go home.'

Lola and Lemar walked the short distance to the edge of the forest where an open bank swept down to the mouth of the pitch pool.

Not a sound could be heard on the embankment or inside the dense growth that lay behind them. Death stalked the very air as no living creature could survive such oppressive and benevolent magick. As Lola's eyes skimmed across the lake the hairs on her arms stood to attention and she hoped that she was one living creature that would survive it. A half-moon island swelled out into the water that sat black and still like a sheet of looking glass. The Club's central symbol, the owl, rose odious and menacing thirty feet above the grand altar. The creature's eyes, although carved from stone, plunged downward ready to devour the scene below.

In the middle of the altar lay a huge stone table in the shape of a vulva. Even from her vantage point on the forest side of the lake, Lola could see the deep crevices that radiated towards the edges of the sacrificial table like razors. Ceremonial braziers burned and spat sending golden red flames slashing and cutting across the glass water.

Lola took off her coat and without hesitation she stepped out into the frigid depths and plunged in. She had experienced many moments of nakedness where she felt exposed to the blasts of doubt that her mind blew at her but Lola's eyes and heart were fixed on that altar and she was sure that what she was doing was the right thing. Lemar melted back into the shadows and willed his friend across the lake.

The drone of an approaching engine made Lemar retreat a little further. He cursed himself as the speedboat rounded the corner of the lake disturbing the tranquillity and stillness of the scene; despite his diligence he'd overlooked this one possibility. He shouldn't have worried because as the boat slowed down, casting the baleful eye of its spotlight across the surface of the water, Lola was already submerged, her lungs screeching for air as she swam as hard as she could away from its amber stare.

Opening her eyes Lola momentarily panicked when she saw beams of light penetrate the depths of the water. Below in the mist of silt and murk Lola thought she could see pale forms lying on the bed of the lake.

Her lungs burned but she forced herself to wait until the light moved before emerging to the surface choking and coughing as her lungs drank in the air, gasping for more. She had just a little bit further to go.

Her clothes were beginning to drag her down and slow her movements. Pulling off her hoodie and her shoes she was able to move more freely. She had identified a small jetty covered with reeds that would allow her some cover and help her gain access, unseen, to the grand altar. Lola secured the ring on her finger and bid it into action.

Her head was heavy and her nose began to leak blood again. Her limbs were tired and fatigued from the exertion and she could feel the same magick that protected the perimeter and the same nefarious presence that had stalked after her in New York, she felt it radiate from the altar; the ring obeyed but neither she nor it was strong enough to go untouched.

As she slid out of the water like a shadow, Lola scanned the altar. Everything seemed to be in place. Incense burned in a large urn, it smelled of pine needles and lemons and moss. Lola's eyes searched for another veil that her gut told her was there. She closed her eyes and called in her mind's eye to the Bile Màthir, sure she would answer, but no response came only the sound of the fire cracking and the wind as it disturbed the coven of trees that bent their boughs around the circumference of the sacrificial altar.

This time Lola took a deep breath and tried again but again her call remained unanswered. A blue wave of terror shot through her veins like ice and in desperation Lola turned her attention to the Cosmic Cube.

Letting her lids close she began the process again. She visualised it and beckoned the Cube to come to her.

Something stirred on the table forcing Lola to crouch lower still. Looking from behind one of the seven stone columns her eyes were drawn to the large granite table, which lay vacant but expectant. Again she heard the groan of stone on stone and then the image of the Cosmic Cube presented itself before her mind's eye and Lola felt that all was not lost.

The unidentified object on the table moved again. Crouching ever closer Lola took sanctuary under the rigid effigy. Now that she was able to scrutinise the table from a much closer angle she could see that there were chains with iron cuffs bolted deep into the stone, cuffs for the arms and cuffs for the legs.

An ancient rage rose in Lola's breast and this time she allowed it to surge and rise as the delicious flame scoured and ignited through her veins. Lola thought of all the women who'd met their deaths on that table and determined that she would not be one of them.

It was a perfect replica of the table at Mussenden Temple back home in Ireland, the one that had almost claimed the life of Celeste. The grind of granite on granite slapped Lola in to focus.

'What lies within, reflects without,' she whispered and a laser of glacial blue light shot skyward like a beacon out of the Cosmic Cube. Breaking her cover she raced to the table.

The Cube now in its solid granite form rushed to her out-stretched arms like a child to its mother. For a moment Lola thought it was all too easy. She glanced across the water again to where Lemar was urging her across from the edge of the darkness but something was preventing her from moving.

It wasn't the book because by now Lola understood that it wasn't there, that it had never been there, such was her bond and connection with it. She had been duped, they knew she would come after the book and she had obliged. Lola crept to the water's edge and was about to swim to safety when a shrill scream shattered the silence and with it any notion Lola had of leaving.

Lying down on her belly she watched as a young woman, no older than herself, was pulled towards the table by her hair. One of the men slapped her across the face momentarily quieting her sobs for help. He motioned towards the two other men to hold her down on the ground while he adjusted his trouser belt.

'No! No!' sobbed the young woman. 'Please, not again. Not again.'

Lola couldn't stand it anymore; she could feel the young woman's torment and anguish as if it were her own. She could feel her desperation and allowing that ancient fire to explode, Lola broke her cover and rushed to the scene as the first man was about to take his turn.

'Now, now, boys,' boomed Lola, standing tall and magnificent in her power. 'What would your mothers think?'

All three men spun around startled and bemused by the incursion into their fun, leaving the young woman to scramble to her freedom.

'That's no way to treat a young lady now is it?' said Lola feeling in total control. 'After all didn't you hear her say no? No means no.'

The woman scrambled behind Lola, cowed and shivering from her ordeal.

'Who's this bitch?' laughed the first man buttoning up his trousers casually. Lola could feel her veins hiss.

'This bitch,' smiled Lola, 'is your worst nightmare.'

This made them all laugh which only emboldened her further.

'You're going to pay for what you've done to this young lady,' smiled Lola serenely. She could feel the fire rise in her like a wild animal but this time she refused to tame it, up it swelled and swelled until the tips of her fingers and the palms of her hands trembled. The men widened out surrounding the girls like a noose.

'Can you swim?' asked Lola over her shoulder to the young woman who stood sobbing behind her. One of the men took out a dagger and stood eyeing up his shot.

'Yes,' she nodded. 'But I can't... I can't go in there,' she sobbed harder now. 'That's where all the others are.'

'I need you to focus,' said Lola firmly. 'If you don't want to join them, you need to go to the water, where the reeds are on the left hand side. Swim directly across to the other side. There'll be someone waiting there for you. His name is Lemar,' she instructed never taking her eyes of the three abominations in front of her who stood with smug grins.

'This one's feisty,' said one of the men. 'Mr Stein likes them feisty. I say we keep this one, Hank, and let the other one go,' he laughed. 'I mean we've all had our turn there.'

The men laughed. The girl behind Lola broke down again.

'Go,' demanded Lola. This time the girl ran as fast as she could to the water. Lola could see she was limping and in pain and blood streamed from between her legs.

The sight made the rage roar in her again and Lola thought not of Brigid but another great Irish triple Goddess, The Morrígan, the Goddess of War and Carnage. So cloaked in black and in full control of her inner darkness she let the chaos that raged in her build.

She felt the wrongs of every woman at the hands of men like these and she consumed it and turned it into power, to energy and vibration. Lola felt the defilement of that sacred body and again she used it as kindling for the fire that she was about to send forth.

The one they called Hank moved the dagger around in his hand playfully eyeing up his shot but Lola didn't flinch or run. Instead her eyes burrowed into his flesh like a drill and smiling she inched closer and closer.

Hank and his men stepped back casting furtive looks to one another. Lola could see the doubt and uncertainty as it crept across their faces now.

'I suppose you'd better make your move, Hank.' Lola smiled. 'I don't have all night to stand and dance with you boys.'

As instructed Hank took aim and loosened the dagger, aiming for Lola's leg. But it didn't hit its intended target. As if slowing time itself with the flick of her wrist, Lola commanded the sliver blade into her own hands as she felt her sacred magick pour from her like a furnace.

Exhaling, Lola pushed her hands out into the energy field in front and around her and watched Hank's body and head come raining down on the stone table. The others were foolish enough to move towards her but she dispatched them both with a flick of her head.

Hank stirred writhing in pain as his head gushed blood. The owl looked on, its sharpened beak contorting in pleasure. Adjusting the dagger in her agile hands Lola slowly walked towards him.

Standing over him she felt full of disgust and whatever compassion she once held in that moment seemed to be dead. She wanted revenge she wanted Hank to suffer the indignity that he'd thrust on that poor girl.

Lola smiled calmly as he begged her to spare him. She leaned over and unbuttoned his trousers slowly pulling down the zipper. Hank tried to plead with her but Lola's eyes looked at him dispassionately.

'No. No. Please. No. Don't. Don't.' But his pleas dropped from her ears as if into an abyss.

'No?' sneered Lola. 'According to men like you, Hank, no means yes. Isn't that right? Now let's see how you enjoy being penetrated.' Without hesitation Lola took the knife and lunged into Hank's crotch.

A slow clap sounded behind her and it seemed to bring her back to herself.

'Well, well,' laughed the slow southern drawl of Carl Stein, 'all my dreams have come true on this most auspicious of nights. What darkness you cradle, Miss Paige. I dare say all those dalliances with my son seem to have infected you.'

Lola looked across the lake to where the clearing lay dead and empty, happy that Lemar had done as she'd asked and gotten himself to safety and hopefully the poor soul that she'd sent to him.

Lola turned to face the lone voice only to find that he was not alone. Behind him was gathered at least thirty cloaked and masked members of the Hell Fire Club. Carl took off his golden Scaramouch while the others remained veiled.

He looked around him in bemusement and with a flick of his hands, a group moved to dispose of the men Lola had expired.

'I didn't think you had it in you, Ms Paige, to kill another human being. Isn't that against the Order's rules? I must say,' said Carl flashing his politicians smile at Lola, 'I'm quite aroused by the sight. Doesn't it feel great to walk on the dark side?'

Lola watched tentatively as the group widened out into a wide prison around her. She wondered where he was, all the other masks were white apart from Carl's and Lola wondered what mask concealed Alex and Prospero tonight.

'Imagine you walking right into my play garden, Miss Paige. What a delight.' Carl moved in closer to her. 'And to think that this pleasure was almost denied me when you became entangled in my plan to destroy that book.'

'You?' said Lola genuinely confused.

'Yes me,' Carl smiled laconically. 'Who else? Miss Delaney had informed me that you had taken quite an interest in the book and the visiting professor and after our search at Ur left us empty handed, I just wondered if this might have been the Lost Oracle we were seeking. I mean why else would my sister-in-law have permitted you to come to New York, they were testing you out, Lola. You see they really don't care about you, all the Order cares about is their cause. I couldn't take the chance so I arranged for a little accident, neither Moriarty nor you was our intended target. We had to dispatch of Susie, she knew too much, but your friend was a bonus I suppose. The book and the world's leading expert, expired in one neat little explosion. Except you were there and as I've seen your powers have grown immensely.'

Lola shouldn't have been delighted but she was, this meant that the book was out there and if Carl Stein didn't know that then it must be in safe hands. Lola wanted nothing more than to throw that back in his smug face but she wasn't that foolish, her duty was to protect the book even if it meant that she'd risked her life for nothing. Well perhaps not nothing. She had saved that girl, Lemar was safe and she had found the Cosmic Cube. It was time for her to leave.

'How foolish you are, my dear child. Wasn't escaping from the preservation lab enough for you? Now you have come here. Why have you come here?'

'The Cube,' lied Lola, she could see the suspicion form in Carl Stein's mind and she feared he would figure out that the book was safe – why else would she risk this if not for something that important?

'Why did you destroy the book?' asked Lola trying to distract him from his own reasoning.

'Well I understood that if the book was what we suspected it to be there was no way it would ever answer to me. I see you and Mr Kane have created quite a storm digging and trifling in very grown up affairs,' said Carl moving around the centre of the altar with dramatic flair.

'You've made things very difficult for me, Miss Paige.' Carl Stein's face darkened. 'There is no way they will link me personally to this but you have complicated things immensely.'

Lola's mind raced searching for a way out. She urged herself to play it cool, to stay calm. So far the ring was doing its job and she had been so preoccupied that she had forgotten all about the pain and drumming ache in her head.

'I came here for the Cube,' said Lola steadying her nerves, 'and this time, I'll be leaving with it.'

'I admire your tenacity, Ms Paige, and that fight in you but you must understand,' smiled Carl, 'that us southern boys may be slow with our words but we ain't half fast on our feet.'

Lola had been straining so hard to keep Carl Stein's force at bay that she was unaware of the cloaked figure that had crept up her blindside. It was the familiar smell of orange, bergamot and ylang-ylang that made her turn around but it was too late because the hot blade had already been thrust into her side. She could feel her blood, like liquid ice, trickle out of the small puncture wound as a hand slid around her throat restraining her.

The power drained from Lola and no matter how she fought, her magick seemed to have evaporated. She could feel her assailant's warm breath on her neck and with a flick of his wrist, Carl Stein relegated Lola to her knees, where she slumped over paralysed and unable to get up.

Two anonymous men pulled her to her feet while the person who had stabbed her used the blood-stained blade to cut off her sodden clothes. The golden blade shone and glistened, it was a broad oval shape that looked like it belonged on the end of spear rather than the short ivory handle it now rested on. Lola wondered what magick it possessed. From the agony she was in she knew it was stronger than any she had. The blade didn't look particularly sharp but it cut through her leggings and t-shirt like a hot knife through butter.

The smell of perfume grew stronger as Lola focused her clouded brain to place it. It smelt like Jodi's perfume, musky and expensive but the cloak fell all the way to the ground and the hood and mask obscured any chance Lola had of identifying her attacker. The person who had torn off her clothes, leaving her semi-naked may have smelled like a woman but even Lola knew the Hell Fire Club was exclusively male.

Then she dropped her hood and mask to reveal a head of blazing red hair and face like alabaster. Olivia Van der Vart's painted red lips parted into a smile, her eyes moistened with pleasure as she stood back to look at Lola's dying body. Stepping forward she ran her tongue along the side of Lola's cheek, biting at her ear before standing side by side with Carl Stein, who gave her an approving smile.

Lola's pale and wet body shivered against the gathering cold.

'I must admit,' said Carl Stein coming closer and licking the dry blood from behind her ear. 'I will be sorry to see you go, Miss Paige. You have been such a fun little thing but you're no match for me. You never have been and that old fool was negligent to believe that you would be.'

He was so close now that Lola could feel his warm breath on her breasts. He ran his fingertips between her cleavage stopping just above the line of her underwear. Her skin burned and she let out a gasp of pain.

'You see, Lola, I've been in this mean old chess game for so long I can smell what direction the wind is blowing. Now I admit, I never imagined that you'd walk right into my path, but I must say,' chuckled Carl, 'I'm mighty glad you did.'

He put his hands on Lola face and stuck his tongue in her mouth. Lola with her hands pinned could only bite down on his lip; it was the only form of protest she had left.

Pulling away from her he slapped her face cutting her cheek. She spat out the blood from her mouth but this only earned her another blow, this time it buckled her legs.

Strange hands lifted her and placed her on the cold stone table and although she could feel the sensation of being cold Lola couldn't focus on it. Her nose had started to bleed ferociously and the blood leaked down into her throat blocking her airway.

'Sit her up, boys,' commanded Carl Stein as he stalked around the table with all the pageantry and drama of a ringmaster. 'I don't want this to be over too soon.'

A warm gentle pair of hands came from behind tilting Lola's head up so she could breath. They moved about her face wiping the blood away with their cloak. Then a voice that she would recognise in any lifetime spoke into her ear. The whisper was like low thunder as it cursed her coming. 'Why?' It agonised. 'Why did you come here? The book is safe. I told the old man. I told him that you would try and come after it but he wouldn't listen. All this was for nothing, everything I did was for nothing!'

Alex's voice was vivid and passionate, full of resentful sorrow and unsated hatred. It was beautiful and Lola smiled and choked through the blood because she understood it all now. He had chosen her after all, he'd been helping Prospero all along.

It was too late for her but the book was safe – Prospero, Rocha, Aíbgréne and Celeste, they all would look after it and they would finish what had been started.

As the cloaks gathered around the table, her airway constricted again, but this time it wasn't from the blood, she could feel Carl Stein's magick enter her veins and arteries like scalding liquid ice. Her hands and legs were bound in the cast iron cuffs but they needn't have bothered. Lola was spent and the pain that tore through her body made her wish for death. The same pair of hands lifted her head again to aid her breathing and rubbed the blood from her nose away.

Alex Stein had never felt the pain and sheer agony that had gripped him now. This had not been part of the plan and if he exposed himself they both were dead. So he stood his ground and held Lola's head, the only comfort he could offer her as she was dying.

Lola did not ask him for help and in that moment Alex Stein understood the meaning of true beauty as it lay dying in that boundless, all-forgiving love that brought such light and warmth into the chaos of his life. He felt all the poetry of Lola Paige's heart and how she had remained true to the old man and the Order and her damned cursed legacy. She had remained true to them all and it was taking her to the grave.

Alex despised himself, he should do something, but he wasn't like Lola, he wasn't compassionate and brave. He was wrong, broken and selfish.

'Brothers,' declared Carl Stein, standing at the foot of the table. 'Behold the great Goddess in all her majesty and splendour.' A sea of laughter erupted around them. 'This pitiful child is the Goddess that was promised by the Tùatha Dé Danann and the great Equinox Oracle. Because of my son's obvious weakness for her, she was able to avoid her destiny with this spear head some time ago, but tonight, thanks to my new second in command,' Olivia Van der Vart positioned herself by Carl Stein's right side, 'she has not avoided this ancient blade for a second time.'

Carl Stein's aim was to humiliate his son for his weakness. 'You see, Alex my boy, I knew you would never be able to do it. Tonight our world hangs on a precipice and tonight we celebrate our victory over this sick and lame prophesy of light. There is no way but our way and as we offer this blood sacrifice to our Great God and as we drink the blood of the last Dé Danann, let us consummate the death of this false light.' Again another roar of approval rang out.

By now Lola was growing faint, but she focused on Alex's smooth hands, as they held her head like a cushion of air. Alex pulled off his mask, his tears fell on her face and a piercing scream tore from his throat as he fell prostrate at the side of the table. What had he allowed to happen?

Carl Stein slowly approached his son commanding him to his feet. 'Your weakness disgusts me, boy,' he spat, slapping Alex across the face. 'You will have to earn your future place at this table and when she is gone so too will your foolishness.'

Alex rose and looked down into his father's eyes with his habitual expression of self-worth having returned.

'What?' derided Carl. 'You think we didn't know about your little meeting in St Patrick's with that old bum from Liberty Plaza and how it was you that was bankrolling him? You have too much of your mother in you, boy, and I hoped that I had removed it from you, but like her you are sentimental. You think I didn't know about your dalliances with the beautiful Miss Paige here?'

The blood continued to gather in Lola's throat and her lungs begged for breath as the hole in her side bled out into the sundial crevices on the table.

'You failed,' said Alex echoing his father's contempt. 'The book is safe and you will never have it.' The sneer slid from Carl Stein's face and with a flick of his wrist Alex was propelled against one of the stone columns. Carl Stein looked down on his son's crumpled body with derision.

'This is a new day for the Hell Fire Club,' shouted Carl Stein. 'Miss Vander Vart has shown more guile and grit than all of you gathered here and I'm ashamed to say, including my own son. But in this game we must be prepared to make any or all sacrifices.'

A blast of light boomed from the embankment shaking the foundations of the altar like an earthquake, forcing the celebrants to the ground. Lola's vision was blurred and it dipped in and out of consciousness. She knew she was close to death and she was able to think of a million things and places and experiences, all simultaneously. She thought of her distraught family and friends, she thought of Ireland, her sacred home.

It was funny how you had to leave a place to really see it, thought Lola, as the chaos broke out around her. Being so far from her home served to illustrate just how attached she was to her tiny corner of the world. She was Ireland and she was innately connected with the energy of the land and of the people who inhabited the acres in the field of her life. This was all for them.

Lola could feel the Brón Trogain. She was acutely attuned now to the sorrowing of her homeland because it was her sorrow too. She could feel the eons of division and injury the land and her people had endured. She felt sorely the dark and festering wound of the border and understood that a land separated could never be healed. For Lola, this was not political but spiritual, the once sacred land of the Dé Danann had been fouled and infected and a once proud people had lost all sense of their royal lineage. The Bile Màthir called to her and her soft whisper lulled Lola to her side.

Lola's eye drifted open again and now five beams of light moved towards her. Each was a different colour and a different shape and soon she realised five individuals stood behind a piece of the Cosmic Cube. The Hell Fire Club were powerless against them, only Carl Stein and Olivia managed to offer a fight as their black merged with white creating a grey mist; eventually Carl was forced to retreat by another blast of light and out of the tumult emerged a man with a staff and beard.

At first Lola suspect she had died, because behind the principal indigo light stood Prospero, flanked by Rocha, Aíbgréne, Daithí and Celeste. The absurdity of the scene convinced Lola that she had passed but the pain and cold told her otherwise. Alex was back on his feet again supporting her head to allow some precious oxygen into her lungs.

'You're too late.' Alex Stein's face looked down on Lola's; even upside down his face was still perfect. His tears fell on her bruised and bloodied face berating the silhouette that came towards them.

'You're too late, you're all too late and now she's going to die.'

'And what did you do to protect her?' boomed the angry voice in reply,

444

only it wasn't Prospero's voice that came out, it was Arthur's. 'You made a vow and you failed to keep it!'

As Lola looked down at her side she could see the red blood, laced with the most beautiful pale golden light. Her life's blood, she thought, as life itself trickled out of her body. She had no fight left. As her lids fluttered closed and open again her fading sight latched to a single umber leaf, dead and dry, she watched as it sky-waltzed to the ground. All around her there was chaos but in that single moment the cogs of the seasons seemed to click into place and Lola understood that everything was connected, as the trees and leaves breathed their last delicious sigh of life and gave way to the autumn and coming winter so too would she.

Only a shimmer of life fizzed in the last of her blood. A familiar face looked down on her and the kindest pair of earthen eyes she had ever seen, eyes that she had longed to see again. Lola smiled to greet them. 'Arthur?' she murmured.

'Yes, my child,' cried the familiar voice. 'What have I done? What have I done? What have I done?' He sobbed.

'Arthur,' murmured Lola. 'Arthur, you're here. It's you!' she whispered from her cracked and blue lips. 'Ní thuigeann an sách an seang,' smiled Lola.

'You can't understand what you haven't experienced,' repeated Arthur between sobs. 'Yes,' he wept, 'but I fear I'm too late, my child.'

With that Lola's eyes of emerald closed for the last time, the darkness stole in and Lola Paige was gone.

To be continued...

Acknowledgments

Firstly, I would like to thank you the reader. I want to thank you specifically because as an independent author I could not do this without your support. You, my lovely readers, have given me the mandate to write, and the growth of Solstice, book one of The Goddess Trilogy to where I am today was largely down to your support and encouragement.

With that in mind, if you have enjoyed book two of The Goddess Trilogy, please get in touch to let me know, or simply pass it on. Word of mouth, reviews and recommendations are the currency of every indie author – we simply need them to survive. So, thank you!

I would also like to give a very special mention to my husband Neil, for the countless cups of tea you made, the dinners you prepared, the piles of washing and drying you did. Because you kept your feet firmly in reality, in the everyday mechanics of life, you gifted me the freedom to live in the realm of my imagination, to walk the streets of New York with my characters, navigating and unearthing, plotting and scheming. You were the light that guided me in those dark days – and there were a few – when I questioned whether I should be writing at all.

I'd like to thank my editor Dr Emma Warnock, without whose expertise, patience, honesty and gentle encouragement you would not be reading this. Going into the second book in my trilogy I was very conscious of strengthening my writing and my craft and I firmly believe that she has helped me achieve that, so thank you, Emma, for not giving up on me!

I would also like to thank the talented Gemma O'Hagan for creating this lovely cover and for her patience and professionalism throughout. Last, but by no means least, a huge word of gratitude to my comrade Barry Rooney, who like a super hero is always there in the nick of time to save the day! Through writing The Goddess Trilogy, I have meet so many amazing people and I hope you will all stay on this exciting journey with me.

Yours in deepest gratitude,
J.S. Comiskey